SIMON BOOKER

WITHOUT TRACE

D0109397

twenty7

First published in Great Britain in 2016 by Twenty7 Books

This paperback edition published in 2016 by

Twenty7 Books
80–81 Wimpole St, London W1G 9RE
www.twenty7books.com

A CIP catalogue record for this book is available from the British Library.

Paperback ISBN: 978-1-78577-022-7
Ebook ISBN: 978-1-78577-021-0

1 3 5 7 9 10 8 6 4 2

Printed and bound by Clays Ltd, St Ives Plc

Twenty7 Books is and imprint of Bonnier Zaffre,
a Bonnier Publishing company
www.bonnierzaffre.co.uk
www.bonnierpublishing.com

For Mel

One

Nine days before her daughter disappeared, Morgan Vine paid her twenty-third visit to HMP Dungeness. She knew the prison officers mocked her naïvety *(Start a book group! Heal the world!)* but she didn't care, nor did she mention her real reason for staying in touch with a man convicted of murder.

'You don't look like a do-gooder.'

Morgan decided to take the screw's jibe as a compliment. She watched him cast a wary eye over her scuffed leather jacket, skinny-fit jeans and high tops.

'I'm planning a mass breakout,' she said. 'The reading group's a front.'

A frown.

'You realise aiding and abetting an escape is a criminal offence?'

'*Now* you tell me.'

The man sniffed and exchanged her keys and iPhone for a plastic tag. He placed her belongings in a locker then buzzed her into the holding area where another officer, her escort, was leaning against an out-of-order vending machine. The man folded a tattered *Daily Express* and unlocked the first of many gates.

Morgan followed him across the exercise yard, glancing at the loops of razor wire, the barred windows of the cells.

Top floor, third from the left.

His cell.

Did he get any sleep last night or lie awake until dawn?

Fretting.

Hoping.

Planning.

The officer unlocked the side gate to C-Wing. Morgan paused, savouring a last taste of autumnal fresh air before entering the dingy corridor that reeked of stale sweat, bad food and low-level fear. More clanging gates. More jangling keys. Down a flight of concrete steps, along another fetid corridor and into the rec-reation room. The ten men were seated in a circle, legs splayed, staking out their personal space.

Feeling his eyes on her, she was glad she'd risen early to wash her hair. More blonde-ish than blonde, she would have opted for a shorter cut years ago had he not had a 'thing' for long hair. Still the right side of forty, her slimness was the result of regular swimming combined with a surfeit of nervous energy, and her eyes had kept their youthful sparkle.

Aside from Danny himself, no one in the room was aware of the history that bound Morgan to Prisoner FF7836 and that was how it would stay. She'd started the group as a pretext to rekindle regular contact but even if tomorrow went well – even if his appeal were successful – she wouldn't abandon 'her boys'. They had come to trust her. There was no question of bailing out simply because Danny might get his life back.

As usual, he was sitting opposite Gary Pascoe, a bull-necked cage fighter serving a lengthy sentence for garroting the pregnant mother of his five children with a bicycle chain. The man had commemorated the event by having a teardrop tattooed under his eye.

'Hello, gorgeous.'

Pascoe was always first to speak, jousting for control from the moment Morgan arrived.

'Morning, Gary.'

'Not got a smile for me?'

'Make me laugh and we'll see.'

'I only know dirty jokes.'

'Then let's stick to the book.'

'You're the boss.' The man cracked his knuckles, reached into the waistband of his trackies and produced a copy of *To Kill a Mockingbird*. 'But I've got a question about the lawyer in the story. What sort of stupid name is Atticus Finch?'

Morgan said nothing. Taking her seat, she flipped open her dog-eared paperback. The book fell open at a page that bore minute traces of chocolate, a smear of Cadbury's Flake from twenty-five years ago. Traces of the past.

'If you ask me, he's a twat,' said Pascoe, 'but teacher's pet says I'm wrong.'

He glared at the man opposite, giving Morgan an excuse to look directly into Danny's grey-green eyes. She saw bruising on his cheek and a grubby bandage around his left hand. Another shank in the shower?

'Want to tell us how you see Atticus, Danny?'

Kilcannon leaned back in his chair and considered the question with what seemed to Morgan a Zen-like calm. She'd never understood where this inner stillness came from but even at school he'd exuded quiet authority.

'He's the archetypal hero. Always does the right thing.' Danny raked the fingers of his good hand through his thick, blue-black hair. 'People turn on him because he's defending someone they're prejudiced against but he sticks to his principles, whatever it takes.'

Pascoe revealed a gap-toothed grin.

'He's a twat and the book's shite.' He winked at Morgan. 'Kilcannon only chose it because you like the film and he wants to get in your knickers.' His grin became a leer. 'Which is a shocker 'cause we all know he likes 'em barely legal.' He sucked his teeth. 'Still, tomorrow goes his way, he's on a dead cert with you, right?'

Morgan felt her cheeks burn.

'Not cool, Gary.'

'See?' said Pascoe, looking around the room. 'They'll be at it the moment he gets out.' He winked at Morgan. 'I'm up for parole. Wanna wait for a real man?'

Danny's jaw tightened as he leaned towards Pascoe.

'Show some respect.'

'Relax, Danny boy.' Pascoe waved airily towards the bandage. 'Something wrong with your hand?'

The men stared at each other. Undisguised loathing. Morgan knew the next few seconds would decide if the session continued peaceably or ended in a brawl. The trick was to assert her authority without humiliating the cage fighter.

'Play nice, lads,' she said, 'or I'm cancelling Disneyland.'

Pascoe threw back his head and laughed.

'Disneyland?' he said. 'Wouldn't go there for all the hooch on C-Wing.'

Laughter all round. Morgan felt a flicker of relief. Most of these men were on medication. You never knew if a joke would backfire. And when something big was brewing – like Danny Kilcannon's appeal – you could feel the tension.

The papers had revived the story over the last few days. The *Post* ran a readers' poll. *Danny Kilcannon: wrongly convicted or guilty as sin?* Eighty-two per cent had voted 'guilty' but the case still had the power to trigger debate.

- *He's guilty.*
- *He's innocent. Whoever killed Zoe was a stranger, a burglar.*
- *Most murder victims are killed by someone they know.*
- *Doesn't prove Danny did it.*
- *What about the missing wife? He killed her too. Dumped the body at sea.*
- *No way. Rowena had a breakdown, like he told the jury, then topped herself.*
- *You just fancy him.*
- *Who doesn't?*

Morgan had chaired the book group for two and a half years but had no idea why most of 'her boys' were behind bars. Prison etiquette was strict – *don't ask, don't tell* – but nobody needed to enquire why Danny Kilcannon was serving a life sentence.

Although never a household name, his face was vaguely familiar even before the trial. A carpenter by trade, he'd earned a few quid as a TV extra, graduating to a single speaking part as a murderous priest in a BBC drama. During his trial, the role had been a gift to tabloid editors casting around for a nickname. To the world at large, Danny was now 'Killer-cannon'. Except in here. Here he was 'The Luvvie', or 'Filthy Murdering Bastard', depending on your point of view.

Although popular with some of his fellow inmates, he was loathed by those who believed that four summers ago he tried to rape his fifteen-year-old stepdaughter before cracking open her skull with a thirty-two-ounce claw hammer.

Ninety minutes later, Morgan leaned against the door of her Mini and put a roll-up between her lips. A stiff wind was blowing in from the sea, buffeting the vast expanse of shingle surrounding the network of buildings that made up HMP Dungeness.

'Morgan!'

Getting into the car, she tried to pretend she hadn't heard the man's reedy voice but it was too late; he was hurrying across the car park, bicycle clips hooped around corduroy-clad ankles, paperwork flapping in the wind. She glimpsed his name on a pamphlet.

The Psychology of Socialisation into Criminality by Nigel Cundy.

She lit her cigarette and rolled down the window.

'Hi, Nigel.'

The sandy-haired man made an attempt to smooth his comb-over.

'Wondered if you fancy a drink tomorrow.'

'Sorry, I'm busy,' she said. 'Maybe another time?'

He was struggling to keep his smile in place.

'Will you still be "busy" if his appeal fails?'

'Excuse me?'

'I assume you're hoping to see Kilcannon on the outside,' said Nigel. 'Candlelight, champagne, violins.'

She felt a flicker of annoyance.

'Not sure what you mean.'

'You'll need cheering up when his appeal gets thrown out,' said Cundy. 'Especially after all that blogging and tweeting, keeping his case in the public eye.' A sniff. 'Pity a hack like you couldn't get a proper article into a proper paper.' Morgan could feel her jaw clench as he continued. 'Plus it's his second attempt at an appeal. Doesn't bode well.'

'Maybe you're forgetting the fact that he's innocent.'

'Maybe you're confusing fact with opinion.'

'A major miscarriage of justice right under your nose, Nigel. Doesn't that bother you?'

'If it *was* a miscarriage, yes. But if you look at *all* the evidence—'

Morgan felt her face flushing with anger.

'Don't you ever get tired?' she said.

'Of?'

'Defending the system, no matter how much it screws up.'

'He's guilty.'

'I know Danny,' said Morgan.

'Knew. When you were a kid. Now you're in your forties—'

'I'm thirty-seven.'

'Old enough not to allow the good old days to cloud your judgement and get in the way of facts.'

The man's smile was growing more glacial. He handed her a copy of the *Daily Telegraph*.

'Souvenir,' he said.

That photo – the one snatched at the window of the meat wagon just after Danny's conviction – appeared alongside a headline posing the question that cut to the heart of the matter.

Innocent or Guilty? Killer-cannon faces appeal court tomorrow.

'The *Daily Telegraph*?' she said. 'Seriously?'

He sniffed. 'We're not all Guardianistas.'

She sighed.

'Ever wonder if you're in the wrong job, Nigel?'

'Beats writing about fourth-rate celebs.'

Morgan knew her smile didn't reach her eyes. She sucked on her roll-up, plucking a strand of tobacco from her tongue.

'Is this really your idea of how to chat up women?'

Nigel's grin vanished as Morgan started the car. He raised his voice to make himself heard above the engine.

'One last time: Danny Kilcannon is not the man you want him to be.'

But his words were lost on the wind.

The place Morgan called home, one of a scattering of converted railway carriages that had housed fishermen and railway workers in the 1920s, was five minutes' drive from the prison, three hundred yards from where the shoreline met the shingle beach.

A succession of owners had extended the structure, cladding the walls and erecting a clapboard lean-to on the side facing the old lighthouse.

There were two bedrooms, a bathroom and a kitchen-cum-living room that gave on to a timbered deck festooned with hanging baskets of red geraniums. The splash of colour always raised Morgan's spirits, especially on those graveyard-grey days when the sea spray assaulted the windows like machine-gun fire and the wind howled like a ghost train.

With its huge power station, gravel pits and heaps of rusting scrap, Dungeness Nature Reserve was nobody's idea of a resort but Morgan loved every scrap of shingle, every spear thistle, every clump of sea kale. She got a thrill from sharing her habitat with pipistrelle bats, foxes, stoats, badgers, hares and weasels, not to mention dragonflies, a hundred species of beetle, and, according to the RSPB Reserve, enough birds to enthral the most passionate twitcher – from peregrine falcons to avocets, wheatears to corn buntings.

Stepping out of her car, she scanned the windswept beach, deserted except for three teenage boys in the distance. One was kicking a can, another hurled stones at an abandoned fishing boat. She could hear the tinkle of breaking glass. As the boys chased after the can, heading for the Dalek-like pylons that pointed their death rays at the power station, Morgan stepped onto the deck bordering her house.

She heard the seashells before she saw them. Felt them crunching underfoot. For a second, she wondered if they'd been scattered by the wind or left by the boys – some kind of game – but on closer examination she saw they'd been arranged, neatly and deliberately, to spell out three words.

Don't trust him

She turned to scan the beach. The lads had disappeared. The shoreline was deserted, as was the single-track road that ran parallel with the railway line snaking towards Romney Marsh.

Without making a conscious decision, Morgan lashed out, kicking the shells onto the beach, scattering them far and wide. Then she let herself into her house and poured a glass of wine, trying to ignore the trembling of her hands and the hammering of her heart.

Two

Waking before five, Morgan tried in vain to push the message from her mind. The obvious culprit was Nigel Cundy – petty, jealous – but maybe the warning had nothing to do with her. Just a teenage prank.

As dawn broke she gave up on sleep, took a shower then spent half an hour deciding what to wear. With a knot of apprehension curling in her stomach, she got into her car and headed for London. She'd had the Mini serviced last week. Today had been a long time coming. Her car breaking down was out of the question.

After parking in an underground NCP, Morgan walked through the bustling streets, taking up position on the south side of the Strand, opposite the Gothic extravaganza that housed the Royal Courts of Justice. She'd decided not to sit in the public gallery, knowing she would struggle to control her reaction if the wrong verdict were announced. Time to keep a low profile. Every TV in HMP Dungeness would be standing-room-only tonight. Even on a red-letter day for Prisoner FF7836, she couldn't risk compromising her relationship with the other members of the book group.

The chilly October sunshine seemed to have triggered a burst of bonhomie among the reporters milling around the Court of

Appeal. Surveying the satellite vans – Sky News, BBC, ITV – she couldn't help wondering what had happened to her own journalistic career. The plan had been simple: a first at Oxford then important work as a fearless investigative reporter combined with appearances on *Question Time,* pronouncing wisely and wittily on the issues of the day.

The reality had been bewilderingly different: pregnancy; redbrick dropout; single motherhood. Not one editor had accepted her impassioned, forensically researched articles putting the case for Danny's innocence. Far from being hailed as champion of the wrongly convicted, she'd been dismissed as a crank, a member of the green ink brigade.

The start of her career had coincided with the acceleration in the decline of the newspaper industry, so she survived by hacking out articles on C-list celebs, topping up her income by scrubbing seaside bolt holes belonging to smug second-homers and their floppy-haired children with names like Sholto, Candida and, for all she knew, Chlamydia.

Feeling a vibration in her jeans pocket, Morgan fished out her phone and checked her email. Most waking hours were spent in a state of low-level anxiety, hoping editors would deign to respond to pitches where her breezy tone fooled no one.

Hi! Ever wondered what happened to (name of ex-soap star/ disgraced footballer/long-forgotten boy band member)? Wonder no more. He/she is in rehab/panto/flipping burgers. Thought I'd give you first dibs.

Her weekly column, Me and My Fridge, had been a surprise hit for *Plus One*, a lowbrow glossy. For three years, micro-celebs had lined up to *exclusively reveal!* their favourite recipes and, inadvertently, their eating disorders, but a new-broom editor had arrived and Morgan's only regular source of income had been swept away.

Even now, awaiting the verdict from the Court of Appeal, the freelancer part of her brain was keeping an eye out for responses to a pitch for a piece on pets that resembled their celebrity owners. But instead of a message that might put food on the table *(OK, 1500 words by Monday)* the email proved to be from her daughter's father.

Your pal Danny K is making another appeal! In court now! Thought you'd like to know! Cx

Typical Cameron: head in the Californian clouds, too many exclamation marks.

About to compose a reply, Morgan had the powerful feeling that she was being watched. She scrutinised the reporters on the other side of the road but no one seemed to be taking an interest. Passers-by hurried along. Nobody gave her a second glance.

But someone was watching. An animal instinct. She could *feel* it.

Shivering, she saw a stir outside the court. The hacks surged forward, jostling for position ...

And there he was ... Danny Kilcannon ... emerging through the archway with his lawyer, Imogen Cooper-Price, a pencil-skirted redhead who waited for the jostling hacks to position their microphones.

Dodging traffic – the hell with being spotted; she'd striven for this moment! – Morgan ran across the road. The fact that Danny was here, standing on the pavement, could mean only one thing. He was free after four years inside! Jostling amid the throng of reporters she strained to catch the lawyer's statement.

'Today,' said Imogen, 'following a long fight for justice a terrible wrong has been righted. After considering fresh forensic evidence – and following a recanting of testimony by the only so-called eye witness at the original trial – the Court of Appeal has declared Danny Kilcannon's conviction unsafe.'

Standing on tiptoe, eyes stinging with tears, Morgan tried to quell the feeling that *she* should be the one delivering this victory statement. She forced herself to concentrate on Danny. His impassive face.

'Let's be clear,' continued the lawyer, 'Mr Kilcannon is innocent. His conviction is quashed. The Crown Prosecution Service will not be seeking a retrial. As of this minute he is exonerated, totally innocent in the eyes of the law.' She paused and looked at the cameras. 'And every right-thinking person.'

Morgan knew the statement had been packed with sound bites to ram home the message not just to viewers, but to every editor in the country. The tone of the media coverage would determine how Danny was perceived for the rest of his life: as an innocent wrongly convicted, or a liar who got away with murder. How many people had stood on these steps, vindicated by the system, only to remain vilified in the court of public opinion?

Imogen was still speaking.

'Danny will not be making a statement. He's asked me to say one final thing: today marks the end of his nightmare but not the end of the fight for justice for his stepdaughter, Zoe. Nor the end of the search for his wife, Rowena.'

The lawyer had barely finished before Danny was bombarded with questions.

How does it feel to be free?

Why did your wife go missing?

Engulfed by the crush of journalists, Morgan tried to wave to the man at the centre of attention but her arms stayed pinned to her sides.

Do you think Rowena is still alive?

If you didn't kill Zoe, who did?

Danny ignored the questions and headed for a waiting taxi. Morgan watched as the lawyer ushered her client into the cab then climbed in beside him. As the taxi pulled away, Morgan stared, willing him to turn around.

Stop the cab. I need to thank Morgan.

But all she saw of him was his back, ramrod-straight, as he headed away with Imogen Cooper-Price. The stab of jealousy hit Morgan like a fist. She turned and headed towards the car park, striding through the crowded streets.

Minutes later, hurrying down the piss-stained staircase into the gloom of the NCP, she fed her ticket into the machine. She could ill afford the fifteen-quid fee and her resentment at being ignored – *after all she'd done* – was growing with every passing second. Today was not going well.

As she approached the Mini, she stopped. A parking ticket? *Seriously?* She snatched it from the windscreen. It wasn't a fine but a slip of paper on which someone had printed two words.

You're next

Three

By the time she got back to Dungeness darkness was falling and wisps of fog were swirling in from the sea. She climbed out of the car, stomach still churning with resentment and anxiety. She dreaded finding another message but the deck was bare. No shells. No note. No warning.

Hurrying inside, into the kitchen, she locked the door and shrugged off her leather jacket. The hot tap was running (she must have forgotten to turn it off this morning) and the bin stank of last night's prawn shells. Chucking the rubbish bag onto the deck, she closed the door against the wind then sat on the sofa. For a full minute, she tried to banish the messages from her mind while wondering what you were supposed to do when four years of work paid off and there was no one to tell.

The possibility that Danny might waltz away with his lawyer had never crossed Morgan's mind. There had been no discussion between them about tonight, she'd simply assumed he'd want to be here, with his champion and oldest friend.

More than friend.

Her eyes roved the room. She'd laid in Belgian beer and Cadbury's Flakes, the chocolate he'd loved as a kid. These she had wrapped in yellow tissue paper and tied with yellow ribbon.

One corner of the *Congratulations!* banner had peeled free from its Blu-Tack and was drooping onto the sofa next to two half-deflated helium-filled balloons. She chucked the banner into the bin then lit a roll-up and popped both balloons.

Two beers later, she booted up her laptop then checked her mobile. No emails. No messages. No texts. She ripped the paper from one of the Flakes then paced the room while giving herself a talking to. OK, this wasn't how she had envisaged tonight, but Danny was free and that was all that counted. He'd be in touch when he was ready. And if he was currently licking champagne from Imogen Cooper-Price's breasts or peeling off her stockings (she looked like that kind of woman), who could blame him?

Recoiling from the image, Morgan bit off a chunk of chocolate and told herself to get a grip. She turned on the TV, where Danny's release was the lead on the *Six O'Clock News*. And there was that lawyer again, bloody Imogen bloody-Cooper-bloody-Price, the woman who had declined Morgan's offers of help, dismissing her as a lovesick loony. Her statement outside court was shown in full. Then, as the camera showed her climbing into the taxi with Danny, Morgan found herself reliving the stab of jealousy she'd felt. She forced herself to focus on the BBC's jowly reporter.

'According to his lawyers the case against Danny Kilcannon was always purely circumstantial. Prosecutors alleged he was violent towards his wife Rowena – who remains missing – and behaved 'creepily' towards her fifteen-year-old daughter Zoe. But the so-called hard evidence was sparse. Firstly, the prosecution argued that blood spatters on Kilcannon's clothing could only be explained if he were the killer. Although accepted by the original

jury, this evidence has since proved to be flawed, resulting in the disbarring of the expert witness who made the claim. But on its own, this wasn't enough to secure Kilcannon an appeal. The man who completely turned things around was Dover Holiday Park manager Caleb Quirke. He told the original jury he'd seen Danny running from the crime scene shortly after midnight on the night Zoe died.'

As the reporter continued speaking, the camera cut to archive footage of Danny alighting from a prison van on the first day of the Old Bailey trial. Suit. Tie. Gaunt face. Hollow eyes.

'But when Quirke recanted, confessing to having perjured himself at the original trial, the Criminal Cases Review Commission finally agreed to refer the case to the Court of Appeal. With advances in forensic techniques, the discredited bloodstain evidence came under renewed scrutiny. Professor Dorothy Greenberg, one of the UK's leading forensic experts, testified that Zoe was still breathing when Kilcannon found her in the family's holiday chalet. Contradicting the original expert witness, the professor said it was the teenager's dying exhalation of a bubble of blood that sprayed the mist of drop-lets onto her stepfather's clothing. Had Kilcannon been responsible for the brutal hammer attack, said Professor Greenberg, his clothes would have been spattered with a lot more blood, as well as particles of tissue.'

Now the screen filled with another piece of archive footage: the familiar home video of freckle-faced Zoe, then thirteen, hula-hooping in the chalet park.

'Eighteen months ago, Kilcannon's first appeal was rejected by the Criminal Cases Review Board – a crushing blow.'

The reporter reappeared onscreen, standing outside the Court of Appeal.

'But with the new forensic evidence, and with Caleb Quirke recanting, the CCRC agreed to refer the case up the chain. Following today's ruling, the Crown Prosecution Service announced there was no realistic prospect of Kilcannon's being convicted at a retrial – with the result that he is now innocent in the eyes of the law, and no doubt celebrating his first night of freedom in four years.'

Morgan turned off the TV. She stared at the blank screen then picked up her phone and scrolled through her contacts. One by one, her friends had given up on her, exhausted by her obsession with Danny's innocence. Her mother was lost to cancer, her father to dementia, her daughter still holidaying in America. Nigel Cundy's face flashed across her mind, only to be dismissed straightaway. There was only one person she wanted to talk to tonight and he had other plans.

Which was fine.

Absolutely fine.

On the verge of opening another beer, her third, she thought better of it. She should have made a Plan B. The beer buzz had lifted her spirits but another bottle would start a downward spiral.

She stood up.

Tea.

That was the thing.

Camomile tea.

Hot bath.

Early night.

Waiting for the kettle to boil, she stared out of the window, listening to the sound of waves on shingle. Reaching into the pocket of her jeans, she pulled out the pebble she'd carried since the age of nine, feeling its reassuring weight in her palm.

Almost thirty years ago, another beach.

A girl. A boy. Eight years old.

Danny's voice.

'Let's swap pebbles.'

She frowned. 'Why?'

'It's like having a bit of each other. In our pockets, all the time.'

She shrugged. It sounded silly. But she was pleased. Had a funny feeling in her belly. A warm glow, like porridge, only nicer.

'OK,' she said. 'Let's swap pebbles.'

Four

It was 3.06 a.m.

The blood-red digits of the bedside clock cut through the darkness.

3.07

3.08

Morgan had not slept. Overtired. Resentful.

And jittery.

Had she really left the kitchen tap running? Or had someone been here?

Slipping out of bed, she walked into the kitchen and stared at the sink, hoping to jog her memory, but her morning rush to get ready was no more than a vague blur. Shivering, she checked the locks, cursing herself for choosing such isolation. The nearest house was almost a mile away, an architect-designed folly once featured on *Grand Designs* and occupied only on summer weekends.

When the rental agent had suggested Morgan's meagre budget might stretch to a converted railway carriage on the beach, she'd laughed, not because it seemed improbable but because of the sheer serendipity.

Danny.

The prison.

The book group.

If she was going to spend so much time in Dungeness, why not live here too?

She tried to immerse herself in *Lord of the Flies*, next on C-Wing's reading list, but concentration proved impossible so she fired up her laptop and updated the *Justice for Danny Kilcannon* website. After four years' chronicling every twist of the appeal process, the best she could muster for the climactic entry were the only words that mattered.

HE'S FREE!

She stared at the screen for a moment then shut down her laptop and turned off the light.

3.17.

She turned her pillow over, laying her head on the cool cotton and closing her eyes. An image of Danny swam into her mind. In the taxi. With Imogen Cooper-Price. She tried to banish the tableau from her head.

And then she heard it.

Footsteps on shingle.

Her eyes sprang open. She slipped out of bed and parted the curtains.

No sign of life.

She stood still, aware of the triple-quick beating of her heart.

There it was again.

A crunch of pebbles underfoot.

She snatched up her mobile, about to dial the police, but froze as she heard a familiar voice. A young woman's.

'Hello?'

Relief mingled with adrenaline.

'Are you trying to scare me to *death?*' Morgan shouted through the window.

A slender teenager with a heart-shaped face, bright red lipstick and long blonde hair stared back at her.

'Hi, Mum. Nice to see you too.'

The eighteen-year-old looked like the kind of girl you'd see on someone's shoulders at Glastonbury, brimming with the insouciant confidence of youth and beauty. She dumped a Louis Vuitton holdall onto the shingle, drawing Morgan's eye to a pair of black Doc Martens and cut-off jeans.

'Is it just me or are all men shit?'

'You left the tap running.'

Morgan sat at the kitchen table, trying not to glare at her daughter.

'At least I washed up my coffee mug,' said Lissa. 'Wanted to surprise you.'

'At three in the morning?'

'I'm on LA time. Got talking in the pub. Met this biker bloke, went to his place. Total loser. He threw up after, like, half a spliff then passed out.'

Alcohol. Bikers. Weed. Morgan didn't know where to begin. She studied her daughter's face, trying to recall a single conversation that hadn't been full of recrimination. There must have been *one* in the years before Lissa had declared that living with Morgan was 'worse than being sentenced to actual hell, like, forever' and campaigned to be allowed to live with her father.

Exactly what was it about your rich, easy-going dad that made you think living with him would be fun? After I'd done the hard graft. What was so tempting about the big, posh house in Notting Hill and the holidays in Malibu?

Why have you ignored my calls?

Since when did you wear Lolita-red lipstick?

And is that a tattoo on your ankle?

Lissa was staring at the fridge.

'Do we have any, like, coconut water?'

Morgan fought the urge to roll her eyes.

'Not unless you brought some from LA.' A thought flashed into her mind. 'Have you been leaving me weird messages?' She was sure she knew the answer.

'No. What kind of messages?'

'Never mind. How long are you staying?'

'You might pretend you're pleased to see me.'

'I *am* pleased to see you.'

She took a sip of tea then reached across the table and stroked her daughter's slender wrist.

'Hungry?'

Lissa stretched her arms above her head. Three bracelets jangled.

'Just tired,' she said. 'No sleep on the flight.'

Morgan smiled. 'Time to get as snug as a bug in a rug?'

'Shit, Mum, I'm eighteen.'

'I know. I was there when you were born.' She nodded towards the bracelets. 'You got my present, then.'

The three silver hoops. Simple. Elegant. Worth the hike on the overdraft. Lissa gave a sheepish smile.

'They're beautiful. I should have, like, emailed or something?'

What's wrong with the phone?

'Was it a good birthday?'

Lissa's smile vanished.

'Are you pissed off because I had the party at Dad's?'

'No,' said Morgan. 'But it's late and I've had a crap day.' She headed out, pausing in the doorway. 'For the record, it's good to see you.'

And it was.

Five

The next morning, Morgan donned her red swimsuit and walked barefoot along the deserted shoreline, heading for the water's edge. Shivering, feeling the mud ooze between her toes, she carried on without pause then plunged beneath the waves. The ice-cold water made her gasp and triggered an instant endorphin rush. Swimming was her sole concession to the Health Nazis. She didn't do it every day, just often enough for it to feel like a habit. Usually, battling with the waves gave her respite from over-thinking the past, forcing her to take a break from the voices clamouring in her head. But today was different. Lissa's absence had felt like a bereavement; her return had rekindled resentments Morgan would never voice aloud.

Your father wanted me to have an abortion. He said I'd tricked him by getting pregnant. He may be generous now but he refused to contribute a penny towards your care, never called, never wrote, never came to see you. You only have contact today because I kept the lines of communication open. A girl needs her father. No one knows that better than I do.

There had been other love affairs, of course – the workaholic lawyer (too neurotic), the would-be poet (too self-absorbed), the wily reporter (too married) – but thanks to Lissa, Morgan would be forever tied to Cameron, just as she would always keep a place in her heart for Danny Kilcannon. *The first cut is the deepest.*

Morgan towelled herself dry and headed for home. She dressed quickly then took her daughter for a windswept walk along the shoreline. She didn't say much, content to listen to Lissa's account of life in Range Rovia, the *'so boring'* school prom *('Why are boys my age crap?')* and her post A-level summer in Malibu.

'Dad's thinking of selling the house. Says he's, like, down to his last Porsche.'

'Poor thing.'

Morgan knew how much Cameron adored the place over-looking the Pacific, along with the other perks enjoyed by an Oscar-nominated screenwriter: the cash, the kudos and the come-hither smiles of pretty young wannabes. She'd never seen the beach house, of course – he'd hit the big-time long after their fling – but Lissa said he called it his *reward for all the Hollywood shit.*

Not for the first time, Morgan wondered how life might have been if she and Cameron hadn't fizzled out. Twelve years her senior, he was kind, smart and sexy. There were worse combinations. But he was also incapable of monogamy, once cooking her a *paella* while nonchalantly explaining his idea of fidelity: restricting himself to one mistress at a time. He had also shown his true colours by refusing to acknowledge his daughter until she was old enough to be 'interesting' – by which he meant interest*ed*. In him.

'I'm pretty sure he's broke,' said Lissa. 'Or maybe the latest child-bride has her eye on somewhere bigger.'

'Do you get on with her?'

Morgan could see her daughter choosing her words carefully.

'Her name's Kristina. She's a classical pianist, five years older than me, and thinks it might be "fun" to be a Hollywood agent, or design baby clothes for oligarchs' wives, or be Miss Ukraine – but I'm not going to, like, slag her off, if that's what you're hoping.'

'I'm not asking you to take sides,' said Morgan, stooping to pick up a discarded fast-food container, 'but it would be nice if you'd stop being spiky.'

She crumpled the litter into her pocket and looked out to sea. Seagulls were swooping around a flotilla of fishing boats. Further out, an oil tanker crawled across the horizon. There was litter everywhere. A black bin bag had been ransacked by the gulls. Cans, sweet wrappers, crisp packets ...

Lissa chewed the inside of her lip, a tic she'd inherited from her father.

'Can I stay for a bit?'

Morgan felt a warm glow.

'Of course,' she said. 'As long as you like.' She brandished a polystyrene container. 'Join me on litter patrol?'

Lissa rolled her eyes but couldn't resist a smile.

'*Seriously*?'

They spent the next hour cleaning up the beach, stuffing their pockets with food wrappers and plastic packaging. Morgan had never been the most doting mother, not even when Lissa was little, but a constant overdraft had forced her to find inventive ways to keep her daughter occupied. In the pre-teen years, litter patrol had been a favourite.

Later, after Eggs Benedict (Lissa was a natural in the kitchen, a trait she'd inherited from Cameron, along with her blue eyes), Morgan fell silent as her daughter reapplied her lipstick while describing a visit to her grandfather's care home in Sandwich Bay.

'I spent the afternoon with him before I flew to LA. I don't think he knew who I was but he smiled a lot and kept singing "You Are My Sunshine". Maybe he thought I was you.'

'Mmm.'

'Are you OK?'

'Fine.'

'I was thinking ... if he doesn't recognise me, chances are he might not recognise you either.'

'Why are you looking at me like that?' said Morgan.

'Maybe you could bluff your way in, without her knowing.'

Her. Morgan's stepmother. Ursula. Manipulative. Prim. Poisonous.

'Mmm,' she said. 'Maybe.'

'Or write to him. Might make you feel better about ... all the stuff.'

'I'll think about it.'

'Which means no.'

'Are we still talking about this?'

'Now who's being spiky?'

Morgan sighed. 'I *have* written. Many times.'

'And?'

'Ursula sends the letters back, unopened.' She started to clear the plates, adopting what she hoped was a breezy tone. 'You know the upside to Alzheimer's? You can hide your own Easter eggs.'

Lissa smiled.

'Changing the subject much?'

'Coffee?' said Morgan. 'Or how about a poke in the eye with a sharp stick?'

Later, on the sofa, half-watching Lissa's favourite show (a dating format featuring elderly widows and widowers flirting with young gerontophiles), Morgan brought her daughter up to date with the success of Danny's appeal.

'The experts came up with new evidence, and the eye witness – a guy called Quirke – recanted his testimony.'

Lissa frowned.

'Why did he lie in the first place?'

'He was threatened by Zoe's real killer,' said Morgan. 'The man crept up, held a Stanley knife to his throat and threatened to come back and flay him alive unless he lied about seeing someone else running from the chalet.'

'And that "someone else" was Danny?'

Morgan nodded.

'Did the police find the guy with the Stanley knife?' said Lissa.

'No.'

Morgan could see her daughter thinking things through.

'So what made Quirke change his mind?'

'Conscience,' said Morgan. 'His change of heart wasn't enough on its own, but add the new blood-spatter evidence, along with a discredited expert witness, and Danny's a free man.' She quoted the red-haired lawyer. '"Innocent in the eyes of the law. And every right-thinking person."'

'That's *so* not what Dad says.'

'Dad doesn't know him.'

'Neither do you.'

'Of course I do.'

'No,' said Lissa. 'You *knew* him.' She fell silent for a moment, chewing on a strand of long blonde hair. 'Have you tried, like, internet dating? Maybe you could be a cougar on Tinder? How about it, Tinderella?'

'I am so not having the hook-up conversation,' said Morgan, lighting a roll-up. Lissa made an elaborate pantomime of waving away the smoke.

'What is it about Danny?' she said. 'Thirty years and you're still carrying a torch.'

Morgan exhaled twin plumes of smoke. She was tempted to tell her daughter that life hadn't always been like this. That there had been a time when it was possible to believe in people – police, bankers, priests, even politicians – a time when you didn't have to invest all your trust in those closest to you.

'There's no torch,' she said. 'I just know he's not capable of murder.'

'Even so,' said Lissa, 'there must have been more to it than puppy love.'

Morgan's roll-up had gone out. She let the seconds tick by.

'How about hot chocolate?'

Lissa gave a theatrical sigh.

'Why won't you tell me what happened?'

'Is that a tattoo on your ankle? A devil?'

'Want to know what I think?' said Lissa.

'Certainly *looks* like a tattoo.'

'I think Danny *did* kill his stepdaughter. And his wife. And everyone I know agrees.'

'They're wrong.'

Her daughter sighed.

'I get it,' she said. 'Maybe the eye witness *did* lie about seeing him on the night of the murder, and maybe the blood-spatter evidence *was* flawed – but you can *still* only ever be ninety-nine per cent certain Danny didn't do it.'

Morgan suppressed a stirring of irritation but remained silent. Her daughter needed to have her say.

'If the system can mess up once, it can mess up twice,' continued Lissa. 'We just don't know which order they cocked up in. And you weren't there when Zoe died so ninety-nine per cent is as sure as you're ever going to be, unless someone finds out what happened to his wife and who killed his stepdaughter.'

'By "someone", you mean me?'

'Might make a change from writing about celebrities' fridges.'

'None taken.'

Lissa plucked the roll-up from Morgan's hand and took a drag. Exhaling smoke through her nose, she glanced out of the window, scanning the deserted beach.

'Just the thought of you seeing him – especially here – it totally freaks me out.'

'He's my oldest friend.'

Lissa shrugged.

'It's *so* obvious you never even had sex with the guy. If you had, you'd have got him out of your system years ago.' She took another drag on the cigarette. 'In my experience, if you're crazy about someone ...'

'Did my eighteen-year-old daughter just say, "in my experience"?'

'Yes,' said Lissa. 'If you want to get over a guy, get *under* him or he'll always be, like, the one that got away.'

'That's exactly what he was.' Morgan's voice had become smaller.

'Well, now he's a bed-blocker.' Lissa's tone was unforgiving. 'The guy who stops you finding Mr Right. Last word? Check out what really happened to Zoe and the wife, but for God's sake let go of Danny. Swipe left, and get on with your life.'

Morgan stared at her daughter, trying to remember a time when the world was black and white, people were good or bad, and all things were possible.

Six

1989

Sitting on the shady side of the playground, Morgan made sure she couldn't be seen by the teachers, switched on her Walkman and let Donna Summer's voice wash over her; a song about a girl trying to play it cool while desperate to attract the attention of the boy of her dreams.

Keeping an eye out for Danny, she let her gaze rove across the school's three principal cliques. By the gates, members of the Big Hair Coven were flicking through the *Sun*, ignoring the headline about a disaster at Hillsborough football stadium, focusing instead on the antics of Dirty Den and Angie in *EastEnders*.

Outside the Science Block, members of the Football Brigade were making the most of the final minutes of break, one playing kicky-uppy, another jeering as a gaggle of smokers, the Nico-teenies, emerged from the girls' toilets. As one of the furtive fourteen-year-olds handed round a tube of Trebor mints, another caught Morgan's gaze and flicked a V-sign. She pretended not to see and cranked up the volume on the Walkman.

A shadow fell. Stevie Gamble was staring at her, motioning for her to remove her headphones. Morgan ignored him but the acne-faced youth snatched away the Walkman, holding it out of her reach.

'Your dad's making me miss the First Eleven match next week.'

'What was it this time?' said Morgan. It would be uncool to grab for the Walkman. 'Gin? Windolene?'

'Cider,' said Stevie Gamble. 'Everyone drinks cider.'

'Not in Geography.'

'Did you grass me up?'

Morgan shook her head. 'No need,' she said. 'Your breath stank and you were being a pillock.'

There was no warmth in his smile.

'He's still a bastard.'

The bell rang. The Football Brigade and the Big Hair Coven began to shuffle in the same direction as the Nico-teenies, joining the rest of the pupils funnelling towards the main building. Morgan tried to follow but Stevie puffed out his chest and blocked her way. He was close enough for her to smell his cheese-and-onion breath.

'And he's a poof,' he said.

Morgan rolled her eyes.

'Which is why he married my mum. And why they had me.'

'Loads of pillow-biters have kids.' Stevie smirked.

'Get lost,' said Morgan. 'You're pathetic.'

She walked around him and followed the others as they streamed towards the main building.

'We all hate you,' said Stevie, falling into step and handing back the Walkman. 'Everyone hates you because of your pervy dad. I'd shag you, though. Maybe a blow-job for starters.'

'Dream on, needledick.'

He clenched his jaw. Morgan broke off as he grabbed the Walkman, raising it in the air.

'Take it back, slag.'

'N-E-E-D-L ...' said Morgan.

She heard another voice.

'Give her the Walkman.'

She turned to see Danny Kilcannon, shirt untucked, face covered with a sheen of sweat from playing football.

'Piss off, pretty boy,' said Stevie Gamble.

'I'm counting to three,' said Danny.

'It's sod all to do with you.'

'One, two ...'

Without warning, Stevie hurled the Walkman at Danny's head. Morgan heard a crack of bone then watched as the two fourteen-year-olds laid into each other, arms flailing, punches flying, feet kicking.

Another familiar voice. Older. Angry.

'Enough!'

Morgan turned to see her father striding across the playground, tweed jacket flapping. She retrieved her Walkman, slipping it under her jumper.

'Kilcannon! Enough!'

But Danny couldn't hear the headmaster or perhaps didn't want to. Morgan could see blood seeping from the cut where the

Walkman had struck, just above his eyebrow. Her father prised the teenage combatants apart. The boys glared at each other, both breathing heavily.

'He threw something at me,' said Danny.

'Threw what?' said Morgan's father.

She tightened her grip on the Walkman beneath her sweater.

'Not sure,' said Danny, 'but it hurt. And he was bullying Morgan.'

Leo turned to his daughter.

'What did Mr Gamble say, exactly?'

'Can't remember.'

Her father folded his arms, exposing the leather patches on his elbows, and turned back to Danny.

'Your third fracas this week.'

'Yesterday wasn't my fault either.'

'When I want your opinion, I'll give it to you.'

Morgan watched as her father shook his head slowly.

'What are we going to do with you?'

'Don't know, sir.'

'I do.' Leo leaned closer, breathing in Danny's ear. 'I'm sending you home.'

The boy's face fell. 'I'm excluded?'

Morgan winced as her father nodded.

'One week,' he said. 'Go home at the normal time and don't come back until next Wednesday. Ask your mother to telephone me.'

'Stevie started this, sir—'

'Perhaps you'd prefer two weeks?'

Morgan could see Danny swallowing his anger. He turned away and strode towards the cloakroom, muttering under his breath. Morgan looked her father in the eye.

'He's right,' she said. 'This wasn't his fault.'

He ignored her, calling after Danny.

'Tuck that shirt in!' He turned back to focus on Stevie Gamble. 'Cider for breakfast, now this.' Morgan watched as her dad took off his glasses and began to polish the lenses on the hem of his V-neck. Never a good sign. 'Care to tell me what you were saying to Miss Vine?'

'Can't remember, sir.'

'See if this helps your memory. The First Eleven will have to manage without you for the rest of term.'

The boy looked stricken.

'Are you serious?'

'"Avaunt, and quit my sight."'

'What?'

'Shakespeare, Mr Gamble. You might have heard of him. It means, "go away".'

Morgan watched as Stevie drew breath to protest then changed his mind and headed in the direction taken by Danny. Leo waited until both boys were out of earshot then donned his glasses and raised an eyebrow in his daughter's direction.

'Three things.' He ticked them off on his fingers. 'One: if I see that Walkman again it goes to Oxfam. Two: do up your top buttons. Three: stay away from Kilcannon. "Mad, bad and dangerous to know".' He gave a tight smile. 'Source?'

Morgan sighed. 'Byron.'

'No, it was said *of* Byron by …?'

'Lady Caroline Lamb. Can I go now?'

It was the end of the day before Morgan had a chance to seek out Danny, catching up with him during the exodus through the school gates.

'Sorry about earlier.'

His shoulders were hunched, his expression grim.

'Mum's going to kill me,' he said. 'Assuming she's not too pissed.'

Morgan shot him a sympathetic smile.

'Has my dad ever been … weird with you?'

'Define "weird".'

She shrugged.

'You know – weird.'

Danny gave her a sideways look.

'Oh. That.'

The rumours had been around for as long as Morgan could remember; first whispered behind her back then deployed to taunt her, or – worse – used as a pretext to ignore her completely.

'All that "Mr Vine's a perv stuff" is bollocks,' said Danny. He took his pebble from his pocket, tossed it in the air then caught it and gave her a reassuring wink.

'Right,' she said, smiling back. 'That settles it. He's not gay.'

'How do you work that out?'

'"Cause if he were he'd be all over a pretty boy like you faster than you can say George Michael.'

Morgan could tell Danny was embarrassed but she didn't care. It would be a week before she saw him next; she wanted to part on an upbeat note.

And when they did meet again, after Danny's exclusion ended, it was at the same spot, by the gates. Along with the rest of the school they watched in stunned silence, Danny placing a comforting hand on Morgan's arm, as her father walked stiffly in front of two plainclothes police officers, climbed into the back of their car and was driven away without a backward glance.

Seven

'Mum?' Lissa poked her head around the door. 'Are you awake?'

'I am now.'

'There's a man. Wants to talk to you.'

'What man?'

'Clive Rossiter.'

Morgan sat bolt upright and blinked at her daughter.

'Ask if I can call back in ten minutes.'

'He's in the kitchen.'

'Shit.'

Five minutes later, Morgan was dressed in jeans and a faded *Buena Vista Social Club* sweatshirt, sitting opposite a silver fox in his forties. Subtle aftershave, expensive suit, shoes from Bond Street, or wherever people like the features editor of the *Post* flashed their Platinum cards.

'Sorry,' said Morgan. 'I don't normally sleep this late.'

Clive Rossiter flashed his Harley Street smile.

'I'm the one who should apologise. Barging in before breakfast. Anyone would think I was a hack.'

Morgan sipped her coffee, tuning in to the sound of the rain on the roof. She'd taken an instant dislike to her visitor.

Half man, half Rolex. But he edited the best features pages in what was left of the newspaper industry so she donned her friendliest smile.

'Something tells me you're not here to talk about my piece on pets that resemble their celebrity owners.'

He crossed his legs, revealing an unexpected pair of red socks.

'No,' he said, feigning nonchalance, 'but I glimpsed your pitch in my inbox then someone happened to mention your name.'

She could hear Lissa clattering in the bathroom.

'Who mentioned me?'

'Forgive me,' said Rossiter. 'We hacks must be discreet, *n'est-ce pas*?'

Smarmy *and* pretentious – Morgan's least favourite combination. She tried another tack.

'In what context did my name come up?'

'A Danny Kilcannon context.'

She felt her smile tighten but was distracted by the sound of dripping, coming from somewhere just beyond her peripheral vision. Glancing to her left, she saw the roof was leaking. In that instant, she became aware of the state of her home. The furniture seemed more shabby than shabby-chic, the 'lived-in' look merely messy.

'You run a prison reading group, am I right?'

Morgan's smile disappeared.

'What's this about?'

'I'm here to make you an offer.'

'Why didn't you phone?'

'I'm old school,' said Clive Rossiter. 'Prefer dealing face to face.' He smiled. 'Couple of questions, off the record?'

Morgan shrugged.

'Fire away.'

'You were at school with Danny, yes?'

'How did you know?'

The man in the red socks nodded towards Lissa who had emerged from the bathroom and was stacking the dishwasher, pretending not to listen.

'Lissa and I were chatting while you were getting dressed.'

Morgan looked at her daughter, still tanned from her Malibu summer, the top buttons of her cream linen shirt undone. The visitor followed Morgan's gaze.

'I must admit,' he said, 'I wasn't aware until talking to the lovely Lissa just how far back you and Danny go, but it makes things even better.'

'The lovely Lissa'? Could you be a little more creepy?

'Better for whom?' Morgan said.

Rossiter sniffed then leaned forward and steepled his fingers. She noticed a leather document case by his feet.

'The Killer-cannon murder is one of those stories people can't get enough of. *Did he or didn't he?* The mob baying for blood, hammering on the van as the monster is driven away. Finally, closure. Peace restored. Order out of chaos.' His gaze held Morgan's as the performance continued. 'But then they tell us the monster isn't guilty after all. So where's the closure now? After all, *we* locked him up, so if he's innocent what does that make us?' The journalist's lips twitched. 'It makes us guilty, Morgan. And we can't stand that. We're the good guys. So a handful, like you, think he's innocent – but the majority need to believe that he killed Zoe and murdered his wife, because if he didn't then *we're* the guilty ones for wanting him locked him away. And that's unbearable.' He leaned back into the sofa. 'Have you heard from him since his release?'

'Why do you ask?'

He flashed his expensive smile.

'I'm not here to steal your story.'

'I don't have a story.'

He sniffed again.

A cold? Or was he a coke freak?

'That's where you're wrong,' he said, shooting his cuffs. 'At the risk of descending into cliché, I intend to make you an offer you can't refuse.'

It proved to be an exaggeration, of course – journalistic hyperbole – but the offer was simple: should Danny Kilcannon get in touch, it would be 'splendid' if Morgan could keep her 'eyes and ears open'.

'For?'

'Anything of interest.'

'You mean, anything to confirm he's a monster?'

'Not necessarily,' said Rossiter, flicking a speck of something invisible from his lapel. 'Could be something to prove he's innocent.'

'But then the story would be over,' said Morgan. 'Which wouldn't sell papers. Whereas confirming his guilt would be good for circulation.'

'Ah—' Rossiter dragged out the single syllable into a drawl. 'Well, that would be of interest. But uncertainty, mystery, that's what keeps a story alive. Jack the Ripper, JFK, the *Mary*

Celeste ... Unsolved murders ... missing children ... And now Danny Kilcannon.'

Drip.

The sound was growing more regular, like a metronome.

Drip.

He looked up at the ceiling.

Drip.

'I find there's something uniquely depressing about a leaky roof.'

'The landlord's on the case,' said Morgan.

Rossiter gave a thin smile.

'To put it bluntly,' he said, 'your old friend is the star of one of the biggest stories in years. Every time we splash "Killer-cannon", or feature him on Post Online, we add readers and get a zillion hits. Like today.'

He reached for his document case and took out a copy of the *Post*. Morgan read the headline: *Killer-cannon Witness Hit-and-Run.*

'Mum? Are you OK?'

Morgan felt her daughter's hand on her shoulder. She scanned the byline above the article. By Clive Rossiter.

'The story is everywhere,' he said. 'Even the *Guardian*.'

Lissa was reading the paper over Morgan's shoulder.

'Is this the eye witness who lied about seeing Danny the night Zoe died?'

Rossiter nodded.

'Caleb Quirke,' he said. 'The chalet park manager. Run over by a car and in hospital, "fighting for his life", as hacks like me and your mother might say.'

Another attempt to ingratiate himself.

The man's gaze lingered on Lissa's tattooed ankle then he dragged his attention back to Morgan.

'He's under police guard.'

'Why?' Lissa was twirling a strand of blonde hair between her fingers.

'In case whoever ran him over has another go,' said Rossiter.

'Maybe it was the guy who murdered Zoe,' said Morgan. 'The one who threatened to flay Quirke alive with a Stanley knife.'

'Possibly,' said the journalist. 'It's a confused picture at the moment.' He paused for effect. 'But it happened shortly after Danny was released. Quite a coincidence, don't you think?'

Morgan's grip tightened around her mug.

'What exactly do you want?'

'To put you on a retainer.'

'I told you, Danny hasn't been in touch.'

'He will be,' said Rossiter. 'You tweeted and blogged about him for years. Ran the campaign website, kept the flame alive. Started a reading group so you could see him behind bars. Even moved to the back of beyond to be near him.'

'You make me sound like a stalker.'

'Not at all. Such loyalty is rare.'

Could you be a little more patronising?

'He's probably holed up somewhere discreet,' said Rossiter, 'screwing some Broadmoor Babe. Beating women off with a stick.' A thin smile. 'Or a thirty-two-ounce claw hammer.'

Morgan stood up. 'I need to get on with my day.'

Rossiter remained seated.

'I'm the editor's representative on earth. She's keen to nail this deal.'

Morgan heard Lissa's voice.

'What does that mean, exactly?'

'A thousand a week, minimum of six months,' said Rossiter. 'A retainer to give us the inside track on what Danny says, where he goes, who he sees.'

'Spy on him?' said Morgan.

The man in the red socks pretended not to hear.

'If you were actually to write anything we'd double our top rate.' He paused for effect. 'Which beats scrubbing other people's houses for minimum wage.'

How did he know she worked as a cleaner? Lissa must have told him that too. Morgan flashed a glare at her daughter while doing some lightning calculations. The man's offer was worth £26,000 for starters. Most importantly, her byline would appear in the *Post* – a proper newspaper.

'I expect you'd like to think about it,' said Rossiter, getting to his feet and placing a business card on the table. 'Call me anytime.'

'The answer's no,' said Morgan.

Lissa's eyes widened.

'*Mum...*'

'I don't spy on friends.'

She was surprised by how resolute she sounded but the journalist acted as if she hadn't spoken. 'The offer's good till Friday,' he said, heading for the door. 'And I might even be able to push the editor to fifteen hundred a week.'

His hand was on the doorknob.

'Clive?'

He turned.

'I could do you a great piece on lookalike celebrity pets.'

Another thin smile.

'You're sitting on the biggest story of your life, Morgan. Make the right decision.' He opened the door. 'Good to meet you. And your lovely daughter.'

He stepped out into the rain.

Lissa stared at her mother.

'You just turned down fifteen hundred pounds a week!'

Morgan glanced out of the window and watched Rossiter drive away in a silver BMW. She headed for the bathroom.

'I need a shower.'

Letting the lukewarm trickle of water wash over her, she tried to suppress a surge of panic. Two days ago, she would have given anything to have the *Post* deign to respond to an email, let alone promise to publish anything she wrote. She tried not to think about her overdraft.

'Mum – phone!'

'Take a message.'

'It's Danny Kilcannon.'

Eight

Morgan closed the door of the huge beachfront house and listened to the silence. She had once arrived at a cleaning job to find the husband, a stockbroker, splayed on the staircase, wearing a gimp mask while being straddled by the Hungarian au pair. Morgan's red-faced apology hadn't saved her from the sack. Not a mistake she intended to repeat.

'Hello? Anyone home?'

Silence.

She checked her watch. Six and a half hours before she finally got to see Danny on his own, a rendezvous she'd looked forward to for years. She opened the cupboard where the owners kept the mop and bucket, thankful for the chance to keep busy. The work was tedious but it would stop her counting down the hours. Tea and homemade chocolate cake, as per Danny's request.

She decided to tackle the grottiest jobs first. Entering the downstairs loo, she took a fresh pair of rubber gloves from the packet and stared at the note taped to the cistern.

No TAMPONS or LOO PAPER down the bog!
Spare a thought for the poor septic tank!

No mention of a thought for the cleaner. Nine quid an hour for sprucing up the second homes of best-selling novelists, advertising execs and other weekenders was hard to swallow, but emptying bins full of used Andrex and tampons *really* stuck in the craw.

Morgan's attempt to set up a property management company servicing holiday homes had started well but fizzled out when the recession hit. Still, people always seemed to need cleaners. One 'temporary' job had led to another. And another and another. Then the freelance journalism had dried up altogether and now here she was, doing what her stepmother would have called 'charring'.

For a second, she imagined setting fire to the house then running outside, yelling at the top of her voice, but her bank statement flashed before her eyes so she snapped on the yellow gloves and prised open the lid of the bathroom bin.

Five hours later, she cast a glance around the immaculate steel-and-granite kitchen. The Aga shone, the work surfaces gleamed and the windows sparkled, even the skylight. She picked up the envelope propped against the Gaggia espresso maker and extracted five crumpled tenners and a Post-It.

Thanx Morgen. P.S.: don't worry about the change.

Gee, thanks.

And '*Morgen*'? Seriously?

She contemplated calling Clive Rossiter to tell him she'd changed her mind but the impulse died in a second. She was a good hack, just stuck in the doldrums. She needed to redouble her efforts. Yes, there were good reasons for the state of her finances – the climate for freelancers had never been so brutal – but she needed to work harder, have bolder ideas, find smarter ways to pitch.

Her mobile rang.

'Hi, Lissa.'

'You're not going to be late, are you?'

'Why?'

'Because if you invite a killer to tea, the least you can do is not leave your daughter to make chit-chat. *How was prison, Danny? Where's your missing wife? Murdered anybody lately?*'

'You don't have to be there.'

'You don't think I'm going to leave you alone with *him*?'

'I'm on my way,' said Morgan. 'Don't touch the cake. I was up half the night baking the bloody thing.'

She made it back to Dungeness in record time and parked outside the converted railway carriage. Lissa was on her hands and knees, scrubbing bird shit from the deck.

'Who are you and what have you done with my daughter?'

Lissa continued to scrub, keeping her voice low.

'I needed an excuse to come outside.'

'Why are you whispering?'

'I told you: I'm not being alone with a man who picked up a hammer and …'

Morgan felt her heart rate quicken.

'He's here?' She checked her watch. 'An hour early?'

'Got the train times mixed up.'

'Terrific,' said Morgan. She fingered her grimy fleece.

'You smell like shit,' said Lissa.

'Because I've been up to my elbows in …'

She broke off as the door opened. Out stepped the man she had last seen on the steps of the Court of Appeal. She registered his new haircut and a black cashmere polo neck that made him resemble a sixties beatnik.

A present from Imogen?

His smile was warm, his voice low.

'Here she is,' he said. 'The woman who saved my life.'

Tea was a strained affair. Just the two of them. Not even the onset of rain could drive Lissa inside.

'Suppose I'll have to get used to people snubbing me,' said Danny, gazing out of the window. Her hoodie raised against the elements, Lissa was sweeping shingle from the deck. 'I've only been out a couple of days and I've already been spat at and called a "murdering bastard".' His knee was jiggling. 'It'll only get worse after what happened to Quirke.'

Morgan sipped her tea.

'People are idiots.'

Danny nodded, letting the silence stretch. He picked at his chocolate cake then put his hand in his pocket.

'When they let you out,' he said, 'they give you fifty-three quid and a plastic bag with the stuff you had when you were arrested. Wallet, watch, keys.' He drew something from his pocket. 'And this.'

He put his pebble on the coffee table.

Morgan drew her own pebble from her pocket, placing it next to his.

'Funny old world.'

He smiled.

'Yep.'

Another pause. Awkward. Like she'd forgotten how to talk to him.

Drip.

He looked up at the ceiling.

'I could fix that.'

Drip.

She pointed to a card on the coffee table.

Dungeness Handyman. No job too big or small.

'My landlord sent him to check it out,' she said. 'He says he'll come back when he gets the time.'

Danny examined the card's toolbox logo. He replaced it on the table, next to the pebble and a posy of wild flowers Morgan had noticed while making tea.

'You shouldn't have,' she said.

He winced. Embarrassed.

'They're not for you. Sorry.'

Oh.

'It's OK, Danny. I'm not expecting anything.'

Read into that what you will.

'Always been rubbish about presents.' He sucked cake crumbs from his fingers. 'I could make you a piece of furniture though. As a thank you.'

'A kitchen table?'

'You're on.'

He swallowed the last of his tea then took a breath. Something on his mind.

'I know what you did for me, Morgan. I know how tough it was keeping the faith. Seeing you every few weeks, with Pascoe and the others, not being able to talk properly – it drove me nuts.'

You don't know the half of it.

She smiled. 'Well, here you are.'

'Because of you.'

Morgan felt a warm glow. Until he spoiled it.

'And Imogen.'

'Ah, Imogen.' She suppressed a flicker of irritation. 'Quite a character.'

'You mean a bitch?'

'She wouldn't even meet me,' said Morgan, choosing her words with care. 'But she did a brilliant job. And only a bitch would call another woman a bitch.'

Danny leaned closer. She could smell the soap on his skin.

'I wouldn't be here without both of you,' he said. ' "Thank you" isn't enough but it's the best I can do. Till I make your table.'

He cracked his knuckles and stared at the floor for a moment. She braced herself for more about Imogen, but Danny got to his feet.

'Mind driving me somewhere?' He picked up the flowers. 'These are for Zoe. Today would have been her nineteenth birthday.'

Morgan's smile faltered.

'Is this a good idea?'

A shrug.

'They wouldn't let me go to her funeral so—'

He tailed off abruptly as the door opened, ushering in a blast of cold air. Lissa entered, stamping the rain from her Doc Martens. She ignored Danny and glared at her mother.

'Is he ever going to leave?'

'Where are you staying?' asked Morgan.

Danny looked out of the car window.

'With a friend.'

She tightened her grip on the steering wheel. Unbidden, an image of Imogen flitted through her mind. In a shower. With Danny. His head bending to kiss her pale neck ...

Forcing her attention back to the road, Morgan swerved to avoid a pothole.

'For God's sake, Mum!'

Squashed onto the back seat, Lissa radiated disapproval.

You don't think I'm going to leave you alone with him?

Banishing the image of Imogen, Morgan tried to think of a neutral topic. Her daughter had a point. What were you supposed to talk *about*? All recent conversations with Danny had revolved around books. Dickens ... Greene ... Orwell ... *Down and Out In Paris and London* ... *The Catcher In The Rye* ... Before he'd re-entered her life – before the C-Wing reading group – she hadn't seen Danny in two decades.

She'd heard he'd married, of course – a young widow with a daughter from a first marriage – and that he was working as a carpenter, making furniture for people who valued proper craftsmanship. Then came the Deal Secondary School reunion, always a minefield, especially after the fate that had befallen her father. Danny had been a no-show – a crushing disappointment – but someone mentioned that he was on the books of an extras agency, doing occasional TV work to supplement his income. Morgan had tried to watch *EastEnders*, hoping to glimpse him propping up the bar of the Queen Vic, but found the storylines too depressing. She'd caught an ad for car insurance, the one where he played a superhero rescuing a damsel in distress. Then, just weeks before his arrest, she'd made a point of watching his first speaking part – as the murderous priest in *Guilty As Sin*. Small role, big impact. It had earned him fifteen minutes of fame and the nickname 'Killer-cannon'.

He turned to face Lissa.

'OK in the back?'

'Nope.'

Morgan stole a glance at her daughter in the rear-view mirror.

'When are you going to get a proper car, Mum?'

Morgan rolled her eyes in Danny's direction but he didn't seem to be listening.

'Nearly there,' he said.

Dusk was closing in and the roads were almost deserted as a succession of Kent villages flashed by. Danny rolled down the window and breathed in the air, still rainfall-fresh.

'I missed this,' he said. 'Bonfires. Pint in a pub. A Labrador kipping by the fire.'

'You sound like Dad,' Morgan said, immediately wishing she'd kept her mouth shut.

'How is he?'

'He has dementia,' said Morgan. 'Lives in a care home. Ursula still won't let me see him.'

Danny nodded.

'She always reminded me of Cruella de Vil.'

A voice from the back seat.

'Can you, like, close the window? It's freakin' freezing.'

Danny obliged. Silence descended for the final mile as Morgan steered the car through a deserted hamlet. A church loomed out of the darkness.

'This is it,' said Danny.

His voice was hoarse. Morgan pulled onto a grass verge, turned off the engine and killed the lights. Danny stared at the church for a long moment. Clutching the posy, he got out of the car and walked up the grassy slope towards the arch leading to the churchyard. Morgan watched as he disappeared into the darkness beyond.

She heard Lissa's sigh.

'Must do this more often.'

'You didn't have to come,' said Morgan.

'Oh, yes, I did.'

The ensuing silence was punctuated by Morgan's sporadic attempts to mollify her daughter.

No, Lissa didn't think Danny was nicer than expected.

No, the church wasn't Norman.

No, she wouldn't like a bloody Tic Tac.

Three minutes passed. Five. Ten.

'OK, that's enough,' said Lissa. She reached across to open the passenger door.

'Where are you going?' said Morgan.

'Where do you think?'

Morgan hesitated then got out of the car. The moon had yet to make an appearance through the clouds that scudded across the night sky. The church stood on an incline, set back from the road. She followed Lissa up the path, through the gate, under the ivy-clad arch. Most of the headstones were centuries old, leaning at angles, like a giant's jagged teeth.

No sign of Danny.

Morgan reached out to take Lissa's hand then recoiled as she grazed a knuckle on a serrated blade.

'What are you doing with a knife?'

'Stupid question.'

And then Morgan saw it. The headstone. White marble. No dates, as if recording the brevity of this stolen life would be too much to bear.

> *Zoe Munro*
> *Beloved*

She folded her arms against the cold. Still no sign of Danny but someone else had been here. They'd left white lilies by the grave. Morgan stared at the flowers. She heard a footstep on the path behind her.

'Jesus!' said Lissa.

Danny emerged from the shadows.

'Sorry,' he said. 'I didn't mean to scare you.'

He was still holding the posy. His eyes were puffy, as though he'd been crying. For an instant, Morgan thought she caught a look of compassion flicker across Lissa's face but then it was gone.

'I wanted to go inside the church but it's locked,' said Danny. He stooped to place the flowers by the headstone. The seconds ticked by. Morgan caught the scent of the white lilies.

'Who left these?'

He shook his head and shrugged.

'No idea.' His voice was hoarse. 'No signature.'

Only now did Morgan see the small, white card nestling among the flowers. A single word printed in black ink.

Sorry

Lissa reached towards the card but Morgan stayed her hand.

'Don't touch. There might be fingerprints.'

She turned to Danny.

'Will you tell the police?'

'Of course.'

He stared at the flowers then turned and walked back to the car in silence. Following close behind, Morgan watched him cast a final look at the churchyard. As he bent his frame into the back of the Mini, Lissa placed a hand on his shoulder.

'I'll go in the back.' Her voice was gentle, conciliatory. 'Open the window if you like.'

A tiny concession but it would do, thought Morgan, turning the key in the ignition. As fast as seemed decent, she drove away from the churchyard and the young girl's grave.

Nine

Shielding her eyes from the sun, Morgan looked up at her roof. Danny had laid down his tools and was sitting, cross-legged and barefoot, on top of the converted railway carriage, staring out to sea. She watched for a moment, imagining how dearly Clive Rossiter would love a photo of Killer-cannon with a claw hammer in his hand.

'Ready for more tea?'

He wiped his brow with the hem of his T-shirt, revealing a livid scar on his stomach and a six-pack that would put many Hollywood stars to shame.

'No, thanks,' he said. 'Nearly done.'

Morgan didn't know where to look and couldn't think of anything else to say. She let her eyes rove over the beach. In the distance, a three-legged dog was sniffing around an abandoned fishing boat. She'd seen the dog before but never in the company of people. Another Dungeness stray, perhaps, like herself.

Inside, she rummaged in the fridge, found the remains of a lamb kebab and left it out on the deck. Then she turned her attention to her daughter.

Lissa was slumped on the sofa, playing a game on her iPad. They hadn't spoken for hours. The no-show by the handyman had coincided with a call from Danny. After demurring briefly, Morgan had accepted her old friend's offer to patch up the leak.

A couple of hours later, as he'd set to work with roofing felt and a can of bitumen, Lissa had marched her mother inside and volunteered her latest theory: Morgan's old flame was so devious that he'd beaten up the handyman who was now hospitalised, just like Danny's hit-and-run victim, Caleb Quirke. Danny had then offered his services as a knight in shining armour.

'Why would he do that?'

'To make you think he's Mr Nice Guy.'

'What if he *is* Mr Nice Guy?'

Lissa had yet to master the art of disagreeing without being disagreeable.

'For God's sake, Mum. If you want to have a grown-up conversation then at least admit my scenario is, like, possible?'

'OK,' said Morgan. 'Let's call the handyman and check he's not in Intensive Care.'

Lissa pouted and stuffed her hands into the pockets of her cut-off jeans. Morgan leaned across the table.

'I was watching you last night,' she said. 'In the churchyard. You felt sorry for him.'

'Doesn't mean he didn't do it.'

'So the new evidence counts for nothing? The appeal court got it wrong? He's conned me all these years? The boy I've known since I was eight?'

'He's not a boy anymore. Plus, he's an actor. And you're behaving like a lovesick kid.'

'Maybe,' said Morgan. 'But is it possible that you fell for the press hysteria? That you hate to admit you misjudged him? Is it possible there are millions of people who feel the same way?' Recalling the speech made by Clive Rossiter, she answered her own question. 'Because that's why they hate him, Lissa. That's why they spit at him in the street ... It's easier than hating themselves for locking up an innocent man.'

Lissa tapped her hairbrush on the table. Pink. Plastic. A relic from childhood.

'Shall I brush your hair?' said Morgan.

Lissa nodded. A thaw was coming. Morgan led her to the sofa.

'So who left the lilies?' said Lissa.

Morgan shrugged, brushing her daughter's hair in long, even strokes.

'No idea. But he's told the police. Maybe they'll trace the flowers, get prints or DNA from the card.'

'Who'd need to say sorry to Zoe?' said Lissa. 'Apart from the obvious.'

Morgan loosened a tangle in her hair.

'Maybe Zoe's mother.'

'Rowena? Why?'

'For not protecting her daughter,' said Morgan. 'If anything happened to you ...' Her voice tailed off.

'Let's think this through.' Lissa's tone was still sceptical. 'Rowena vanishes for years – no proof of life, no ATM withdrawals, no passport activity. Then she pops up and leaves flowers on Zoe's grave? Like, *seriously*?'

'If you want a grown-up conversation,' said Morgan, echoing Lissa's jibe, 'at least admit it's possible.' The hairbrush strokes were rhythmic, soothing, the way Lissa liked. 'But to play devil's advocate,' Morgan continued, 'it's also possible that Danny bought the lilies himself.'

'To divert suspicion?'

'Maybe. Say he went to the churchyard earlier, planted the flowers then conned us into going with him so we could "discover" that someone had beaten him to it.'

'To make us think that this "someone" was the real killer?'

'It's possible.'

'But you don't believe it,' said Lissa.

'Nope. Just keeping an open mind.'

Lissa fell silent then stretched her long, tanned legs. Morgan took stock of the devil tattoo and a delicate silver anklet. Not the sort of trinket Cameron would buy. A gift from a boyfriend? Now was not the time to ask.

'OK,' Lissa said, 'an open mind would have to allow the possibility that the appeal court got it right.' She scratched her nose. 'And I admit he's different when you get to know him.'

Another concession. Morgan felt a small stir of triumph. She handed the pink hairbrush to her daughter then got to her feet. They heard Danny clambering down from the roof. Seconds later he was at the door, shirtless, toolbox in one hand, sweat-soaked T-shirt in the other.

'The dog ate the kebab,' he said. 'OK if I use your shower?'

'Help yourself,' said Lissa.

Morgan watched her daughter track Danny's progress. As he disappeared into the bathroom, revealing his bare back, Lissa's eyes widened in shock. Across his broad shoulders was a series of small red marks. Dozens, no, *scores*. Morgan frowned, trying to fathom their origin, then stifled a gasp as realisation hit home.

They were scars left by the burning tip of a cigarette.

The lunchtime crowd had dwindled. The fish and chip shop was almost deserted. Morgan sprinkled vinegar on her haddock and pulled up a stool at the counter, next to Danny's. Lissa was posing for a selfie in front of a sign that announced the chippy's name: There's a Plaice for Us.

'One for Dad. He loves puns.'

She preened as she took the photo then tapped away at her iPhone.

'I'll never understand the whole selfie thing' said Danny. 'Why does every second have to be photographed?'

'Rembrandt did selfies centuries ago,' said Lissa. Raising her gaze, she seemed to be taking stock of him for the first time, her eyes travelling over his upper body.

'You look like a swimmer. Like Mum.'

'Not lately,' said Danny. 'How about you?'

'In Malibu, every day,' said Lissa. 'Here, no. But I did have a dip this morning. Completely naked.'

'Thank you for sharing,' said Morgan.

Lissa ignored the jibe, her eyes still on Danny.

'How did you get the scar on your stomach?'

'He doesn't want to talk about it,' said Morgan. 'Let him eat.'

She was wrong: he did want to talk about the scar. She picked at her fish, listening as he related how Gary Pascoe had taken a dislike to him from day one. How a heroin dealer who'd murdered the mother of his five children had decided Killer-cannon was the lowest of the low. The intimidation and violence had been relentless: knife attacks; beatings with a sock full of batteries; and one summer night, a 'lock-in'.

'Pascoe bribed a screw to unlock my cell so he and his cronies could get at me.'

'What happened?' said Lissa.

A thin smile.

'We played Monopoly.'

'Couldn't you have transferred to the Vulnerable Prisoner Unit?'

'Someone knows their jargon.'

'I Googled prison stuff while you were fixing the roof.'

'VPU is for sex offenders,' said Danny. 'Blokes the others want to lynch.'

'Exactly,' said Lissa. 'It's for the prisoners' own safety.'

Danny's voice was quiet.

'That's what they tell you,' he said. 'And that's why I was sent there at the start of my sentence.'

'What happened?'

Danny snapped open his Coke. Morgan sensed he was playing for time.

'The truth is, VPU is not much safer than anywhere else. It's where I got the scar on my stomach. Half an inch higher, I wouldn't be here.' He swigged from the can. 'But since I'd done nothing wrong, I figured I might as well take my chances in gen-pop. Made my case to the Governor, he said yes.'

'What about the burns on your shoulders?' said Lissa.

Danny looked away.

'More Monopoly,' he said. Then he fell silent for a moment before making a determined effort to change the subject. 'What about you, Lissa? Gap year? University? Travelling?'

She shook her head.

'Not if Dad's girlfriend has anything to do with it.'

Morgan raised an eyebrow.

'Oh?'

'Kristina says I have a window of, like, two years – three max.'

'To do what?'

'Cash in while my boobs pass the pencil test,' said Lissa. 'Get famous.'

'Famous for what?' said Danny.

Morgan listened with mounting dismay as her daughter outlined her career plan.

'Find a guy – actor, singer, sports star, whatever. Piggyback on his profile, do the sex-tape thing. Leak it to TMZ. Then work my arse off till the rest falls into place.'

Danny frowned.

'Rest of what?'

'Kristina's career strategy,' said Lissa. 'Reality TV in the US. Suck up to Mail Online, establish a UK profile. Then do the relationship break-up exclusive for *OK!*, invite *Hello* into my "lovely home", all that cheesy shit. Plus PAs. Dee-jaying, making music, my own perfume.' She took a sip of Coke.

'I thought Kristina was a classical pianist,' said Morgan.

'She is,' said Lissa. 'But she's also got an eye for the main chance, which is why she's with Dad and why she spent a year studying celeb-ology.'

'Is that a thing?' said Danny.

Lissa gave a sly grin.

'Gotcha.' She turned to Morgan, still smirking. 'Both of you.'

Morgan was confused. Was her daughter serious? Surely no one could be as venal as Lissa made Kristina sound?

As Lissa freshened her lipstick, Morgan became aware of the dumpy woman behind the counter. She was whispering to the fish fryer, a middle-aged man in a bad toupee. The woman cast a disdainful look in Danny's direction then disappeared into the back.

'You need to leave,' said the man.

Morgan narrowed her eyes.

'Excuse me?'

'Your boyfriend understands.' The fish fryer opened the till and took out three five-pound notes, slapping them on the counter. 'Take your money and go.'

Morgan could feel a red mist starting to descend.

'Maybe you don't read the papers,' she said. 'He's innocent.'

'Really?' said the man. 'And I'm Mary Poppins.'

Danny laid a hand on Morgan's arm.

'It's OK,' he said. 'I'm done.'

Morgan stood up, scraping her stool on the floor. Lissa remained seated, finishing her lipstick, then she turned on the man in the toupee.

'Do you have any idea what this guy has been through?' The eighteen-year-old glared at the fish fryer, picked up the bank-notes and ripped them in half. 'Stick these together, buy yourself a new wig.' She let the fragments flutter onto her plate. 'The one you're wearing looks like a rat died on your head.'

She slid from her stool then slammed out, linking arms with Morgan and Danny as they headed for the beach.

It was Lissa who first floated the idea of Danny giving her driving lessons. She'd been mad about cars since she was six. Her father had offered to pay for lessons but reneged following a row.

'About what?' said Danny.

He was sitting on Morgan's deck, emptying the dregs of his tea onto the red geraniums.

'Sex,' said Lissa.

Morgan watched as her daughter licked an ice cream and gazed across the beach. In the distance, a small boy was flying a kite.

'My own fault,' said Lissa. 'I made the mistake of telling him about a guy I was seeing when I was over there last Christmas. His name was Carlos. Lived in Santa Monica. Gave me my first driving lesson in his Maserati. I hit ninety-eight on the freeway.'

Morgan winced, wondering if the silver anklet had been a gift from the man with the Maserati.

'If I meet Carlos,' she said, 'I'm going to skin him alive. I'm guessing he wasn't your age?'

'Thirty-six,' said Lissa, feigning nonchalance. 'Said he was in real estate. Might have been a coke dealer on the side.'

'And still your dad wasn't happy?' said Morgan. 'Go figure.' She poked Lissa in the ribs. 'No more driving till you pass your test. And no more Carlos.'

'No chance of that,' said Lissa. 'He went back to his wife.'

'Tell me you're kidding.'

Lissa gave a coquettish smile.

'That's for me to know and you to wonder.'

'Nothing beats a Maserati,' said Danny. 'Except my old Merc.'

Lissa turned towards him, eyes wide.

'You drive a classic Mercedes?'

'It was my dad's. He died while I was in prison so it's been rusting for years.'

As Morgan knew only too well, Danny's life had been in a state of suspended animation for years. Rowena had disappeared days after Zoe's death. Danny had been charged with his stepdaughter's murder, denied bail then placed on remand while awaiting trial. There was still no sign of his wife but their cottage remained in joint ownership. He couldn't sell until she'd been missing seven years.

There had been no trace of Rowena. Privately, Morgan thought it likely the police had scaled down the search after Danny's conviction (at least the bastard was banged up for *something*) but that the hunt would resume following the controversial decision to set him free. For the police – humiliated by the appeal court's verdict – there was now renewed urgency to find the wife of Killer-cannon. Preferably dead.

'What sort of Mercedes?' said Lissa, taking another lick of ice cream.

'It's a 230SL,' said Danny.

The blue eyes widened.

'OhmyGod. 'Sixty-three?'

''Sixty-four.'

'Colour?'

'Burgundy.'

'Leather upholstery?'

He nodded.

'Cream.'

Lissa grinned.

'When you get it working, will you teach me how to drive?'

As the two petrol-heads began to discuss six-cylinder engines, fishbowl headlamps and chrome grilles, Morgan realised she was no longer listening. Instead, she was staring in dismay at her daughter, her long-legged, doe-eyed daughter, who was hanging on Danny's every word while licking her ice cream and twirling a strand of long blonde hair between her fingers.

Ten

Morgan was on a short fuse after a bad morning at HMP Dungeness. One of the prisoners had pronounced *Lord of the Flies* a 'shit kiddie book' then called her a bitch when she'd suggested, albeit gently, that he might not have entirely grasped the point. Gary Pascoe hadn't bothered to show up. She refrained from asking why, reminding herself that he was due for release and probably terrified at the prospect. Of all 'her boys', she would miss the cage fighter least.

An hour later, Nigel Cundy soured her mood further by falling into step on the landing. Would she have a drink with him later? She didn't think it was a good idea. Why not? Because they were colleagues – well, sort of. He'd persisted. She'd run out of excuses. They were on for tonight.

To make things worse, en route to five back-breaking hours cleaning a beachfront house for a property developer with more money than taste, she'd maxed out her Visa filling up the Mini, winced at two emails snubbing her latest magazine pitches, and made it home through torrential rain to find her T-shirt-and-knickers-clad daughter sprawled on the sofa, soldered to her iPad.

'Are you ever going to get dressed?'

'Shhh …'

'Excuse me?'

'I'm watching him on YouTube.'

Morgan bit her lip. Any relaxation of hostilities towards Danny counted as progress. She grabbed Lissa's hairbrush and began to brush her own rain-frizzed hair while glancing at the iPad screen. She'd seen the original police appeal on the news – and replayed in the 'Danny Kilcannon: Justice on Trial' *Panorama* investigation – but never failed to be moved by the sight of Danny's haunted face.

'If anyone knows anything … or suspects anything … no matter how insignificant it seems – please …' His voice tailed off, his glassy eyes stared into the camera. 'People must know *something* … Maybe someone at home is behaving oddly… or someone at work … maybe they can't account for their movements last Thursday. Maybe you've just got a feeling something's not right. Anything at all … and if you have, *please* contact your local police or the incident room, in the strictest confidence.'

The stout policewoman next to him nodded earnestly.

'I'd like to echo what Mr Kilcannon has said,' said Detective Inspector Jacqui Farmiloe. Morgan watched as the reassuringly stolid Senior Investigating Officer reiterated the plea for information then gave out a telephone number.

'She thinks he did it,' said Lissa. 'You can see it in her eyes.'

Morgan watched as DI Farmiloe handed back to Danny for the second part of the appeal.

'If Rowena is watching,' he said, 'please come home ... or at least call. I know how hard this is for you ... even harder than it is for me ... but we'll get through it together, so *please*, Rowena, get in touch. Even just a text to let me know you're OK.'

As Danny spoke, the DI turned towards him, her eyes fixed on his face. Morgan knew – *everyone* knew – that the police set great store by the way victims' families behaved on camera. Especially the stepfather of a murdered girl. She suspected that a battalion of body-language experts and criminal profilers had been scrutinising every nuance of Danny's performance. After all, he was an actor, albeit one with limited experience.

Morgan's suspicions were confirmed during the trial. From the start, Jacqui Farmiloe made it clear she believed that Zoe Munro had been murdered by her stepfather. There hadn't been a peep out of the woman since Danny had walked free from the Court of Appeal.

As the YouTube clip continued, a photo of fifteen-year-old Zoe's smiling face appeared on the iPad screen.

Lissa peered closely.

'Do you think she looks a bit like me?'

Morgan found the question unsettling. About to answer, she was interrupted by the sound of a car crunching on the shingle outside. Lissa sprang from the sofa and hurried to the window.

'Oh. My. God.'

Following her daughter's gaze, Morgan saw Danny at the wheel of a burgundy two-seater Mercedes. She had no idea what 230SL stood for but knew he'd been waiting all week for spare parts, working on the car late into the night. No doubt about it: the 230SL was a beautiful machine. The contrast with her Mini couldn't have been more stark.

'Looks like we're going for a drive,' she said. Then, in what she hoped was a neutral tone of voice, 'You'd better put on some clothes.'

'Can I ask a question?' said Lissa. 'About Zoe?'

Squeezed into the rear bucket seat of the Mercedes, Morgan decided to say nothing. Danny could take care of himself. She tried to shift position, so she could see her daughter's face, but Lissa was peering out of the passenger window. The rain had stopped falling but the skies were heavy with cloud, the Romney Marsh roads still slick with water.

'OK,' Danny said. 'Ask away.'

'Did you kill her?'

Morgan saw his hands clench on the wheel.

'Jesus, Lissa . . .' she said.

'It's OK,' said Danny. He turned a level gaze towards Lissa. 'No. I didn't kill her.'

'What about Rowena?'

'I didn't kill her either.'

'Did you hit her?'

'No.'

He turned to look back at the road.

'She said you did.'

'No, the *newspapers* say she *said* I hit her. Big difference.'

'Will you sue?'

'And spend the rest of my life trying to prove a negative, fighting the best lawyers money can buy? No, thanks.'

'What about suing the police? For compensation?'

He shook his head.

'Four years in prison, Lissa. Four birthdays, four Christmases. I couldn't go to my own father's funeral. That's enough criminal justice for one lifetime. And that's before you even get to the Antisocial Behaviour, Crime and Policing Act 2014, which – and here I'm quoting Justice, the human rights organisation – "makes an award of compensation almost impossible to achieve".'

Lissa thought for a moment.

'What about your mother? Did she support you?'

His jaw tightened.

'Too busy boozing it up in Tenerife.'

Morgan remained silent, watching as her daughter began to brush her hair with the pink hairbrush.

'OK,' said Lissa. 'So what do you think happened to Rowena?'

There was a brief silence before Danny spoke again.

'Post-partum depression. She had a terrible time after Zoe was born.'

'For fifteen years?'

'No,' said Danny. 'But she had a history of depression – and I don't mean "down in the dumps", I mean not eating, not washing, not speaking.' He slowed the car, guiding it through a patch of standing water. 'Then she lost the baby.'

Lissa's eyes widened.

'Your baby?'

Danny nodded.

'The miscarriage triggered another bout of PPD, more severe this time.' He took a breath. 'So ten days before Zoe was killed Rowena took an overdose. They said if I'd found her any later she'd have died.'

'God,' said Lissa softly. She turned towards Danny. 'Poor you.'

He shook his head. 'Poor Rowena.'

Lissa fell silent for a moment, staring out of the window.

'So you think she couldn't cope? Just ran out on her life?'

He nodded.

'That's exactly what I think.'

Morgan realised she'd been holding her breath. She knew the story backwards, what had she been expecting to hear?

'Do you mind me asking this stuff?' said Lissa.

'Not in the least. But saying "I didn't do it" doesn't help much, does it?'

'Of course it does,' said Lissa. 'So long as people can look you in the eye while you're saying it.'

'I can hardly pay house calls,' said Danny. 'I have to accept that most people believe I'm guilty. Nothing I can do about it.'

'Wrong,' said Morgan.

'Wrong how?'

His eyes met hers in the mirror.

'If you want to lead a normal life, you need to find out who killed Zoe. And what happened to your wife.'

No one saw the fox in the middle of the road.

The impact slammed Morgan's face into the back of the headrest.

Lissa screamed.

The tyres screeched.

The car skidded.

Then silence.

'Everyone OK?' said Danny.

Lissa managed a shaky nod.

Danny unclipped his seatbelt and got out. Lissa followed. Morgan extricated herself from the back seat. She stared at the bloodied fox on the road. Lissa raised a hand to her mouth.

'Is it dead?'

'Alive,' said Danny. 'But only just.'

'Oh my God . . .' said Lissa.

'Get back in the car,' said Danny. Morgan saw him open the boot.

'We should take it to the RSPCA,' said Lissa.

Danny said nothing. He produced a tyre jack.

Lissa's voice was shrill.

'What are you doing?'

'Look away.'

'Danny, no!'

Lissa buried her face in her mother's shoulder. The last thing Morgan saw before closing her eyes was Danny wielding the jack, raising his arm in the air. The sound was sickening. A thud. A yelp. Then it was over.

'Sorry you had to see that,' said Danny.

Lissa glowered at him, her eyes glistening with tears, her voice hot with anger.

'We could have taken it to a vet.'

Ignoring her, he picked up the fox and gently placed it on the verge.

'Let's go,' said Morgan.

Lissa folded her arms and slumped in the passenger seat, falling into a tearful sulk. Morgan got into the back as Danny replaced the jack then settled behind the wheel.

'It was the only thing to do,' said Morgan, mainly for Lissa's benefit. But she knew that when she next closed her eyes she would see the look on his face as he'd raised the jack in the air.

They drove on in silence. It was dark by the time they reached Dungeness and pulled up outside the converted railway carriage.

'I'm sorry,' said Lissa quietly. 'Mum was right, you had no choice.'

Danny said nothing. She raised her eyes to look at him then gave a gasp.

'There's blood on your face.'

Glancing in the mirror, he winced. Lissa produced a Kleenex and dabbed the spatters from his cheek.

'Will you still give me driving lessons?'

'Better ask your mother.'

'Let's think about it,' said Morgan.

Lissa's voice took on a petulant tone.

'What is there to think about?'

Morgan thought for a moment.

'Fine,' she said. 'If Danny doesn't mind.'

Lissa's face brightened. She reached out to take his mobile from the dashboard. Her fingers danced across the keyboard as she entered a series of numbers.

'Let me know when,' she said as her own mobile rang in her pocket. The ringtone was a jaunty tune Morgan recognised from TV cartoons. *Popeye the Sailor Man.*

'Keen on spinach?' said Danny, smiling.

Lissa shook her head.

'I just like his muscles.' She handed him the phone. 'Now I've got your number,' she said, 'and you've got mine.' She began to scroll through her contacts. 'Anyone hungry? I'm ordering pizza. With extra pepperoni.'

Morgan watched, her skin prickling with a combination of embarrassment and apprehension.

A Prius drew up alongside the Mercedes. Danny narrowed his eyes.

'Is that who I think it is?'

Morgan had forgotten about Nigel Cundy.

'Oh, God,' she said. 'He's taking me for a drink.'

One of Lissa's spaghetti straps slipped from her shoulder.

'At least someone's got a date,' she said. Then she went back to fiddling with her phone, the fingers of her free hand straying down her leg, drawing the eye towards the silver anklet and the devil tattoo.

Eleven

The pub was noisy, the wine corked and the menu like an ironic tribute to the 1970s. Morgan braced herself for a barrage of anti-Killer-cannon remarks from Nigel. She didn't have long to wait.

'I can't believe you're spending time with that man.'

The shrink had made an effort to spruce himself up. Not a bicycle clip in sight. But he was sporting short shirtsleeves (Morgan's number one fashion no-no) and his aftershave was sickly-sweet.

'I have a cousin in the police force,' he said. 'High up. I could ask him, if you like.'

'About what?'

'Kilcannon. The inside track. Why the police are still convinced he killed that girl.'

Morgan sighed.

'Can we change the subject?'

Giving up on her Chicken Kiev, she wondered if it would be rude to order more wine. She was no connoisseur but the Merlot was corked; the smell reminded her of old hymn books.

Nigel managed to avoid mentioning Danny for all of five minutes. Conversation turned to his hobby, photography. As part of a long-term project, he was researching the network of tunnels under Dover Castle. Originally an underground barracks for troops, the labyrinth was constructed in the Middle Ages then expanded during the Napoleonic Wars in readiness for a French invasion. In 1940 the tunnels served as the HQ for the planning of the Dunkirk evacuation. Morgan's interest was genuine – she was relieved not to be talking about Danny – but the conversation soon switched back to the matter uppermost in Nigel's mind.

'Promise me one thing,' he said. 'You won't ever be on your own with him.'

He forked a piece of scampi into his mouth. Morgan stole a glance at her watch.

'You know, it's been a long day so ...'

It was as if she hadn't spoken.

'And never leave him alone with your daughter.'

'He's not alone with her, he went home.'

'Sure about that?'

'Yes.'

Was she?

Morgan summoned the memory of the scene outside her house: Danny declining Lissa's offer of pizza; the Mercedes driving away; her daughter's face as she stomped inside and slammed the door.

'I know I'm a pain in the posterior,' said Nigel, 'but I am a man.'

'Pain in the posterior'? Who talked like that?

He leaned across the table, resting his elbow on a half-empty sachet of tartare sauce. The contents oozed onto the mat.

'If you ladies had any idea what goes on in our heads when we see a pretty thing like Lissa – a luscious, ripe young peach …' He looked away. 'The stuff we think – you'd be *horrified*.' He picked up his glass. 'And I'm one of the good guys.'

Morgan wiped her mouth with her napkin.

'Did you call my daughter a "luscious, ripe young peach"?'

Nigel looked unabashed.

'Every man would know what I'm talking about,' he said. 'Women have no idea.'

'Peach? Seriously?'

'Just trying to make a point.'

'Job done. Change the subject.'

But any topic other than Danny proved impossible. After a few minutes discussing the C-Wing reading group, debating whether or not its members would 'get' *Lolita*, they were back to Killer-cannon. According to the papers, Caleb Quirke, the eye witness who'd recanted, was still in hospital, still under police guard after the hit-and-run attempt on his life. Meanwhile, the *Post's* Clive Rossiter had been sniffing around prison staff, trying to identify other inmates due for release.

'Why?' said Morgan. 'To pump them for stuff about Danny?'

'Presumably,' said Nigel, pouring the last of the wine. 'I also had a visit from DI Farmiloe. Tricky old bird.'

Morgan hated Jacqui Farmiloe but not as much as she loathed Nigel's attitude.

'You mean, she doesn't take any crap?'

He held up a hand in mock surrender.

'Relax, Big Chief Feminist. I come to smoke pipe of peace.'

She fought the urge to throw her wine in his face.

'What did Farmiloe want?'

'The police are reviving the hunt for Rowena,' said Nigel. 'I'm guessing they're determined to prove that Danny killed her, if only to save face over the Zoe fiasco. Jacqui wanted to know if he'd mentioned anything useful during our sessions.'

'Had he?'

'No,' said Nigel with the air of a man who had given up all hope of making a difference in the world.

'Would you have told her if he had?' said Morgan.

'If it could lead to finding his wife, then possibly.'

'So it's a grey area?'

'Isn't everything?'

'Not when it comes to old friends. Trust. Loyalty.'

'You still believe Kilcannon's innocent? One hundred per cent?'

Morgan swirled the wine around her glass.

'I'm as sure as it's possible to be.'

'Ah-ha.' Nigel's eyes lit up. 'I detect a scintilla of doubt.'

She studied his face, the shaving rash around his neck.

'Not really.'

'Perhaps one day you'll enlighten me as to the origin of this unshakable faith.'

Morgan hated the man's pomposity but his question was fair.

'My dad was pilloried when I was a kid,' she said. 'The world decided he was guilty of something terrible. Danny was the only one who kept an open mind.'

An image came back to her. Fourteen-year-old Danny poring over *To Kill a Mockingbird*, mesmerised by the story of Atticus Finch and Scout.

'Was he right?' said Nigel. 'About your father?'

Morgan hesitated.

'Long story,' she said. 'It's getting late.'

Nigel let the seconds tick by then gave a heavy sigh. For a moment she thought he was about to soften his stance but he was merely preparing a fresh onslaught.

'I had extra sessions with Kilcannon,' he said. 'To address his anger-management issues.'

He played the revelation like a trump card.

'Are you supposed to tell me this?'

A shrug.

'You should know the type of man you're dealing with.'

'Are you saying he's a sociopath? That he's fooled me all these years?'

'Your words, Morgan, not mine.'

She leaned forward.

'Have you been leaving me messages, Nigel?'

He frowned.

'Messages?'

'*Don't trust him,*' said Morgan. 'Written in seashells.'

'Seashells?'

'Or notes on my car.'

He met her gaze.

'I've no idea what you're talking about.'

She studied his face. Impenetrable. Inscrutable. Infuriating.

He drained his glass then leaned closer, propping his chin on his hands. She could smell the wine on his breath.

'Do you know what a MILF is?' He moistened his lips with the tip of his tongue. 'It stands for Mum I'd Like To—'

'I know what it stands for.'

'Well, that's what you are. My favourite MILF.'

She counted silently to five.

'Piece of advice, Nigel?' He nodded. 'Rethink your approach to women. I think you're probably OK, deep down, but you act like a dick. Not just a dick – a dick's dick.'

His smile vanished. He leaned back, weighing his next sentence in his mind.

'Something else you should know,' he said. 'Someone tried to kill Gary Pascoe. Snuck up on him in the shower, slashed his throat. Usual story: no one saw a thing.' He leaned forward again. 'Happened on Kilcannon's last night inside.'

Morgan felt her pulse quicken. Pascoe had failed to show up for the book group. Now she understood why.

'Is he OK?'

'He'll live. He's in Intensive Care.'

'You think Danny put him there? Pascoe makes his life hell so he takes revenge just before he gets out?'

'Well, it's one heck of a coincidence, don't you think?'

Nigel's smile was more smug than ever. He clicked his fingers at the waitress, scribbling in the air, then turned back to face Morgan.

'Now, what were you saying about trust?'

Twelve

The house was dark when Morgan got home. Passing the kitchen table, she heard a beep and saw Lissa's iPhone light up. She scanned the text. It was from Danny.

Just got your pic. Bad idea. Sleep well.

The screen faded to black. Replacing the mobile on the table, next to an empty pizza box, Morgan considered checking Lissa's texts and photos. Staring hard at the phone, the urge was almost overwhelming but she decided against taking any action that could compromise her position on the moral high ground. 'Happening to see' a message was one thing; scrolling through a teenager's mobile was a declaration of war.

Brushing her teeth and donning her old *Buena Vista Social Club* sweatshirt, she climbed into bed. She glanced at her pile of books but knew concentration would elude her so she turned out the light, resigned to another bad night.

Just got your pic. Bad idea. Sleep well.

What 'pic'?

What 'bad idea'?

She stared at the blood-red digits of the bedside clock. Just past midnight. It was going to be a long one.

In the morning, she showered then made coffee and sat at the kitchen table, waiting for her daughter to emerge from her bedroom.

'How was the hot date?' said Lissa, yawning.

'Not a date. He works at the prison.'

'Nigel,' said Lissa, rolling her eyes. 'Loser's name.'

She shuffled into the bathroom. Morgan heard clattering. The loo flushed. Then silence. Moments later, Lissa reappeared and sat at the table. Morgan chose her words with care.

'Your phone pinged last night,' she said. 'I happened to see the text.'

Lissa snatched up the mobile and read Danny's message.

'OhmyGod, you're spying on me!'

'It beeped as I was passing.'

'Wow, look – a flying pig.'

'What was the "pic"?'

'Nothing.'

'So why does he say it was a "bad idea"?'

'Fuck's sake, Mum, it was just a selfie.'

'Can I see it?'

'I've probably, like, deleted it already.'

'Your nose just grew two inches.'

Lissa glowered, scrolled through her photos then sulkily held the phone up for inspection. The photo showed her smiling to camera and giving a thumbs-up. She was wearing a T-shirt taken from Morgan's wardrobe. On the front was *that photo* of Danny – the one of him inside the prison meat wagon – and the slogan in red.

Justice for Danny Kilcannon.

Morgan counted to five but it was no use; the row that had been simmering for days boiled over.

'What are you playing at?' she said.

'OhmyGod,' said Lissa, 'you're actually jealous.'

'No, I'm worried.'

'You're jealous because you think Danny fancies me, not you.'

'Don't be absurd.'

'What's absurd? That he wants to fuck me or that you're jealous?'

'Lissa, you're smart and beautiful and you know exactly what's going on. I need you to stop before …'

'Before what?'

'Before we have a problem.'

'We already have a problem. My mother is a jealous bitch.'

Morgan stood up and placed her mug in the dishwasher.

'I'm going to work.'

'Whose house are you cleaning today?' said Lissa. 'Which successful person with two homes is buying your services?'

Morgan felt a flush of anger.

'When did you become such a snob?'

'I am what you and Dad made me,' said Lissa. 'And guess what: people like it. Maybe your little friend likes me too. And if he does, you'll just have to get the fuck over it.'

She jumped up, knocking over her mug and slamming into her room. Morgan counted to ten before calling through the door with all the calmness she could muster.

'We'll finish this conversation tonight. Please clear up the coffee.'

She snatched her keys from the table and crossed to the front door, yelling towards her daughter's room.

'Your turn to cook tonight.'

Stepping outside, Morgan felt a pang of remorse. She was on the verge of going back, of trying to smooth things over, but held her nerve. Lissa was a spoiled brat. Let her stew.

Driving away, Morgan's unease gave way to a sense of foreboding. About what, she couldn't say.

She surveyed the results of her work – the pristine kitchen, the gleaming floor – then picked up the envelope resting against the Gaggia. Inside was a familiar message.

Thanks Morgen! P.S.: Don't worry about the change. x

She ripped the Post-It in half then pocketed five £10 notes and slammed out. Battered by the wind blowing in from the sea, she climbed into the Mini and checked her mobile. Her early-morning anger had cooled and she had texted to ask if Lissa was OK. All day, throughout both cleaning jobs, she'd been on alert, hoping for a response, but when it came to stand-offs Lissa was capable of staying stubbornly silent for days, sometimes weeks. There was usually a cursory *I'm OK* message within twenty-four hours, a tacit acknowledgement that going off the radar was callous bordering on cruel. Then the sulky silence – the *real* punishment – would begin.

Arriving back on Dungeness beach, fumbling for her key, Morgan stopped dead. Someone had left another message on the deck, a careful arrangement of seashells that sent a prickle of fear down her spine.

U R not safe

She scanned the beach.

Not a soul in sight, just the three-legged stray dog sniffing around the abandoned fishing boat in the distance.

Inside, Morgan could tell Lissa had gone. The open-plan kitchen-cum-sitting room was silent, the spilled coffee mug lay as her daughter had left it. The anxiety Morgan had been fending off tightened its grip. She pushed open Lissa's bedroom door. No sign of life, no make-up, no clothes. Even the iPhone charger had gone.

U R not safe

She reached for her mobile and tapped her daughter's number.
'Hi, this is Lissa. Leave me a message.'
Beep.

There were two likely explanations: either Lissa couldn't hear the phone or she was avoiding her mother. Morgan made herself wait five minutes before trying again. She passed the time by booting up her laptop.

Trust.

That was the theme of Clive Rossiter's column in Post Online.

'*In a cynical age, where Britain's so-called elite has forfeited any right to be trusted, who can we believe?*'

According to the 1,000-word rant, there was no longer anyone worthy of trust. Forget the soft targets – estate agents, lawyers, journalists – all fish in a barrel. Nowadays, priests were paedophiles, bankers were bastards and the police were up to their necks in cronyism and corruption. No one was surprised when politicians lied ten times before breakfast or when Big Pharma allowed people to die needlessly, or pop stars and DJs used their celebrity status to dazzle fans into staying silent about abuse, but when priests, NHS execs, high-street banks and even the forces of law and order were believed '*by ordinary, hard-working families*' to be guilty of cover-ups and conspiracies, something was rotten, '*and not just in the state of Denmark*'.

Morgan didn't care for the tone of Rossiter's article. Its subtext seemed to suggest that only the white middle class had reason to feel aggrieved by '*broken Britain*' – but it was hard to disagree with the thrust of his argument. Harder still to answer his central question.

Who can we trust?

She sat back, lit a roll-up and dialled her daughter's number.

'*Hi, this is Lissa. Leave me a message.*'

Beep.

Morgan scrolled through her contacts and tapped Danny's number. As the phone rang, she felt stirrings of relief. She'd let her imagination run riot. There was no need to worry. He would answer – or Lissa would call – and everything would be fine.

The ringing stopped.

'Hi, this is Danny. You know what to do.'

Shaking off another tingle of anxiety, Morgan decided against leaving a message. Hanging up, she glanced again at the *Post's* website. Rossiter's eyes stared from the photo above his column, under the headline that Morgan knew would do nothing to help her sleep.

Who can we trust?

Thirteen

1989

'Did your father ever touch you inappropriately?'

Inspector Barry Younghusband had a weird name and a kind face but Morgan wasn't fooled by his patronising smile.

She shifted position on the sofa, her legs crinkling the plastic cover her stepmother still refused to remove, four years after the purchase of the brown velvet three-piece suite.

'No,' Morgan said. 'He never touched me like that.'

'You're sure?' said the policeman. 'Not even when you were little?'

'Never.'

'How old are you, Morgan?'

'Fourteen.'

'So you know what I'm talking about?'

She nodded then studied her shoes.

'Are we nearly finished?'

He stood up and handed her his card.

'In case there's anything else you want to tell me.'

She'd been off school since her father's arrest. For the first two days she'd blamed her period but after a week her stepmother had lost patience.

'You can't hide forever.'

Ursula took a Findus crispy pancake from the microwave and placed it on a plate, alongside two tomato halves and a scoop of potato salad. The smell clashed with her perfume – cloying overtones of vanilla – making Morgan feel sick.

'Besides,' Ursula said, 'you've no reason to be ashamed. Your father's done nothing wrong.'

But that wasn't what the Nico-teenies said the next day at Woolworths Pic'n'Mix.

'Hi, weirdo. How's your dad? Buggered any boys lately?'

She knew her father was taking what he called 'a leave of absence' from his job. She also knew he'd been sleeping on the sofa-bed in his attic study; she could hear him pacing there at night, or trying to soothe himself to sleep with classical music on the radio. But there was no mention of the police investigation. Family supper – a strictly enforced ritual, no matter how hard Morgan might try to avoid it – was an agony of tasteless food and desultory chat, the three occupants of fourteen The Grove united in grim determination, trying desperately to ignore the elephant in the room.

Even Morgan's champion was keeping his distance. Every time the phone rang she hoped it might be Danny but it never was. In theory, she could have taken the initiative and phoned him, but 'in theory' didn't take into account the hell of being the daughter of a small-town headmaster arrested on suspicion of raping a male pupil.

Stevie Gamble had been questioned by the same chain-smoking policeman. The *Deal Guardian* ran a story filled with innuendo and quoting Inspector Younghusband. He wouldn't comment, 'except to hope that there will be no rush to judgement by the community'.

Fat chance.

Morgan knew from eavesdropping on her father's calls with his lawyer that 'no smoke without fire' was how most people saw the world, especially in a small town on the Kent coast. She'd grown familiar with other phrases, too.

Sub judice.

Innocent until proved guilty.

Other press reports of her father's troubles were not only full of innuendo but inaccuracies too: his age; the fact that Ursula was his second wife, not his first; his interest in 'astrology' (sic) as opposed to astronomy. When Morgan became an award-winning reporter she would ensure that there were never any mistakes in her copy. And she would never smear someone, no matter how damning the circumstantial evidence.

On the day she finally resigned herself to returning to school, the walk through the gates seemed to take forever. The stares were unforgiving, especially from the Big Hair Coven and the Nico-teenies. A hush seemed to envelop the building like a strange acoustic mist.

Reaching the classroom, she was relieved to find it empty except for Danny. He was in the front row, shirt untucked as usual, eating a Cadbury's Flake while finishing his homework.

'Did you read the book?' he said without looking up.

'Finished it last night.'

She closed the door then hesitated before sitting three desks away and delving into her bag for her copy of *To Kill a Mockingbird*.

'Why was Atticus Finch the only one who could see the guy was innocent?' said Danny, raising a hand to flick at a fly buzzing around his head.

Morgan shrugged.

'It's how things were in the South.'

Danny looked up and grinned.

'You're a bit like Scout,' he said. 'Total tomboy.'

She didn't know whether to feel crushed or pleased.

Suddenly, he slapped the paperback on the desk. Morgan gave a start then wrinkled her nose as he raised the book and inspected the dead fly.

'Great book,' he said. 'Unless you're a bluebottle.'

She returned his smile. They were OK. Maybe everything would be fine. Her father would clear his name and life would go back to normal.

She watched as Danny scribbled the final sentence of his essay then bit into the Flake. A crumb of chocolate fell onto the book. He didn't notice but she held her breath, transfixed. The chocolate had fallen from his mouth. His lips.

'Why didn't you call me back?' he said.

'When?'

'Last week. I phoned to ask if you wanted to see the new *Indiana Jones*. Your stepmum said you were out, both times.'

Morgan's frown deepened.

'You called my house? Twice?'

A nod. 'Didn't Cruella de Vil tell you?'

Before she could reply, the door burst open to admit an invasion of pupils letting off a blast of energy before the first lesson. A dumpy brunette Nico-teeny called Wendy skidded to a halt and glared at Morgan.

'That's my desk, Paedo-girl.'

Morgan considered her options. Fight or flight. She glanced over the girl's shoulder and saw Stevie Gamble, her father's accuser, swaggering into the room. The class immediately quietened down.

'I said, that's my desk,' said Wendy.

Morgan remained seated, splaying her legs, laying claim to the chair.

'Plenty of others,' she said.

The girl folded her arms.

'I'm counting to three.'

'Are you sure you can?'

It was nowhere near Danny's best joke but it did the trick, lightening the mood. Even Stevie smiled, stretching his acne-scarred features into a grin while brushing past Morgan on his way to the rear of the class. Wendy scowled at Danny then fell in with the rest of the pupils as the bell rang and they scrambled for seats.

Danny patted the chair next to him, raising an eyebrow at Morgan. Feigning nonchalance, she got to her feet and took a seat next to her friend – the good-looking boy with the easy smile and skin that smelled as nice as toast.

She thought of the chocolate crumb that had fallen onto the book. She'd noted the page number: sixty-seven.

Snooping. That was the only word for it. She was snooping around her father's inner sanctum. His attic study smelled of old books and wood polish. Bare floorboards, dusty beams. A day-bed, a desk and a telescope for star-gazing.

On the desk was a framed photo of his widowed mother, taken shortly before her death. Morgan barely remembered the woman. But she'd overheard her drunken dad on the phone to a distant relative, a second cousin. His mother's passing was 'a blessing for all concerned', he'd said. Her illness – dementia – had blighted not just her own life but her son's too. For years he'd been run ragged, trying to hold down a job while raising a child and meeting the needs of two dying women – his mother and his wife Bronwyn. 'And now I'm scared,' he'd told the cousin. 'Not just for me but for Morgan. If I get dementia, what happens to her? I can't bear the thought of her having to feed me, watch me drool, and wipe my arse like I wiped Mother's. I'd sooner top myself.'

His desk drawers yielded nothing of interest, nor did his battered briefcase. The shelves were crammed with books on astronomy and English literature. To Morgan's relief, there was no sign of any unhealthy interest in young boys, no secret stash of porn. Then again, if Leo did have something to hide, wouldn't he have got rid of it by now, before Inspector Younghusband came back?

She heard the hall clock strike six. Ursula had persuaded her husband to accompany her to Safeway.

'You've nothing to hide. Get out there and look the world in the eye.'

They would be back any minute. Morgan stood in the doorway, taking a last look around the attic. Her eye was drawn to the telescope. Her father had tried to share his enthusiasm with her, but had met with little success. She'd feigned interest, to show willing, but the only Mars and Milky Ways she cared about were in the shop on the corner.

She frowned. Usually, the telescope was angled upwards, towards the skylight. Today it was horizontal. She put her eye to the peephole. It took a few seconds for things to come into focus and for Morgan to realise that she was looking at a poster of a scantily clad Madonna. The house across the road belonged to Mrs Jenks, a single mother who lived there with her son. Morgan guessed the boy was a similar age to her – thirteen, maybe fourteen – but he went to a different school. They'd never exchanged a single word. Insofar as she thought of him at all, she thought of him as The Boy Across The Road.

And there he was now, entering his bedroom and closing the door. Her eye pressed against the telescope's peephole, Morgan watched as he lay on his bed. She saw him unzip his fly and gaze at the poster of Madonna, his hand creeping inside his trousers ...

She sprang back. Her heart was hammering. Fleeing the attic, she felt as if she might burst at any minute, or cry, or throw up. Perhaps all three.

She finished laying the table as the microwave pinged. Ursula removed three baked potatoes and served them with a small dollop of Stork and a pinch of Cheddar. Leo was staring into the middle distance. He hadn't shaved and was in need of a change of shirt.

'Eat while it's hot,' said Ursula, mashing the cheese into her potato.

Her husband didn't seem to hear.

'Not hungry, Leo?'

'Not really.'

Silence descended like fog.

'I see the Princess of Wales visited the Hillsborough survivors,' said Ursula. 'Despite their appalling behaviour. That woman's a saint.'

'I'm not sure you should believe everything you read in the papers,' said Leo, pouring himself a glass of Frascati.

'May I have a drop?' said Ursula with a chilly smile. 'Or are you saving all the wine for yourself and Mr Rude?'

'Sorry.'

As Leo raised the bottle to fill his wife's glass, Morgan thought back to her mother's death and the arrival of her stepmother at number fourteen The Grove. The first few weeks had passed uneventfully. Ursula had tiptoed around Morgan, careful not to boss the grieving girl. Such niceties had been short-lived. On the first of each month, Ursula made a point of taking a fresh J-Cloth from the packet. It was supposed to last exactly one month. Three weeks into June, Morgan had broken a glass, used the cloth to clear up the mess then thrown it away, fearing it might contain splinters of glass. Ursula had told her she should have washed the cloth then hung it out to dry. 'They don't grow on trees.' She would have a word with Leo, suggesting he dock the cost of a new J-Cloth from next week's pocket money. Morgan had assumed her father would ridicule such pettiness but she was wrong. Her pocket money had been short by five pence.

'Sorry.' He had given a sheepish shrug. 'That's how things are now. We'd better get used to it.'

'Had enough to eat, Morgan?'

'Yes, thank you, Ursula.'

She put her knife and fork together. Leo pushed his food around his plate.

He turned to his daughter, his eyes watering, his voice husky.

'You know I didn't do anything wrong, don't you?'

Then came the moment Morgan would remember for the rest of her life. Her father – never a tactile man – placed a tentative hand on her arm. She tried not to flinch but tension must have got the better of her. She recoiled, snatching her arm away, just a fraction of inch, but enough to confirm his worst fear.

She wasn't sure of him.

Ursula's eyes widened.

'How could you? To your own father?'

'I didn't do anything.'

Morgan felt a prickle of anger radiating through her body. Ursula's vanilla perfume was nauseating but the memory of her father's telescope trained on The Boy Across The Road made her sick to her soul.

'It's OK,' said Leo, forcing a smile. He withdrew his hand then did something he'd never done before. Looking his daughter in the eye, he began to sing "You Are My Sunshine".

Morgan looked away, embarrassed. Ursula stared in bemusement. After a moment, Leo rose from the table, clutching the bottle of wine.

'Excuse me.' He planted a kiss on the top of Morgan's head. 'There's a symphony on the radio by ...' He frowned and tailed off. 'Austrian chap ...'

Cheeks still flushed with embarrassment, Morgan said nothing. Her father was becoming more forgetful lately. Probably stress. But the word 'dementia' came to mind and she remembered her grandmother. The vacant stare. The 'goldfish' memory. The endless repetition.

'Mozart?' said Ursula.

Leo shook his head, furrowing his brow as he groped for the composer's name.

'No ...'

'Strauss? Bruckner?'

'No,' said Leo, still frowning. 'It'll come to me in a moment.'

He left the room. Ursula gave a heavy sigh.

'Man plans, God laughs.'

'Laughs about what?' said Morgan.

Her stepmother picked up her glass.

'Never mind.'

She finished her wine in two gulps, swigging it like medicine.

The brick came crashing through the hall window while Morgan was in the bathroom brushing her teeth. She ran downstairs. Her father emerged from the sitting room, the sound of classical music (a symphony by Schubert) merging with Ursula's frightened whimpers. All three stared at the brick on the carpet and the shards of glass.

'Stay here.'

Leo yanked open the front door and stepped outside.

'I'll call the police.' Ursula's voice was shrill.

Morgan picked up the brick. Dimly aware of her stepmother jabbering on the phone, she joined Leo on the pavement. There was no one else in sight. On the far side of the tree-lined road, Mrs Jenks appeared in an upstairs window, took stock of the situation then closed her curtains. There was no sign of The Boy Across The Road.

'Don't worry,' said Leo. 'They're cowards, they won't be back.'

Morgan knew his words were empty. She didn't want his meaningless attempt at reassurance, she wanted him to go away and never come back. She despised herself for having disloyal thoughts and wished she'd never looked through the telescope at the boy with the Madonna poster. She hated her father for living under the same roof as her and for making everyone at school hate her, and she detested herself for hating him, and so it went, on and on and on ...

Danny.

She wanted Danny.

He would know what to do, how to make her feel better.

Out of the corner of her eye, she caught a glimpse of movement. Something – someone – was lurking behind Mrs Jenks's hedge. Was it The Boy Across The Road? She yelled out.

'Dad!'

But her father had disappeared around the corner, in search of whoever had thrown the brick. Morgan felt her heart rate quicken.

'We've phoned the police,' she called out, her voice shaking. 'They'll be here any minute.'

At first, there was no response. Then a man emerged from behind the hedge and stepped out onto the pavement. He wore a business suit and shiny black brogues. His face was familiar but it took a moment before she could place him.

Stevie Gamble's father.

She'd seen him at school, attending a parents' meeting. He was holding something. A can – hairspray, perhaps. He met her gaze.

'Your word against mine, kiddo.'

Morgan watched as he rounded the corner and disappeared from view. Clenching her fist, she turned to call out for her father. But she stopped as she saw the wall by the front door.

Scarred with fresh graffiti.

Red spray paint.

One word.

PERVERT

Fourteen

'Have you heard from Lissa?' blurted Morgan as soon as Danny answered the phone. He sounded surprised.

'No. Why?'

'She's disappeared.'

'Since when?'

'The night before last.'

'Have you told the police?'

'Obviously.'

She put a roll-up between her lips and waited for him to speak again.

'Has she gone AWOL before?' he said.

'Never this long without letting me know she's OK.' Morgan lit the cigarette. 'And someone keeps leaving messages outside my house.'

'What kind of messages?'

'The crazy kind.'

Don't trust him.

U R not safe.

Clamping her mobile to her ear, she tried to strike a casual tone while remaining vigilant for any sign of tell-tale hesitation.

'Did you get my voicemails?' she said.

'When?'

'Yesterday and today. Must have called you six times.'

'Sorry,' said Danny. 'Reception here's pretty patchy.'

It was an opening. She took it.

'Where exactly are you, Danny?'

Two days ago she might have felt jealous of whoever was giving him a bed but no longer. Imogen Cooper-Price and the 'Broadmoor Babes' were the least of her worries. Thirty-six hours since she'd slept. Thirty-six hours since Lissa had disappeared.

'I told you,' he said. 'With a friend.'

'How nice.'

She let the silence stretch, flicking her cigarette into the ashtray.

'You sound as if you don't believe me,' said Danny.

'That's because I don't.'

She heard his sigh.

'Fair enough,' he said.

She waited. Then she waited some more. When he finally spoke again, he talked quickly, as though racing through what he had to say would somehow make things better.

'I've been – what's the phrase? – economical with the truth. It's all a bit awkward. But I haven't been staying with friends, like I told you, I'm at the cottage.'

'Which cottage?'

'Home.'

The home he'd shared with Zoe and Rowena. The thought made Morgan feel queasy.

'So why lie?'

'Because people would think it's weird and I don't want to have to explain myself.'

The truth didn't make her feel less uneasy. If anything, it made things worse. He'd never lied to her before. Or so she told herself.

'What's your address, Danny?'

'Why?'

'We need to talk.'

Silence. Then another sigh.

'I warn you, the place hasn't been lived in for years. It's a mess.'

'I'll bring rubber gloves.'

Danny's cottage stood in the shadow of Dover Castle at the dead end of a tree-lined track. A derelict, ivy-covered Martello tower sat near a layby, facing out to sea and marking the entrance to the lane. The small circular fortress was a relic from the nineteenth century, part of the network of defences against Napoleon. Scars of graffiti (*Asylum Seekers Out!*) suggested the locals were as welcoming as ever.

Morgan drove past the tower, bumping down the unmade track and pulling to a halt in front of the cottage. A broken window gave onto what had once been a front garden but was now a waist-high tangle of weeds and brambles fenced in by struts of rotting wood that needed repainting or replacing altogether. The graffiti vandals had been here too. But this was more personal, directly targeting the occupant of the cottage.

Kiddie killer!

Scum!

The daubs looked weather-beaten, as though the culprits had struck years ago, while Danny was in prison. Maybe they'd be back. Google was no friend to those seeking privacy or a quiet life.

Climbing out of the Mini, Morgan glimpsed Danny's Mercedes peeping out from beneath a green tarpaulin. The front door was ajar. She knocked, listening to rooks cawing in the trees and a dog yapping somewhere in the distance, but there was no sign of life. She stepped across the threshold.

'Hello?'

The smell of decay and mould struck her straight way. She could feel the spores hitting the back of her throat. Cobwebs and dust were everywhere. As her eyes grew accustomed to the gloom, she saw a narrow wooden staircase leading to the right. On the left, a door led into the kitchen.

'Danny?'

It was the bulging bin liner that brought things home. A tangled strip of plastic ribbon – crime-scene tape – snaked from the top; blue and white with black lettering.

Police Line. Do Not Cross. Police Line. Do Not Cross. Police Line.

With a start, Morgan realised what Danny had meant when he'd said that being here would strike people as 'weird'. The police tape dated back four years. The cottage was almost exactly as it had been left in the aftermath of Zoe's death. The murder scene, the holiday park, was two miles away but this had been Zoe's home. And Rowena's. The forensic team had scrutinised every inch and the jury had paid a site visit during the trial.

Then Danny had been locked up and the cottage had remained empty, falling into disrepair.

A sound made her jump.

'Hello?'

The noise – a distant, rhythmic banging – was coming from the rear of the house.

'Danny?' The urge to flee was outweighed by the need to look into his eyes when she asked about her daughter. 'Anyone home?'

Leaving the cluttered kitchen, she found herself in a scullery reminiscent of one of those TV documentaries about compulsive hoarders. The plastic corrugated roof had been leaking for months, perhaps years. Every surface was piled with greasy pans, cereal packets, dirty plates, discarded food cartons, smeared glasses and mould-encrusted mugs. A plate of still warm, half-eaten baked beans sat on the worktop, the sole clue that the house might be inhabited.

Morgan walked through the scullery, opening the door to the garden – a jungle of weeds, brambles and overgrown shrubbery bordered by trees that had shed their leaves, carpeting what had once been flowerbeds.

The banging was louder now. As she rounded a decrepit greenhouse, passing a water butt, she could see him standing in the doorway of a ramshackle shed, hammering a length of pine.

'Danny?'

He turned from his workbench. No trace of a smile.

'I should have told you not to come,' he said. 'I didn't want you to see me like this.'

'This place might need more than a squirt of Mr Muscle,' said Morgan. She nodded at the hammer in his hand. 'What are you making?'

'Your table,' he said. 'Nearly done.'

He holstered the hammer in his toolbelt, like a gunfighter in a western, and wiped his hands on a rag. She noticed that he was barefoot.

'Tea?'

Morgan forced a smile.

'If you can find the kettle.'

As they stood in the kitchen, waiting for the water to boil, she took a gamble.

Look him in the eye.

Put him on the spot.

'I thought Lissa might be here.'

He met her gaze and frowned.

'Why would you think that?'

'She was coming on to you,' said Morgan. 'Like a heat-seeking missile.'

The frown deepened.

'You asked if I'd heard from her. When we spoke on the phone.'

'Yes.'

'And I said no.'

'Yes.'

The kettle started to whistle.

'So you didn't believe me?'

Morgan maintained her steady tone, raising her voice above the whistling.

'Even I can see she's sex on legs. Nigel Cundy called her a "ripe young peach".'

'Cundy's a sleazebag.'

'Maybe he was just saying what others think.'

She saw Danny's jaw tighten.

'He obviously managed to convince you that all men lust after your daughter or you wouldn't be making accusations.'

The shrieking kettle reached a crescendo.

'I haven't accused you of anything.'

She turned off the gas. The whistling died away. Danny began to rinse two mugs under the tap.

'This "peach",' he said. 'You're wondering if I'm tempted to take a bite?'

Yes.

No.

Yes.

'Are you?' she said.

He stared.

'Seriously?' he said.

Too much caffeine and not enough sleep got the better of Morgan.

'Seriously,' she said. 'Because I know a lot of men think horrible stuff, even while they're smiling and talking about the weather. And no matter how well you know someone, you can never be sure what's inside their head.'

Danny puffed out his cheeks.

'As my dad used to say, "Better out than in".' He narrowed his eyes. 'Is this about *your* father? Your inability to trust men?'

Morgan felt her cheeks burn.

'No, it's about my daughter. My missing daughter.'

Danny lifted the kettle and turned away to make the tea.

'For the record,' he said, 'Lissa hasn't been here. I have no intention of inviting her over, unless she's with you. She's very pretty and a flirt, but she's virtually a kid. Most importantly, she's your daughter.' He turned to face her. 'My oldest friend. The one who keeps a pebble in her pocket.'

They searched each other's eyes, neither finding the reassurance they sought. In the distance, Morgan could hear the sound of the yapping dog. Danny's jaw tightened.

'Bloody animal,' he said. 'Barks all bloody day, all bloody night.'

He handed her a mug of tea.

'When did you last hear from her?'

'The morning after that business with the fox,' said Morgan. 'I came home from work and Lissa was gone.' She sighed, relieved to unburden herself in spite of everything.

'You said this isn't the first time she's gone AWOL,' said Danny.

'It's a pattern. Ever since she was thirteen. We argue, she disappears then punishes me by not responding to calls or texts.'

Or by going to live with her father.

'So what's different this time?'

'She's never been off the radar this long before. Usually it's twenty-four hours then she texts to put me out of my misery.'

'What do the police say?'

'Not much. I've reported her missing before so she has a history of wasting police time. And she's over eighteen now so there's not a lot they can do except put her on the missing persons list.'

Morgan swallowed. Tears were not far away. 'Sorry if I'm being a bitch. I haven't slept.'

But Danny wasn't ready for apologies.

'Sounds like you've done all you can,' he said, heading for the door. 'I'll be in the workshop. Feel free to look around.'

She watched him go then heard the scullery door close. Leaning against the counter, she cursed herself for not being more subtle, more strategic. But at least things were out in the open. She put down her mug and checked her mobile in case she'd missed a text.

Then she saw it.

A rat. Grey. Fat.

It scuttled across the floor, headed for the scullery then disappeared. Shuddering, she hurried into the hall and shut the kitchen door behind her.

Spiders she could cope with. Mice even. But rats ...

She stood in the dark hallway, feeling her heart flutter. Then she forced herself to get a grip and remember why she was here.

Feel free to look around.

Folding her arms against the chill, she walked into the sitting room.

Cobwebs everywhere. Dirty plates. Low wooden beams. An inglenook fireplace filled with grey-white ash from a recent fire. And tucked into the side of the sofa, a pink plastic hairbrush.

Fifteen

Behind her, a floorboard creaked. She turned.

'Jesus ... You scared me.'

She forced herself not to look at the hammer dangling from Danny's toolbelt. Tried to block out the image of the tyre jack in his hand ... his arm raised in the air ... the yelp of the dying fox.

'I forgot,' he said. 'Lissa sent me a selfie. I thought you should know.'

Morgan nodded. 'That was what we argued about.'

'I texted her to say sending photos wasn't a good idea. Not to Killer-cannon of all people.' She looked away. He followed her gaze. The hairbrush. She let the seconds tick by. 'Lissa left it in my car the other night,' he said quietly. 'But you'd figured that out, right?'

He raised an eyebrow but she didn't answer straightaway. Too busy trying to recall the sequence of events.

The churchyard.

The white lilies on Zoe's grave.

The injured fox.

Had Lissa used the brush while in the Mercedes?

Morgan summoned a clear recollection of her daughter in the car, brushing her hair while talking to Danny. The memory flooded her with relief.

'Yes,' she said. 'I remember.'

He was telling the truth; he'd simply found the brush in the car and brought it inside.

On the other hand … This wasn't some poor kid on the news, this was her daughter …

Her mind spinning, Morgan forced herself to get a grip. This was *Danny*, for God's sake. The workings of his mind, the secrets of his heart, were as familiar to her as her own. Weren't they?

'Sorry for giving you a hard time,' she said. 'No sleep, anxious mother. Bad combination.'

He nodded.

'Forgiven,' he said. 'And forgotten.'

Thank God. Change the subject.

'There was a rat,' she said. 'It ran into the scullery.'

He nodded.

'They're in the tunnels under the house. Old military defences hidden in the cliffs.'

Morgan nodded but she wasn't thinking about rats, she was staring at the hairbrush.

'Would you like me to help find her?' said Danny.

A tingle of relief coursed through Morgan's veins. But it was tinged with something else.

What was the phrase Nigel Cundy had used?

A scintilla of doubt.

They spent the next half-hour sitting on the bench by Danny's allotment, running through possibilities, discussing Lissa's childhood friends, habits, haunts. Both left pleading messages on the teenager's voicemail. If she wouldn't respond to Morgan maybe she'd talk to Danny.

'Does she have any money?'

'Her father gives her an allowance every month,' said Morgan. 'Enough to pay her mobile, get a taxi if she's out late. And she has a credit card. He pays that too.'

'Have you told him she's missing?'

'Of course.'

'And?'

'He said she's a spoiled little mall rat and she'll come back when she's ready.'

'He's probably right,' said Danny.

Morgan looked into his eyes. The seashells message flashed across her mind.

Don't trust him.

She fought to remain calm, trying to ignore the mound of earth she could see over his shoulder. A flowerbed. Freshly dug. A spade jutted from the soil.

Danny followed her gaze and fell silent for a long moment. Then he sighed.

'Go ahead,' he said.

'Sorry?'

'Ask why I've been digging.'

She flushed. He knew her too well.

'Why have you been digging?'

'Tulips.' He folded his arms. 'We planted them every autumn. Me, Rowena and Zoe.'

Morgan faked a smile.

'It's only October,' she said. 'My stepmother never planted tulips before Guy Fawkes' Night.'

Danny flicked the dregs of his tea onto the compost heap then stared at her. Morgan could hear the quiet anger in his voice.

'Your imagination is driving you nuts. But I understand. This is your daughter that's missing so everything looks different – even a bed of tulips. That doesn't make you a bad friend, it makes you a mother worried about her child.'

Calm. Reasonable. Reassuring. Where was this going? She focused on his body language, searching for a tell. Why talk so much? Wasn't that what people did when they had something to hide?

'You stood by me,' he continued. 'But now you're thinking, "Can I trust him?" His eyes never left hers. 'I get it,' he said. 'But it breaks my bloody heart.'

He stood up, tugged the spade from the flowerbed and began to dig.

'What are you doing?'

'Saving this friendship.'

Dig.

'Danny …'

'You don't trust me.'

Dig.

'Please, stop …'

Dig.

One spadeful of soil followed another. As he forced the spade into the ground, again and again, Morgan saw a crimson gash appear on the sole of his bare foot.

'For God's sake, you're bleeding ...'

He ignored her, his face set hard.

Dig.

'Happy now?'

He jabbed a finger towards the mound of earth. Morgan saw three tulip bulbs.

Dig.

More earth. More bulbs. She moved towards him, laying a hand on his arm.

'Please,' she said. 'Danny, stop.'

Dig.

More earth. More blood. He flung the spade away. It landed with a thud. In the distance, the dog was still barking.

Danny wiped away a bead of sweat.

'Jesus Christ,' he said, half to himself. 'That bloody dog.'

Morgan stared at the tulip bulbs. How could she have been so idiotic? How could she have doubted him?

'I need your help,' she said quietly. 'To find Lissa.'

He turned to face her.

'Of course.' There was no warmth in his voice. 'What are friends for?'

Sixteen

The episode Morgan dubbed 'Danny's outbreak of tulip fever' did nothing to ease her suspicions but made her doubly ashamed of doubting him. Truth was, she was confused. This was Danny. Her friend. For thirty years.

The most likely explanation for her daughter's disappearance was a teenage strop. The first of these had seen the precocious thirteen-year-old hitch to London and sleep rough for five days and nights. The second, nine months later, involved a stolen car, two quarts of vodka and a thirty-six-year-old fairground worker complete with ASBO and nose-ring. Morgan took comfort from the likelihood that this latest vanishing trick was yet another petulant stunt, designed to forestall any criticism of her daughter's bad behaviour.

So I flirted with Danny. Big fucking deal.

She would show up in a couple of days, or weeks, or whenever she liked, with tales of coke-snorting Hell's Angels or feral bareknuckle fighters, possibly both. Killer-cannon would prove to have nothing to do with her disappearance.

On the other hand, eighty-two per cent of people believed he was guilty of murdering his stepdaughter and doing away with his wife.

If they were right ... it didn't bear thinking about. And Lissa had now been missing for three days.

The idea of their sharing the search had come from Danny himself. His high-profile face made him the last person able to roam the streets enquiring after a missing girl. But he could hit the phone and work through a list of names, trying to trace Lissa's old friends, the ones she'd ditched so unceremoniously after going to live with her father. There was no need to give his full name. He was 'Dan', just a friend of the family. Meanwhile, Morgan would badger the police then visit Lissa's old hangouts in the hope that someone had spotted her.

'Sounds like a plan,' said Danny.

She took two photos of her daughter to Canterbury police station and answered questions from a lugubrious desk sergeant sucking a cough sweet. No, Lissa didn't have medical issues. No, Morgan wasn't able to supply bank or credit-card details but she'd get them from Cameron. No, she couldn't in all conscience say that Lissa was at imminent risk – unless you counted being grounded till she was eighty. The sergeant advised Morgan not to worry. Ninety-four per cent of Mispers turned up within days. The signs were good, especially for a headstrong teenager with a history of going AWOL.

Gee, thanks.

Couldn't they track Lissa's mobile? Monitor her computer activity?

In theory, yes, said the sergeant, but cell-site analysis would kick in only if 'things moved up a gear or two', which in all likelihood they wouldn't because Lissa would turn up safe and well.

As for her computer, it wasn't wise to believe everything you read in the papers, especially the effing *Guardian*. This was Canterbury nick, not GCHQ. Lissa was an adult, she had the right to disappear. The UK Border Police would be notified in case she tried to leave the country. (Morgan had confirmed her daughter had taken her passport.) In the meantime, why not download a fact sheet from www.missingpersons.police.uk?

Thanks. Again.

She was tempted to mention the spate of anonymous messages but worried it would confuse matters so said nothing. All the same, she was relieved not to find another warning when she got home. Sitting at the kitchen table, she Skyped Cameron in Malibu. The conversation – their second in twenty-four hours – went as expected.

She's being a teenager. Relax. She'll show up any minute.

Nice job, Cameron. Dad of the Year.

There was no sign of their daughter in Malibu. His London housekeeper would have told him if she'd pitched up in Notting Hill, but yes, of course he would check, and he'd be more than happy to get on a plane and look for Lissa himself if it weren't for this piece-of-shit romcom. Just two weeks from shooting, he had four egomaniacal producers, warring co-stars and a Xanax-addled director issuing demands for rewrites. If he left LA he'd be in breach of contract. Then he'd go broke, lose the beach house and the girlfriend. Oh, and speaking of Kristina, her psychic insisted Lissa was fine, just hanging out with friends. Somewhere near water.

Morgan used a lot of bad language then took down the number of Lissa's Visa card. Hunched over her laptop, still in her fleece, she glimpsed her ex's twenty-four-year-old girlfriend sashaying past the pool in fuck-me heels and spray-on jeans. Moments later, the faint sound of piano music came wafting from the house. Kristina was practising. Mozart. Talented, sexy, young. Morgan was so happy for her.

Terminating the call, she downed a glass of wine and smoked two roll-ups in quick succession. Feeling no better, she picked up the phone and relayed Lissa's Visa details to the police sergeant. When she got to the part about her ex's beach house in Malibu she could hear him roll his eyes.

Her next calls were to the weekenders she worked for. She was sorry but she'd be unable to clean for a while. Responses ranged from indifference to outrage at being 'so badly let down at such short notice'. As her anger boiled, Morgan decided this was one of those moments that called for the old saying, 'Never waste a good crisis'. For too long she'd scraped by on her cleaning jobs and hacking out pieces about C-list celebs, along with the occasional restaurant review. Time to burn a few bridges. Once this was over, once Lissa was safely home, she would refocus on her career and get back to *proper* journalism.

The owner of the Gaggia, the woman who felt 'so badly let down', could go to hell. Oh, and for the record, the invisible skivvy who'd been emptying all those bins full of used tampons and shitty Andrex? Her name was Morgan, not Morg*en*.

She was about to pour another glass of wine when Danny called.

'Just got a text.'

'From Lissa?'

'Yes.'

Thank God!

'What does she say?'

' *"Got your message. All OK wiv me. Tell Mum to chillax."* '

'Wiv me?' said Morgan. 'Spelled how?'

'W-I-V,' said Danny. 'Is that important?'

It might be. Lissa's messages often contained deliberate misspellings and pointless abbreviations. But the surge of relief was extinguished by a fresh flicker of doubt. *Tell Mum to chillax.* Did teenagers really say stuff like that or was it an adult's idea of how young people spoke?

'Can you forward it to me?'

He didn't reply.

'Danny?'

'Oh, Christ ...' he said.

But he wasn't talking to her.

'What's wrong?'

'I can't talk now. Someone's here.'

'Who?'

She heard a woman's voice.

'Hello, Danny.'

The voice sounded familiar.

'Mind if we come in?'

'Who's there?' said Morgan.

But he'd gone.

By the time she got to the lane leading to his cottage the sun was setting behind Dover Castle. She could hear the yapping dog, still barking somewhere in the distance. A police car was parked by the Martello tower.

'Sorry, Madam. No entry.'

The officer wore a high-vis jacket and a thin smile.

'I'm visiting a friend,' said Morgan. 'Everything OK at the cottage?'

'I need you to turn around and go back to the main road,' said the policeman. His tone brooked no opposition.

About to protest, Morgan saw an old Ford pull up in the layby. At the wheel, a familiar face. Clive Rossiter. She performed a U-turn and drew alongside the journalist. He rolled down his window.

'Where's the BMW?' she said.

'Long story. What are you doing here?'

'You first.'

'We had a tip-off.'

'About?'

But he wasn't listening. Instead, he was staring over her shoulder at an unmarked police car emerging from the lane. A woman was at the wheel. Thirties. Slim. Long brown hair. In the passenger seat sat a second female police officer – larger, older. Morgan recognised her immediately. Danny's nemesis, Detective Inspector Jacqui Farmiloe.

'Why the hell is she here?'

'They're doing a dig at Kilcannon's cottage,' said Rossiter.

'A dig?'

The reporter nodded.

'Looking for Rowena.'

Seventeen

The following afternoon, three and a half days after Lissa had disappeared, Morgan responded to a summons from DI Farmiloe.

'Just a few questions about Danny. Bit of background. I'd be very grateful.'

The interview suite was sparsely furnished. Strip lighting. A desk. Four bucket chairs. Recording equipment. CCTV camera on the wall.

'Thank you for coming in,' said Farmiloe, sitting down heavily next to her slender, glossy-haired colleague, DS Donna Goshawk.

Morgan put Donna Goshawk at thirty-five and Jacqui Farmiloe in her late forties. Auburn bob cut, austere manner. The younger of the two looked as if she'd stepped out of a shampoo commercial.

'Can I get you anything?' said Donna. 'The tea's dishwater but you might survive the coffee.' Her lips twitched into a smile.

'I'm fine, thanks,' said Morgan.

'I take it you remember me?' said Jacqui.

'How could I forget?' said Morgan. Four years ago, they'd clashed in a room like this during the investigation into Zoe's murder. As Senior Investigating Officer, Farmiloe had quizzed all Danny's old friends and acquaintances, building up a picture of the man she believed to be a killer. Morgan had made it clear *she* knew Danny was innocent. The stout policewoman had made it plain she believed the opposite.

'I gather you run a reading group at HMP Dungeness.'

'How did you know that?'

'I'm a police officer,' said the DI. She sprinkled a sachet of sweetener into a polystyrene cup. 'Was it just coincidence your book club is where Kilcannon got banged up?'

Morgan shook her head.

'I'd been thinking about setting up a prison reading group for a while. He wrote from Belmarsh saying he was being transferred to my neck of the woods. It seemed serendipitous.'

Jacqui Farmiloe gave a thin-lipped smile and turned to Donna Goshawk.

'"Serendipitous". Not a word we hear a lot, is it? Ms Vine's a journalist.'

The DS nodded, leaning back in her chair.

'I'll have to watch what I say.'

Jacqui faced Morgan.

'I saw your name on a restaurant review in the local rag,' she said. 'That fish place in Folkestone. Took Colin for our twenty-fifth. Cost an arm and a leg, gave him food poisoning.'

'Sorry to hear it,' said Morgan. She remained on her guard, watching as Jacqui stirred her coffee with a Biro.

'Was the book group your way of staying in touch with Kilcannon?'

'I'm not some kind of prison groupie, if that's what you're thinking.'

What had Rossiter called those women? *Broadmoor Babes.*

Farmiloe gave another watery smile.

'Why would I think that?'

Morgan shrugged.

'Just trying to be clear.'

Jacqui sucked coffee from the pen.

'Have you seen Kilcannon since his release?'

'Several times.'

'May I ask if you and he are in a sexual relationship?'

'We're just good friends.'

'Same as four years ago?'

'Same as when we were kids.'

'Yes, I remember.' A sip of coffee. 'Has he said anything about his wife?'

Morgan shrugged. 'She liked tulips. Does that count?'

Donna Goshawk leaned forward. Morgan noticed a silver locket on a chain around her slender neck.

'He said Rowena liked tulips?' said the softly spoken DS. '*Liked?*'

'They planted tulips every autumn,' said Morgan. 'I don't think you should read anything into my use of the past tense.'

'You're aware that Rowena Kilcannon is still missing?' said Donna.

'Of course,' said Morgan, fixing the DS with a polite smile. 'I'm also aware how humiliating it must have been for Inspector Farmiloe to see the appeal court overturn Danny's conviction for a murder he didn't commit. Maybe the embarrassment would be easier to bear if the police could pin something else on him. Like another murder.'

The two women stared at her. She stared back.

'We don't "pin things" on people,' said Jacqui quietly. 'The enquiry into Zoe's murder is ongoing. So is the enquiry into the whereabouts of her mother.'

'Good,' said Morgan. 'In the meantime, have you discovered anything from the card at Zoe's grave? DNA? Fingerprints? Any clue as to who left the lilies?'

'We're following all lines of enquiry,' said Farmiloe.

'What about the so-called eye witness?' Morgan could feel herself getting worked up. 'The one you relied on at Danny's trial. The one who recanted?'

'Caleb Quirke is still in hospital,' said the DI. Her voice was calm. 'Again, we're following all lines of enquiry.'

'Including his claim to have been threatened by a man with a Stanley knife on the night Zoe was murdered?'

'Naturally.'

'But I assume you think Danny was behind the hit-and-run?' said Morgan. 'Taking his revenge on Quirke for helping you to secure a wrongful conviction?'

Jacqui Farmiloe was growing increasingly tetchy.

'I was hoping *I'd* be the one asking the questions.' She swept a non-existent crumb from the table. 'Tell me about the night you drove Kilcannon to Zoe's grave.'

'Someone left lilies,' said Morgan. 'You know the rest.'

'Can you describe his frame of mind?'

'He was visiting his stepdaughter's grave,' said Morgan. 'Upset, emotional, angry.'

'About?'

'The fact that the real killer is still out there.'

Jacqui Farmiloe tightened her jaw and pushed a card across the table.

'In case anything else comes to mind,' she said, getting to her feet.

Morgan stared at the card. She was already regretting her belligerent tone but years of battling the system had taken its toll. Once, she might have felt intimidated in the presence of a police officer, now she felt only furious and cynical.

'Was there something else?'

Jacqui was looking at her, raising a quizzical eyebrow. Morgan met her gaze. She knew what would happen if she told Farmiloe and Goshawk that Lissa was missing. Increased suspicion around Danny. A leak to the tabloids faster than she could say 'grease my palm'. The story was irresistible.

Killer-cannon pal's teenage girl missing!

Suddenly, she felt lightheaded and anxious. So many conflicting feelings. For years, she had despised Jacqui Farmiloe for persecuting Danny. Yet the DI was now in a position to help her. On the other hand, if Danny *was* innocent, if Lissa *was* merely playing games, it followed that there was no danger, so no sense in alerting Farmiloe to Lissa's disappearance. Canterbury police station was a busy nick and Morgan and her daughter had different surnames. There was little likelihood of a humble Misper case coming to DI Farmiloe's attention unless Morgan herself joined the dots. Let sleeping dogs lie.

On the *other* other hand, Lissa had now been missing for four days . . .

'I could use your help,' said Morgan. 'My daughter has disappeared.'

Jacqui exchanged a look with Donna then resumed her seat at the table.

'OK,' she said. 'I'm listening.'

It took fifteen minutes for Morgan to relate the sequence of events since Lissa had returned from California. The senior policewoman listened carefully, leaving it to her colleague to take notes on everything from Lissa's hangouts to her use of social media, which was precisely zero. Contrary as ever, the eighteen-year-old had dismissed Facebook, Twitter and Instagram as 'a waste of time for losers'.

'Just to be clear,' finished Morgan. 'My hunch is that she's simply punishing me. I don't believe her disappearance has anything to do with Danny. And I don't want the press adding two plus two to make mischief.'

'No leaks from us,' said Jacqui. She shot a look at her DS. 'Not how we roll, is it, DS Goshawk?'

'No, ma'am.'

Morgan couldn't resist.

'In that case, how did Clive Rossiter get a tip-off about your "dig" for Rowena?'

She watched as Jacqui's expression darkened at the mention of the journalist's name.

'I've no idea,' she said. 'But do you mind a word of advice?'

'Feel free.'

'If that man comes near you, waving his newspaper's chequebook, remember what they say: "Sup with the devil, use a long spoon."'

'No chance of me supping with Clive Rossiter,' said Morgan. 'Not after the stuff he wrote about Danny.'

Farmiloe nodded then capped her Biro. The meeting was at an end.

'Anything else?'

Morgan hesitated. She decided not to mention the pink hairbrush. Danny deserved the benefit of the doubt. Besides, his explanation was plausible: Lissa had left the brush in his Mercedes; he had simply brought it into the house.

'No,' she said. 'That's everything.'

'I'll make sure Lissa goes to the top of the Misper pile,' said Jacqui. She leaned forward and gave a sympathetic smile. 'I have a daughter, too. Same age as yours.' She fished her wallet from her pocket and produced a photo of a blonde girl in her late teens. Her pale, pretty face was disfigured by piercings in her lower lip. There was a snake tattoo on her neck.

'That's my Chelsea. Beautiful. Bolshie. Clever. Light of my life, bane of my life – all rolled into one.'

'Sounds familiar,' said Morgan.

They exchanged a small smile, almost conciliatory. Then DI Farmiloe got to her feet. Her sidekick followed suit.

'Meet me at the car,' Jacqui told Donna Goshawk, checking her watch. The younger woman nodded and smiled at Morgan.

'Nice meeting you,' she said as she left the room, high heels clacking on the floor. Farmiloe drained her cup and dropped it in the bin.

'Off the record?' she said. 'Mother to mother?'

'Sure.'

'I know Danny is your friend,' said the DI, 'but I remember what my dad used to say. He was a copper, too. Sat me on his lap and warned me about the Bogey Man. I said, "How will I know who he is?" And Dad said, "Aha, that's where the Bogey Man is so clever. He doesn't wear a black hat like a cowboy, or an eye-patch like a pirate. In fact, do you know why the Bogey Man is so dangerous?"' Morgan found herself holding her breath as the policewoman paused for effect. ' "Because he looks like everyone else."'

Outside, while climbing into the Mini, Morgan saw Jacqui Farmiloe again. The portly DI was at the wheel of the unmarked police car as it emerged from a set of tall black gates. Donna Goshawk was in the passenger seat. Morgan watched as the car jerked to a halt inches from a teenage girl who'd stepped onto the road without looking. Peering closely, she saw that the girl was Farmiloe's own daughter.

Beautiful. Bolshie. Clever.

She watched the DI get out of the car, her face flushed with anger.

'Chelsea! Where have you *been*?'

Morgan couldn't hear the reply but a snatched, ill-tempered conversation culminated in Farmiloe handing her daughter some cash from her wallet. There was another brief exchange then the teenager's face contorted with fury, her eyes bulging as she spat venom at her mother.

'I wish you were dead!'

The girl seemed to be drunk, or stoned, maybe both. Morgan watched as she hurried away, unsteady on too-high heels, hands plunged into the pockets of her long black coat.

'Chelsea?' The DI called plaintively after her daughter. 'Chelsea! Please!'

The girl with the snake tattoo flicked a V-sign, revealing bright green fingernails, then disappeared around the corner. Her mother hung her head for a moment, a picture of misery and defeat, then slammed back into the car and drove away in the opposite direction.

Light of my life, bane of my life – all rolled into one.

Morgan couldn't have put it better herself.

Eighteen

She was being followed. The car had been on her tail for almost an hour, first on the motorway then every side road, every country lane. Now, as the Mini rattled through the dark wasteland of Romney Marsh, Morgan's pursuer was still close behind.

It was the end of a long day. Since leaving Farmiloe and Goshawk, she'd had a series of dead-end conversations with café baristas, bar staff and bouncers. No one had seen Lissa. Morgan had no idea if Danny was keeping his promise to ring around her daughter's old friends. He had yet to return her calls, leaving her anxious and on edge. But most of all she was angry at being pursued by someone who didn't even have the decency to dim his headlamps.

As Lissa would say, *WTF?!*

Ahead was a petrol station, the only pit-stop between here and Dungeness. If Morgan wanted to confront her pursuer in public – and safety – this was her last chance. She steered the Mini onto the forecourt. The other car slowed, engine idling, then pulled up alongside her. Seeing the driver's face, Morgan didn't know whether to be relieved or alarmed.

'Why are you following me?'

Clive Rossiter got out of the Ford. He'd swapped his expensive suit for chinos and a leather coat with a button missing. She glimpsed his signature red socks and detected the smell of fast food. Big Mac and fries.

'Just wondered if you'd changed your mind,' he said. 'About the retainer.'

'Bullshit,' said Morgan. 'You were hoping I'd lead you to Danny.'

The reporter smiled and held up his hands in defeat.

'Busted.'

He leaned against his car. The petrol station was deserted except for an attendant manning the shop.

'How did you get on at the police station?'

Morgan ignored the question. She looked at his car.

'What happened to the Beemer?'

He gave a resigned shrug.

'It was a company car. Like they say, "One minute you're the cock of the walk, the next you're a feather duster."'

'You've been fired?'

He shook his head.

'Demoted. To general reporter. The editor thinks I have "an unhealthy obsession" with your pal Kilcannon so I may as well cover the story myself.' Morgan saw his jaw tighten. 'My successor is about twelve. Maybe she's screwing him.'

Morgan narrowed her eyes.

'Have you been drinking, Clive?'

'Depends what you mean by drinking.'

'Should you be driving?'

'I'm too drunk to walk.' He flashed a smile. 'Only kidding.'

Unexpectedly she found herself warming to the man. Without his flashy suit he looked less like a banker, more like a proper human being. Even his silver-grey hair wasn't so overgroomed today.

'I don't know where Danny is,' she said.

'That makes two of us.'

He proffered a pack of cigarettes. Morgan shook her head.

'Some stories get under your skin,' said Rossiter. 'This is one of them. Ever since Zoe was murdered.' He shook a cigarette from the pack. 'Sorry about the other day. Barging into your place. I was a prick.'

Morgan recalled the glint in his eye as he'd ogled Lissa.

'Yep.'

He gave a rueful nod, acknowledging the tacit rebuke, then put the cigarette between his lips.

'We're on the same side, Morgan. We both want to get to the truth about Danny.'

She counted to three, choosing her words carefully.

'I already know the truth about Danny.'

He studied her for a moment, registering her hesitation.

'Has something happened?' he said. 'You don't sound like you believe in him anymore. What's changed?'

Morgan met his gaze, trying to sound more confident than she felt.

'Nothing's changed,' she said. 'Everything's fine.'

He gave her a sideways look.

'Methinks the lady doth protest too much.' He got back into his car. 'If you change your mind about the retainer, you know where to find me.' He took an envelope from his pocket. 'And when you see Romeo, give him this.'

She took the letter.

'What does it say?'

'That's between me and him.'

Morgan watched as the man lit his cigarette, performed a U-turn and drove away. Settling behind the wheel of the Mini, she found herself shivering – with cold or dread, she couldn't be sure – then she locked herself inside the car and headed for home.

The encounter with Rossiter was unsettling. Morgan preferred the humbler version to the smarmy sleazeball she'd first met but there was still something about him that made her uneasy. After making one last, fruitless attempt to call Lissa, she wolfed down half a bar of chocolate then climbed into bed and listened to the waves pounding the beach. It was an hour before she fell into a fitful sleep.

The rumble of an engine filtered into a dream about Lissa as a baby, lost at sea in a pink plastic bucket. As Morgan slowly became aware of tyres crunching on the shingle outside, she wasn't sure if she was resurfacing into consciousness or still dreaming.

Suddenly she was on high alert, sitting bolt upright.

She heard the engine stop.

The clunk of a car door.

Footsteps on pebbles.

Then silence.

She slipped out of bed and parted the curtains a crack.

No sign of life.

Grabbing her bathrobe, she moved quickly into the kitchen. Her eyes darted to the knife block.

Footsteps on the deck.

The door handle turned.

The lock rattled.

The footsteps receded.

Then she heard them again. On the shingle. Heading for the back door. She unsheathed the carving knife. Her eyes flew to the door. Had she fastened the bolt?

Another rattle: metal against metal.

Then a voice from outside.

'Morgan?'

His voice.

'What do you want, Danny?'

He didn't answer immediately.

'I need a friend.'

She was trembling. DI Farmiloe's words came flooding back.

Do you know why the Bogey Man is so dangerous? Because he looks like everyone else.

'Give me a second.'

She switched on the light and caught sight of herself in the mirror. *Wide-eyed woman clutching a knife.* She sheathed the blade in its wooden block then drew back the bolt and opened the door. Danny was silhouetted in the moonlight.

'A posse of drunks,' he said. 'Six of them. Bricks through my window. Tried to torch the Merc.'

She recalled the graffiti at his cottage.

'Did you call the police?'

He shook his head.

'Just needed to get away fast,' he said. 'I was planning to sleep in the car but it's freezing out here.'

She ushered him inside. He wore the black polo neck, the one that made him look as if he belonged on a stage with a script in his hand.

'Sorry if I scared you,' he said.

She could feel adrenaline flooding her system.

'Did you not get my messages?'

He shot her an apologetic look.

'I would have called back if I'd discovered anything about Lissa. I phoned all the names you gave me, drew a blank.' He paused. 'And there's a lot going on. It's not every day the police dig up your garden looking for your wife.'

Morgan said nothing. She'd imagined this scene many times. Alone with Danny in the small hours. But never like this. She saw his eyes flicker to the letter on the table. His name on the envelope.

'It's from Clive Rossiter,' she said.

A shadow fell across Danny's face. He ripped open the envelope and scanned the note.

'Bastard.' She waited for him to speak again. 'He's door-stepped me twice in two days. I keep saying no to an interview so he's trying every trick in the book.'

He handed her the note.

Dear Danny

We've had tip-offs about sightings of Rowena. The editor is keen to run the story. I'm not sure how long I can hold her off. Contact me ASAP. Day or night.

The journalist's card was stapled to the note.

'Will you call him?'

'Of course,' said Danny. 'And he knows it.'

'Maybe it's a ruse, just trying to get some quotes.'

He shrugged.

'Either way, he's a shit. What he wrote about me when Zoe died set the tone for the rest of the pack. Plus he's in deep with Farmiloe.'

If Morgan was going to raise the topic of her encounter with Danny's nemesis, now was the moment. His brow furrowed as he listened to her account of the conversation with the DI.

'I told her I wanted your name kept out of it.'

He gave a rueful smile.

'Won't make any difference. Let's just hope she can find Lissa.'

He fished his phone from his pocket then hesitated.

'Can I use yours? I don't want Rossiter to have my number.'

She handed him her mobile.

'Could I kip on your sofa?'

She hesitated.

'You can have Lissa's room.'

'Great. Any chance of some toast?'

'The bread's mouldy.'

He smiled.

'I'll count it as one of my five a day.'

He dialled the number on Rossiter's card. As Morgan bus-ied herself with the toaster, she could hear the conversation. Danny's tone was curl bordering on rude.

'This is Danny Kilcannon,' he said. 'Tell me what you know about Rowena.' He listened then his voice grew quiet. 'I'm hang-ing up in three seconds,' he said, clicking his pen. 'One … two …'

The threat seemed to work. He listened for a moment, scrib-bling on the kitchen notepad. Then he ended the call abruptly, tore off the slip of paper and put it in his pocket.

Morgan buttered two slices of toast and placed them on the table alongside a glass of red wine. Folding her arms, she took stock of Danny's dishevelled appearance: three days' stubble, rheumy eyes that spoke of sleepless nights.

'Are you going to tell me what he said?'

Danny was staring into the middle distance.

'Two sightings of Rowena.'

'Says who?'

'Rossiter's readers.'

She could feel her pulse quicken. If Rowena were alive it would not only vindicate Danny, but also go a long way to quashing suspicion over his part in Zoe's death.

And it would soothe Morgan's fears over Lissa.

I need you to be the man you say you are, the boy with the pebble in his pocket.

'Where did they see her?'

He hesitated, picking up his glass of wine.

'Not far from here.'

His tone didn't invite a follow-up. Morgan frowned.

'Are you not going to tell me?'

'I need to do this alone.'

She let the words sink in.

'After everything we've been through? Seriously?'

He sipped his wine then turned to look her in the eye.

'I've been doing a lot of thinking,' he said. 'About us.'

Morgan stood perfectly still.

'And?'

He crinkled his eyes and gave a small smile.

'Can I be with you tonight? Just to hold you?'

A few days ago his words would have made her heart leap. But this time there was no hesitation.

'Sorry,' she sighed. 'Bad idea.'

Avoiding his gaze, she picked up the bottle of wine, went into her bedroom and closed the door.

Waking at daybreak, groggy and thirsty, Morgan was immediately assailed by the thought that her daughter had been missing for five days. Dressing quickly, she found Danny's door still closed. She drank two glasses of water then left yet another message on Lissa's voicemail, made a pot of coffee and stared out to sea.

The idea began to dawn slowly.

It wasn't a plan for now, but for when all this was over... when Lissa was safely home.

A non-fiction book. Based partly on Danny's case and her role in helping to secure his release. But that was just the beginning. The book would broaden out to cover other miscarriages of justice. Derek Bentley. The Guildford Four. Timothy Evans. The Birmingham Six. The countless wretched mothers wrongly convicted of killing their babies. Colin Stagg. The Bridgewater Four. The list was shamefully long. Maybe Morgan could even find a way finally to write about her own father's trauma, how the saga had scarred her childhood, how it had spurred her to fight for justice for Danny, to give her old flame the benefit of the doubt long after others had given up.

Booting up her laptop, the title – *Trial and Error* – came to her straightaway and the rest followed quickly, as though a flood of pent-up creative energy had at last been undammed. Within two hours, she had completed the proposal for the book. A search online produced a list of literary agents. She wrote a covering letter and emailed the outline to three likely candidates then made a second pot of coffee and checked her watch.

Still only nine thirty.

No sign of Danny.

She rapped on his door and pushed it open.

The bed was rumpled but empty. A wave of disappointment washed over her, quickly turning to confusion. Surely he couldn't have taken offence at her refusal to sleep with him? *Could he?*

A thought struck.

A trick she had seen in the movies. Sitting at the kitchen table, she began to brush the tip of a pencil over the blank notepad from which Danny had torn a page after his call with Rossiter.

His pen had left indentations.

Two words.

Deal market.

Nineteen

The bustling seaside town was livelier than Morgan remembered. Just off the high street, where there had once been a few trestle tables piled with cheap shoes and mouldy paperbacks, there was now a vibrant street market. Stalls selling flowers, artisan breads, cheeses and sausages sat alongside higgledy-piggledy displays of paintings, vintage clothes and what her father had called 'junk-tiques'.

She lucked into a parking space near a row of Georgian houses. Ten years since her last visit to her hometown, the place looked smarter, busier, richer. Savouring the autumnal tang in the air, Morgan scanned the crowds, searching for familiar faces. Sooner or later she would bump into someone she knew but for now she was focused on finding the woman the tabloids called *Tragic Zoe's Missing Mum*.

An internet trawl had elicited dozens of newspaper photos of Rowena, snatched after her daughter's murder and in the days leading up to Danny's arrest. In each picture, the pale, black-haired woman looked gaunt and hollow-eyed. According to the press, she was prone to depression. Her first husband, an IT specialist, had died in a climbing accident, leaving her to raise their daughter alone.

Rowena had married Danny when her daughter was ten. Three years later a miscarriage triggered a profound post-partum psychosis, forcing her to leave the teaching job in a primary school that she'd loved. Her sudden resignation was accompanied by whispers of heavy drinking and attempts at suicide. Then came Zoe's murder. Within a week, Rowena had suffered a breakdown, disappearing days before Danny's arrest. Rumours that she was living rough remained unverified, as did sightings as far afield as London, Glasgow and Penzance. The police drew a blank. They could find no reason to charge Danny. People disappeared every day.

Five months later, the murder trial took place without Rowena's testimony. Her absence cast a long shadow. DI Jacqui Farmiloe was suspected of briefing the press off the record, hinting at a marriage troubled by secrets, lies and violence, but no charges were brought against Danny. The police focused on securing his conviction for Zoe's murder. Locked up on remand, he was in no position to challenge the accusation that defined the way the public still saw him.

The wicked stepfather.

Too handsome for his own good.

A bloody actor.

That he was a carpenter by trade counted for nothing as far as the headline writers were concerned. *Killer-cannon* sold papers. *Skilled Carpenter* did not.

There was warmth in the sunshine as Morgan mingled with the Saturday morning shoppers. The smell of frying sausages wafted around the market, making her hungry for the first time in days. She bought a croissant and a cappuccino, sipping it as she scanned the crowd.

No Rowena.

No Danny.

Just a familiar face at a café table across the road.

Clive Rossiter.

The reporter was discreetly surveying the crowds, half-hidden behind a copy of the *Times*. His presence came as no surprise but Morgan knew he was the last person Danny would want to see.

If this was a tabloid sting, where were the photographers? Except for one smartly dressed woman (an American tourist?) there was no sign of anyone with a camera. If the *Post's* tip-offs were real, if Rowena *did* make an appearance, there was no possibility that a hack like Rossiter would miss the moment when *Killer-cannon* was finally reunited with *Tragic Zoe's Missing Mum*.

Finishing her cappuccino, Morgan froze as she saw another familiar face. The man had put on weight and lost his hair but there was no doubt: it was her childhood tormentor – her father's nemesis – Stevie Gamble. He was accompanied by a short, dumpy woman with a tanned face. Both of them wore tracksuits and trainers.

'Jesus H. Christ,' said Stevie, catching sight of Morgan. 'I don't bloody believe it.' An Australian twang. He and his mother had emigrated years ago, fleeing the town's net-curtain twitchers. Melbourne? Adelaide? Morgan couldn't remember.

'Hello, Stevie.'

The greeting was out of her mouth before she knew it, politeness trumping the impulse to kick him in the balls. He turned to his companion.

'This is Morgan,' he said. The tanned woman looked blank. 'The one I told you about? The headmaster's daughter?'

'Oh. Right.'

She folded her arms. No smile. No handshake.

'This is Marie,' said Stevie. 'My wife.'

Morgan said nothing. What could you say to a man who had caused such misery? When he spoke again, his words came out in a rush.

'My aunt died. We're back for the funeral.' He swallowed, ill at ease. 'Got two boys back home. Sammy and Bobby. They're staying with Marie's sister ...'

He babbled on but Morgan wasn't listening. She was adjusting to the way his features had changed and knew he was thinking the same about her.

Christ, you're getting old.

A memory bubbled to the surface. Her father at the dining table, smelling of alcohol, singing "You Are My Sunshine" in a feeble voice.

What if Stevie had never made the rape accusation? Everything would have been different. For Leo. For Morgan. For her stepmother. Ursula's words were as fresh as ever, the pain as sharp.

'Your father doesn't want to see you or hear your name ever again.'

Life boiled down to a few key decisions, a handful of roads less travelled or not taken. Stevie's allegation had sparked a chain of events that remained toxic, even today. If Morgan hadn't flinched that night at supper – if she hadn't recoiled from Leo's attempt to reach out to her – so much pain and strife could have been avoided. Ursula wouldn't have driven a wedge between father and daughter. Morgan's relationship with Leo would never have broken down. She wouldn't feel in Danny's debt, wouldn't be his champion. And she wouldn't be here now, staring at Stevie Gamble's receding hairline and po-faced wife.

She voiced none of this. It was all much too complicated, much too late. But she couldn't let the moment pass without venting her feelings.

'You're a despicable human being, Stevie.'

Later, she would think of cleverer insults but at least her words came from the heart. She saw his eyes widen. People didn't say things like that, not people like Stevie Gamble. They smiled to your face then whispered poison behind your back. He opened his mouth then closed it again.

The woman in the tracksuit glared at Morgan and tugged her husband's sleeve.

'Come on, babe,' she said, leading him away.

Morgan was trembling. The caffeine hit her system along with a surge of adrenaline.

Brandy.

That was what she needed. She turned and headed for the pub on Middle Street.

Then she stopped in her tracks.

Danny was at a clothing stall, trying on a black trilby, the kind Morgan associated with her stepmother's Sinatra albums. Over by the fruit and veg stall, a couple in matching anoraks were staring at him, whispering behind their hands. Morgan could imagine their conversation.

'It's Killer-cannon.'

'No, it just looks like him.'

'I'm telling you, it's him. Murdering bastard.'

Suddenly, the object of their fascination was on the move. Danny replaced the trilby on the stall and strode into the market, following a woman with long black hair.

Late thirties. Pretty. Petite.

Rowena?

Morgan began to tail Danny but lost him in the crowd. Quickening her pace, she swerved to avoid a couple pushing a double buggy then hurried past a group of dawdlers.

There he was, close behind his quarry, staring at her back as she said something to a man selling plants. The woman was slim and well dressed in a Boden way. Gilet. Pale blue scarf tied around her neck. Danny was rooted to the spot, staring at the back of her head.

Suddenly, acting on some kind of instinct, he swivelled to face Morgan. She saw the shock on his face as he registered her presence. He glanced over her shoulder, his surprise turning to anger.

A voice behind her.

Rossiter.

'Is it her?' The reporter ignored Morgan, bearing down on Danny. 'Is it Rowena?'

At the hack's side was the woman Morgan had taken for an American tourist. The woman raised her camera to photograph

Danny, shutter whirring. He stood still, staring defiantly into the lens.

'No,' he said. 'It's not her.'

Rossiter's face fell.

'Shit. *Shit.*'

He put a restraining hand on the photographer's arm. The woman lowered the camera. Rossiter reached into his pocket and produced a snapshot of Danny's wife. Even at this distance, Morgan could see that the picture bore a strong resemblance to the woman in the blue scarf, but that's all it was – a resemblance.

Danny was stony-faced. He stared at Rossiter then turned his gaze onto Morgan, his eyes searching her face.

'Did you set me up? Are you working for this bastard?'

'No.'

'So why are you following me?'

'I needed to see if it was Rowena,' said Morgan. 'This isn't just about you, Danny. Not anymore.'

He stared at her, his eyes filled with disappointment. She tried to hold his gaze but a wave of shame swept through her. No getting away from it: tailing him was a crappy thing to do, but doubting him was worse.

He studied the ground for a moment, gathering himself, then looked up at the reporter and photographer.

'Do you have any idea how shitty my world is, thanks to people like you?' He glanced at the woman in the gilet. She was still talking to the plants man, oblivious to her role in the unfolding drama. 'What if it *had* been Rowena?' said Danny. 'You take a few photos, run a headline. *The Killer-cannons reunited! Roll up, roll up, see their anguish.* Is that it?'

'Just doing my job,' said Rossiter.

Morgan saw Danny's jaw tighten. A flash of anger. Without warning, he drew back his fist and punched the journalist in the stomach. The photographer began to capture the scene.

Click whirr …

Rossiter doubling up in pain.

Click whirr …

Danny delivering an uppercut to his face …

Click whirr …

Rossiter crashing into the bookstall …

Click whirr …

Consternation on shoppers' faces …

Danny walking away …

Morgan watched him go. Her eye was drawn to something on the ground.

His mobile. It had fallen from his pocket. She picked it up. No one seemed to notice. A few rubberneckers were already dispersing as Rossiter dusted himself down, exposing a glimpse of his customary red socks while muttering to his colleague. He was trying to laugh off the brawl; an unconvincing show of bravado.

Morgan hurried away, through the market. Reaching her car, she sat behind the wheel then unlocked Danny's mobile with a sliding motion of her thumb. She scrolled through his texts.

None from Lissa.

Morgan frowned. He had messaged her daughter, she'd seen the texts. So why delete them?

She tapped the camera app and scrolled through his photos. For a fleeting moment, she wondered if she might come across images of Imogen Cooper-Price but the pictures were mostly of Zoe's grave. One, taken at night, showed the card that had accompanied the white lilies.

Sorry.

But it was the final image that quickened Morgan's pulse. A freeze-frame from a video. She pressed 'play'. The image jerked to life. Two naked bodies: a gym-fit man and a young woman, their faces out of shot. The smartphone appeared to have been propped alongside a bottle of wine in a candlelit bedroom. The couple were lost in a bout of frenzied, sweaty sex.

A familiar voice. Female.

'*Fuck me!*'

The girl's face came into view, lips parted, jaw slack, as she stared towards the camera with glazed, unseeing eyes. She was astride the man, grinding her lithe young body into his. As she moaned, moving her arms to grip the brass bedstead, the man's face was revealed.

Danny.

Morgan gasped. She shut her eyes tightly but there was no way to escape the sound of her daughter's voice.

'Fuck me, Danny. *FUCK ME!*'

Twenty

1989

Morgan tried to put the telescope out of her mind. If her father was a Peeping Tom – if he had an unhealthy interest in The Boy Across The Road – she didn't want to know. And she had absolutely no idea what to do about what she did know.

Besides, there were other things preoccupying her.

She and Danny went to a chemist's in Dover, where no one would recognise them, and bought the condoms together. Two awkward fifteen-year-olds determined not to giggle or be too earnest. Morgan didn't know a lot about sex but she was sure that being overly serious would be the kiss of death. On the bus home, she steered the conversation to neutral topics: Kylie versus Madonna; the lame end-of-term play; Stevie Gamble's father, the unlikely graffiti vandal with his spray can of red paint and his vendetta against Leo. Danny was monosyllabic, nerves getting the better of him. As Morgan inserted her key in the front door he stayed her hand.

'Sure about this?'

She smiled.

'They're in London. Relax.'

But upstairs it was her turn to be apprehensive. He sat on the bed, watching her draw the curtains. She began to babble nervously, talking about the night the brick came through the window. Danny knew the story, of course – he'd helped her cover up the graffiti – but never before had she mentioned the crucial detail, the moment at the supper table when Leo had touched her arm and said, *'You know I didn't do anything wrong, don't you?'*

She'd wanted to believe him, more than anything. But she couldn't be sure. Those rumours at school. The visit from the policeman with the stupid name – Younghusband. Above all, the telescope trained on the bedroom of The Boy Across The Road. How could there be an innocent explanation? Why was life so complicated? One thing was clear: her stepmother would never forgive her.

'Your own father. How could you not trust him?'

Morgan's flinch – a tiny reflex action – had poisoned her relationship with Ursula. Her father had pretended not to notice Morgan's tell-tale reaction but his depression deepened from that moment on. He slept most of the day, pacing the house at night, surviving on Weetabix.

The household was on tenterhooks, waiting to hear if the CPS planned to prosecute him for the rape of a fourteen-year-old boy. By eavesdropping, Morgan had learned that Stevie Gamble had been admitted to hospital with mysterious 'injuries' whose severity had obliged doctors to alert the police. They in turn had questioned Stevie and extracted a tearful admission: he'd been raped. He identified his attacker as his headmaster, Leo Vine.

Morgan was still babbling. Danny reached out and placed a gentle finger on her lips, silencing her nervous chatter.

'It's fine if you don't want to do this,' he said. 'I'm nervous too.'

'Might help if you kissed me.'

It wasn't their first kiss. That milestone had passed weeks ago in the back row of the Odeon. But it was the best yet. Tender, tentative, increasingly urgent as the tip of Danny's tongue teased her lips.

A crash from the attic. They sprang apart.

Danny stared at the ceiling.

'I thought no one was home.'

Morgan's eyes were wide, blood thudding in her ears.

'They said they wouldn't be back till seven.'

Danny grabbed her hockey stick and headed for the door.

'Stay here.'

She heard his footsteps mounting the stairs. Then his cry of alarm.

'Morgan!'

She took the stairs two at a time, entering Leo's attic to find Danny on his knees, next to her father, his fingers frantically struggling with the rope around Leo's neck.

Morgan took stock of the scene. The telescope on its side. The upturned chair. The beam that had given way under Leo's weight, thwarting his bid for oblivion.

Later, after Danny had gone home and the doctor had left Leo in a tranquillised sleep, Ursula sat on the sofa, white-faced and tearful, fiddling with a loose thread on her blouse. Morgan stared out of the window, replaying her father's apology in her mind.

'I'm sorry. But you know how people are. "No smoke without fire." I may as well be dead.'

The smell of Ursula's vanilla perfume was overpowering. Her voice drew Morgan from her reverie.

'This is your fault.' The woman's hands were trembling. 'Your father's innocent but weak. That boy's accusation is vile enough but it was you who broke his heart, Morgan. Not trusted by his own daughter. No wonder he wants to end it all.'

She got to her feet, smoothed her skirt and headed for the door.

'I married that man for better or for worse, till death do us part. I'll stand by him, no matter what. Pity the same can't be said for you.'

'I don't understand,' said Morgan. 'This has been going on for ages. What's changed?'

Ursula looked tired, as though the fight had gone out of her.

'Surely you've worked it out?'

'No.'

'The police are going to prosecute. Your father's going on trial.'

Twenty-One

Morgan strode past the Mercedes and hammered on the cottage door until her fist hurt.

'Danny!'

No sign of him. Just the rooks cawing in the trees and the dog yapping in the distance.

Morgan thumped on the door again. Both fists at once.

'We need to talk!'

Silence.

'Get out here *now*!'

Her voice was getting hoarse.

'*Danny!*'

The door opened. He was out of breath, eyebrows arched in surprise.

'I was in the workshop.' He wiped his hands on a rag. 'What's wrong?'

Morgan's hand trembled as she held his iPhone at arm's length. She pressed 'play' and let her daughter's voice do the explaining.

'*Fuck me, Danny. FUCK ME!*'

Danny's eyes widened in horror.

'Oh, Christ …'

The video ended. Morgan pressed 'replay', holding the screen inches from his face – the face she longed to punch. Lissa's voice emanated from the tinny speaker, cutting through the quiet afternoon air.

'*Fuck me, Danny. FUCK ME!*'

'Oh, Christ Almighty …'

He closed his eyes, shaking his head, as though trying to block out what was happening.

'I. Am. So. Sorry.'

Morgan hurled the phone to the ground then lashed out with a half-clenched fist, catching his jaw with a blow. He staggered back, into the doorway.

'OK,' he said, blinking hard. 'I deserved that.'

'Tell me where she is.'

Danny shook his head again.

'I swear, Morgan, I honestly don't …'

Another blow, this time to the side of his head.

'*Where's my daughter?*'

Danny hunched his shoulders and splaying his hands in a pleading gesture.

'If I knew, I would tell you. She stayed two nights, left three days ago. I haven't heard from her since. I have absolutely no idea where she is.'

The sound of a car coming down the track.

Two cars.

Morgan didn't need to turn. She knew who was arriving. She'd made the call herself then driven here at top speed, determined to beat them to it, to look into Danny's eyes as she confronted him.

His face fell as he gazed over her shoulder at the new arrivals.

'Oh, Jesus … You told *Farmiloe*?'

Morgan's gaze was unflinching.

'What did you expect?'

She turned away, unable to look at him as the police officers pulled to a halt. DI Farmiloe clambered out of the unmarked car, pulling on her jacket. She was followed by her glossy-haired sidekick, DS Donna Goshawk. Three male officers in uniform brought up the rear.

'Christ alive, Danny,' said the senior policewoman, shaking her head from side to side. 'What were you *thinking*?'

He said nothing, head lolling onto his chest, a picture of guilt and shame.

There was a rushing in Morgan's ears. She could hear someone talking … ordering a fingertip search of the cottage … something about a warrant. She turned and stumbled towards the Mini but was only halfway there when the urge to vomit became overwhelming. She bent double and dry-heaved twice before emptying the contents of her stomach onto the gleaming grille of Danny's Mercedes.

Twenty-Two

'What did he say they argued about?' said Morgan quietly.

She watched Jacqui take a sip of lager then place the glass on the table.

The country pub was almost deserted; the 'swift half before supper' crowd had yet to arrive.

'He tried to end the fling with Lissa,' said Jacqui. 'She hit the roof.'

'Do you believe him?'

The policewoman shrugged.

'I don't know,' she said, looping a strand of hair over her ear, avoiding Morgan's gaze. 'But I shouldn't be having this conversation.'

'So why did you come?'

'Sympathy ... solidarity,' said Jacqui with a shrug. 'Your daughter's been gone six days. I can only begin to imagine how you must be feeling.'

Only six days? Felt like a lifetime.

'Kilcannon's done nothing illegal, so far as we know,' said Jacqui, 'but Christ, what a bastard.'

'Tell me what else he said.'

The DI gave an apologetic shrug.

'In a nutshell, his story goes like this: after four years inside, poor, helpless Danny was easy prey for a pretty young thing, especially one as determined as Lissa. He tried to resist but she wouldn't take no for an answer. So, what's a red-blooded guy to do? Blah-blah-blah ...'

Morgan swallowed, trying to banish the sex tape from her mind. She reminded herself that bad though things were, they could get worse.

'Did you find the hairbrush?'

A frown.

'What hairbrush?'

'Pink, plastic,' said Morgan. 'Lissa never goes anywhere without it. I saw it at his cottage the other day.'

His cottage.

She couldn't bring herself to say his name.

The DI nodded and tugged open a bag of crisps.

'We found the hairbrush,' she said. 'He said she left it in his car, after you all went out together. Is that right?'

She waited for Morgan's nod before continuing. 'Apart from that, there was no sign of Lissa's stuff or anything untoward.'

'Apart from my old flame having sex with my eighteen-year-old daughter?'

'I mean, nothing to suggest she's come to any harm. We're checking the hospitals. No record of Lissa.'

Morgan studied her untouched glass of wine. Jacqui munched on a crisp then leaned forward.

'Off the record?' Morgan nodded. 'Kilcannon says he had no idea that Lissa was making the sex tape. First he knew of it was when she forwarded it from her mobile to his. He swears the sex was consensual.' A pause. 'And judging by her performance, I'm prepared to give him the benefit of the doubt.'

Morgan checked for a smirk. There was none.

'I'll step up the Misper enquiry,' continued the policewoman. 'I'll let you know the second we get any news.'

'Thank you,' said Morgan. 'But I should warn you, I'm going to do some digging.'

A frown.

'For what?'

'I don't really know but I can't sit around doing nothing. God willing, she's fine, just playing games. But the *not knowing* is unbearable.' She stared into Farmiloe's eyes. 'I understand that you think Danny got away with murder but I've no idea what to believe anymore so I need to get to the truth about him, once and for all.'

Jacqui stared at her.

'Is he going to sue for compensation?'

Morgan frowned. The question seemed to come out of the blue.

'Not so far as I know.'

'Odd, don't you think?' said Jacqui. 'He swears he's innocent but now he's out, it's like the whole thing never happened. He hasn't even demanded an official apology.'

'He just wants to get on with his life.'

'Hmm.'

The policewoman raised a sceptical eyebrow then fell silent. Morgan let the seconds tick by.

'Where can I find Caleb Quirke?' she said.

'Why?'

Because if Danny was behind the hit-and-run, he's not the man I think he is. Is Quirke still in hospital?'

The DI licked salt from her fingers.

'One thing you need to remember about our friend Mr Quirke. He's bipolar.'

Morgan frowned.

'I don't recall that coming out in court. Or at the appeal.'

'He's undiagnosed so it wasn't admissible. But it's true.'

'Says who?'

Jacqui took a sip of her drink.

'I know people with mental illness, Morgan. Trust me, the man is bipolar.'

'How is that even relevant? It's not as if it makes him a liar.'

'No,' conceded Jacqui, 'but it might make him unreliable, unpredictable. The trial jury believed him, then the appeal court bought his change of heart when he recanted. But I'm sure he was telling the truth first time round: he saw Kilcannon running away on the night of Zoe's murder.'

'So why would he recant? After all these years?'

Jacqui shrugged.

'I have absolutely no idea.'

She sipped her drink. Morgan studied the policewoman's face. Tired. Harried. Too many responsibilities, not enough time.

'Quirke wasn't the only reason the conviction was quashed,' said Morgan. 'The blood-spatter evidence was discredited. Your whole case collapsed.'

The policewoman's face flushed with indignation.

'I could cite dozens of cases where some scumbag has got off on a technicality. Murderers, rapists, terrorists. We know they're guilty but we have to keep quiet while their lawyers tell the world how rubbish we are, or how the CPS isn't fit for purpose.' She took another sip of lager then made an effort to soften her tone. 'Tell me you don't still think Danny's whiter-than-white. Not after what he did with Lissa?'

Morgan hesitated.

'I'm sure of only one thing: I can't sit around watching you eat crisps.'

Jacqui crumpled the packet.

'Most Mispers turn up unharmed,' she said. 'Lissa has form. There's every reason to think things will work out fine.'

The door opened. Two men in hoodies headed for the bar.

'Could you track her mobile?'

'Maybe, if I had a decent budget,' said the DI.

Morgan said nothing, letting the silence wear away the woman's resistance.

'OK,' sighed Jacqui. 'I'll see what I can do.'

Morgan glanced towards the bar. The new arrivals were ordering pints. One had a tattoo on his forearm, a snake, similar to the one sported by Jacqui's daughter. Morgan remembered the girl's green fingernails, how her face had contorted with anger as she'd flicked a parting V-sign at her mother.

'Your daughter looks like a handful,' said Morgan. 'I saw her outside the police station.'

Jacqui's face darkened.

'Chelsea's going through a rough patch. I do my best.'

'Is her dad around?' said Morgan.

Jacqui nodded curtly.

'Yep.'

Terse. Shutting the conversation down. Draining her glass.

'I'm sorry for your trouble,' she said, 'but stay away from Caleb Quirke. No good can come of it.'

Morgan couldn't resist one final turn of the screw.

'Face it,' she said. 'You messed up.'

'We did our job,' said Jacqui evenly. 'We got the right man. You helped to put him back on the street.'

Morgan stiffened but this wasn't the moment for a showdown.

'Maybe someone had it in for Danny,' she said. 'Maybe he was framed.'

The DI stared at her as if she were mad.

'Who by? Why?'

'The man with the Stanley knife? The one who threatened Quirke? Or maybe it's something to do with Quirke himself. I don't know,' said Morgan. 'But whoever killed Zoe is still out there. Maybe someone set Danny up, maybe they didn't. Maybe there's a link to Lissa disappearing, maybe there isn't. Either way, I need to know.'

Jacqui got to her feet. 'Word to the wise,' she said. 'Don't waste your time on Kilcannon. And leave finding Lissa to us.'

'I'll think about it,' said Morgan.

But there was nothing to think about. She would find Quirke. She would find Lissa, please God. Then she would discover the truth about Danny.

Twenty-Three

The A-frame chalets and mini-golf course of the Dover Holiday Park were deserted as Morgan pulled up outside the manager's office. She'd seen the place before but only on news reports about Zoe's murder and on the *Panorama* special, 'Danny Kilcannon: Justice on Trial'. The programme had played a pivotal role in convincing the Criminal Cases Review Board to refer Danny's case to the appeal court. The so-called eye witness, Caleb Quirke, had been door-stepped by the BBC reporter and challenged over evidence he gave at the Old Bailey.

You told friends you'd lied in court, Mr Quirke. Why?
I've nothing to say ...
Not even when a man is in prison because of your testimony?
No comment, sorry ...
Why tell friends you'd perjured yourself if you hadn't?
Leave me alone!

Morgan rapped on the manager's office door.
'Anyone home?'

The door was opened by a man in his sixties. Tousled white hair. Mutton-chop sideburns. Like a character in a Dickensian drama. No hint of a smile.

'Can I help you?'

Behind him, a grey-haired woman in a yellow overall was mopping the floor.

'Sorry to trouble you,' said Morgan. 'Do you know where I can find Caleb Quirke?'

'Nope.'

Morgan was thrown by the brusqueness. She increased the wattage of her smile.

'He used to work here.'

'What's this about?'

'I'm a journalist. Making enquiries about—'

'I'm busy.'

The man with sideburns was about to close the door when the woman put down her mop.

'Don't be such a rude beggar,' she told the man before turning to smile at Morgan.

'Sorry, love. Caleb hasn't worked here for years. And it's not that we're unfriendly but we still get ghouls wanting to take pictures of where that poor girl died.'

Morgan followed her gaze to a chalet that stood apart from the others.

'That's where it happened?'

The woman nodded.

'Nice kid,' she said. 'Bright as a button, pretty as a picture.' She reached into the pocket of her overalls and pulled out a packet of cigarettes. 'How could he do such a thing?'

'He?'

The woman stepped out of the office and lit a cigarette.

'Killer-cannon,' she said. 'Who else?'

Morgan studied her face.

'You know he's been exonerated.'

'Exonerated, my eye,' said the woman, drawing on her cigarette. 'No doubt in my mind. Or his.' She nodded towards Mutton Chops and raised her voice. 'That man's as guilty as sin. That's what we always say, isn't it, Alf?'

He nodded then turned his back on Morgan.

'Damn right,' he said over his shoulder. 'Guilty as sin.'

Twenty minutes later, as dusk was falling, Morgan parked outside a row of terraced houses and checked the scrap of paper given to her by the woman in yellow overalls. Long accustomed to receiving short shrift from people wary of hacks, Morgan had played the sympathy card, explaining how tracing Quirke might lead on to finding the eighteen-year-old girl who had now been missing for a week.

Caleb Quirke. 6c Lister Street, Dover.

The ground floor of number six was boarded up. Flat C was on the top floor, its net curtains facing a café whose windows badly needed washing. Behind the counter, a woman in a blue and white polka-dot bandana served a lone customer. He sported the uniform of the twenty-first-century inner-city male: trainers, grey tracksuit, hoodie. Morgan pressed the buzzer. A second later she saw a curtain twitch. She counted to ten then buzzed again.

Silence.

About to head for the greasy spoon, to kill time while planning her next move, she stopped as she heard footsteps coming down the stairs. The door opened to reveal threadbare grey carpet and a scrawny, bald man in a green velveteen dressing gown, a small cross on a chain hanging around his neck. Caleb Quirke was a good deal thinner – and much less healthy-looking – than the last time Morgan had seen him.

Four years ago.

Emerging from the Old Bailey after giving evidence.

Head down, trying to dodge a scrum of photographers as he scurried towards the Tube then disappeared among a crowd of Japanese tourists.

'Hello, Mr Quirke.'

A frown.

'Who are you?'

She had only seconds before the door was slammed in her face. Quirke listened to her opening gambit then coughed and shook his head.

'You're wasting your time. I don't speak to the press.'

'Understood,' said Morgan. 'I'm just trying to find my daughter. And to get to the bottom of what Danny Kilcannon did … or didn't … do.'

He coughed again.

'That doesn't sound very healthy. Have you seen a doctor, Mr Quirke?'

The attempt to ingratiate herself was far from subtle but it did the trick.

'That's all I bloody see,' he said. 'Doctors and nurses, morning, noon and night. And now bloody coppers.'

More coughing.

'If you had a minute to talk, I'd be very grateful,' said Morgan.

'About what?'

'What you saw the night Zoe died; the man who threatened to flay you alive with a Stanley knife; why you recanted your testimony—'

Quirke interrupted.

'I'm ill,' he said. 'I tried to do the right thing – better late than never – but now they're prosecuting me for perjury. So I hope the Good Lord helps you find your daughter but I've nothing to say about Kilcannon. I wish I'd never heard his name.'

He closed the door before Morgan had a chance to reply. She heard another bout of coughing accompanied by footsteps as he went up to his flat. Then there was silence.

She considered buzzing again but there was a fine line between being persistent and being a pest. Turning to leave, she felt goose bumps along her arm. The street was deserted but she had the feeling that she was being watched, not by the man in the top-floor flat but by someone whose eyes she could feel but not see. She turned to scan the dimly lit street. Parked cars. Empty doorways. Silent shadows.

Uneasy and on the verge of heading back to the Mini, the thought of a cup of tea stopped her in her tracks. A reviving cuppa and a rethink.

She crossed the street and entered the café. The man in the hoodie had gone, the woman in the polka-dot bandana was the only sign of life. The place reeked of fried food and disinfectant. Morgan paid for a cup of tea and a bun then sat at a sticky table and checked her phone in the hope of finding a message from Lissa. A call she'd failed to hear. An email she'd missed. A text.

Nothing.

She scrolled through her contacts and came to the photo of her daughter. For what felt like the hundredth time that day she stroked a finger over Lissa's smiling face then held her breath until the call connected.

'Hi, this is Lissa. Leave me a message.'

No point leaving yet another voicemail. Morgan pocketed the phone then looked up at 6c Lister Street. Quirke's window was lit by a bare bulb, visible through a crack in the net curtains that kept the world at bay.

The woman brought the tea and bun, setting them down without a word then disappearing into a room at the back. Morgan sipped the tea. To her surprise, it was delicious – hot and strong.

Eyes still on the house across the road, her hand froze as she saw a figure approaching number six. The tall man in the tracksuit had returned, his back to Morgan, face concealed beneath the hoodie. He was carrying something in his hand. It looked like a magazine. He walked up to the front door and pressed a buzzer.

Moments later, the door was opened by Caleb Quirke, still in his dressing gown. Morgan's eyes widened as she watched the man in the hoodie drop the magazine to reveal something in his hand – a hammer, or length of pipe – then raise his arm high in the air, bringing the weapon down on Quirke's head.

She dropped her cup. Ran out of the café.

'*Stop! Hey … Stop!*'

Without thinking, she ran across the road and hurled herself at the assailant, grabbing his arm as he brought the weapon crashing down again. Quirke cried out. Morgan clawed at the hoodie's hand. Felt her nails digging into his flesh. He grunted in pain. Turned to face her. His features were hidden behind a balaclava. His foot kicked out at her leg. Again and again. She fell to the ground, crashing headlong into a wheelie bin as she heard footsteps running away. Quirke was leaning over her, breathing hard.

'Are you OK?' he panted.

'I don't know.'

In the distance there was the sound of a car engine starting up. A squeal of tyres. The attacker driving away. She got to her feet, watching as Quirke winced while gingerly touching a hand to his head, where the first hammer blow had struck.

'Not serious,' he said. 'Glad for small mercies, eh?'

'Was it someone you know?' said Morgan.

Quirke looked away.

'No.'

A lie.

Morgan reached for her phone.

'I'll call the police.'

'Absolutely not.' He was coughing again, heading back inside. 'I'm sorry you got involved. Better you just go away.'

'But you were almost …'

'Just a silly misunderstanding,' he said. 'Leave me alone. *Please.*'

He slammed the door, leaving Morgan to take stock of the pain in her leg where the man in the balaclava had kicked her.

'Mr Quirke!'

No response. The sound of his footsteps going back upstairs.

'Caleb!'

The slam of the upper door. A distant bout of coughing. Then silence.

Across the road, the café was deserted. No sign of the woman in the blue and white polka-dot bandana. No passers-by. No witnesses. The man in the hoodie had chosen his moment with care.

Morgan got to her feet and hobbled towards her car. Fumbling for her keys, she eased herself behind the wheel and locked the doors. Her body was aching, her hands trembling. The shock had yet to fully register but it would come.

Home. She needed to get home.

But as she turned the key, a thought flashed into her mind. Was her imagination playing tricks or did the man in the balaclava have the same build as Danny Kilcannon?

Twenty-Four

She was woozy when her mobile rang; the bedroom was in darkness. She'd taken a sleeping pill an hour ago, one of a batch left from her last bout of insomnia. When Lissa had insisted on going to live with her father, Morgan had put on a brave face but felt like a failure. Night after night, she'd lain awake, tormented by what her stepmother used to call 'monkey-brain' – a nightmarish kaleidoscope of random thoughts and fears. Her weight plummeted, her confidence crashed and her freelance assignments dwindled. Looking back, she could trace her decline, professional and personal, to the day Lissa had packed her Louis Vuitton trunk (a present from Cameron) and moved out of the cosy two-bedroomed cottage she'd shared with her mother.

On the morning Lissa moved to London, into the six-bedroomed house in Notting Hill, Morgan had waited until she was alone then collapsed on the floor and wept hot, angry tears. She'd never taken 'empty nest syndrome' seriously, thinking it a made-up name for a non-existent condition.

How wrong could you be?

A sleepless night followed. More sobbing. A second night of torment. Then another. Three sleepless nights plagued by guilt, grief and despair. The little yellow pills had saved her. She'd kept a handful in case of emergency.

'Hello?'

She answered without checking Caller ID, hoping to hear Lissa's apologetic tone.

Hi, Mum. Just checking in…

But the voice was male.

'It's me.'

The chemical fog took a moment to clear.

'I've nothing to say to you, Danny.'

'I've found Lissa.'

She sat up and turned on the light.

'Where?'

'In Margate,' he said. 'I remembered her talking about the Turner Gallery and those cute new shops in the old town, so I thought, *give it a go* – and there she was.'

'When?'

'An hour ago. Buying a kebab on the seafront.'

Morgan checked the bedside clock. 12.44 a.m. The bruises on her leg were aching. The man in the hoodie had given her a good kicking.

'Is she OK?'

'Yes,' said Danny. 'Stroppy but fine.'

'Did you tell her to call me?'

'Of course.'

'And?'

There was a pause.

'You know what she's like.'

'Where is she now?'

'I don't know.'

'You don't *know?*'

'She ran off when I started getting heavy about calling you. Threw her kebab at me and disappeared.'

'What was she wearing?'

'Sorry?'

'You heard.'

A pause followed by a sigh.

'I'm a bloke. I never notice what people are wearing.'

'Try. Close your eyes. Visualise her.'

Another pause.

'A coat. Black, maybe dark blue. Three-quarter-length. And those ugly boots. Doc Martens?'

Morgan didn't reply. The description was plausible but proved nothing.

'Ask the kebab guy,' said Danny. 'Show him a photo. He'll confirm what I'm saying.'

A teenage girl, one of dozens buying a Friday night takeaway. Would anyone remember? And since when did Lissa eat kebabs?

'I'll tell Jacqui Farmiloe,' said Morgan. 'Get her to check it out.'

'OK,' said Danny. 'Now turn off your light and sleep tight.'

Turn off your light . . .

Morgan felt her blood chill.

'Danny?' Her voice was barely a whisper. 'Where are you?'

This time the pause was even longer. When he finally spoke she could tell he was making an effort to sound casual.

'Not far away.'

She got out of bed and peered through the crack in the curtains. Heart pounding, adrenaline pumping, slicing through the grogginess in her brain.

The Mercedes was twenty yards away, on the shingle by a clump of sea kale. The driver's door was open. No sign of Danny behind the wheel. No moon, just a bank of cloud and a stiff wind blowing in from the sea.

'Jesus, Danny … You're giving me the creeps.'

No reply.

'Danny?'

Three short beeps.

The call cut out.

Morgan stared at the mobile in her hand. She could feel the blood pulsing in her head, her heart hammering in her chest. She peered out of the window, straining to catch a glimpse of movement. How long had he been outside?

Her phone rang. His name appeared on the screen.

'Sorry. Got cut off.'

'Where are you, Danny?'

'On the beach. Looking at the prison.' He paused. 'I used to fantasise about this when I was banged up. Being on the beach at night, just breathing fresh air.'

'Are you drunk?'

'Maybe.' His voice grew small. 'Still got your pebble?'

For a fleeting instant, she felt the pull of the past. But the memory of the sex tape came flooding back.

'Spare me the little-boy-lost bullshit.'

A crunch of shingle. She turned and gasped.

He was right outside, one hand resting on the windowpane, the other holding his phone to his ear.

'Jesus! You said you were near the prison.'

'I said, looking *at* the prison.'

She tried to keep the fear out of her voice.

'Did you knife Gary Pascoe? The night before your appeal?'

He sighed.

'Why do you care about that sick bastard? He made my life hell.'

'Is that a yes?'

Danny hesitated then gave a sheepish nod. Morgan looked into his eyes, searching for something to cling on to, something black and white – but there were only infinite shades of grey.

'One last time. Do you know where Lissa is?'

'No. I swear.'

They stared at each other as the seconds ticked by then he got into his car and drove away. Only now did Morgan notice that every muscle in her body was rigid with tension. The man was drunk. Shouldn't have been driving. But she'd had a bellyful of looking out for him.

She paced around the house, trying to walk off the adrenaline in her system, then strode into Lissa's bedroom. Without switching on the light, she got straight into bed and buried her face in the pillow, desperate to immerse herself in the lingering smell of her daughter. Soon she was rocked by sobs that convulsed her body. Primal. Animal. And for the first time in her life she knew she was capable of doing something terrible.

If Danny were lying – if he had harmed Lissa – she would kill him.

Twenty-Five

She was back at the café just after dawn, in time to see the woman in the blue and white bandana catering to the breakfast crowd. Despite the little yellow pill, Danny's visit had induced another semi-sleepless night, leaving Morgan groggy and exhausted. Her bruised leg was aching and the shock of the hoodie's attack had yet to fade. She'd returned to the scene of the previous night's fracas without a plan, just a series of questions that could only be answered by Caleb Quirke.

It was 7.25.

Eight o'clock on a Saturday morning was the earliest she could reasonably call Jacqui Farmiloe. There was much to tell but first she needed coffee. A handful of customers queued for bacon sandwiches, others tucking into a 'full English' while reading the *Sun* or *Mirror*. One man was flicking idly through the *Post*. A photo of Danny caught Morgan's eye. It captured him mid-punch, hitting Rossiter's jaw. The headline read 'Killer-cannon attacks Post reporter'. The man barely glanced at the story, moving briskly on to the sports pages. Morgan felt a flicker of relief. Her obsession with finding the truth about Danny was not shared by the rest of the world and she was relieved that Lissa's disappearance didn't seem newsworthy.

Teenager argues with mum, has consensual sex then goes off radar.

Move along. Nothing to see here.

What had Farmiloe said?

'*Most Mispers turn up unharmed … There's every reason to think things will work out fine.*'

The thought was briefly reassuring but the sight of a businessman in a red car caused Morgan to jolt upright and spill her coffee.

When the man had first parked outside, minutes earlier, she had paid no attention. Now, as he tapped his fingers on the steering wheel, he seemed to be directing his gaze at the upstairs window of six Lister Street. Morgan's eye was drawn to the back of his hand. A large sticking plaster was visible.

The man's face was cast in shadow. Early forties with an athletic build, not unlike Danny's – or the man who had kicked her so savagely last night, the man whose hand she had scratched, drawing blood. She cast another look at the plaster then slipped out of the café.

The car was new, pristine except for a dent on the front panel, the kind of damage that might have been made by something solid but soft – a dog, say. Or a person – maybe one called Quirke. The 'evidence' was only circumstantial, like the plaster on the man's hand – but *what the hell*?

'Back for another crack at Quirke?' she said, leaning into the open passenger window.

He jerked his head towards her.

'*Excuse me?*'

Middle management. Wire-rimmed glasses. Tall. Fit. Same build as Danny. Hair greying at the temples. Kind face. Weak, perhaps, but decent. A surge of adrenaline told Morgan her instincts were correct.

'Is the balaclava in the boot?' she said. 'With the hammer and the hoodie? Or maybe you dumped them.'

The man reached towards the ignition.

'Piss off.'

He didn't seem accustomed to swearing, more a mild-mannered type putting on a display of bravado.

'I told the police,' she said, rising anger fuelling her confidence. 'They scraped skin and blood from my fingernails.' She nodded towards the plaster. 'From where I scratched you.' He opened his mouth but she was in full flow. 'You seem like a decent bloke so either I give your registration number to the police, which means they'll trace you and take a DNA swab ...'

She paused. He had yet to start the engine.

'Or?' he said.

She looked into the man's eyes. He was no threat, not in broad daylight.

'Or you can let me buy you a cuppa and tell me why you've got it in for Caleb Quirke.'

His name was Allan Maitliss and Morgan's 'middle-management' guess was correct: he worked as an accountant for a software company in Folkestone. Stirring his tea, he had difficulty meeting her eye as he told her about his daughter.

'Suzi wanted to be a nurse,' he said. 'Ever since she was a kid. Didn't care about ponies or pop stars, all she wanted was to help people, have kiddies and live happily ever after.' He sipped his tea then glanced up at Quirke's flat. 'That bastard took it all away.'

He took off his glasses and wiped them on a napkin. Morgan knew better than to hurry him. She watched as his eyes roved across the terrace opposite, coming to rest on number six. The grimy top-floor window with the net curtain.

'I've never told the whole story,' he said. 'Not to a stranger.' He composed his features into a watery smile. 'But like Suzi used to say, "a stranger is just a friend you haven't yet met".'

Morgan smiled back.

'Take your time.'

He took a deep breath.

'Caleb Quirke raped my daughter.'

He let the words hang between them for a few seconds before continuing.

'She was nineteen, staying in one of those holiday chalets, on a hen weekend with friends. The other girls left on Sunday night but she stayed on. "Last night of freedom", she called it. She was due to start college the next day. But the manager – Quirke – let himself in while she was asleep. He tied her up with his belt and raped her.'

Allan Maitliss's eyes were shiny with tears, his Adam's apple working overtime.

'She was so brave,' he said. 'Went straight to the police. No bath, no shower, just into a special room and on with the overalls they give you. She gave a full statement, let them do the swabs and everything they needed to get the ... evidence.'

Morgan remembered her bluff about having the man's DNA under her fingernails. Feeling a pang of guilt, she bit her lip and bided her time.

'The case looked open and shut,' said Allan. 'Quirke denied rape, of course, but they had his DNA. We got word his lawyer was advising him to plead guilty, hoping for a reduced sentence.' He pushed the mug away, his voice tightening with anger. 'A week before the trial, the police came to see us.'

'Us?'

'Me and the wife. "Sorry," they said, "there's been a cock-up. The evidence – Quirke's DNA – is inadmissible in court." *Inadmissible?* I said. *What do you mean?* "Happened during a move," they said. "Backroom staff shifted a load of evidence files from one storage facility to another. The packaging got damaged."' His voice cracked. '*The packaging.*' She saw his fingers tighten around the mug, his knuckles whitening as he continued. 'Bottom line: Quirke's sample was contaminated. Which meant the evidence wouldn't have stood up. His lawyers would have trashed us.'

This time the silence was hard to bear. Morgan's voice was as gentle as she could manage.

'So Suzi never got her day in court?'

Allan shook his head.

'No DNA, no prosecution.' His voice was quieter now, harder to hear. He studied the sauce bottle. 'On the day the trial should have started, Suzi got into a bath with one of my razor blades.'

Morgan held her breath and took his hand.

'I'm so sorry.'

It was several seconds before he spoke again.

'Me and the missus stuck it out for a bit but we were never the same.' He gave another unconvincing smile. 'She lives in Marbella now. Looking for answers at the bottom of a bottle.' He picked at the plaster on his hand. 'So maybe you can see why I had a go last night.'

Morgan nodded.

'I'd feel the same,' she said, fending off the image of Lissa in a bath, the water crimson with blood. 'But I'm not sure I could bring myself to run someone over then leave them for dead.' He looked away. She pressed the point, needing to know. 'The hit-and-run attempt on Quirke,' she said. 'That was you, too, right?'

The man gave a small nod. Morgan was about to reply but the woman in the bandana arrived to wipe the table. Allan Maitliss fell silent, waiting for her to finish.

'Sorry for your loss,' said the woman.

Allan looked up and raised an eyebrow.

'You knew Suzi?'

The woman shook her head.

'Recognise you from the paper.'

He nodded.

'Saw her picture too,' said the woman. 'Lovely girl.' She finished wiping the table. 'Next time,' she said, 'breakfast's on the house.'

A small smile.

'Appreciate it.'

The woman went back to the counter. Allan Maitliss fell silent for a moment then cleared his throat.

'Will you tell the police?'

Morgan studied his face.

'Depends. What are you planning to do about him?'

She nodded towards number six.

Maitliss sighed.

'You can't possibly understand. You've never lost a child.'

Not yet ...

'True,' she said. 'But would Suzi want you to go to prison?'

Her mobile beeped. *Please let it be Lissa ...*

She forced herself to wait.

'You're right,' he sighed. 'I'll leave Quirke alone.'

She nodded then checked the text. An apology from Danny.

Sorry about last night. But I DID see Lissa in Margate. PLEASE believe me. xx

She stood up, scraping back her chair.

'Got to go.'

Maitliss nodded. Smiled. A belated attempt at normal conversation.

'Boyfriend?'

Morgan didn't hesitate.

'No,' she said. 'Just someone I used to know.'

Twenty-Six

Speeding towards Margate, she allowed herself a pat on the back. By following a hunch, by asking the right questions, she'd established that Danny was not behind the hit-and-run attempt on Quirke's life, or the previous night's hammer attack.

OK, hardly Watergate, but she was glad to be regaining her mojo, reviving her appetite for the buzz that came from chasing a lead, following a story, finding the truth. So many questions. Who murdered Zoe? What happened to Rowena? Above all, where was Lissa? But at least she'd made a start.

Back in the game.

By the time the clock on the seafront struck ten a.m. she'd already dialled Jacqui Farmiloe's mobile, brazenly interrupting the DI's round of golf to alert her to Danny's sighting of Lissa. She'd also found the seafront kebab shop. Seagulls cawed overhead as the bleary-eyed owner scrutinised the photo of Morgan's daughter then went back to washing his windows.

'Friday nights are the worst.' He shrugged. 'Payday drunks and screeching girls. I don't look at their faces, I just count their money.'

She found a café and settled in a booth, scrolling through her mobile, working her way through her list of Lissa's childhood friends. Danny had promised he'd spoken to them, but then Danny had promised a lot of things.

Calling around, double-checking with Lissa's friends and their parents, Morgan drew a blank. No one had heard from her daughter since her return from California. There was nothing untoward in this; Morgan knew Lissa could be unsentimental about friendships and was capable of severing ties without misgivings, moving on without a backward glance. At just eighteen, there was already something disturbingly ruthless about the girl, a conscience-lite insouciance that enabled her to sleep with married men (with Danny even) and tune out her mother's feelings.

The TV was showing the mid-morning news. An image of a high-speed train flashed onscreen, part of a report on delays caused by a fatality at Dover Priory station. Morgan shuddered, banishing from her mind's eye a picture of Lissa's mangled body on the tracks. She grabbed her keys and fled outside, into the chilly sunshine.

None of the staff at the Turner Gallery recognised Lissa's photo, and a painstaking trawl of cafés, pubs and shops proved fruitless. In desperation, Morgan forced herself to comb the amusement arcades, even though she knew Lissa was allergic to places that were so noisy and garish. As a last resort, she bought a ticket to Dreamland, the retro amusement park, but here too the story was the same. *Sorry, haven't seen her.*

Then she caught sight of Chelsea Farmiloe.

Emerging from a seafront café.

High heels. Long coat. Head down.

On the verge of turning away, Morgan gave in to a sudden impulse to follow the teenage girl. Feeling ridiculous, like someone who has inadvertently strayed into a spy movie, she maintained a discreet distance as she tailed Chelsea several hundred yards to a seafront shelter overlooking the harbour. There was a bus stop nearby. Morgan feigned interest in the timetable, watching out of the corner of her eye as Chelsea sat on a bench, lit a cigarette and fiddled with her phone. Moments later, the teenager with the green fingernails and the snake tattoo was joined by two scrawny men in their twenties, both sporting tracksuits and trainers.

Morgan couldn't make out their conversation but didn't need to. The gist was obvious: a furtive exchange, cash slipped into Chelsea's palm in return for a small wrap of paper. Cocaine? Weed? Crack? Morgan had no idea but she'd seen all she needed. As a bus approached she walked away, wondering what to do with the knowledge that Detective Inspector Jacqui Farmiloe's daughter was a drug dealer.

Light of my life – bane of my life.

Her watch showed nearly four thirty as she hurried towards the car park tucked away in the backstreets. She slowed her step. Had someone *painted* the car's roof? No ... but someone *had* covered it with a layer of sand. And in that sand they had traced a familiar message.

Don't trust him

Morgan felt a surge of fury. Didn't she have enough to worry about? She fished her phone from her bag and took a photo of the message. She had no idea what to do with it but the act of taking it made her feel as if she was doing *something*. Nine long days and nights had passed since Lissa went missing. She needed to take some kind of action, gather evidence. Against whom and for what reason she had no idea.

Casting a glare around the car park, she brushed away the sand then got behind the wheel of the Mini, and headed for Dungeness.

To her relief, there were no more messages at home, no sign of anyone following or lying in wait. All the same, as she locked the doors of the converted railway carriage, she couldn't shake the sense of unease that came from knowing that someone was watching her every move.

She had no appetite but made spaghetti with chilli, garlic and olive oil, poured a large glass of red wine and turned on the TV. Fingering the remote, she was about to click away from the local news when she saw footage of Dover Priory station. A bearded reporter was covering this morning's fatality: the body on the tracks. Morgan's fork was halfway to her mouth as the thought struck again, this time with the force of a punch.

Please God, not Lissa . . .

She turned up the volume. The reporter was talking about the casualty.

A man.

Thank God.

But Morgan's eyes widened as a photo of a familiar face flashed onscreen.

'*The dead man was forty-two-year-old Caleb Quirke from Dover. Police have appealed for witnesses and released CCTV footage appearing to show Mr Quirke being pushed onto the tracks by a man wearing a hoodie. Some viewers may find these images distressing.*'

Morgan held her breath. She watched as the blurry CCTV footage filled the screen. There could be no doubt about it: one minute Caleb Quirke was standing at the platform's edge, the next he was being shoved onto the tracks, into the path of an oncoming train.

Mercifully, the footage froze before the impact. The assailant wore a black hoodie. His face (and surely it had to be a man) was angled away from the camera, but he shared the same build as two people Morgan knew who bore grudges against the hapless Mr Quirke.

One was Allan Maitliss.

The other was the man whose pebble she carried in her pocket.

Twenty-Seven

'Sorry to call on Sunday,' said Morgan. 'I need to talk about Caleb Quirke.'

Jacqui sounded exhausted.

'Sunday? I hadn't noticed.'

Awake since dawn, Morgan had taken an icy swim, deliberating long and hard before deciding to phone the DI a second time. She had more than a little sympathy for Allan Maitliss: even if he *had* pushed his daughter's rapist under the train, the mild-mannered accountant was no serial killer. From now on he would almost certainly live a blameless life, tormented by his own conscience. It was tempting to stay silent, to let him get away with murder and achieve some sort of closure.

But if Maitliss *was* guilty of killing Quirke, then Danny *wasn't*. In which case he was possibly unworthy of the other suspicions swirling around him. The temptation to let things lie was outweighed by Morgan's need to find her daughter and that meant shopping Maitliss to the police, providing them with another crucial piece of the jigsaw.

'Any chance we could meet today?' she said, aware of the croak in her voice. The DI's reply was laced with concern.

'Are you OK?'

Morgan felt a surge of raw emotion. She was thankful the DI couldn't see her eyes glaze with tears.

'My daughter's missing. My oldest friend's a liar. No, I'm not OK.'

Silence then a sigh.

'I shouldn't do this,' said Jacqui, 'but why don't you come over for breakfast?'

It turned out the DI had been up all night, working as Senior Investigating Officer at the scene of Quirke's murder. She'd returned home for a shower and a breather.

'Thank God for caffeine,' she said, pressing the plunger into the cafetiere and motioning for Morgan to sit down at the kitchen table. 'I take it you're here as an actual human being not a journalist?'

'Everything's off the record,' said Morgan, glad of the no-nonsense approach.

She took stock of the view from the cliff-top bungalow's picture window. The green of the golf course tapered towards the Dover Straits and the white cliffs. Photos chronicling Chelsea's childhood were everywhere – on fridge magnets or pinned to the corkboard. Her penchant for green fingernails seemed to date back to her early teens, the snake tattoo appearing later, around the age of sixteen.

Morgan decided not to mention Chelsea's drug dealing. It was none of her business. More importantly, she needed Jacqui focused on the search for Lissa not fretting about her own kid.

As it was, a fresh murder enquiry centred on the victim on the train tracks would leave little time for a Misper.

Over coffee and scrambled eggs, Morgan brought the DI up to date. Her attempt to question Quirke. The hammer attack by the man in the balaclava. Her grilling of Allan Maitliss.

Jacqui took no notes but it was clear she was absorbing every detail, processing all angles. The more Morgan saw of Detective Inspector Farmiloe, the more impressive she found her. A committed professional at the top of her game.

'Did you see the CCTV footage we released?'

Morgan nodded.

'Whoever pushed Quirke under the train has the same build as Maitliss.'

The policewoman leaned forward.

'And Danny – who hated Quirke because he lied at the trial, or so Kilcannon says.'

'Which would give Danny motive,' conceded Morgan. 'Theoretically.'

Jacqui raised an eyebrow. 'Only theoretically?'

Morgan shrugged. It was as far as she was prepared to go. She could feel the DI sizing her up.

'Between you and me,' said Jacqui, 'that's the only CCTV angle we've got. Chances of seeing the guy's face are zero, which means—'

She was interrupted by a crash from another room. Sighing, she got to her feet.

'Excuse me.'

A man entered, naked except for a single black sock. Nudging seventy, he was unshaven with wispy grey hair and a sagging belly. He ignored Morgan and glared at Jacqui.

'Can't find my other sock.'

'Jesus ... Colin.' Jacqui handed him an apron to cover himself. 'Can't you see someone's here?'

The man turned to Morgan.

'Where's my sock?'

'Sorry. Haven't seen it.'

'Damn and shit and piss,' said the man. Then, in a moment that Morgan would remember as half tragic, half comic, he spread his arms and sang a jingle from an old TV ad.

'*Washing machines live longer with Calgon!*'

Jacqui shot Morgan an apologetic look then steered the naked man out of the kitchen.

'Back in a sec.'

Morgan turned her attention to a wedding photo on the fridge. It showed Jacqui and Colin in front of a village church, flanked by a handful of relatives. Even all those years ago, one thing was glaringly obvious: the age gap. Jacqui was a good fifteen years younger than her husband, possibly more.

It was ten minutes before she returned, offering a single word by way of apology.

'Dementia,' she said. 'He was the smartest copper I ever knew, now he can't wipe his own arse.' She resumed her seat. 'The carers cost a fortune so I take over when I can. I'm trying to keep him at home as long as possible.'

Morgan glanced at the other family photos.

'Does Chelsea live at home?'

'Nope,' said Jacqui.

Once again, the DI was quick to shut down any mention of her daughter.

Morgan heard a TV in the distance – the roar of a sports crowd – and thought of her own father in the Sandwich Bay care home. Was he too watching TV? Sitting slack-jawed in a semi-circle of high-backed chairs? A sudden wave of guilt engulfed her but it was tempered by the knowledge that their estrangement was at his insistence. And Ursula's.

She brought herself back to the here and now.

'You've got a lot on your plate,' she said. 'Doesn't leave much time to look for Lissa.'

'I checked an hour ago,' said Jacqui. 'No sightings, no sign she's used her ATM card or passport.' She sipped her coffee then made an attempt at reassurance. 'We never work just one case, Morgan. I'm breathing down my sergeant's neck every day.' That muscle twitched again. 'And Donna Goshawk is a star. On the fast track. If anyone can find your daughter she can.'

She began to clear the table and stack the dishwasher. Something on her mind.

'I need to know I can trust you.'

'Of course,' said Morgan.

'I went to Dungeness prison.' Jacqui set the dishwasher. 'An inmate asked to see me. Said he had information about Danny.'

'Are we talking about Gary Pascoe?'

Jacqui nodded. Morgan recalled Danny's attempt on the cage fighter's life.

'Is he still in hospital?'

The DI shook her head.

'A man like that would never let a knife-wound stop him from getting out on time.' She hesitated. 'But he told me that Kilcannon made a confession.'

'To what?'

'Killing Zoe,' said Jacqui evenly. 'And Rowena.'

Morgan frowned.

'Danny hates Pascoe. Why open up to him of all people?'

'I got the impression the confession was extracted under duress.'

Morgan's frown deepened as she remembered the cigarette burns on Danny's back.

'A confession extracted by torture and given to a convicted killer? Worthless.'

'In court, yes,' nodded Jacqui. 'Prisoners often try these stunts to make a trade-off. Extra visits, maybe a reduced sentence. But Pascoe was released on Friday. Hard to see what he had to gain.'

Morgan raised an eyebrow.

'You mean, he's out?'

The DI nodded, chewing the inside of her lip. 'Did you give him any indication that you might see him on the outside?'

'Of course not. Why?'

'Because he seems to like you. A lot.' Morgan felt her shoulders tense. 'I told him that he should forget his past. And everyone in it. Especially you.'

Morgan was holding her breath.

'I'm not sure what you're trying to say.'

A look of concern flitted across the policewoman's face. When she spoke again her tone was gentle.

'As I was leaving, he asked something I found disturbing.'

'Define "disturbing".'

'He asked me how to trace people.'

Twenty-Eight

As Morgan pulled to a halt in the prison car park, half a dozen screws were arriving by minibus. She grabbed the opportunity to quiz them. Had Pascoe talked about her? Had he said he was trying to find out where she lived? Blank faces all round.

Inside the visitors' reception area she waited for the gate officer to process her admittance then followed her escort along the labyrinth of corridors, down into the basement. The recreation room reeked of disinfectant, its striplight emitting an intermittent buzzing like an angry trapped fly.

Taking her seat, she was struck by Pascoe's absence. At six foot five, he had been the most imposing member of the group as well as its most vocal. She greeted the regulars and one new participant then did her best to focus on a discussion about George Orwell. She was relieved when the session limped to an end, leaving her to go in search of the man who might be able to shed further light on what Jacqui had said about Gary Pascoe.

She found Nigel Cundy striding along the admin corridor. His keys jangled on his belt as she kept pace while filling him in on her conversation with the DI. She could almost taste the man's disappointment; it was as if he'd wanted to be the one to break the news about Danny's confession. She liked Cundy less with each encounter. The niggling feeling that he was responsible for the spate of anonymous messages wouldn't go away.

'Did Pascoe mention me during your last session?'

A thin smile.

'Because everything's about you?'

'He murdered the mother of his kids, Nigel. If he's trying to find out where I live it would be good to know.'

The shrink had the grace to sound apologetic.

'He's at a halfway house in London. I bet you never hear from him again.'

He walked on, leaving Morgan to head for reception, her stomach still churning.

Retrieving her keys from the locker, she exchanged pleasantries with the guard. Flourishing a copy of *Midnight's Children*, he urged Morgan to put the book on the group's reading list. She told him it would be a tough sell but was glad to have a normal conversation, one that didn't include murderers or missing girls. As she exited through the gates, into a burst of midday sunshine, she chastised herself for assuming that all prison officers were the same: witless boors who'd missed their vocation as bouncers. That was the thing about people: the surprises kept on coming.

Settling behind the wheel of the Mini, she inserted the key in the lock then looked up and gasped – part shock, part fear – as she saw Pascoe, a bandage across his throat, his face at the window.

'We need to talk,' he said.

She started the engine. Hands trembling.

'Just talk, I swear,' he said. 'Then I'll go.'

She was about to slam her foot on the accelerator when he planted himself in front of the car. He held out both hands – a pleading gesture.

Morgan caught sight of a prison officer emerging from the staff entrance. The man was carrying a holdall, leaving at the end of his shift. She slammed her hand on the horn. The officer raised his head. Saw Pascoe. Dropped his bag. Ran towards the Mini.

'What are you doing, man?' The screw's voice was weirdly high-pitched. 'You shouldn't be here.'

'Free country, pal,' said Pascoe. 'I go where I like.'

The officer looked at Morgan.

'Want me to get someone?'

She considered her options. She could talk to Pascoe now, in view of the guard, or risk antagonising someone determined to track her down. She opened the window, just a crack.

'It's OK,' she told the screw. 'Mind sticking around?'

The man shrugged, folded his arms and fixed his gaze on Pascoe.

'Why aren't you in London?' said Morgan.

Pascoe gave a gap-toothed grin.

'I came to see you,' he said. 'My brother gave me a lift.'

She followed his gaze. A large, shaven-headed man sat at the wheel of a plumber's van, picking his nose. His face looked untouched by thought or feeling. Clearly, Gary was the brains of the family.

'I've got a plan,' said Pascoe. 'You're a journalist. You can make it happen.'

The plan was simple. He wanted advice on how to cash in on what he knew about Danny.

'Depends what you know.' Morgan needed to hear it from his own lips.

'He killed his stepdaughter,' said Pascoe. 'And his wife.'

She made an effort to keep her voice steady.

'You come up with this now – after four years – and you expect people to take you at your word?'

Pascoe grinned and took a mobile from his pocket.

'I nailed him. On this.'

Morgan's eyes widened.

'You had a phone inside?'

He sucked his teeth, scoffing at her naïvety.

''Course I had a fucking phone. That's why he shanked me, trying to get it off me.' He brandished the mobile. 'What's on here means lover boy is up shit creek.'

Morgan kept her tone light.

'OK, let's hear it.'

A smile spread across Gary's face. He had her attention and he knew it.

'Soon as you hook me up with the right people.'

Twenty-Nine

An hour later Morgan pulled up outside the country pub where she'd met Jacqui Farmiloe. The cage fighter was next to arrive, following in his brother's van. Clive Rossiter joined them five minutes later.

Morgan made the introductions, settled the two men in a booth then went to the bar. Waiting for drinks, she fought a wave of exhaustion, braced herself for what lay ahead then paid for a pint of bitter, orange juice for Rossiter and a Diet Coke for herself. At the table, Pascoe sipped his pint and closed his eyes, savouring the moment.

'You have no idea how good this tastes.'

The ex-prisoner wiped a hand across his mouth. He reached into his pocket, took out his mobile and placed it on the table in front of Rossiter.

'Morgan told you the deal?'

The journalist nodded, keeping his voice low even though the pub was empty and the barman out of earshot.

'She says you've recorded Kilcannon confessing to murder.'

'Two murders,' said Pascoe. 'So what's it worth?'

Mistake number one, thought Morgan: never let the buyer set the terms.

'Depends,' said Rossiter. 'I'd need to hear it.'

Pascoe shook his head, his voice taking on a C-Wing swagger.

'Money first, pal. My game, my rules.'

Rossiter met his gaze.

'Let's be clear: you're a convicted murderer. No matter what's on your mobile, no newspaper is going to make you rich.'

Pascoe sucked his teeth and turned to Morgan.

'You said he was serious.'

'Listen to him,' she said.

But the man was getting to his feet, in a display of bravado.

'You're full of crap,' he said, staring at Morgan. 'Same as everyone else.'

'Sit down, Gary.'

Rossiter's voice was calm. He produced an envelope from his pocket.

'One thousand pounds.'

Pascoe gave a mirthless laugh.

'You shitting me? Multiply that by twenty then we start talking.'

Rossiter shook his head.

'This is the starter not the main course. A gesture of goodwill so I can hear the recording.' He patted the envelope. 'Whatever happens, you keep this.'

Pascoe eyed the envelope then sank back into his seat.

'Ten grand for the starter,' he said. 'Fifty for the main.'

Rossiter shrugged. 'Try any paper you like. No one will touch you.' He sipped his orange juice. 'Facts of life, Gary,' he said. 'Read 'em and weep.'

Morgan knew he was right. Whatever the contents of Pascoe's mobile, no newspaper could be seen to pay a drug dealer who'd murdered the pregnant mother of his five children. But this didn't mean a confession by Killer-cannon – even a spurious one – wasn't newsworthy. Rossiter needed to hear the recording. A thousand pounds would be a bargain. At the same time, Pascoe hadn't thrived behind bars without learning how to negotiate every advantage, every spliff, every favour. Morgan watched as he assumed a poker face.

'Eight grand for one listen,' he said. 'Then we talk about the main course.'

Stalemate. Morgan rolled her eyes.

'Just give him the money, Clive.'

The journalist glared but she didn't care. The more she discovered about Danny, the greater the chances of finding Lissa. A confession, even one obtained under duress, might bring her closer to the truth. And a bigger question was nagging at her: had the police simply cocked up the investigation into Zoe's murder or had someone set out to frame Danny? If so, was there a link to Lissa's disappearance?

'Five grand,' said Pascoe, tracing a finger around the rim of his glass. 'I'll wait while you get it.'

Clive gave a tight smile.

'No need.' He took another envelope from his pocket. 'Two grand.' He pushed the envelope across the table. 'That makes three. Final offer.'

Pascoe opened both envelopes and scanned the contents. Satisfied, he pocketed the money then looked over to the bar, making sure no one was within earshot. He picked up his mobile, wagging it at the journalist.

'Listen good.'

Morgan watched as he swiped to the voice memo app then pressed 'play'. A voice emanated from the tinny speaker.

A man. Breathing hard. In pain.

Danny.

'*OK.*' He was panting. *'Jesus Christ ... OK!'*

Pascoe's voice.

'*OK, what?*'

'Jesus! Stop and I'll say it.'

Danny let out an agonised howl unlike anything Morgan had ever heard. Pushing away a wave of nausea, she closed her eyes, remembering the cigarette burns scarring his back.

Pascoe again.

'*What will you say, Danny boy?*'

'*I did it.*'

'*Did what?*'

'*Killed Zoe.*'

'*Who else?*'

'*Rowena.*'

'*Again.*'

Another cry of agony. Like an animal thrashing around in a trap.

'*I killed them both.*'

'*You lying, Danny boy? To get me to stop?*'

'*No! I did it.*'

'*So you're a lying, murdering piece of shit?*'

'*Yes!*'

'*Say your name.*'

'*Danny Kilcannon.*'

'*Say what you did.*'

'*I killed Zoe and Rowena.*'

The recording cut out. Pascoe grinned, cupping the phone in his hand.

Morgan stared at the teardrop tattoo under his eye. She could feel her anger rising. This was Danny. *Her* Danny.

'Clearly a false confession,' she said, struggling to keep her anger from showing. 'Obtained by torture and totally worthless, Gary. Like you.'

The man's grin died. He pocketed his phone.

'She's right,' said Rossiter. The journalist had got what he wanted; the nonchalance was back. 'This proves nothing. It'll only bring you grief.'

'Bugger that, pal,' said Pascoe, patting the phone. 'This is my pension.'

'In your dreams, *pal*,' said Rossiter, getting to his feet and buttoning his jacket. 'Have a nice life.'

'Fuck off,' said Pascoe. He glowered at Morgan. 'Who else do you know?'

'No one who'll give you a different answer.'

The man leaned closer. She could smell beer on his breath.

'Not good enough, bitch.'

'This isn't C-Wing,' said Morgan, trying to keep her voice steady. 'You need to learn how to ask nicely.' Without waiting for a reply, she raised an eyebrow at Rossiter. 'Are we done?'

The hack nodded and followed her out of the pub, leaving Pascoe at the table, cracking his knuckles. Outside in the car park, Morgan felt a combination of anger, disappointment and exhaustion.

'You OK?' said Rossiter.

She didn't reply, her eyes fixed on the plumber's van. Pascoe's burly brother was at the wheel, smoking a joint. She let out a sigh.

'He's trying to find out where I live.'

The journalist thought for a moment then zapped his fob, unlocking his car.

'Follow me.' He cast a glance at the man in the van. 'Till we're clear of these idiots.'

She fumbled for her keys, embarrassed by the tears that were springing to her eyes.

No! Not here.

These fretful, anxious days were taking a toll. Having no one to share the anguish made everything a hundred times harder. Even ordinary days – when your child was safe, when your old friend had your back – even those days could sometimes feel as if *alone* was bleeding into *lonely*. It wasn't that Morgan needed people to do things with – she liked her own company – but she missed someone to do *nothing* with.

'Still living out at the beach?' said Rossiter.

'Yep.'

She could see him thinking.

'Spare room at my place,' he said. 'Might make you feel better. Safer.'

The swiftness of her own reply took Morgan by surprise, as did the surge of relief.

'If that's a serious offer,' she said, 'I'll take you up on it.'

Thirty

She followed Clive to London, stopping at a supermarket to pick up overnight essentials: toothbrush, knickers, wine. The traffic was snarled along Holloway Road but she found a parking space directly behind his car, at the end of a scruffy Victorian terrace. Stepping onto the pavement, her nostrils were assailed by a stench that made her gag. Rossiter looked away, embarrassed.

'I bought the house ages ago. A year later, they built a recycling centre two streets away. A huge, stinking rubbish dump for north London.'

Morgan cupped her hands over her nose.

'So why not move?'

'Would you buy a house here?'

'No way.'

'Exactly.'

He darted inside to fetch a parking permit. Morgan watched as he emerged and foraged in a hanging basket of dead geraniums. He fished out a small plastic bag containing a spare key. Handing it to Morgan, he told her he was off to a 'quick meeting' and would be back in an hour.

Nosing around the house – magnolia walls, beige carpet – she found a stack of M&S ready meals in the walk-in pantry, no trace of a woman's presence and the Serenity Prayer taped to the bathroom mirror.

God grant me the serenity to accept the things I cannot change, courage to change the things I can, and wisdom to know the difference.

Now his 'quick meeting' made sense: he'd gone to a local branch of Alcoholics Anonymous. She recalled their encounter at the Romney Marsh petrol station. He'd been drinking, she was sure of it, rocked by his demotion from features editor to lowly reporter. Still, people leaped off the wagon every day then managed to clamber back on. He'd drunk only orange juice in the pub.

Morgan wondered if she too should give up alcohol for a while but the thought lasted no longer than the time it took to find a corkscrew and open her bottle of Chianti. Glass in hand, she continued to explore, rifling through a stack of paperbacks on anger management and a shelf of books on addiction. Drugs. Alcohol. Sex. Gambling. Her host was a man with issues.

Darkness had fallen by the time he returned with a Chinese takeaway. He arranged the food on the coffee table in front of a huge TV. She could tell he was uneasy, unaccustomed to having someone in the house. He insisted she relax in his Charles Eames chair while he assembled chopsticks and plates. Then he perched on the leather footstool, drinking fizzy water.

Morgan had decided to keep quiet about Lissa's disappearance. The hack had ink for blood. The story would be irresistible.

Killer-cannon sex romp with ex's missing teen daughter.

The conversation turned to Danny and Quirke instead. Clive focused intently on Morgan's account of her encounter with Allan Maitliss, the accountant whose daughter had killed herself after the rape case against Quirke collapsed. The reporter listened without interruption but soon steered the conversation back to Killer-cannon.

'What do you make of the CCTV? Does it show Danny pushing Quirke under the train?'

She toyed with a ring of salt and pepper squid.

'Could be Maitliss.'

'Still giving Danny the benefit of the doubt?'

'Just keeping an open mind.'

He selected a piece of chicken, holding it between his chopsticks.

'Gun to my head, I'd say it was Kilcannon He's had years to plan his revenge against Quirke – and why would Maitliss strike now? But I take your point. Danny's not the only one with motive.'

They fell silent for a moment. Morgan poured herself another glass of wine. The nagging doubts were back.

'What if someone framed him for Zoe's murder?' she said.

Rossiter's eyes widened.

'Excellent,' he said. 'It would keep the story alive for years. But *cui bono*?' He sipped his water. '*Cui bono* is Latin for "to whose benefit"?'

'Thanks,' said Morgan. 'I know what it means.'

He smiled, accepting the rebuke.

'So, what's the answer?'

She took a sip of wine and considered the question. She didn't want to sound like a conspiracy theorist and yet it was surely possible that Danny had been set up.

'The real killer,' she said.

'Do we have a suspect?'

'No. Apart from the man who threatened Quirke with the Stanley knife.'

'Who has never been found.'

'But what if Danny *was* framed?' said Morgan. She watched as Rossiter wiped his mouth with his napkin.

'Find me a suspect with a plausible motive to frame Danny,' he said, 'and I'll guarantee you a front-page splash. Plus a picture byline that will make your career.'

She raised her glass in a mock toast.

'It's a deal.'

There was no mention of the retainer he'd mentioned during their first encounter. Perhaps the offer was no longer on the table. Or maybe he'd simply taken her at her word. *I don't spy on friends.*

Supper over, he insisted on clearing away while she took a bath. Immersed in the water, she scrutinised the bruises on her leg. Listening to her host clattering around the kitchen, she felt ill at ease. She didn't linger in the bathroom, swathing herself in a towel and emerging to discover that Clive had made up the bed in the spare room. She could hear him in the kitchen, murmuring down the phone.

One final attempt to reach Lissa then she'd try to sleep. She scrolled to her daughter's number, a flicker of optimism flaring for a second before being snuffed out.

'Hi, this is Lissa. Leave me a message.'

A floorboard creaked. She looked up. Clive was in the doorway, a glass of water in his hand.

'Don't panic,' he said. 'I don't bite.'

He took a step closer and handed her the glass. His fingers brushed hers. His eyes held her gaze. She looked away.

'Thanks,' she said briskly. 'Sleep well.'

He gave a knowing smile, taking rejection in his stride. Then he left the room and closed the door.

When Morgan awoke at six thirty he was gone. There was a Post-It by the kettle. *Make yourself at home. C.*

She was relieved he hadn't signed with an *x*. She should never have accepted his offer. Restored by sleep and feeling idiotic for succumbing to what Ursula would call 'a fit of the vapours', Morgan dressed and scribbled a thank-you note. Then she let herself out onto the rain-slicked street, returning the key to its place in the basket of geraniums. The stench from the rubbish dump was almost overwhelming.

The sight of a piece of paper sticking to her windscreen increased her heart rate but proved harmless – just the parking permit. She climbed into the Mini, lit a roll-up and headed for Dungeness, trying to quieten the mounting sense of dread. Eleven days since Lissa had vanished without trace. Two hundred and sixty-four hours, each longer than the last.

It was still daylight as she pulled up outside her home. Out at sea, a flock of seagulls circled a fishing boat, their cries echoing far and wide. Morgan frowned. Someone had left a table outside her house. On top was a posy of wild flowers. The table was old pine, a drawer at one end. Inside was an envelope. She opened it. Something slipped out onto the deck.

Danny's pebble.

She picked it up, feeling its heft in the palm of her hand, then took a note from the envelope.

Thank you for believing. Hope you like the table. Glad I was able to keep one promise.

Morgan re-read the note, unsettled by its valedictory tone. She reached for her mobile and dialled his number.

'*Hi, this is Danny. You know what to do.*'

The journey to his cottage normally took thirty minutes. She made it in twenty-five, as dusk was falling. Slewing to a halt, she saw his Mercedes and felt a wave of relief. She'd been plagued by images of him slumped over the wheel, a hosepipe snaking from window to exhaust ...

She ran to the door.

'Danny ...?'

She hammered with her fists then ran around the side of the cottage but there was no gate to the garden, just a hedge bordering the property.

'*Danny!*'

No response, only rooks cawing in the trees. She looked up to the bedroom windows. No sign of life.

And then came his voice in the distance.

'Morgan?'

She turned. He was walking along the track that sloped down from the hill behind the cottage, pushing a wheelbarrow. As he drew closer, she saw his boots and face were spattered with mud.

'What are you doing?'

She stared.

The wheelbarrow – empty.

The spade resting on the handles.

His eyes met hers.

'Christ,' he said softly. 'Here we go again.' He let the wheelbarrow rest on the ground. 'I know what you're thinking, Morgan. Let's stop the crap and do this, now.'

She found her voice.

'Do what?'

'There was a dead sheep,' he said with a sing-song air of exaggerated patience. 'It was blocking the stream that irrigates my allotment. I dragged it out and buried it.' He picked up the spade, growing more irate with every syllable. 'But you don't believe me so let's dig it up.'

She stared at him.

'I thought you were dead, Danny. Your letter was like a suicide note.'

He stared back at her, frowning. She could read his thoughts. Where there had once been trust there was now only mutual suspicion.

'If I was going to kill myself, I'd have done it years ago.'

She tried not to look at the spade. His muddy boots. The wheelbarrow.

'Nice table. Thank you. How did you get it to my place?'

He shrugged.

'Hired a van.' For a moment, the only sound came from the rooks in the trees. 'Sorry about the other night. I was drunk.' He took a breath. 'As for what happened with me and Lissa …'

She raised a hand, stopping him mid-sentence.

'I went to Margate,' she said. 'The kebab guy doesn't remember her.'

He studied her face.

'But you do believe I saw her?'

'Yes.'

It wasn't quite a lie, more like wishful thinking. He raked his fingers through his hair then hoisted the wheelbarrow and pushed it towards the cottage. She followed, trying to keep the anxiety from her voice.

'Rossiter and I met Gary Pascoe,' she said. 'He played us your confession. Clive told him to forget it. Said it was obvious you were lying – just saying whatever Pascoe wanted, to get him to stop hurting you.'

Danny downed the wheelbarrow and reached for his key.

'Rossiter thinks I killed Quirke.'

A question, not a statement.

'Yes.'

He turned.

'And you?' he said. 'What do you think?'

Say what you need to say.

'I don't think you're capable of killing anyone.'

He studied her face for a moment then went into the house, turning on the lights. Following him into the kitchen, she drew his pebble from her pocket.

'Why did you leave me this?'

He shrugged.

'A reminder. The good old days. When you trusted me.'

She placed the pebble on the pine dresser. He ignored it then took two beers from the fridge.

'I saw Jacqui Farmiloe,' he said. 'She interviewed me under caution.'

'Did you have a lawyer?'

A nod.

'Imogen came down from London. But Farmiloe really went to town. *Where were you when Quirke was killed*? At home. *Do you have an alibi*? No. Total waste of time. Hers and mine.'

In the distance, the sound of the yapping dog.

'Jesus ... that animal never stops!'

He snapped open a can of beer, proffering the other to Morgan. She sipped it while filling him in on the saga of Suzi and Allan Maitliss. But as she talked, she wondered how soon she could return with a spade of her own to dig for what she prayed would be a dead sheep, not a teenage girl with blue eyes and blonde hair.

Thirty-One

1989

Leo's bail conditions allowed him to live at home during his trial. Every evening, he moped around the house, ignoring the nervous prattle of his wife who had taken up smoking menthol cigarettes. 'Cool as a mountain stream,' she muttered several times a day. Morgan wondered if she was cracking up.

Ursula went to any lengths to avoid referring to Stevie Gamble's rape allegation in front of her stepdaughter. Pilfering a cigarette, Morgan found a blister pack of Valium, along with a list of suitable topics of conversation designed to perpetuate the charade of normality.

1) New parking restrictions.

2) Release of Guildford Four – disgrace!

3) Mrs Thatcher – true grit!!

All three came up over supper, eliciting zero interest from Leo and cursory replies from his daughter. To her credit, Ursula drove her husband to court each day, ironing a fresh shirt and laying the breakfast table every night before bed. Morgan had glimpsed her stepmother on the news, immaculate in twin-set and pearls, smiling at reporters as she clutched Leo's arm and steered him into the courtroom.

Supper on the third day of the trial was especially subdued. Morgan knew from the radio that the jury had retired. One way or another, tomorrow would likely bring an end to the proceedings.

'If you go to prison, will it be nearby?'

Leo sipped his wine.

'Sit up straight and eat your sardines,' said Ursula.

'I hate sardines.'

'Do as you're told,' said Leo.

He'd barely spoken since his attempt to hang himself – crippled by shame or despair, Morgan supposed, or a combination of the two. But she felt sure his new attitude towards her – stern, aloof – was a result of Ursula's campaign to poison their relationship. She'd heard their whispers.

'The girl doesn't trust you – her own father. It's shameful.'

Perhaps the woman would have felt differently had she known about the telescope trained on The Boy Across The Road but Morgan couldn't tell her. She couldn't tell anyone – not even Danny.

Leo's voice. Weary.

'Put yourself in her shoes. School gossip. Peer pressure. She's confused.'

'The word you're looking for is "disloyal". One of these days you'll see her for what she is. I'm not saying you're going to have to choose between me and your daughter ...'

But that was exactly what she was saying.

Morgan knew Ursula was right about one thing: her father was weak. Terrified of being lonely, he'd married the pretty widow within months of Morgan's mother's death from cancer, plucking up courage to tell his eleven-year-old daughter only the day before the wedding.

Morgan had refused to attend. Ursula had never forgiven her.

On the morning the verdict was due, Morgan arrived at the school gates then hesitated before turning and running away. She knew Danny wasn't in class – recovering from 'flu – but she needed his company, now more than ever. Exhilarated by her act of defiance, she hurried to his house, the scruffy two-up-two-down to which he and his mother had been reduced when his father, a car salesman, ran off with the boss's daughter.

His mother answered the door in her dressing gown. Morgan could smell alcohol on her breath.

''Morning, Mrs K. Is Danny in?'

The mottled-faced woman nodded her inside then flicked cigarette ash into a yoghurt pot. She sank onto the red leather sofa and went back to watching TV. Morgan glimpsed what looked like a legal letter on the coffee table. The words *decree nisi* jumped from the page.

'Might have known Madam wouldn't be at school today. Not with Daddy in the dock.'

'Is Danny in his room?'

The woman remained glued to the screen. A game show was starting. She nodded towards the staircase.

'Go on. But no funny business.'

Upstairs, Morgan knocked on Danny's door. He was on his bed, reading *Animal Farm*.

'Thought it might be you.'

She saw the pebble on the desk, next to his French homework.

'Are you infectious?'

His wan smile widened to a grin. He brandished a French dictionary.

'*Oui. Beaucoup.*'

To Kill a Mockingbird lay on the floor. She picked it up.

'Can I borrow this? I've lost mine.'

The lie was easier than the truth. She wanted his book, the copy with the smear of chocolate on page sixty-seven, the fragment of Flake that had fallen from his lips.

He shrugged.

'Keep it.'

She smiled.

They spent the day eating toast and Marmite, resorting to Monopoly to stave off boredom (his) and anxiety (hers). There was no mention of what had happened (or not happened) the last time they'd been alone together in a bedroom. Nor did they speak of the drama reaching a climax in Canterbury Crown Court.

At twelve thirty, Danny's mother barged in without knocking. She was off to the cash-and-carry. Would they keep an ear out in case that bastard Reece popped in?

Reece was a timeshare salesman she'd met at Weightwatchers. According to Danny, he 'popped in' whenever he could get away from his wife.

They listened to the news every hour, neither mentioning the reason for their newfound interest in current affairs. As three o'clock approached, Morgan felt her stomach lurch. Perhaps the verdict wouldn't come today. Maybe her agony would be prolonged.

A ring on the doorbell. Danny made his way downstairs. Morgan followed, intrigued to see what 'that bastard Reece' looked like.

But the visitor wasn't Mrs Kilcannon's boyfriend, it was Ursula.

'I knew you'd be here. I promised your father I'd let you know the verdict. Before it's on the news.'

Morgan caught the familiar smell of vanilla perfume. Her mouth was dry.

'And?'

A catch in her stepmother's voice. Her eyes were watery but she made no attempt to soften the blow.

'Guilty.'

Thirty-Two

Crouched among the bamboo canes bordering Danny's vegetable patch, Morgan watched his bedroom light go out. She forced herself to wait fifteen minutes before making her move. Somewhere in the distance a church clock struck midnight then silence was restored. Even the yapping dog was quiet tonight. She'd bought the spade on the outskirts of town, along with boots and gardening gloves. A good move, but she should have worn more layers. She was chilled to the bone.

Climbing the hill, she checked his cottage was out of sight then switched on her torch. She kept her ears peeled for running water. The dead sheep had blocked a stream. Or so he'd said.

There was no moon, no break in the cloud, only a light shining from Dover Castle. Rain had been falling all evening. Morgan's boots squelched in the mud, chafing as the incline grew steeper. Her heart rate seemed to double every few yards and her breathing grew laboured.

Cursing today's tally of cigarettes (twenty … more?), she panted past a decrepit barn. She had little idea about the workings of country life. Was this where sheep were penned at night or did they stay in their field? Either way, surely one dead animal couldn't cause a problem with irrigation? Water took the path of least resistance; it was hard to see how a small blockage could divert a stream far enough to deprive Danny's allotment. But if it wasn't a sheep he had buried, what was it?

She brought herself up short. The only thing of which Danny was guilty – having sex with Lissa – was not a crime. At least, not the kind that put you behind bars.

Negotiating a stile, picking up a splinter in her thumb, she refused to let the pain break her stride. Then she heard it. *Baa-ing* in the distance. Tacking to the left, she followed the sound, cresting a hillock to see a small flock of sheep penned inside a lean-to abutting a rickety barn.

Suddenly, the hillside was seared by sheet lightning, illuminating the sky long enough to give her a glimpse of Danny's cottage down below. Just yards from where she stood, next to a brook swollen with rainwater, was a mound of newly turned earth. Another flash of lightning, a rumble of thunder. The storm was closing in. Leaning on her spade, Morgan took a moment to catch her breath, trying to gnaw the splinter from her thumb. Determined to ignore the sting, she donned her gloves and began to dig the mound of earth, trying to focus on an image of what she *hoped* to find.

Dig.

A dead sheep was not a happy prospect but better than the alternative. Another flash of lightning was followed by a crack of thunder. The rainclouds broke with pent-up fury.

Dig.

Turning over spadeful after spadeful of sodden earth, she recalled Danny's crimsoned sole as he'd unearthed the tulip bulbs outside his workshop, his face set with righteous indignation, his foot bleeding.

Dig.

With the rain streaming down her face, she forced the spade into the earth, again and again. Feeling the blade strike something solid, she stopped to gather her breath, raising her face to the rain. Her eyes were drawn to a light down below. The cottage. Danny's bedroom. He was awake.

Feeling a sudden surge of panic, she sank to her knees and began to scrape at the mud. The gloves were cumbersome, making it harder to dig. She flung them away, scrabbling at the earth, feeling the splinter's sting, unable to stop digging even as the pain intensified.

Another glance down the hill. The light was no longer shining. Had he gone back to bed or had he seen her? Was he pulling on his boots? Heading up the hill? Her eyes searched the darkness. No sign of life.

Then her fingers touched fabric.

Hessian?

A sack?

A shroud?

Who would bury a sheep in a shroud?

A foul smell assaulted her nostrils. She felt sick, glad of the driving rain – it kept the nausea at bay as she scraped away yet more earth, revealing more hessian. And beneath the sacking, something firm but pliable.

Deep breath.

Ignore the stench.

Forget the splinter.

Push through the pain.

She dug her fingers into the hessian, tearing at the sack. She could feel the coarseness of the weave. A rip in the material. Dimly aware of another crack of thunder – this time directly overhead – she pulled at the hole with bleeding fingers, tugging at the sacking, feeling it stretching, ripping, the hole widening to reveal the sight she had been praying for since encountering Danny with his wheelbarrow.

The fleece of a dead sheep. Filthy. Matted.

There was no one to hear her sobs of relief or witness the tears that sprang to her eyes. Still on her knees, long past caring about the rain, she scraped the mud back over the carcass, hiding the animal from view and leaving the burial mound as she'd found it.

Exhausted, she slithered down the hill, away from the cottage, sucking on her bleeding thumb and weeping tears of relief and guilt and shame until she could weep no more.

Ten minutes later, she was in the lane that led to his cottage. She'd parked in the layby, hiding the Mini behind the Martello tower. She sank into the front seat of her car, shook the worst of the rain from her hair then shone the torch onto her thumb. Raw. Bleeding.

She checked her watch. Just past one in the morning. Chances of finding a local A&E department were nil. The nearest was miles away, at Ashford. Only one option. She rummaged in her bag for a safety pin. Two excruciating minutes later she'd sterilised the tip with her lighter and gouged out the splinter, almost fainting in the process.

But – and this was the weird thing – even completely soaked, even with her thumb bleeding and the rain pounding the car, even alone in the middle of nowhere, she couldn't recall the last time she'd felt so alive, so filled with relief. But there was also shame. Yet again she'd doubted Danny's innocence. Yet again she'd been wrong. The sceptics – the eighty-two per cent … Farmiloe … Rossiter – they all wanted her to believe Danny was not the man she needed him to be.

True, the sex tape had helped to bring her round to their way of thinking. But the betrayal with Lissa didn't make him guilty of abduction or capable of murdering Zoe. Or Rowena. It was surely at least *possible* that someone had framed him. Once again, Morgan had let fear and jealousy get the better of judgement.

Turning the key in the ignition, she reviewed the idea that Allan Maitliss might have killed Quirke. For years, she'd believed Danny to be the victim of a miscarriage of justice. His prison attack on Pascoe notwithstanding, there was no proof to the contrary. As for the anonymous messages, the campaign had begun while Danny was behind bars. He had no case to answer.

All things considered, when it came to Lissa's disappearance, surely he deserved the benefit of the doubt? For a moment, the thought made her feel lighter. There was hope – perhaps even a future for her and Danny.

But the flicker of optimism was short-lived. Without Lissa, there was no future, no happy ever after. Tears threatened to return as Morgan steered the car onto the main road and peered out into the rain. She thought of Maitliss. How did he get out of bed every day? How did anyone survive the death of a child? What would be the point in going on?

Thirty-Three

On the twelfth day since Lissa's disappearance the call from Jacqui Farmiloe came just after eight a.m.

'We've had news from her bank.'

Morgan sat up in bed, groggy from her sleeping pill.

'What news?'

'Her ATM card was used at two forty-six this morning. Two hundred pounds withdrawn from NatWest in Cecil Square, Margate. We're checking CCTV to confirm it was used by Lissa herself.'

Morgan ran through the possibilities.

Lissa was alive and well, just being selfish.

Someone had found her card and discovered the PIN.

She'd been abducted and forced to reveal it.

'How long will it take to check the CCTV?'

'Assuming it exists, a day or so,' said Jacqui. 'I've told DS Goshawk to make it a priority.'

Morgan remembered the DI's second in command, the woman with the slim, elegant hands and lustrous hair.

'Can't you do it yourself?'

A sigh. Farmiloe was struggling to stay on an even keel.

'Morgan, I've half the resources I had five years ago. My boss insists I "do more with less", as though clichés make up for budget cuts. Meanwhile, Colin's going from bad to worse. As for Chelsea …' She tailed off and gave another sigh. 'Sorry. Overshare.'

Despite a stab of sympathy these were not Morgan's problems.

'Chelsea's not missing. Lissa is.'

A note of steel entered the DI's voice.

'I'm aware of that. I'm also flat out on other cases – including the murder of Caleb Quirke.'

'Any news?'

'We're investigating all avenues,' said Jacqui. Her tone was frosty, professional once again.

'Thanks for keeping me posted.'

Morgan had no intention of waiting for Donna Goshawk to establish who had used Lissa's ATM card. She made it to Margate in record time, bought coffee and stood outside the bank, scanning the area for CCTV. There was only one camera, across the square, angled away from the bank, towards the main road. The chances of seeing whoever had used the card were nil, but the possibility that Lissa had stood here just hours ago was hard to bear. Morgan scrutinised the gutter, peering into bins and under parked cars, hoping to find a clue, some proof of life.

Making her way down the hill, heading for the seafront, she entered the maze of cobbled streets that Lissa had dubbed 'quaint'. In a trendy-looking café, jazz playing softly in the background, she showed Lissa's photo to a waitress with dreadlocks. A smile of recognition.

'Popular girl.'

Morgan raised an eyebrow.

'How do you mean?'

The waitress began to clear a table.

'A guy came in earlier. Asked the manager to put up that photo.'

Morgan followed her gaze. A flyer was stuck to the pin-board. A photo of Lissa was displayed alongside Danny's mobile number and a handwritten slogan.

Have you seen this girl?

'When did he come in?'

'About an hour ago.'

'Did you recognise him?'

Morgan was intrigued to know if Killer-cannon was still at the forefront of people's minds. The waitress frowned, eyes widening as realisation struck home.

'Now you mention it,' she said. 'Didn't he kill that girl?'

'People say he did. There's a difference.'

Morgan spent the morning scouring the area around Dreamland, stopping strangers in the street, visiting every café, every shop, every pub. Always the same story: Danny had beaten her to it but no one had seen Lissa. If people found it odd that Killer-cannon was trying to find a missing teenager, only one – a publican with a strawberry birthmark – brought it up.

'Should have strung the bastard up while they had the chance.'

Walking along the sea front, Morgan turned her collar up against the stiff wind that was blowing in across the beach. She crossed the road, heading for the sleek, modern building that housed the Turner Gallery, then stopped in her tracks. Danny was at a table on the terrace, eating a sandwich. As she drew closer, she saw he was wearing a sweatshirt emblazoned with Lissa's photo.

Have you seen this girl?

He raised a hand in greeting.

'Must stop meeting like this.'

Morgan sat and nodded towards his sweatshirt.

'A very good idea,' she said. 'Should have thought of it myself.'

He dug into a carrier bag and fished out an identical sweatshirt.

'Had them done in the place that printed these.'

He produced a stack of flyers. Morgan studied the photo of her daughter's face: the long hair, blonder than ever after her summer in the Californian sun, the mischievous grin, the smiling eyes.

'Where did you get the photo?'

He looked down at his cup.

'A selfie. She sent it to me.'

Morgan took off her coat and donned the sweatshirt. She let the silence stretch, gazing out towards the windswept beach. A woman was throwing a Frisbee for her black Labrador. In the distance, a teenage boy was trying to hoist a kite into the wind but with no success. Normal people doing normal things. Morgan wondered if her life would ever be normal again. Maybe she was destined to be one of those people she saw on TV every year, on the anniversary of a loved one's disappearance, telling their story for the thousandth time.

Should she update Danny about the ATM withdrawal? If the card user was Lissa this was a crucial piece of the jigsaw. On the other hand, if Danny himself had used the card – to make it seem as if Lissa was alive ...

Morgan couldn't bring herself to finish the thought. She forced her mind back to last night.

The storm.

The mud.

The sheep.

She'd left the lane near his cottage just after one o'clock. His car had been parked outside but that proved nothing. He could have driven to Margate in the early hours, used Lissa's card as a red herring then returned with his flyers and his sweatshirts and his kind eyes.

Who can we trust?

'The police say someone used Lissa's ATM card.'

His eyebrows arched in surprise.

'When?'

'Middle of the night.'

'Brilliant.' Big encouraging smile. 'You must be so relieved.'

She shrugged.

'There's no guarantee it was her.'

His smile faltered as he nodded and pushed his cup away. Getting to his feet, he delved into the bag and drew out the flyers, dividing the stack in two.

'We'll cover more ground on our own. You choose: precinct or arcades.'

She took the flyers, barely able to look at Lissa's face.

'Arcades.'

'Deal.' He tossed his sandwich wrapper into a bin. 'I'll call if there's any news.'

She watched him cross the road then turned and headed into the wind.

The skies over Thanet are the loveliest in all Europe.

Not today. The clouds were gravestone-grey, the wind fierce and the rain threatening to return. Skirting the harbour, she headed for the row of arcades lining the promenade, garish relics of the resort's heyday. Despite Dreamland, the Turner Gallery and other signs of regeneration, Margate remained defiantly seedy, an air of dowdiness and resentment permeating everywhere.

A skinny man was raising the shutters outside an amusement arcade called the House of Phun. Morgan handed him a flyer and asked if he'd seen Lissa. He lit a cigarette.

'If I had a quid for every poor sod looking for their kid, I'd be out of this shithole faster than you can say Bangkok titty-bar.'

Morgan managed a smile then moved on. Out of the corner of one eye, she saw him crumpling the flyer into his pocket. It would be in the bin by the time he'd finished his smoke.

Thirty minutes later, she'd trawled the other arcades, drawing a blank. She was about to head for the shopping precinct when a white Range Rover drove past, Sinatra's *Fly Me To The Moon* blaring from an open window. The pristine SUV looked out of place on the shabby seafront: showroom-fresh, whitewall tyres, chrome bull bars. Morgan couldn't make out the driver's face but she glimpsed a man's hands on the steering wheel, a glint of cufflink gold. She narrowed her eyes as she saw a familiar figure in the passenger seat.

Chelsea Farmiloe, sullen-faced, smoking a joint.

And a third person in the backseat.

A teenage girl?

Morgan couldn't be sure.

As the Range Rover slowed, she quickened her pace. The SUV headed up the hill to a Regency terrace then stopped outside the Pleasureland Hotel. Morgan watched as Chelsea stepped out, followed by the driver. A dapper man in his sixties. Mediterranean complexion. Navy blazer. Yellow cravat. Even at this distance, Morgan could make out white loafers and a gold watch. He looked like a cruise-ship crooner.

She watched him open the door of the white Range Rover, delivering a mock salute as the girl stepped onto the pavement.

Younger than Morgan had thought.

Fourteen?

Thirteen?

As the odd-looking trio entered the hotel, it wasn't the girl's age that made Morgan uneasy nor the fact that she wore school uniform, it was the look of fear on her face.

Thirty-Four

Standing on the doorstep of Jacqui Farmiloe's bungalow, listening to the gulls shrieking overhead, Morgan wondered if she should have brought a bottle of wine. The phone call had been brief.

> *'Can I come and see you?'*
> *'I've no news, Morgan.'*
> *'This isn't about my daughter, it's about yours.'*
> *'What about her?'*
> *'This might be better in person.'*
> *A pause.*
> *'I'll be home by eight.'*

Morgan rang the bell and checked her watch. Eight twenty-five. She'd allowed time for the overworked policewoman to decompress and say goodbye to her husband's carer. Not for the first time, she wondered how her stepmother – fastidious, bordering on squeamish – had coped with Leo's dementia during the early stages, before he'd moved to the care home. Morgan had offered help – practical, financial, emotional – on many occasions but the response was always the same.

Your father doesn't want to see you or hear your name ever again.

All day, she'd agonised over whether to tell Jacqui what she'd seen. She'd decided that, had their roles been reversed, she'd want to know.

Morgan wasn't sure exactly what she'd witnessed outside the Pleasureland Hotel but she was ninety-nine per cent certain that Chelsea Farmiloe was dealing drugs, probably cocaine and/or heroin. A criminal conviction would ruin her life.

Jacqui opened the door, whisky tumbler in hand.

'Will this take long?'

Morgan gave what she hoped was a reassuring smile.

'I'll be as quick as I can.'

But an hour later they were hunched over the kitchen table, the policewoman picking at a microwaved lasagne while Morgan toyed with an apple, trying to recall when she'd last felt hungry.

'You didn't get the registration number? The Range Rover?'

Morgan shook her head.

'I missed a trick. But it looked new. Shouldn't be hard to track down.'

'Would you recognise the man again?'

Morgan nodded.

'Not the type you forget.' She cut a slice of apple. 'Maybe he was the girl's father or granddad.'

Wishful thinking and she knew it.

She should have intervened, asked the girl if she was all right. The odd-looking trio had disappeared inside the hotel before she'd had a chance to gather her wits. Now she was plagued by the sense of an opportunity missed and a horrible feeling of guilt.

Jacqui downed her fork.

'I'll ask Chelsea who the man is.' She glanced at her mobile. 'If she ever calls back.'

'Did you know she was dealing drugs?'

Jacqui didn't answer straightaway.

'I've had my suspicions but she's a law unto herself. If there was a rule, she broke it, a weak spot, she'd find it, a plan, an ambition, a dream, she'd mess it up. Bunking off school, flunking exams, smoking dope, not going to uni, not looking for a job.' She finished the litany of disappointment then sank the whisky, her second since Morgan's arrival. 'She's eighteen so there's bugger all I can do.' She raised the empty glass in a mock toast. 'Welcome to my world.'

As the woman lapsed into silence, staring into the middle distance, Morgan tuned in to the sound of a TV in another part of the house: an ecstatic sports crowd cheering.

'How's your husband?'

Jacqui propped her elbows on the table.

'I had to beg for two hours off last Saturday,' she said, her speech now slightly slurred. 'To take Colin to the specialist. Psych assessment. Told my guv'nor, "Wait till your family falls apart then we'll see how you cope." ' She splashed more Johnnie Walker into the glass. 'Last Friday, I get home and Renata –

his carer – she's hysterical.' She flapped a hand, mimicking what Morgan took to be a Polish accent. '"Husband gone! He stole car keys."' She swilled the whisky around the glass. 'Turns out he'd made it to the M20. I managed to get Traffic to flag him down.' Her voice cracked with emotion. 'I'm going to have to do what I should have done ages ago and put him in one of those places.'

'That's a tough one,' said Morgan.

Jacqui got to her feet and scraped her supper into the bin.

'I don't get much time for friends,' she said, turning away, 'but it's good to talk.' She put her plate in the dishwasher, avoiding Morgan's eye. 'And this is between us, right? About Chelsea?'

Morgan nodded. 'Of course.'

She reached for her coat as Jacqui's mobile rang. Caller ID showed the name of her sidekick, *Donna Goshawk*.

'I need to take this,' she said, reverting to her professional persona. 'Give me two minutes.'

Morgan replaced her coat, watching as the policewoman walked into the hall. She let her eyes rove across the kitchen. There were few signs of domestic bliss; desiccated cacti on the windowsill; over-ripe bananas in the fruit bowl; countless pictures of Chelsea.

'Washing machines live longer with Calgon.'

The voice made her jump. She turned to see Jacqui's husband in the doorway, wearing a dressing gown that gaped open revealing his hairy belly and erect penis. He was stroking it.

'Unzip a banana,' he sang, his hand moving faster as he continued to masturbate, staring straight into Morgan's eyes. She felt strangely calm, moved to pity rather than disgust.

'Colin,' she said quietly, 'you shouldn't be doing that.'

The man gave a lopsided grin.

'*Unzip a banana,*' he said. '*Unzip a banana.*'

'*Jesus Christ!*'

Jacqui was back, rushing towards her husband.

'For God's sake ...'

She placed her hands on the man's shoulders, ushering him from the room. Morgan tried to imagine herself in the DI's shoes. Leaving without saying goodbye would make the woman feel worse. She busied herself by washing her plate and watering the cacti.

When Jacqui returned, she was red-eyed and clearly mortified.

'I'm *so* sorry ...'

Morgan cut her short, gently placing a hand on her shoulder.

'That was much worse for you than for me.'

Jacqui gave a grateful half-smile. Fumbling for a tissue, she blew her nose. Morgan could smell her whisky breath.

'We were all set to buy a place in Spain,' she said. '*Dun-Sleuthin'.* Then he got ill.' She fell silent for a moment. With the air of a decision made, she said, 'I'll check out care homes first thing.'

Another inch of whisky.

Morgan picked up her coat.

'I should be going.'

Jacqui gave a brittle smile. An understanding had been reached: Colin's behaviour wouldn't be mentioned again. She followed Morgan to the front door.

'That was Donna Goshawk,' she said, brandishing her mobile. 'I told her to check out the Pleasureland Hotel, see if they can shed any light on the man in the Range Rover. The manager wasn't there. She'll go back tomorrow.'

There was more to come. Morgan let the silence run.

'I probably shouldn't be telling you this,' said Jacqui, 'but she also double-checked Allan Maitliss's alibi for the time of Quirke's murder.'

An exchange was being offered: Morgan's sensitivity over Colin's behaviour in return for privileged information.

'And?'

'Looks pretty solid.'

Morgan felt her stomach lurch.

'Which makes Danny prime suspect?'

'Definitely a person of interest.'

If Morgan had been keen to leave before, now she was desperate.

'Have a good evening.'

Jacqui gave a rueful smile then closed the door, heading back to her rendezvous with Johnnie Walker.

Getting into her car, Morgan felt a wave of sympathy. A family in pieces: hopes dashed, dreams denied. Trying to picture herself at Chelsea's age – Lissa's, too – she wondered if her goals – a career, a life with Danny – had ever stood a chance, or if she'd just been building castles in the air.

Either way, her stepmother had been right.

Man plans, God laughs.

Thirty-Five

Definitely a person of interest.

Morgan was back at Danny's cottage by eight a.m. Standing on the doorstep, collar turned against the drizzle, she glanced at the hill behind the house, recalling the stench of the dead sheep.

He didn't seem surprised to see her. Sporting his *Have You Seen This Girl?* sweatshirt, he led her through the scullery into his garden workshop.

'You look terrible,' he said.

'She's been gone nearly two weeks. What do you expect?'

He picked up a screwdriver and set to work fixing a castor into a piece of wood. His tone was unforgiving.

'Come to check on me?'

She shook her head and nodded towards his sweatshirt. The photo of Lissa.

'I need to know what she said before she disappeared.'

'About what?'

'Anything that might tell me where she's gone.'

He set the screwdriver down on the workbench.

'We've been through this.'

'Let's go through it again.'

Leaning against the wall, she listened to his account of the affair with Lissa. *Just a fling.* Three days, two nights. She tried to banish the sex tape from her mind and suppressed an urge to stab him with the screwdriver. The 'fling' was irrelevant. Only one thing mattered. Finding Lissa.

Sipping coffee, Danny gave his side of the story. Wracked with guilt, he'd tried to break things off but Lissa had refused to accept his decision. Carried away by some kind of adolescent fantasy, she'd tried to talk him into running away with her. South America. Africa. Anywhere.

He'd rejected the idea out of hand. Betraying Morgan was unforgivable, the affair had to stop.

The eighteen-year-old had become hysterical (why did men always use that word?) and stormed out. He hadn't seen her since.

To the best of his recollection, Lissa had shown no inter-est in contacting old friends or returning to California. But she *had* talked about how much she loved Margate. The old town was 'quaint', the vintage dress shops 'brilliant', the bars and cafés 'cool'.

Morgan dismissed the idea of searching in London. Like looking for a pebble on a beach. Besides, there was no evidence to suggest that Lissa would go there. Morgan would urge Jacqui and Donna to focus on Margate. Two possible sightings already: the kebab shop and the ATM. But first, she needed an excuse to search Danny's cottage.

'Can I use the loo?'

He picked up the screwdriver.

'Top of the stairs.'

She watched as he turned his back, smoothed his fingers over the piece of oak and began to screw in another castor.

The bathroom showed no sign of a female presence. Morgan scrutinised the plugholes – bath and basin – for traces of long blonde hair. There were none. And even if there were, what would it prove? Lissa had spent three days here; Danny had admitted as much.

On the landing was a gun cabinet – the kind she'd seen in country houses. She wondered why Danny needed a shotgun. Self-protection? Did his conviction make it harder to get a licence? Perhaps he hadn't bothered to apply. Or maybe the weapon pre-dated his time behind bars.

Pushing open the bedroom door, she took stock of his unmade bed, the floor strewn with clothes. A sense of déjà vu. Why was the brass bedstead familiar? The realisation hit with the force of a speeding truck.

It was the bed in the sex tape.

Fuck me, Danny. FUCK ME!

Morgan took a breath, trying to shake off the memory of Lissa astride Danny – lost in the moment, lips parted, eyes glazed. She snatched up a paperback from the bedside table.

Life After Prison. An inscription on the flyleaf. *To Danny. Today is the first day of the rest of your life. Imogen xxx*

The book had been lying on top of the local newspaper. A headline caught her eye. '"Nuisance dog" shot dead'.

She remembered the yapping dog. Danny's face, taut with anger.

Jesus ... that animal never stops!

Somewhere below, a door closed. Softly.

'Danny?'

Silence.

She put the book down and walked onto the landing.

'Hello?'

He stepped into view, staring at her from the foot of the staircase. No hint of a smile. He started up the stairs, taking each step slowly.

'Lissa's not here.'

'I know. I was just—'

'Snooping.'

She said nothing. He reached the landing. Close enough for her to smell the coffee on his breath.

'I think you should leave.'

She met his gaze.

'I needed the loo.'

'If you say so.'

Over his shoulder, she saw a handwritten sign on a bedroom door.

Adults keep out!!!

He followed her gaze then nodded her into the empty room. Yellow walls, an IKEA wardrobe, a pine bed – handmade, presumably by Danny. But no flavour of the girl who had once occupied this space, no sense of her fate.

'The police tore the house apart,' said Danny, gazing around the room. 'Gave it a going over the other day, too. Prints, luminol, the lot.'

'Luminol?'

'To look for traces of blood.'

The unspoken accusation hung in the air.

Because you told them about me and Lissa.

He was too close for comfort, his body blocking the doorway. She could smell his skin.

'Am I making you nervous, Morgan?'

'Of course not.'

Trying to sound sure of herself. Sure of *him*. Edging towards the door, her eye was drawn to a photo of Zoe on a corkboard. The freckle-faced fifteen-year-old wore a pale blue T-shirt emblazoned with a slogan. *Teen But Not Heard*.

'The last photo,' he said. 'I took it the day she died.'

Morgan fingered the image of Zoe's face.

'*Teen But Not Heard*?'

'We argued,' said Danny. 'About me searching her room. She said I'd violated her human rights.'

Morgan gave a half-smile.

'Sounds like a handful.'

A shrug.

'We had a lot of "*You're not my dad*" crap. But the problem wasn't me, it was classic teenage rebellion plus anger at her real dad for dying. She was just a kid.' He nodded to the bookshelf. A complete set of *Harry Potter*. 'She liked me to read to her at night.'

'At fifteen?'

'She liked my voice. Said a bedtime story made her sleep better.'

Morgan let the silence stretch.

'Why did you search her room?' she said.

He raked his fingers through his hair.

'I caught her smoking weed. She swore it was the first time, begged me not to tell Rowena, so I gave her a second chance. But she was going off the rails in a big way, staying out late, refusing to say where she'd been, stealing cash so she could run away from home, She told her mum, "I need two grand then you won't see me for dust." '

'Was she serious?'

'Rowena didn't think so. Neither did I.'

Morgan studied the photo of the teenager.

'I don't remember any of this coming out at the trial.'

'The lawyers said it wasn't relevant.'

He searched her eyes. Then, out of the blue ...

'I know you dug up the sheep.'

'I did *what*?'

Morgan's attempt at outrage was greeted with a cold smile. He turned away, staring out of the window towards the hill behind the house.

'Well, someone did. Went up there in the middle of the night.' He turned to face her. Took hold of her wrists. 'Why would anyone do that?'

'Danny ... you're hurting me.'

He stared for a moment then released her wrists.

'What happened to you?' he said. 'What happened to us?'

She had no answer. He shook his head then headed down the stairs.

'Danny—'

He cut her short, calling over his shoulder.

'I didn't hurt Lissa.' He paused at the foot of the staircase. Turned. 'Let me know when she turns up. But that's the last I want to hear from you.'

Then he was gone.

Thirty-Six

Have you seen this girl?

Parked on the Margate seafront, listening to the rain spattering the car's roof, Morgan stared at the sweatshirt. The picture of her daughter's face. The blue eyes seemed to be dancing with anxiety, sending out a plea.

Find me.

Help me.

Save me.

Morgan felt on the verge of tears. She was tempted to bury her face in the sweatshirt, as if holding Lissa's photo to her cheek would somehow bring the girl closer. The moment passed. She took a breath, donned the sweatshirt instead and grabbed a handful of flyers from the passenger seat. Then she climbed out of the Mini and headed into the rain.

The promenade was all but deserted. A hardy dog-walker, a hoodie on a bike, a morbidly obese young woman with a screeching toddler in a pushchair. The child's cries reminded Morgan of Lissa's tantrums during the 'terrible twos', a constant stream of hot, angry tears cascading down chubby, livid cheeks, accompanied by screams of rage. What wouldn't she give to hear those cries now?

She made her way into the cobbled back streets of the old town, bracing herself for another day of apologetic shrugs and smiles.

Sorry, haven't seen her.

Two hours later, she was sipping coffee in a café, staring at the rain, when she glimpsed a familiar face in a passing car. The driver was Jacqui Farmiloe's sidekick. What had the DI said?

If anyone can find your daughter, it's Donna Goshawk.

Morgan hurried outside. Weary from lack of sleep, the sight of the DS came as a huge relief. Morgan headed after the car, cautioning herself not to get over-excited.

The car pulled up outside the Pleasureland Hotel. Morgan watched the woman get out and tighten the belt of her trench-coat before walking inside. Slow, sure steps, authority beyond her rank, confidence beyond her years.

Hovering in a shop doorway, Morgan smoked a roll-up, letting five minutes elapse before entering the hotel, part of a Regency terrace. The policewoman was standing in the lobby, towering over the middle-aged manager. Barely five feet tall, he sported a waistcoat over an off-white shirt. Sweat stains under his arms. As Morgan approached, her high tops squeaking on the tessellated floor, she heard him saying something about 'running a respectable establishment'.

'No one's suggesting otherwise, sir.'

Donna's manner was friendly, her tone reassuring. Morgan couldn't recall the woman uttering more than a few syllables in the presence of Jacqui Farmiloe. Perhaps she came into her own when operating alone. Hearing Morgan approach, she turned, lips twitching into a wary smile.

'Hello?'

A question, not a greeting.

'I saw you drive past,' said Morgan. 'Hoped you might have news about Lissa.'

Donna held up a finger in a wait-a-moment gesture then turned to the manager, handing him her card.

'Let me know if he comes back. Or the girl.'

The man nodded, slipping the card into his waistcoat pocket. Donna pointed to a CCTV camera bolted to the wall, above the reception desk.

'Might be an idea to get that fixed.'

'Will do.'

Donna gave a sceptical smile then turned to Morgan, gesturing towards the front door.

'After you.'

Outside, they stood under the awning. The rain was easing, softening into drizzle.

'I thought you were looking for Lissa,' said Morgan. She couldn't keep the reproach from her voice.

'The boss wanted me to check out the guy in the white Range Rover. And the girl in school uniform.'

'What about Chelsea?'

The policewoman looked away, squinting in the direction of the harbour wall.

'Her too.'

'And?'

A tight smile.

'Please don't ask me to discuss an ongoing enquiry. I'd hate things to get awkward.'

The smile was warm but there was steel in the voice. Morgan took the rebuff in her stride.

'Do you have kids?' she said.

The policewoman shook her head and fingered the locket around her throat.

'I had a plant once. It died.'

The rain had stopped. Donna stepped out from under the awning, looking towards the arcades.

'If the world had haemorrhoids they'd be in Margate.' She turned to face Morgan. 'I did Pilates at six. No breakfast. Reckon chips'd send me to hell?'

Morgan smiled. She was warming to DS Goshawk but persuading her to open up would be a challenge.

They bought chips then sat on the bench in the seafront shelter. In ten minutes of conversation Morgan managed to extract one piece of information from the policewoman (the man in the Range Rover had paid for the room in cash) but was none the wiser about Lissa.

'No CCTV outside the bank,' said Donna, licking salt from her fingers. 'No further use of her ATM card. Nothing from the Misper team.'

Morgan waited for the inevitable follow-up but it didn't come.

'Thank you,' she said.

'For?'

'Sparing me the spiel about most missing persons turning up fine.'

'Understood,' said Donna. 'But it's true: most Mispers *do* turn up.'

Morgan tossed the chip wrapper into a bin. She cast a glance along the seafront, her eye drawn by three people heading for the shelter: two hoodies following a scrawny teenage girl whose features were becoming a regular fixture in Morgan's life.

'Know who that is?'

Donna's face clouded over. She tucked a strand of hair behind her ear.

'Yep.'

Morgan watched the hoodies catch up with Chelsea Farmiloe. The beefier of the two placed a hand on her shoulder. She shrugged him off.

'Fuck off, both of you! Who the *fuck* do you think I am? *Fucking charity?* Fucking fuck *YOU!*'

If Chelsea had noticed Morgan and Donna, she did nothing to indicate it. As she stomped into the shelter and sat down, texting furiously, the shorter of her two pursuers caught sight of Donna. He dug his companion in the ribs. They slowed, feigning nonchalance before striding away.

'You two can fuck off, too,' said Chelsea, without looking up from her mobile.

'Hey, Chelsea.' Donna kept her tone even. 'Didn't think you'd clocked me.'

'Not fucking blind, am I?'

The girl pocketed her phone and pulled out a pack of Marlboro Lights.

'Give us a light.'

'I don't smoke,' said Donna.

'*She* does.' Chelsea nodded towards Morgan. 'I saw her with a ciggie.'

Morgan produced her lighter. The girl with the snake tattoo on her neck lit the cigarette.

'This is Morgan,' said Donna. 'Her daughter's missing.'

Chelsea examined her fingernails.

'We've all got problems.'

Her mobile chirruped. She scanned the text, glared then addressed the phone.

'Get a move on, bitch.'

'Her daughter's name is Lissa,' said Donna, ignoring the strop. 'Maybe you'd recognise her?'

She motioned for Morgan to open her coat, revealing the photo on her sweatshirt. Chelsea gave it a cursory glance then shrugged.

'Haven't seen her.'

'Look again.'

'Haven't fucking seen her, OK?'

'What about the girl you were with the other day?'

Chelsea scowled.

'What girl?'

'School uniform. And the man in the white Range Rover.'

The teenager didn't miss a beat. It was as if she'd been rehearsing.

'I don't know their names. He's her uncle. They stopped me in the high street, asked if I knew somewhere to stay. I said, the Pleasureland.'

'Didn't look like her uncle,' said Morgan.

The girl shrugged and took another drag on her cigarette.

'Why the Pleasureland?'

"Cause of the dwarf."

'The manager? You know him?'

'No. He's just funny.'

'Funny how?'

'Because he's a fucking *dwarf.*'

Donna said nothing, gazing out to sea.

'Where are you living, Chelsea?'

'Here and there.'

Another drag on the cigarette.

Morgan heard a bicycle bell and looked up. A girl was cycling towards the shelter, riding on the pavement. Fifteen, maybe younger. Chelsea got to her feet.

'Any message for your mum?' said Donna.

'Tell her to fuck off.'

Chelsea walked away. Morgan watched her intercept the girl on the bike, mutter something then quicken her pace and head away, head down, hands in her pockets. The new arrival shot a nervous glance towards Morgan and Donna, then turned and cycled after Chelsea.

Donna puffed out her cheeks.

'Proper little charmer.'

Morgan watched the girls round the corner and disappear from view. She could sense Donna choosing her words with care. This was the boss's daughter.

'She'll come unstuck one day,' said the policewoman. 'But there's nothing her mum can do.'

'When you say, "unstuck" …?'

Morgan let the question hang in the air. Was the DS aware of Chelsea's drug dealing? Broaching the subject felt like a betrayal of confidence.

'I'm glad she's not my responsibility,' said Donna. She checked her watch. 'I'm going to knock on some doors, see about your Lissa.'

'Can I come with you?'

'Not a good idea,' said Donna.

'Why not? She's my daughter.'

The woman thought for a moment then got to her feet.

'Fair enough,' she said. 'But let me take the lead.'

For the next hour, Morgan kept pace with the policewoman, briefing her on the pubs, cafés and arcades she'd visited and pointing out the flyers in shop windows. Outside NatWest, she listened as Donna quizzed two Police Community Support Officers. Then she watched as the DS drew a blank with the kebab shop owner. Everywhere they went, the story was the same: no one had seen Lissa.

As they headed back to the side streets, Morgan caught sight of something on the windscreen of the Mini.

'Shit,' she said, fearing another message from her stalker but it was only a parking ticket. 'Thank God.'

Donna looked bemused.

'You collect parking tickets?'

Morgan explained about the messages.

'Want me to see if I can help?'

'How?'

'Maybe check the notes for fingerprints.'

Morgan shook her head.

'I chucked them away,' she said, silently cursing her own stupidity. 'I'll let you know if I get another.'

Donna nodded then plucked the parking ticket from Morgan's hand.

'Abracadabra,' she said, winking. 'Let's see if I can make this disappear.'

Morgan felt a surge of gratitude. Donna was good company. Smart, sensitive, warm. Perhaps one day, when Lissa was home, they could share a laugh or two over a bottle of wine.

Donna's mobile rang.

'Hello, boss,' she said. 'I'm in Margate with Morgan Vine.'

Farmiloe's voice.

'Let me have a word with her.'

Donna handed the mobile to Morgan.

'You're not going to like this.'

Morgan felt her heart rate quicken.

'Is it Lissa? Is she OK?'

'As far as we know. This is about the sex tape. Someone uploaded it on the internet. It's gone viral.'

Morgan's stomach gave a lurch. Then the phone in her pocket began to ring.

Thirty-Seven

The day took on a surreal quality that Morgan found distressing but also exhilarating. Hour after hour, her mobile continued to ring. Not just the tabloids, the broadsheets too. There was fierce competition for Crassest Question of the Day but the winner came from a squeaky-voiced woman at the *Sun*.

'How does it feel to see your daughter behaving like a porn star with your childhood sweetheart?'

The second most infuriating call came from a TV producer working on a show for Channel 5.

'We're making a documentary on women who have sex with men behind bars.'

'They weren't behind bars.'

'Not technically but Kilcannon had just been released so Lissa still qualifies. And she's drop-dead gorgeous. We're willing to make an exception.'

'You're talking about my daughter. She's still missing.'

He barely paused. 'Yes, and it's good to stay hopeful but we still—'

'I'm hanging up now.'

A fortnight since Lissa's disappearance, the sex tape seemed to have changed the public mood, even among Danny's supporters.

Morgan had checked the Justice For Danny Kilcannon website and the trolls were out in force. *If he can screw his ex-girlfriend's own kid what else is he capable of? ... Maybe he killed Zoe after all. Maybe he knows more about Lissa than he's saying.*

Unwilling to turn off her phone in case Lissa tried to call, by the time Morgan reached Dungeness she'd lost count of the overtures from media outlets. The call that convinced her to go off the radar, at least for a couple of hours, came from Cameron.

'How the hell did you let this happen?'

'Thanks for your support.'

'Jesus, Morgan, do you have any idea what this business is like? Twenty years building a career and suddenly I'm not the "Oscar-nominated Brit", I'm the dude who fathered the hot chick who screwed the kiddie-killer.'

'Right. Because this is all about you.'

He sighed.

'I've told you a zillion times, Lissa is fine, she's just being a gigantic pain in the ass and punishing you – again – because you picked a fight over you-know-who.'

Pain in the *ass,* not *arse.* The man was from Cirencester but he'd become someone Morgan no longer knew.

'Maybe she uploaded the tape herself?' Cameron said.

The suggestion sparked a flicker of hope. It would confirm that Lissa was alive.

'Why would she do that?'

'Fifteen minutes of fame?'

'She's too smart for that crap.'

But was that true? Morgan recalled her daughter outlining 'the Kristina strategy'. Reality TV. Selling photos of her wedding to *Hello!* Her own 'celebrity fragrance'. Lissa had insisted she was joking, but was she really?

'I guess it must have been your pal, good old Danny K,' said Cameron.

'He's hardly in the market for bad publicity.'

She heard the snort of disbelief echoing six thousand miles down the line.

'Never heard of revenge porn? Lissa dumped him, now he wants the world to know she's a slut.'

'Did you just call your own daughter a slut?'

A sigh.

'Morgan, listen, the guy's a jailbird, for Chrissakes. His reputation is in the crapper so he screws a sexy kid then uploads the footage, knowing it'll put him on every front page, every gossip website from TMZ to Gawker. From his point of view, where's the negative?' Cameron drew breath. 'Fuck *all the world's a stage.* He's an actor – all the world's an audience.'

'I don't think he leaked the tape,' said Morgan. 'He wants a quiet life.'

'Who else had access?'

'Only the police.'

'Why would they leak it?'

'I have no idea,' said Morgan. 'But right now, anything seems possible.'

She heard a whispered consultation.

'Hold on,' said Cameron, 'Kristina wants to pitch you something.'

'Don't you dare ...'

But he'd gone, his voice replaced by a woman whose native accent was blended with a Valley Girl whine. She sounded like Ukrainian Barbie with bad sinuses.

'Hey, Morgan, I'm sorry we have to meet this way. I just want to say, I *love* your daughter.'

'That makes two of us,' said Morgan.

'And I wanted to talk to you about her sex tape. It's weird this should happen now because I'm actually going into, like, artist management? So this could be great for the entire family.'

Morgan heard the tinkle of ice in a glass.

'What family?'

'Look, I know the whole sex-tape thing is, like, so *old* but it made stars out of Kim Kardashian and Paris Hilton, so maybe it could work for Lissa.'

Morgan groped for something to say. Something polite.

'I thought you were a pianist.'

'I multi-task,' said Kristina. 'That's what we women do, right?'

Morgan didn't rise to the attempt at female bonding. She heard a sigh.

'Look,' said Kristina, 'I'm guessing you think I'm some kind of gold-digging slut so let me set the record straight. My father's a scientist, my mother teaches maths at university. I've studied piano since I was three, practising five hours a day, seven days a week. But could I make a living from music? No. Do I want to spend my life in Kiev? No. So I'm here, living the LA dream with a man I like. A lot. And I think Lissa's great, which is why I want her to have the same opportunities as me. So I hope you're cool with that but if not, it's your problem not mine.'

'I have to go,' said Morgan. *Before I say something I regret.*

The *Six O'Clock News* didn't deem the sex tape newsworthy (thank God) but Sky made up for the omission, showing a carefully pixelated clip and using the video's *'shocking emergence on the internet'* as a peg to rehash the Killer-cannon saga, *'from the brutal slaying of tragic Zoe and the disappearance of her grief-stricken mum to the controversial success of Danny's appeal'*.

The square-jawed presenter ended the report with a smirking coda: the sex tape had notched up over a million hits. Sky viewers could see more by pressing the red button *now*. Morgan half expected him to sign off with a wink.

That Lissa was missing made things a hundred times worse – or, if you were an editor, a thousand times better. By the time the *Newsnight* presenter began his round up of tomorrow's newspapers, the headline writers had produced gems such as *Killer-cannon's Teen Sex Romp (Star)* and *Danny K Gets the Girl (Mirror)*. The *Mail* went with *Where Is Sex-tape Temptress?* linking to a Mail Online piece on 'teen seducers who target their mums' boyfriends'.

It was past midnight before Morgan turned off her TV and laptop (she hadn't even started on her emails) and switched her mobile back on. Twenty-two missed calls. None from Lissa.

Jacqui Farmiloe had left a message offering her spare room 'for when the hacks find you'. It would break all the rules, but what the hell? Morgan might have been grateful if the offer hadn't meant taking refuge in an isolated house with a sexually incontinent husband suffering from dementia.

On the good news front: the media blitz seemed to have galvanised Jacqui into stepping up the search for Lissa. 'We've doubled the team. We're pulling out all the stops. Leave things to us.'

Clive Rossiter had left two messages. The first promised a six-figure sum for Morgan's exclusive on 'the whole Lissa-Danny thing'. The second was another offer of sanctuary, this time in London.

'*You know where the key is. I'm calling as a friend, not a journalist.*'

Yeah, right.

The only offer Morgan didn't dismiss out of hand came from Donna Goshawk. Again, a spare room was at her disposal – this time in Canterbury. She didn't return the call, even though the DS's voice sounded full of sympathy and compassion. Bottom line, Morgan could trust no one.

She'd left two messages for Danny. He had yet to call back. Just as well. She couldn't think of anything to say that wouldn't involve swearing like Chelsea Farmiloe.

Fuck off, you fucking FUCKER!

Exhausted and demoralised, Morgan took a shower. When that failed to make her feel better, she drank half a bottle of red wine, swallowed two Zopiclone and pulled the duvet over her head. Three hours later, thick-tongued and disorientated, she awoke to the sound of a ringtone in the distance.

Not just any ringtone.

Popeye the Sailor Man.

Adrenaline overriding the other chemicals in her body, Morgan ran into the kitchen and snatched a knife from the block. Heart hammering, she unlocked the door and stepped out into the night.

Thirty-Eight

The lights from the power station were visible through the mist. She stood on the deck, her eyes combing the shoreline. Out at sea, a tanker crossed the horizon, its flashing beacon a warning to passing ships.

The ringtone had stopped as abruptly as it began. Aside from the *whoosh* of the waves there was silence, no sign of life. Morgan's eyes roved the darkness. Had she imagined the sound of Lissa's mobile? Had her mind conjured the *Popeye* tune from nowhere, a combination of anxiety and wishful thinking? She could feel the blood pounding in her ears, her heartbeat pulsing. Her senses were on full alert, straining to catch the slightest movement, the faintest sound ...

There it was again. The tinny *Popeye* music cutting through the darkness, emanating from near the wrecked fishing boat beached fifty yards from Morgan's front door.

'Lissa?'

No reply, just the music in the distance and, further off, the soft, slow rhythm of the waves. Bare feet squelching in the mud, she moved swiftly towards the boat, her grip tightening around the handle of the knife. The ringtone stopped, silence descending once more.

And then a sound from inside. Someone moving? She held her breath.

'Hello?'

Her voice was thin and reedy. She cleared her throat.

'Who's there?'

No response.

She picked up a pebble and threw it at the boat, jumping back in alarm as the three-legged dog emerged, equally startled, and scampered away into the shadows. Had the stray adopted the place as its home or was it someone's companion? A rough-sleeper, waiting to pounce? Turning to flee, Morgan stopped as she caught sight of a glint in the mud. A mobile phone.

It began to ring.

The ringtone seemed louder, the jaunty music filling the night air. She scanned the beach again. The dog had disappeared. Not a soul in sight. She ran forward and snatched the phone from the mud. A familiar face stared from a photo on the screen: Danny. Morgan answered the call.

'Hello?'

She heard his voice.

'Lissa?'

'No ... it's Morgan.'

He sounded confused.

'Morgan?'

'I found Lissa's phone.'

'Jesus ... Where?'

'On the beach.'

'Which beach?'

'My beach,' she said. 'Dungeness.'

'Is she there?'

'I don't think so.' Her eyes darted around the deserted shore.

'Lissa!'

Her voice echoed far and wide.

'*Lissa!*'

No response, just the shrieking of a distant seagull. She put the phone back to her ear.

'Why are you calling her?'

'Because I've been trying to find her ever since she went missing. Like you.'

Was this a lie? A ruse to throw Morgan off the scent? Had *he* left the mobile, to sow yet more seeds of confusion?

He was saying something …

' … obviously you need to give it to the police so they can check it out but I guess this means she's OK, just playing one of her games.'

'Where are you, Danny?'

A pause.

'Does it matter? What's important is we're closer to finding Lissa.'

Her eyes scanned the mud, looking for footprints. She kept her voice steady.

'I asked where you are.'

'Better you don't know.'

Her brow creased into a frown.

'Why?'

'So you can't tell them.'

' "Them"?'

'The press. They're all over my place like a pack of wolves.'

Morgan's eyes narrowed.

'*You* don't trust *me?* Do you have any idea how messed up that is?'

'That's not what I meant ...'

The part of her that wanted to hang up lost out to the part that needed to believe he could help find her daughter. She began to rotate in a circle, swivelling on her heels, eyes scanning the darkness, keeping watch for the slightest movement.

'Lissa!'

Her cry echoed into the mist, the darkness beyond.

'Can you see her?'

'No.'

'Well, she obviously *was* there,' Danny said. 'Unless ...' His voice tailed off.

'Unless?'

'Look, Morgan, I don't like to think this way but ...' He faltered.

'Say it.'

'Unless someone is leading you a merry dance.'

She clamped the phone to her ear and picked up her pace, combing the shoreline for footprints.

'Who might that "someone" be?'

A pause.

'Judging by your tone, you think it's me,' he said.

Morgan let silence do the talking. Then she heard another weary sigh.

'Look,' he said, 'the sex-tape thing, it's horrible and I've no idea why she did it but ...'

'Why *she* did it?' said Morgan. 'You're saying Lissa put it on the web?'

'Well, it wasn't me,' said Danny, sounding affronted. 'But it's got to be a good thing, right? In the long run?'

She felt her jaw tighten.

'How is being a global porn icon "good"?'

'Be glass-half-full for a moment,' said Danny. 'Her face is on every front page. Sooner or later someone will spot her or she'll come out of hiding, and we can all get on with our lives.'

'Unless she's dead,' said Morgan.

The brutal truth took her breath away. She'd had the thought before, of course, countless times, especially in the small hours, but she hadn't voiced it aloud. Until now.

'She'll be fine.'

It was the best he could do and she hated him for it.

'Whatever happens, she's all over the internet because of you, Danny. She'll always be "the sex-tape girl". And I hate you for that. I *really* hate you.'

'I'm so sorry.'

Morgan let the silence stretch between them. Then she gave a start as she caught a glimpse of movement just beyond a ridge of shingle, but it was only a seagull preparing to take to the air. She watched the bird lift off, spreading its wings as it flew out to sea, heading for the tanker.

Cameron's words were still fresh in her mind.

Fuck "all the world's a stage". He's an actor – all the world's an audience.

'What will you do?' she said. 'When this is over?' She was quickening her pace, heels grinding into the mud, trying to walk off the worry, the confusion, the despair.

'This isn't the time,' said Danny.

'It's exactly the time.'

He didn't respond straightaway but when he spoke again his voice was full of hope for the future.

'Well, I've been thinking about mentoring people coming out of prison, maybe getting involved in some kind of literacy programme for people who can't read or write, but today's been completely crazy. Three calls from TV agents and one from a ghost-writer who's interested in turning my story into a book and . . .'

Morgan terminated the call, cutting him off in mid-sentence. Then she strode on, along the deserted beach, clenching her fists as she made a silent promise.

Lissa, I *will* find you.

Thirty-Nine

1989

With Leo in prison, the new head teacher urged Ursula to move her stepdaughter to another school. Morgan refused to budge. The only good thing in life was Danny, her rock. She would never be separated from him.

December brought rumours of a second suicide bid by Leo – an attempt to hang himself in his cell. Morgan was unclear exactly what had happened and couldn't face visiting him behind bars. Ursula was refusing to speak to her, blaming her for crushing her father's spirit. The atmosphere at home was barely tolerable, like living in a fug of poison gas.

Although ashamed of her own disloyalty, Morgan couldn't shake the certainty that Leo was guilty of being a Peeping Tom. And if he had one secret – spying on boys while they masturbated – who was to say he didn't have a hundred more, even worse?

She spent little time at home. When not asleep or running the gauntlet at school, she hunkered down at Danny's house, surviving on toast and Marmite, doing her homework on the floor. She didn't discuss their abortive attempt at sex, nor did she talk about her father, beyond telling Danny about the telescope in the attic. Leo was the elephant in the room, always present, never mentioned.

School was different. There was no getting away from what the *Deal Guardian* called *Headmaster's Rape Shame*. Every weekday, Morgan was bullied or ignored.

Things came to a head on a Friday afternoon. Not for the first time, an increasingly erratic Stevie Gamble hadn't showed up for lessons. He'd developed a vodka habit, drinking with a Nico-teeny called Wendy, an attention-seeking brunette. She blamed Leo's assault for her boyfriend's mood swings and attempts at self-harm. Stevie's wrists bore a tell-tale criss-cross of scars.

Changing after hockey one afternoon, Morgan was ambushed in the locker room by Wendy and her cronies. Shrieking like banshees, they flicked her legs with wet towels then held her down, drenching her with ice-cold water and slapping her face until it was red and raw. She fought back, landing a series of blows, but from that day forward no pupil except Danny dared speak to her. At school and at home she'd been sent to Coventry, the loneliest place on the planet.

Over the Christmas holidays, sinking into depression, she stayed in bed most of the time, re-reading *To Kill a Mockingbird*, occasionally turning to page sixty-seven to trace a finger over the smear of chocolate. No presents, no turkey, no tinsel. The silence at fourteen The Grove was deafening.

'Maybe there's an innocent explanation for the telescope,' Danny said during a Boxing Day walk along their favourite stretch of the white cliffs.

'Oh, look,' said Morgan, pointing at the glowering skies, 'a flying pig.'

The truth was, she didn't know what, if anything, had happened between Leo and Stevie but instinct told her that her father was guilty. Danny accused her of jumping to conclusions. They didn't speak for seven days. Longest week of her life.

As the misery deepened she stockpiled pills. Paracetamol, aspirin, ibuprofen, all from different chemists so as not to arouse suspicion.

There was nothing melodramatic about her plan. Suicide simply seemed like the next logical step. But she hadn't counted on Danny. Somehow he read her mind. On the morning of New Year's Eve there came a familiar rat-a-tat on the front door. He was on the doorstep, flipping his pebble in the air.

'Don't do anything stupid, OK?'

'Like?'

'You know.' He pocketed the pebble. 'Come over tonight. It's important.'

She took her first bath for ages then flushed the pills down the loo. Over a can of Heinz tomato soup – her first proper meal for days – she made a decision. Time to have another crack at losing her virginity.

Arriving at Danny's, she was glad to discover that Mrs Kilcannon was 'out on the razz' with her boyfriend, Reece. Danny had laid in pizza and cider but it soon became clear that sex was not on the menu. Instead, he had arranged another surprise.

'He's in the shed.'

'Who?'

'Stevie,' said Danny. 'I told him I had some dope. Lured him inside. Locked him up.'

Morgan frowned.

'Why?'

'Because you need to know the truth.'

She followed him into the garden, along the muddy path leading to a secluded patch bordered by a hedge. The sky was blue-black, like Danny's hair, the air eerily still. He unfastened a padlock and ushered her into the shed. Stevie was on the floor, trussed with a rope, a gag in his mouth. His face was bruised and swollen, his nostrils caked with dried blood. Morgan turned to Danny, eyes wide.

'What have you done?'

Ignoring her, he crouched down and yanked the gag from Stevie's mouth.

'Tell Morgan what you told me.'

Stevie spat out saliva and shook his head.

'Do it,' said Danny. He reached into his pocket and produced a pair of pliers.

Morgan was horrified.

'Danny!'

He ignored her, bearing down on Stevie.

'Tell her!'

Stevie stared in terror at the pliers then at Morgan. When he spoke, the words came out in a rush.

'It wasn't your dad. It was someone else. I had to go to hospital. The injuries were bad. The doctors had to tell the police.'

He faltered. Danny held the pliers closer to the boy's face.

'The whole story.'

Stevie was snivelling.

'I couldn't tell the truth,' he said. 'So I panicked. Told the police it was your dad.'

Morgan's head was spinning.

'What truth?'

The boy's head lolled onto his chest. Danny grabbed his hair. 'Say it.'

A sob escaped Stevie's lips. His eyes filled with tears.

'He gets drunk and does ... stuff. He's a bastard and I hate his guts.'

'What stuff?' said Morgan. 'Who's a bastard?'

The boy looked away.

'My dad,' he said quietly. 'Not yours, mine.'

Morgan recalled the night Stevie's father had hurled a brick through the window and sprayed 'Pervert' on their house. She remembered the smart-suited man hiding behind the neighbour's hedge. His parting shot as he'd walked away.

'*Your word against mine, kiddo.*'

The horror of what Stevie had done made Morgan's head spin. But the cruelty of her own behaviour towards her father made her wish the earth would open up and swallow her alive.

'You have to tell the police,' she said. Her eyes were brimming with tears. 'You're the only one who can make this right.'

Stevie's voice was lifeless.

'I can't,' he said. 'And you can't make me.'

Danny raised a fist. She stayed his hand.

'No!'

Stevie's story came out haltingly. What he called 'the stuff' had begun when he was seven. His mother, a fragile soul suffering from bipolar disorder, had fled her violent husband, taking refuge with her parents. They'd emigrated to Australia. Mr Gamble was a frustrated artist-turned-accountant, filled with rage at a world that refused to recognise his talent. He was also a drunk and an abuser. What began as 'fiddling about' grew steadily worse, culminating in the brutal act of rape that had sent Stevie to hospital and set in train the events that put Leo behind bars.

As Morgan listened, she felt as if her head might explode. If Stevie refused to reveal his father's crime there was no hope for Leo. She could go to the police, of course, with Danny as witness to Stevie's confession, but the chances of being believed were close to zero. For starters, there was the manner in which the admission had been obtained. Whichever way you looked at it, the likelihood of her father's case being reopened was next to non-existent.

Danny stared at Stevie. His eyes were cold.

'If I can't hit you, I'll haunt you.'

The war of attrition began the following day. At six a.m. Danny stationed himself outside the Gambles' house, by the old gasworks, staring up at Stevie's bedroom window. Ramrod-straight, like a sentry outside Buckingham Palace, he stood in silence for two hours, until Mr Gamble emerged and told him to bugger off.

That evening, Danny was back at six p.m. Another two-hour stint of what he called 'the haunting'. The pattern continued for the rest of the school holidays – every morning, every night.

A week into the campaign, Stevie's dad – his name was Bryan – stormed out of the house, smelling of whisky, and asked Danny what the hell he was playing at.

'Ask your son,' said Danny.

As the new term began, Bryan Gamble went back to work, walking to Deal station every morning, returning every evening. Rain or shine, Danny was there, standing on the other side of the road, staring at the house. If Bryan was unnerved, he didn't let it show.

But as days turned into weeks, his son began to show signs of cracking. Stevie was losing weight, his eyes hollow, his nails bitten to the quick. Morgan was increasingly alarmed. The plan was to get the boy to go public, not drive him to a breakdown. Or worse.

As winter gave way to the first signs of spring, Danny stepped up the campaign. Dead pigeons through the letterbox. Live rats. Bricks through the window. Morgan talked him out of it. 'The haunting' wasn't working. They had to find another way.

It was Bryan himself who proved the agent of his own downfall. Word got around that he was planning to remarry – a single mum called Julie. She had a son, Adam. Seven years old. Same age as Stevie when 'the stuff' began.

One misty Friday in March, Morgan fell into step with Stevie on the way to school.

'He'll do it to Adam,' she told him. 'It'll be your fault.'

Stevie stared at her for a long moment but said nothing. On Monday, he didn't show up for school. That evening there was a police car outside his house. As Bryan Gamble was driven away, Morgan overheard the neighbours muttering. She added a phrase to her lexicon. *Helping police with their enquiries.*

The next few days were a blur. The wheels of justice began to grind, but slowly. More than once, Morgan begged Ursula to take her to visit Leo in prison.

Request denied.

Your father doesn't want to see you or hear from you ever again.

A trip to Canterbury library unearthed some encouraging information, words that quickly became seared into Morgan's mind.

'Section 23 of the Criminal Appeal Act 1968 governs the receipt and admission of fresh evidence by the Court of Appeal. The overriding test is contained in Section 23 (1) which states that the Court of Appeal can receive any evidence which was not adduced in the proceedings if it is deemed necessary or expedient in the interests of justice.'

Then came the news that made Morgan weep with relief: Bryan Gamble had confessed, to spare his son the agony of a trial.

On the day Leo's conviction was due to be quashed – Morgan's fifteenth birthday – Ursula had left the house by the time her stepdaughter woke at five thirty. Undaunted, Morgan took a train and two buses then waited outside the Court of Appeal in the rain. During the wait, she thought of Danny and of Atticus Finch, the lawyer in *To Kill a Mockingbird* who did the right thing, no matter what. She made a silent vow to stick to her resolution: never again would she judge someone on circumstantial evidence.

Emerging from court, her father pretended not to see her, climbed into Ursula's car and was driven away. Morgan made her own way home in the rain.

A single birthday card was waiting for her with a message.

From Danny,

I love you.

Forty

Donna Goshawk snapped on a pair of latex gloves and slipped Lissa's iPhone into an evidence bag.

'You shouldn't have touched this.'

'Don't give me a hard time,' said Morgan, pouring coffee. 'I was in no state to think straight.'

She glanced out of her kitchen window, taking stock of the two sniffer dogs and three SOCOs combing the shoreline. The glossy-haired DS had taken her fingerprints – for elimination purposes. At last, something was happening. And the fact that Lissa's phone was still charged was surely a hopeful sign – unless it was now in the possession of someone else.

'The boss apologises for not being here,' said Donna. 'Up to her eyes with the Quirke case. But she's pulling out all the stops for Lissa.' She nodded towards the mobile in the plastic bag. 'Let's hope this helps. As for the sex-tape coverage, we can usually only dream about that kind of publicity for a Misper.'

Morgan said nothing, allowing time for the policewoman's lapse of tact to sink in.

'Sorry.' Donna winced. 'Came out wrong.'

Morgan let it lie. She crossed to the sink and began to wash the ink from her fingertips.

'Can you find out who uploaded it?'

'We're on the case,' said Donna, 'but don't hold your breath. There are a million ways to post things online anonymously. And we're not the CIA.'

Morgan turned from the sink. Despite the lack of sleep and the aftertaste of last night's sleeping pill, she was full of restless energy. Caffeine. Adrenaline. Anxiety.

'What if this were a terrorist case? Would you still tell me not to hold my breath?'

Donna cocked her head to one side.

'You want the hard truth?' She didn't wait for an answer. 'Lissa's an adult Misper. Ten a penny. But there's now an incident room with her name on the whiteboard. The Missing Persons Bureau is making her a priority. The team doubled overnight. Our media handlers are working overtime. But bottom line? There's only so much we can do.'

Morgan stifled her impatience.

'When are you talking to Danny?'

'Next on my list.' Donna seemed to be sizing Morgan up. 'Can I be frank?' she said.

'Of course.'

'Here's the good news,' said the DS. 'Nearly three hundred thousand people go missing every year. Know how many are found dead?'

Morgan shook her head.

'Less than one per cent. Remember that when you're trying to sleep tonight. And let us do our job.'

Morgan flashed a grateful smile and watched as the police-woman fingered the silver locket around her neck.

'Are you on the electoral roll at this address?' said Donna.

'No. Why?'

'That's how hacks find people.' The policewoman fished a card from her pocket. 'I really shouldn't be doing this but if you need a bolt hole, don't hesitate.' She scribbled an address then pushed the card across the table. Morgan felt a surge of gratitude.

'Two kinds of coppers,' said Donna. 'Evidence or instinct. I'm all about the evidence. I like facts, things I can *see*, analyse and dissect. But that doesn't mean I discount gut feelings.' Her eyes searched Morgan's. 'So tell me honestly, what does your intuition say about Kilcannon?'

Morgan closed her eyes, trying to shut out the world, to get in touch with some instinct about Danny, but there was no epiphany, just exhaustion and anxiety.

She opened her eyes. Donna was staring at her.

'I don't know anymore.'

The policewoman leaned across the table, her eyes dancing with concern.

'Bit of advice? Sleep. Swim. Walk. Do something normal.'

Morgan nodded then stared into the middle distance, listening to the sound of the waves.

Later, she watched Donna and the SOCOs drive away. The search of the beach had yielded nothing. Morgan stood on the deck and smoked a roll-up, feeling crushed by a sense of impotence. Later still, she took a long walk along the shoreline, hoping for a sign that Lissa had been there, something the SOCOs had missed, but there was nothing. She made her way home and nibbled some toast, trying to ignore the suspicion that the butter was rancid.

Booting up her laptop, she scanned the latest headlines about Lissa – *Killer-cannon's missing sex-tape girl* – then logged off and rolled another cigarette.

She checked her watch. Still only two o'clock.

Do something normal.

With a start, she remembered an appointment.

C-Wing.

Her boys.

If she left now, she could still make it. Stashing the *Have You Seen This Girl?* sweatshirt in her bag, she grabbed *Catcher in the Rye*, climbed into the Mini and drove towards the prison.

Forty-One

No doubt about it – Cundy was avoiding her. She'd spotted him at the end of the corridor. He'd clocked her too. So why had he swerved into the men's toilets? And was it Morgan's imagination or was her escort oddly monosyllabic?

She stood aside as the prison officer opened the door to the strip-lit recreation room and ushered her inside. The members of the reading group were seated in a circle, as usual, legs splayed in the customary battle for territory, but there was none of the usual banter, just awkward silence.

Do something normal.

Morgan tried to keep her voice breezy.

'Afternoon, all.' A chorus of mumbles. She fished the paperback from her bag then looked up at the expectant faces. 'How's everybody doing?'

There was a brief pause then one of the prisoners – a weasel-faced Welshman called Evans – unfolded a copy of the *Star*.

'We're doing OK,' he said, his face breaking into a grin mirrored by the rest of the group. 'But not as OK as Danny and your daughter.'

He held up the tabloid. Morgan tried to look away but it was too late. A screen-grab from the sex tape filled the front page. Lissa's head was thrown back, her eyes glazed with lust, clearly in the throes of orgasm, her breasts obscured by a judiciously positioned headline.

Killer-cannon sex-tape shock.

The next hour was agony. Try as Morgan might to steer the conversation towards Holden Caulfield or broaden it out to a discussion about disaffected youth, the men kept returning to the photo of Lissa astride one of their own.

Were they shagging behind your back?

Are you jealous?

Does this change your thinking about what Kilcannon did to Zoe?

Most infuriating of all:

If Lissa shows up, get her to start a prison book group. Kick off with Fifty Shades of Grey.

Evans's suggestion earned a raucous cheer. Morgan managed to keep her temper – just – but was relieved when the session limped to an end and the officer arrived to escort her back to the main gate. Halfway along the corridor, she saw Nigel again, locked in conversation with a burly man in a suit. The wispy-haired psychologist was sporting his customary short shirt-sleeves, a style Morgan loathed.

'Hello, Nigel.'

The shrink gave no sign of having heard her. She felt a stirring of anger.

'*Hello, Nigel.*'

He turned. No trace of a smile.

'Everything OK?' she said.

He shrugged.

'Same old, same old.'

The other man wore a blue suit that clashed with his brown shoes. He extended a handshake.

'Christopher Fry. Deputy Governor.'

Morgan introduced herself, averting her gaze from the dandruff on his collar.

'Glad I caught you,' he said. 'Before the email goes out.'

She raised an eyebrow.

'Email?'

'Party's over, I'm afraid.'

Morgan frowned.

'Party?'

'Your book group. All that media coverage about you sneaking in to see Kilcannon? Not a good look for the prison service.'

Morgan felt her face flush.

'I didn't "sneak in". I run a book group. Danny was a member.'

Fry shrugged.

'The Governor's not happy. My hands are tied.'

'Let me talk to him,' said Morgan. 'I'm sure we can sort things out.'

The man gave her a pitying smile, as though she'd requested an audience with the pope.

'This isn't a democracy, sweetheart,' he said. 'It's prison.'

He walked off, shoes squeaking. The prison guard jangled his keys.

'My break's due.'

Morgan held up a finger for him to wait a moment then turned to Nigel, who seemed to be studying the floor.

'Did he just tell me I'm out?'

He met her stare.

''Fraid so.' She detected a softening of his attitude, a hint of sympathy.

'Cuppa?' he said.

She listened as he told the officer not to wait then she followed Nigel along the corridor, into a windowless office. Waiting for the kettle to boil, he commiserated over the Deputy Governor's decision and set a plastic cup of tea in front of her. He sat at his desk, steepling his fingers.

'Is there a massive elephant in this room?' she said, picking up the flimsy cup.

'Elephant?'

'Don't tell me you're the only person who hasn't seen the papers?'

He ran a hand over his comb-over.

'Must be tricky for you,' he said. 'I do hope she turns up soon.' His tone betrayed no compassion. Morgan sipped her tea. Undrinkable.

'Still think Kilcannon is Mary Poppins?' Nigel raised his mug to his lips. She read the slogan. *You don't have to be mad to work here but it helps.*

'I don't know,' she said.

Nigel shifted in his chair. 'I could still ask my cousin about him. You know, the copper. High up. Usually has the inside track.'

Morgan managed half a smile.

'OK,' she said. 'The more info the better.'

She watched as he jotted a reminder on a Post-It.

'Were you avoiding me, Nigel?'

'Why would I do that?'

'Maybe you're embarrassed to be seen with the mother of the "*Kilcannon Sex-romp Teen*"?'

His reply was drowned out by a siren *whoop-whooping* in the corridor. Nigel sprang to his feet, scrabbling for the keys on his belt. He headed for the door, raising his voice to make himself heard.

'Lockdown.' He opened the door. 'Been threatening to kick off all day. I'll have to lock you in ...'

'Nigel—'

' ... for your own safety.'

He was gone, closing the door behind him. She heard the key turn in the lock. The siren blared. Footsteps thundered past, echoing in the corridor outside, competing with the sounds of shouting. She couldn't make out what was being said – something about a strip search? There was the noise of a scuffle then Nigel was joining in the yelling, his voice receding into the distance.

Morgan's eyes roved the office. The room was as charmless as its occupant: a desk, a swivel chair with a cushion for lumbar support, shelves of files. She sat in the chair, revolving slowly as she scanned the alphabetised names. One jumped out.

Kilcannon D. FF7836

What had Nigel said?

I had several sessions with Kilcannon. To address his anger-management issues.

Out in the corridor, the siren was still blaring. Morgan reached for the file. She flipped it open, skim-reading reports in Nigel's spidery handwriting. There wasn't much she didn't know or couldn't guess. Prisoner FF7836 had had difficulty controlling his temper, especially around Gary Pascoe. The men had riled each other many times, often coming to blows. Pascoe had retained his status as top dog through the traditional means: a shank in the shower. There was no mention of Danny's retaliation. He'd been prescribed anti-depressants, but beyond declaring *'I hate the bastard'* and *'I shouldn't even be here in the first place'*, had remained immune to all attempts to coax him into discussing his innermost feelings.

Outside, the siren stopped. Morgan closed the file, reaching up to replace it on the shelf. A photograph slipped out, landing face down on the desk. She turned it over, brow furrowing as she tried to fathom what she was looking at. The photo had been taken outside her house by someone standing at a distance.

No … by someone in a car – the picture was framed by the driver's window. It showed Lissa emerging from the sea, oblivious to the fact she was being watched. The photo conjured up memories of the classic 'Bond girl' shots of Halle Berry or Ursula Andress surfacing from the waves, but with one notable difference: they'd been wearing bikinis. Lissa was naked. Morgan stared at the photo, trying to recall what the shrink had said during their dismal 'date'.

If you ladies had any idea what goes on in our heads when we see a pretty thing like Lissa – a luscious, ripe young peach … The stuff we think – you'd be horrified.

When had he taken the photo?

She recalled another conversation: Lissa and Danny in the fish and chip shop, overlooking the shoreline.

Are you a swimmer, Danny?

Not really, how about you?

Lissa's playful smile as she dunked a chip in ketchup.

In Malibu, you bet. Here, no. But I did have a dip this morning. Completely naked.

She heard footsteps in the corridor.

A key in the lock.

She looked up to see Nigel as he entered, red-faced, dishevelled, shirt untucked.

'Sorry about that. The poor bastard should be in Broadmoor, not here.'

She said nothing.

'Are you OK, Morgan?'

She shook her head. Frowning, he caught sight of the photo. His eyes darted to the shelves – the file on Prisoner FF7836.

'You read his file?'

Ignoring the question, she struggled to keep her voice under control.

'Why did you photograph her, Nigel?'

He sighed.

'It's not what you think.' He took a Nikon camera from a drawer.

'It's my hobby. Photographing landscapes, wildlife, seascapes.'

He pressed a button, flicking through digital images of the Dungeness shoreline: a formation of birds in mid-flight, a clump of sea kale, waves foaming on the beach. Morgan could feel her heart rate quickening.

'My daughter's missing. It's been over two weeks. Before I call the police you'd better tell me what's going on.'

Arms folded, eyes fixed on his face, she listened.

He was a country boy, a member of the Countryside Alliance, and fascinated by wildlife and landscape, in particular Dungeness. A lifelong insomniac, he was often up before dawn, roving with his camera. That was how he'd chanced upon Lissa emerging from the waves. It wasn't as if he'd been stalking her, the photo *just happened*. But he knew it could be seen as creepy which was why he'd stashed it away in a file.

'Out of sight, out of mind,' he finished, with a shrug.

Morgan looked at the photo.

'Do you know where she is?'

He spread his hands.

'No. I never even spoke to the girl, except for two seconds that night outside your place, when I took you out for supper.'

'Is this your only photo of her?'

He hesitated.

'You know what it's like with digital. I probably took a couple of other shots. But if you're asking if this is the only *time* I photographed her, the answer is yes.'

'And the other shots?'

'Deleted.'

'Unlike this one. Which you printed.'

'Come to my flat, Morgan, you'll see what I mean. Photos everywhere.'

She said nothing. His smile faltered.

'I don't mean photos of *girls*. Seascapes, birds, stuff like that.'

She studied his face then opened her copy of *Catcher in the Rye* and slipped the photo between the pages.

'I promise there's nothing to worry about,' said Nigel. 'Not so far as I'm concerned.'

She kept her eyes on his, looking for the slightest tell, the smallest sign that he might be lying.

Who can we trust?

'Have you been stalking me? Leaving messages?'

'Of course not. But I don't blame you for asking.'

'Big of you.'

She headed out, pausing at the door.

'Everything you just said? Tell it to Jacqui Farmiloe.'

A pained look.

'Is that really necessary?'

She didn't bother with a response.

'I need someone to escort me to the gate.'

'I'll take you,' said Nigel.

Morgan shook her head.

'You're not taking me anywhere.'

Forty-Two

The publicity over the sex tape had one positive outcome: the more people saw of Lissa, the more they questioned what the police were doing to find her, compelling Jacqui Farmiloe to step up the investigation.

'We'll pull Cundy in for questioning tonight,' the police officer said when Morgan called from the prison car park. 'I'll let you know how it goes.'

Still no confirmed sightings of Lissa but according to the DI every call from the public was being investigated by the ever-expanding team now dedicated to the case.

Have You Seen This Girl?

'Rest, eat, stay off the internet.' Jacqui's voice was firm. 'Any news, you'll be the first to know.'

Driving home, Morgan took a detour via the Romney Marsh petrol station to stock up on Rizlas, milk and cereal. The idea of cooking seemed frivolous. Her daughter was missing. What was the point of eating? What was the point of anything?

Trying to clear her head, she took another walk on the wind-swept beach, keeping an eye out for the three-legged dog. As darkness fell, she returned home and forced herself to listen to the voicemails that had accumulated during the day. Apart from Clive Rossiter (*'just checking in, as a friend'*) there was not one call she was minded to return. The *Post* seemed to have assigned another reporter to cover the sex-tape story, but elsewhere the intense media interest was already showing signs of losing momentum, the pack moving on to the next scandal, the next broken heart, the next shattered life.

She splashed milk onto a bowl of cornflakes. Three mouthfuls and a glass of wine later she was overwhelmed by fatigue, the kind that usually presaged deep sleep but in her present state – exhausted, hyper-vigilant – would lead to another bout of semi-wakefulness. The prospect of another long, lonely night made her spirits plummet. Her best chance of getting any rest was to stop drinking alcohol and take a bath. Her shoulders were knotted with tension. Relaxing would be impossible but getting properly warm might help.

In the bathroom, she undressed, turned on the taps then reached out to grab her bathrobe from its hook.

She froze, stifling a cry.

The toilet seat was raised.

A man had been here.

Was he still inside? Hiding? Watching? Waiting?

Mind racing, heart thumping, she donned her bathrobe. Then she turned off the taps and scanned the bathroom for a weapon.

Nothing.

She could feel her skin prickling with fear. She called out: 'I've phoned the police!'

But her mobile was on the kitchen table. If someone were in the house, watching, waiting, he would know she was bluffing. He would know she was alone.

Without thinking, driven by anger and panic, she let out a guttural roar drawn from the depths of her soul. Bursting out of the bathroom, she charged into the hallway, stomping like a Maori warrior, banging on the walls, thumping her way into the sitting room, pounding, smashing, kicking anything in her way – chairs, tables, lamps – until she reached the kitchen and her fingers closed around the carving knife. She drew it from the block, yelling, 'COME ON! I'm ready, you FUCKER! COME ON!'

Eyes bulging, panting furiously, she planted her feet a yard apart, brandishing the blade in the air, knowing she looked like a madwoman but not giving a damn because that was how she wanted to appear.

Mad.

Angry.

Lethal.

She let the seconds tick by then lowered the knife, allowing herself to deflate to normal size. Breathing heavily, she took a step forward and kicked open the door to Lissa's bedroom.

Empty.

She could feel her heart rate increasing with every step towards the wardrobe. She reached out and tugged the handle. The door creaked open.

Empty.

Her eyes darted to the bed. The divan was low-slung. No possibility of someone hiding underneath. Unlike her own bed.

She left Lissa's room, taking stealthy steps along the corridor. She raised a finger, gingerly pushing open her bedroom door.

The room was empty, the wardrobe doors ajar, as she had left them.

She turned to look at her bed: the metal bedstead was raised eighteen inches from the floor. Space for someone to hide. She pointed the knife towards the gap between the floor and the base of the bed. Holding her breath, she sank to her knees and peered into the darkness.

Shoes.

Books.

An upturned mug.

No intruder.

Trembling, she sprang to her feet, locked the doors and checked the window catches in every room.

Only then did she allow herself to believe that the house was empty.

That she was alone.

Safe.

In the kitchen she sheathed the knife in the block. Then she picked up her phone, returned to the bathroom and stared at the raised toilet seat for a long moment. Scrolling to a name, she thumbed the number. The call was answered after a single ring.

'Hi, Morgan,' said Donna Goshawk.

'Someone's been here. In my house.'

'Are you safe?'

'I think so.'

A pause.

'We're about to interview Nigel Cundy. Don't move. I'll send a car.'

'No.'

Morgan could feel the blood thudding in her ears.

'Does the offer of a spare bed stand?' she said.

'Absolutely. I'll be back by nine. There's a pub opposite the flat.'

'OK,' said Morgan. 'I'm on my way.'

Forty-Three

To Morgan's surprise, when Donna arrived at the Canterbury Arms she was with Jacqui Farmiloe. After an update on the hunt for Lissa (still no news) and Morgan's recounting of the discovery of the raised toilet seat, the three women sat at a table. The DI sipped Diet Coke and munched on peanuts. Morgan shared a bottle of Shiraz with Donna, one of those mysterious creatures who managed to look as immaculate at the end of the day as at the beginning.

Frowning, Jacqui studied the photo of Lissa emerging from the waves, listening as Morgan gave details of her prison showdown with Nigel Cundy.

'Pretty much what he told us,' said the DI as Morgan finished. 'Of course, the two things – Cundy photographing Lissa; the intruder at your place – aren't necessarily related.'

Morgan frowned.

'But he did photograph my daughter. My missing daughter. Naked.'

Donna nodded.

'We don't like it either but she's an adult. And there's no law against taking photos in a public place.'

'Naked,' Morgan repeated the word for effect, earning a sympathetic smile from Jacqui Farmiloe.

'When she comes home,' she said, 'tell her to stop getting her kit off in front of every Tom, Dick and Harry.'

Morgan felt a flicker of annoyance.

'Isn't that victim-blaming?'

The DI spread her hands.

'She's not a victim. There's no crime. We're hoping it stays that way.'

Morgan didn't press the point. She needed these women – they were out on a limb just being here, breaking the rules by telling her what they could. She turned to Donna.

'So now what?'

'We went to Cundy's flat and interviewed him,' said the DS, lapsing into the sort of 'police-speak' Morgan was finding increasingly grating. 'We've no reason to believe he knows anything about Lissa's whereabouts. His wildlife photos confirm what he says about his hobby. We're continuing to make enquiries.' She looked away and sipped her wine. 'So far, he seems kosher.'

Morgan studied her face. Something wasn't right.

'*Seems* kosher?'

A pause.

'We're off the record, right?' said Donna.

'Forget I'm a journalist,' said Morgan. 'Right now, I'm just a mother.'

The DS's eyes flickered to her boss who gave a brief nod.

'OK,' said Donna, topping up Morgan's wine glass. 'We ran a background check after you called. Seems Cundy got himself into a situation.'

'Define "situation".'

'A complaint from a woman in Essex,' said Donna. 'Couple of years ago she told local police she'd had a six-month relationship with Cundy. But she dumped him when she began to suspect he was using her.'

'Using her for what?'

'To ingratiate himself with her fifteen year old daughter.'

Morgan felt her heart rate quicken.

'He was sleeping with the mother while grooming the daughter?'

'So she was implying,' said Donna, tracing a manicured finger around the rim of her glass. 'Turned out she has a history of crying wolf over supposedly sleazy boyfriends. Daughter insisted Mum was a sandwich short of the full picnic, jealous for no reason.' She selected a peanut and rolled it between her fingers. 'No caution was issued, no action taken, no case for Cundy to answer.'

'Then why are you telling me?' said Morgan.

Another hesitation. Jacqui Farmiloe took up the story, lowering her voice as she leaned in.

'Forewarned is forearmed,' she said. 'And he seems to think you've got a crush on him.'

Morgan's eyes widened in disbelief.

'A crush? On Nigel Cundy?'

The woman held up a hand.

'I'm just saying – woman to woman – when we find Lissa it might be an idea not to have any more cosy suppers with him.'

Quelling a surge of outrage, Morgan tried to stay focused on the matter at hand.

'What about the intruder?'

Donna produced her notebook.

'We checked Cundy's whereabouts,' she said, flicking through the pages. 'He was at work from eight ten till five thirty-five so it's unlikely he could have gone to your place, unless it was while you were swimming or walking on the beach. Even then, he'd have had to slip through the prison-gate system, which seems unlikely.'

Morgan was overwhelmed by a sense of futility. Why would Nigel break into her home? And if it wasn't him, who was it? What had they been looking for?

'Strikes me the intruder wasn't Cundy,' said Donna. 'Maybe it was the same person who leaves those messages.'

Jacqui nodded and turned to Morgan.

'Anything stolen?'

'I don't think so.'

'You'd locked the doors?' said Donna. 'Front and back? And the windows?'

Had she?

'I don't know.'

'Well, obviously some*one* got in some*how*,' said Jacqui. 'We'll send a SOCO first thing.'

It wasn't much but it was something. Morgan felt a flicker of gratitude.

'We also stopped by Kilcannon's place,' said Donna, straightening a beer mat. 'To check his movements today.'

'And?'

'He says he was in his workshop all day. Alone.'

Morgan was feeling increasingly woozy. Exhaustion. Anxiety. Wine.

'You need sleep,' Jacqui Farmiloe said. Her mobile beeped with a text. She glanced at her phone then clambered to her feet. 'And I need to get home. The carer's been looking after Colin since seven. Costing the earth.'

In spite of her own worries, Morgan felt a twinge of sympathy. Tempted to enquire after Chelsea, she thought better of it. The last thing the hard-pressed DI needed was a reminder of her drug-dealing daughter.

'Thank you for coming,' she said.

Jacqui's voice was weary but her smile was warm.

'All part of the service.'

She headed for the door and disappeared into the night. Donna picked up the last peanut and popped it in her mouth.

'Probably best you don't mention kipping at my place,' she said. 'Not done to have a Misper mum in my spare room.'

'Is that what I am?' said Morgan. 'Misper mum?'

Donna shook her head. 'Just someone who needs a break.'

Morgan stared into her glass, thinking about Cundy. And Danny. And Cameron with his twenty-something girlfriend in her fuck-me shoes and spray-on jeans.

'*Men*,' she said. 'What is it with *men*?'

Donna shared out the last of the wine.

'When I'm Commissioner,' she said, 'we'll lock up anyone with a penis, soon as they hit fifteen. Let them out when they're thirty-five. Halve the crime rate overnight.'

Morgan grinned.

'I'll drink to that.' She watched as the elegant DS took a sip of wine, wondering once again how it was possible to look so fresh so late in the day.

Thirty minutes later, Morgan was perched at the breakfast bar in the all-white kitchen of Donna Goshawk's seventh-floor flat, part of a sleek modern development called Canterbury Cloisters. A pair of muddy trainers provided the only hint of disorder, along with insight into how the DS managed to stay in shape.

Morgan savoured the last of the *coq au vin* Donna had conjured from a slow cooker. She was feeling more like her old self, content to let the conversation meander: the drawbacks of inhabiting a city filled with tourists; the pleasures of living alone. But talk soon returned to Lissa, Danny, and Jacqui Farmiloe.

'What's she like to work for?'

'The best,' said Donna. 'God knows how she copes with that horrible husband.'

'Is he horrible or just ill?'

Donna had the grace to look chastened.

'He used to be my Area Commander,' she said. 'Trust me, he was a liability long before the dementia.'

'In what way?'

Donna took a sip of wine.

'Bad case of wandering hands.'

'Sexual harassment?'

The policewoman shrugged.

'Fit woman, macho culture – a bit of hassle goes with the territory.'

Morgan couldn't help admiring Goshawk's insouciance.

'Did you complain?'

The DS shook her head. 'You either grass up the boss or you climb the greasy pole. Can't do both.'

She began to clear away, watching as Morgan stretched her arms, trying to release the tension in her aching shoulders.

'You could use a massage,' said Donna.

Morgan nodded.

'When all this is over.'

She reached for her tobacco and headed for the balcony.

'Roll one for me?' said Donna. 'Be right with you.'

Outside, the air was chilly, the night sky illuminated by a distant orange glow from the cathedral's floodlights. Morgan rolled two cigarettes, placing them on the table. Moments later, Donna joined her, now barefoot and wearing a white towelling robe. She took a seat and cupped her hands around the lighter as Morgan lit both roll-ups.

'Still hung up on Kilcannon?'

'Nope,' Morgan said, handing Donna a cigarette. 'Ancient history.'

'Jacqui says they should never have let him out.'

Morgan felt a stirring of indignation.

'She would, wouldn't she? Protecting her reputation.'

Donna shrugged.

'She has good instincts,' she said. 'I've never known her to be wrong.'

Morgan didn't reply. She didn't want to talk about Danny. She didn't want to talk at all. Donna took a drag on the cigarette.

'Feel free to go to bed,' she said, exhaling slowly. 'I've got an early start: Marlowe Lane Crematorium.'

'Whose funeral?'

'Caleb Quirke's. We've released his body. Pauper's funeral.'

Morgan raised her eyebrows, recalling the CCTV image of the man being pushed in front of the oncoming train.

'No family, no friends?'

'No,' said Donna. 'And not a pot to piss in so the council's stumping up. The vicar, the undertaker and yours truly. Just in case.'

'In case of what?'

'It's not unknown for a murderer to show up at a funeral,' said Donna. 'A long shot but Jacqui thinks it's worth a go.' She flicked ash over the balcony. 'Anyway, I prefer funerals to weddings. No worrying what to wear, no leering blokes.'

Morgan pulled on her cigarette then gestured towards the locket around Donna's neck.

'Is that Mr Right?'

Donna's hand went to the locket, fingering the silver chain. A sly smile spread across her face. 'What makes you assume it's a mister?'

Morgan said nothing. Her heart seemed to be beating at twice its normal rate. She watched as Donna took a drag on her cigarette while reaching out to pluck a piece of lint from Morgan's shoulder. Then she remained perfectly still as the woman in the white bathrobe leaned forward and placed a featherlight kiss on her lips.

'If you feel like that massage,' said Donna, 'you know where to find me.'

Morgan said nothing. She watched Donna walk inside and disappear from view. She finished her cigarette then went into the bathroom. Emerging, she passed the policewoman's bedroom. The door was ajar, a shaft of soft light illuminating the hall. She paused, hearing her father's voice in her head.

Try everything once – except incest and folk dancing.

Feeling more alive than in weeks – months – she let herself into the spare room and closed the door. A handwritten note lay on the white cotton duvet.

I want to lick every inch of you

Morgan sat on the bed and studied the note carefully. Then she folded it and slipped it into the pocket of her jeans. After undressing, she climbed into bed. The lighting was soothing, the duvet warm, the sheets freshly laundered. She stared at the ceiling, luxuriating in a rare sense of wellbeing, then turned off the light. Moments later, her hand crept between her legs and she began to touch herself. Sex was the last thing on her mind but she was desperate for sleep and craved a sense of peace, no matter how brief. Moaning softly into the pillow, she came in less than a minute and was asleep in less than two.

Morgan woke before dawn, refreshed after her first pill-free night in ages. Donna's bedroom door was closed. Morgan made coffee then sat on the balcony, watching the daylight creep over the rooftops.

The search for Lissa was no further forward but the best chance of finding her went hand in hand with unearthing the truth about Danny and the real story of what happened to Zoe and Rowena.

Morgan made a decision. Discovering more about Caleb Quirke – the man whose lies sent Danny to jail – could do no harm. Besides, she had to do *something*.

In the distance, a church clock struck six. She dressed quickly and left a note.

Thank you for everything. M

She didn't add an *x*. Life was complicated enough.

Emerging from Canterbury Cloisters, she walked through the deserted streets, climbed into her car and headed for home, wondering how she was going to cobble together an outfit suitable for a funeral.

Forty-Four

Marlowe Lane Crematorium was shrouded in mist as Morgan arrived, listening to the car radio. P. P. Arnold's "The First Cut Is The Deepest" was playing – a song she'd often played in the small hours, while thinking of Danny.

She switched to the local headlines, dreading hearing Lissa's name. Although confident that Donna and Jacqui would ensure she was the first to hear any news, there was always the possibility of the media getting a tip-off before the police system could kick in.

She'd managed to unearth a black coat and a pair of smart black jeans before remembering that the absence of mourners meant she could have worn almost anything without causing offence.

Climbing out of her car, she saw Donna leaning against the chapel door, wearing a tailored black trouser suit over a crisp white shirt.

'What are you doing here?' said the policewoman.

'Worth a shot.' Morgan shrugged. 'Quirke's testimony sent Danny to jail; any new link to Danny might be a link to Lissa.'

Donna nodded then smiled, her eyes twinkling.

'I got your note.'

Morgan returned the smile.

'I got yours.'

The DS's face creased into a grin. Morgan felt a flicker of relief. No awkwardness, no embarrassment, just two women acknowledging a moment shared, a road not taken.

Yet.

There were no mourners, no sign of Danny Kilcannon or Allan Maitliss, the two men with reason to be pleased Quirke was dead. Morgan watched as a black van arrived. At the wheel was a burly council worker in a yellow tabard.

The customary cliché – *a good send-off* – wouldn't apply today. Quirke had met a gruesome end under the wheels of a train. His final bow would not be an affair to remember. The van's rear doors opened. A second council worker clambered out and was joined by the driver.

'Anyone seen the vicar?'

As if waiting for his cue, a balding man wearing a dog collar and thick black spectacles emerged from the chapel, a professional smile playing on his lips.

'Is this our Mr Quirke?'

The driver squinted at his clipboard then nodded to his co-worker. Morgan and Donna stood aside, watching the men hoist the cheap coffin from the van into the chapel. Not a flower in sight. The vicar clasped his hands together and glanced around the car park.

'All present and correct,' he said, turning to bestow a beatific smile on Morgan and Donna. 'And at least he's got two lovely young ladies to see him on his way.'

As Donna followed the vicar into the chapel, heels clacking on the marble floor, Morgan looked up to see a red Vespa pulling to a halt. The rider was a tall, stocky woman in her forties. Black leather jacket, blue jeans, black boots. She climbed off the scooter, removing her helmet to reveal a blue and white polka-dot bandana. It took Morgan a moment to remember where she'd seen her before: in the café opposite Quirke's flat.

'Thought I'd be the only one.' The new arrival's voice was a rasp, her cough that of a dedicated smoker.

'Not quite,' said Morgan, extending a hand. 'Morgan Vine.'

The woman's handshake was just the right side of painful.

'Rae Slaughter,' she said, studying Morgan's face. 'You're the one with the missing kid.'

'How did you know?'

'Saw you in the paper. Never forget a face.'

The woman wedged her helmet onto the scooter's rack. Her mobile beeped. Fishing it from her pocket, she glanced at the text and curled her lip.

'Twat,' she said, pocketing the phone without elaborating. Then she nodded towards the chapel door. 'I take it you're not family?'

Morgan shook her head.

'Only met him once.'

'Lucky you,' said Rae Slaughter. 'I came to make sure the bastard's dead.'

She marched inside and slipped into a seat in the back row. Morgan let a few moments pass before walking to the middle of the chapel and taking a seat. She saw Donna Goshawk glance at the woman in the bandana, registering the only unexplained presence at the funeral.

The service was a perfunctory affair – a prayer, a blessing – over in five minutes and interrupted twice by beeps from Rae Slaughter's mobile. Unabashed, the woman scanned the texts then yawned as she watched Quirke's coffin disappear behind the red curtain. Morgan allowed a decent interval before leaving the chapel.

Outside, the mist was starting to clear. She rolled a cigarette, watching as the men from the council drove away. Turning to see Donna emerging from the chapel, locked in conversation with Rae Slaughter, Morgan kept her distance, allowing the police-woman to do her work. The vicar smiled wanly as he rattled away in a people carrier, its exhaust rumbling into the distance.

Silence descended over the memorial gardens, broken only by the murmur of the two voices in the chapel doorway. Morgan studied the woman in the blue and white bandana: early forties, angry at life, not someone you'd want to offend. She saw Donna jotting in her notebook then bringing the conversation to an end by answering a call.

'Morning, boss … Yes, just on my way.' She ended the brief conversation then steered Morgan to one side. 'We've confirmed the fingerprints on Lissa's mobile. Hers and yours.' She paused, looking Morgan in the eye. 'And Danny Kilcannon's.'

The revelation came as no surprise.

'She stayed at his cottage,' said Morgan. 'He had plenty of opportunities to touch the phone.'

'Still giving him the benefit of the doubt?'

'Still trying not to jump to conclusions.'

Donna nodded.

'The SOCO team are going back to your place at midday,' she said. 'To check out your intruder. Can you be there?'

Her tone was purely professional, betraying nothing of what had so nearly happened the night before.

'Fine,' said Morgan.

She watched the policewoman drive away then turned to see Rae Slaughter pulling a packet of Marlboro from her jacket pocket.

'Can I cadge a light?' said Morgan. Any icebreaker would do. The woman tossed over a box of matches and gazed at the chimneystack.

'I'd like to see him go up in smoke.'

Despite her tone, Morgan found herself warming to the woman. There didn't seem to be much hair under the bandana. Perhaps she was undergoing chemotherapy. If so, it was doing nothing to diminish her craving for nicotine.

'So,' Morgan said, 'why come to the funeral of a man you hate?'

'How else am I going to spit on his grave?' The woman kept her eyes on the chimney, absent-mindedly flicking ash onto her sleeve. 'I've seen you before,' she said. 'In the café with that nurse's dad.'

Morgan nodded, recalling Allan Maitliss's anguish as he'd confessed to assaulting Quirke.

'Did you know his daughter?'

Rae shook her head.

'I just read about her. Quirke didn't slash her wrists with that razor blade but he might as well have. A man rapes someone then gets on with his life like nothing happened. Think what that does to his victim.'

Morgan gave a sympathetic nod.

'How well did you know him?'

The woman put her cigarette between her lips then used her hands to adjust her bandana.

'He used to come into the café after work. Same every night: sausage, egg and chips. Always writing in his little yellow book. His "autobiography", he called it.' Satisfied with the positioning of the bandana, she took a final drag on the cigarette then flicked it to the ground. 'One day, he came in for breakfast. Told me he'd had to pull an all-nighter – burst pipes at the chalet park. Said he'd seen a man running from the chalet where that other girl was murdered.'

'You mean Zoe Munro?' said Morgan. She was suddenly on full alert. 'Danny Kilcannon's stepdaughter?'

Rae nodded, grinding the cigarette butt under her heel.

'Poor kid died not long after Suzi Maitliss was raped. Same place: Dover Holiday Park. Couple of days later, the police came a-knocking on Quirke's door. I figured they wanted to question him about the night Zoe died. Turned out they were arresting him for raping Suzi.'

She reached for another Marlboro. Morgan returned the box of matches, waiting for the story to continue.

'Then he manages to swing bail,' said Rae. 'Next thing I know, he's all over the papers because the CPS won't prosecute him – something about contaminated DNA evidence – so he comes swaggering back into the café, pissed as a fart, telling me he's "untouchable". And I say, "You're banned, mate." '

'Because?'

'I *knew* he'd raped the nurse,' said Rae, her gaze fixed on the crematorium chimney.

'How?'

'I know things,' said the woman with a shrug. 'Like I know Lissa is alive.'

Hearing her daughter's name on a stranger's lips made Morgan's stomach lurch.

'What do you know about Lissa?'

'Don't panic,' said Rae. 'It's the gift. I see stuff in the papers and I get a feeling. Your daughter is fine and dandy.' She paused, shaking her head. 'As for Danny Kilcannon? Seriously bad news. Like Quirke.'

Morgan's head was full of questions. Was Rae joking or did she seriously believe she was psychic? But the woman was in full flow, steering the conversation back to the man she wanted to see going up in smoke.

'Couple of weeks after I ban Quirke from the café, he barges in one night. Drunk. Tries to rape *me*.'

Morgan tried to visualise the emaciated man wrestling with the hefty woman in the bandana.

'I chucked him out,' said Rae. 'Then I called the police.'

'And?'

Rae shrugged. 'Know how many sexual assaults get to court?'

'Not enough.'

The woman nodded. 'Quirke's word against mine.' She lit another cigarette. 'Last time I bumped into the bastard, we were both in the hospital.' She tapped a finger on her bandana. Morgan's guess was right. *Chemo.* 'He was furious with me for banning him from the café. But he couldn't stay away after that bitch messed up the prosecution case.'

Morgan narrowed her eyes and frowned.

'What bitch?'

Rae rolled her eyes, as though the answer was obvious.

'The policewoman who botched the DNA evidence showing he'd raped Suzi,' she said, dragging on her cigarette. 'After that, he kept coming in, going on about how he was invincible.' She mimicked the man's voice. '"I've got *insurance.*"' She cast another look at the chimney. 'Much good it did him.'

'What did he mean by "insurance"?'

'Your guess is as good as mine.'

The woman's mobile beeped. She glanced at the text and pulled a face.

'Twat,' she said, taking her helmet from the rack. 'He's supposed to be looking after the café but he texts every five minutes asking where stuff is.' She flicked her cigarette to the ground. 'Sorry if I spooked you but your kid's OK.' Morgan said nothing. The woman smiled, climbing onto the Vespa. 'You don't believe me about the gift,' she said. 'But you'll see.'

Watching Rae drive away, Morgan scanned the deserted grounds of the crematorium and listened to the rooks cawing in the trees. Walking around the corner, she entered the garden of remembrance, sat on a bench and smoked another cigarette.

Your kid's OK.

Although every bone in Morgan's body was scornful of Rae's 'gift', she knew that tonight, when she was desperate to sleep, she'd replay the sentence over and over – a crumb of comfort that might serve as a lullaby, allowing a few hours' oblivion.

Getting to her feet, she turned to go. Her peripheral vision caught a glimpse of movement by the chapel. Someone was slipping inside and closing the door.

Forty-Five

Morgan walked quickly and quietly to the chapel. Pausing at the door, she listened for a moment but there was only silence. Her hand closed around the heavy iron handle. She pushed. The door swung open and she stepped inside.

A man was sitting in a pew in the front row, his back to Morgan. Even without seeing his face she knew who it was.

'Danny?'

He turned, eyebrows arching in surprise.

'I thought you'd left.'

Morgan walked down the aisle. Drawing nearer, she saw cuts and bruises on his face. His left eye was swollen.

'What happened?'

'A bunch of blokes recognised me,' he said. 'Called me "kiddie-killer". Decided I needed a kicking.' He winced, clutching his ribs as he got to his feet. In spite of everything, Morgan felt a pang of sympathy.

'What are you doing here?' she said.

'I came to pay my respects.'

She frowned.

'To the man who put you in prison?'

He shook his head.

'To the man who set me free.'

She couldn't hide her scepticism but he pressed on, determined to make his point.

'Quirke did the right thing. I'm a free man, thanks to him, and that's what counts.'

Deep in her belly she felt a stirring of resentment.

'Thanks to *him*?'

He looked abashed.

'And you,' he said. 'I'll never forget what you did.'

She stared at him for a moment then turned towards the door. As he followed she noticed the 'kicking' had left him with a limp. Just a few days ago she would have voiced concern. Was he OK? Had he been to hospital? Reported the assault to the police? Now she stayed silent.

'Any news on Lissa?' said Danny.

Morgan shook her head.

'No, but Farmiloe and Goshawk are pulling out all the stops.'

'They gave me a good grilling after you found Lissa's mobile.'

'Do you blame them?'

He didn't reply. The only sound was the cawing of the rooks in the trees. There didn't seem to be anything else to say.

'I'd better go,' he said.

She couldn't stop the intrusive thoughts.

Go where? To see my daughter? Hide her body? Visit her grave?

'Take care, Morgan.'

But as he turned away, he winced in pain and stumbled, nearly falling to the ground. Instinctively, she reached out a hand, taking him by the elbow.

'I'll walk you to your car.'

They walked in silence, Danny leaning on her arm, limping along the winding path that led to a crescent of gravel by the crematorium gates. Reaching the Mercedes, he drew his key from his pocket and stooped to open the door.

'I guess this is what it's like to be old,' he said, straightening up.

She said nothing. There had been a time when she'd imagined them growing old together. Another world, another life.

'Goodbye, Danny.'

Turning to leave, her eye was drawn to something in his car's passenger footwell. A roll of duct tape. She froze, an image of Lissa bound and gagged flashing into her mind.

Danny followed her gaze.

'What's wrong?'

She couldn't bring herself to reply. Reading her thoughts, his eyes widened.

'What kind of man do you think I *am*?'

'You tell me.'

His eyes were cold, his tone caustic. It was as if a switch had been flicked inside his head.

'For the record,' he said, 'some bastard chucked rocks through my window but I'm completely broke so tape is the best I can do. Any more questions?'

Her eyes flickered to the duct tape. The story was plausible. He'd been labelled a 'kiddie-killer', beaten up; it wasn't much of a stretch to imagine vigilantes following him home and smashing his windows. So why was her flesh crawling, her heart pounding? Why was every bone in her body telling her to run while she had the chance? Rae Slaughter's words came flooding back.

As for Danny Kilcannon? He's seriously bad news.

He held her gaze.

'Maybe you should call your pal Farmiloe.' He mimicked Morgan's voice. ' "Danny's got duct tape. Bring him in for questioning. Better still, lock him up and throw away the key. The man had sex with my daughter. He deserves everything he gets." '

She could feel her cheeks burning. Had he always had a vicious streak she'd never noticed? Or had prison made him hard?

'This has *nothing* to do with you sleeping with Lissa,' she said. 'I just want to know where she is.'

Suddenly, eyes bulging, Danny brought his face close to hers and bellowed. She could feel his breath. Hot. Angry.

'I DON'T KNOW WHERE SHE IS!'

His voice echoed around the grounds of the crematorium and into the woods beyond. As silence descended, Morgan stood firm, staring him in the eye.

'Get away from me, Danny. And stay away.'

She turned and headed for the car park, waiting for the remorse to kick in. She didn't have long to wait.

'I'm *so* sorry ...' His voice was hoarse as he called after her. 'I've no idea what's wrong with me.'

Morgan kept walking. Danny tried again.

'Forgive me, *please*?'

She didn't turn, just kept walking. Moments later, she heard the Mercedes roar to life and the sound of tyres on gravel as his car pulled onto the main road. Then he was gone.

Trembling, heart hammering in her chest, Morgan slowed her pace then stopped in her tracks and narrowed her eyes. A hundred yards away, in the car park, a lone figure – a woman – was slipping something under the Mini's windscreen wipers then hurrying away. Morgan called out.

'Hey!'

The figure kept walking, head down, making for a silver Audi estate. Morgan broke into a run.

'*Hey!*'

The figure got into the car and drove away, speeding for the exit and disappearing as Morgan reached the Mini. Her fingers snatched the slip of paper from the windscreen. On it were printed three all-too-familiar words.

Don't trust him

She stared in the direction taken by the Audi. She hadn't laid eyes on the driver for years but there was no doubt about her identity. Ursula.

Morgan bought a cup of tea from the stall in the layby then returned to her car. She was still trying to absorb the triple whammy of bizarre encounters at the crematorium. First Rae Slaughter. Then Danny and the duct tape. Finally, her stepmother.

Why was Ursula leaving her messages? The seashells, the note in the London car park, the other warnings. True, the woman had never had time for Danny, or for Morgan herself for that matter. But why would she suddenly be taking such an interest in her stepdaughter's wellbeing?

Then there was the question of Danny and the duct tape. His explanation was plausible enough. So why had Morgan felt such fear on seeing it? It wasn't just his angry outburst, there was *something else* – instinct, intuition – warning her to be wary. And yet she knew only too well how unreliable her own intuition could be.

Sitting in her car, sipping tea, she thought back to her suspicions about Leo, how they had led to the estrangement that endured to this day. Instinct had its place, of course, but there were times when all that mattered were *facts*. If she had any hope of finding Lissa she must focus on evidence, follow the trail step by step. Rae Slaughter's words were fresh in her mind, nagging like a troublesome tooth.

The bitch who messed up the prosecution case against Quirke.

The policewoman who screwed up the DNA evidence against him.

Finishing her tea, Morgan drew her mobile from her pocket then Googled Suzi Maitliss's name.

149,000 results.

She tapped the first entry, a Mail Online article on the nurse's suicide. There was a quote from the Senior Investigating Officer in charge of the abortive rape enquiry.

'*Despite Suzi's tragic death we remain committed to bringing her attacker to justice. Our thoughts are with her parents, Allan and Tina, at this difficult time,*' said DI Jacqui Farmiloe.

The sight of Farmiloe's name raised goose bumps along Morgan's forearms. Why hadn't the DI mentioned her role in the enquiry into Quirke's rape of Suzi? Was it coincidence? Or did the woman have something to hide?

Her mind fizzing with questions, Morgan tapped her list of contacts and scrolled to Ursula's name. Dialling, she was greeted by a continuous tone. Number discontinued.

Why didn't Jacqui mention she was SIO in the rape case against Quirke? Most likely, there was nothing to it – a police officer encountering the same person twice, in connection with different enquiries. Must happen all the time. She wouldn't necessarily need to mention it.

On the other hand ...

Quirke had been Suzi's rapist *and* chief witness for the prosecution against Danny. Four years later he was the linchpin of the appeal that had set Danny free. At the heart of both cases, one police officer: Jacqui Farmiloe ...

Morgan lit a roll-up then scrolled to Nigel Cundy's name. He answered after two rings, his voice full of contrition.

'Morgan, I'm so glad you called ...'

'I need your help, Nigel.'

No hint of hesitation.

'Name it.'

'You mentioned a cousin. High up in the police?'

'Yes?'

'I need you to ask him about Jacqui Farmiloe.'

'What about her?'

'Anything out of the ordinary.'

There was a pause.

'Does this mean you believe me?' said Nigel. 'About Lissa and the photograph?'

'Just contact your cousin and call me back.'

She cut him off before he could reply. Then she sat for several minutes, finishing her cigarette while wondering what Quirke had meant when he'd gloated to Rae Slaughter that he was 'invincible'. That he had 'insurance'.

Starting the car, Morgan gunned the engine while making her decision. She'd make it home in time to give the SOCOs access. Then she'd go back to Quirke's place and search for clues. She'd never broken into a house before but there was a first time for everything.

Forty-Six

Skulking in the doorway of a derelict house, Morgan waited for darkness to fall. Then for the café to close and for Rae Slaughter to pull down the shutters, climb onto her Vespa and drive away.

Silence descended. A black cat emerged from beneath a van and padded along the terrace. Scanning the road for signs of life, Morgan emerged from the shadows and walked towards number six. She'd been keeping watch for almost an hour. No lights, no sign of occupants. It was possible the landlord had already cleared out Quirke's flat but the ground-floor windows of the house were boarded up; it seemed unlikely that anyone was in a rush to move in.

The house lay at the end of the Victorian terrace bordered by an alleyway to the rear. Morgan donned her gloves. She'd already identified the most likely means of entry. Now she executed the manoeuvre she'd been rehearsing in her mind: climbing onto a wheelie bin, hoisting herself onto the wall then dropping down into the garden.

Garden was too grand a word. Yard, more like. Slabs of concrete, a rusting fridge, an old sofa, empty bottles.

The back door was padlocked. Of three rear windows, two were boarded up, the other a mosaic of splintered glass. One shove with her elbow was all it took: the cobweb of glass gave way, shards tinkling onto the carpet.

Morgan counted to twenty.

Listening.

Watching for lights.

Nothing.

She extended her arm through the window, avoiding the jagged glass, then released the catch and pushed upwards on the frame. No movement. She heaved again. Inch by inch, the window juddered open. She hoisted herself onto the sill, feeling the rotten wood crumbling beneath her hands, then swung her legs into the house and slipped inside.

The room smelled of damp. Switching on her torch, she made her way across the threadbare carpet, letting herself into the hallway then climbing the staircase to the top floor.

The house had been divided into three flats, one on each floor. There was no lock on the door to flat C. Quirke's idea of security had extended no further than the street door. Morgan tried the handle. The door opened. She stepped inside, letting her torch play over the room.

The flat was crammed with heavy brown furniture. On the ceiling, below a pattern of water stains, was a patch of grey-green fungus. Above the single bed, a crucifix clung to the wall alongside a set of rosary beads dangling from a nail. A cheap bookcase contained a handful of DVDs – mostly action movies starring Stallone or Schwarzenegger – along with a Bible embossed with the initials *CQ* and, to Morgan's surprise, a collection of novels by Graham Greene and Evelyn Waugh.

Her search was swift but thorough, focusing on one thing: the yellow notebook. Quirke's 'autobiography'. Crossing into the kitchenette, she opened a drawer then froze as she heard a noise downstairs.

A key in the front door.

A *click* as the door closed.

She held her breath and switched off her torch. There were footsteps on the stairs, taking each step slowly, drawing closer. A whiff of stale cigarettes. Then the sound of *wheezing*. And a rasping voice. Rae Slaughter's.

'You shouldn't be here.'

The boots took a step into the kitchen. The woman was silhouetted by the streetlamp.

'You're a lousy burglar,' Rae said, recovering her breath. 'I clocked you casing the place. Parked up, gave you five minutes then walked back.' She turned on the light and held up a key. 'Quirke's spare. He was neurotic about locking himself out so he left it at the café. You only had to ask.'

Morgan's mouth was dry.

'I need to know about him,' she said. 'I'm not a burglar.'

The woman drew her cigarettes from her pocket.

'Nothing to steal,' she said. 'Anyway, the police beat you to it.'

'Was it a policeman,' said Morgan, 'or a woman?'

'Woman, apparently. My husband was manning the café that day. I was having chemo.' She lit a cigarette. 'What are you looking for?'

'His yellow notebook.'

'Why?'

'There might be something about Danny Kilcannon in it. I need to know what he's capable of.'

Rae tapped a finger on her breastbone.

'I know what he's capable of. In here.'

She stared through the haze of cigarette smoke, sizing Morgan up.

'A man was snooping around the day before the police,' she said. 'Came in to the café the night Quirke died, asking questions. I told him we had a key.' She held it up to the light. 'He borrowed it, gave us fifty quid.'

'Did he take anything away?'

The woman nodded.

'The notebook.'

Every instinct Morgan possessed was telling her she was getting closer, *but to what?* She scrutinised Rae's face, as if the answer might be hidden in the folds of her flesh, the crow's feet around her eyes.

'Did you tell the police?'

'They didn't ask.'

'Did you get the man's name?'

'No. He was cagey.'

'What did he look like?'

'Forties, silvery-grey hair.' The woman dragged on her cigarette then added two words that confirmed Morgan's suspicions. 'Red socks.'

Rossiter.

Why hadn't he given his name? Why had he been cagey?

Who can we trust?

As the question bubbled to the surface, so did another thought. Rae was close to six feet tall, the same build as Quirke's assailant, the man (*or woman*) captured on CCTV as he (*or she*) pushed the chalet park manager under the train. Quirke had tried to rape Rae. Had she taken her revenge? For herself? For Suzi Maitliss?

Rae's mobile beeped.

'Twat,' said the woman, tutting at the screen. 'He can't even find the sodding Calpol.'

She headed for the door.

'You'll find Lissa,' she said. 'Buy me a drink when you do.'

She flashed a smile and clumped down the stairs. Morgan heard the door close. She took a breath and tried to put Rae out of her mind. The yellow notebook was gone but she still needed to know what Quirke had meant by 'insurance'.

She searched the flat but there was nothing of note except further evidence of Quirke's faith: a book on saints; tacky souvenirs from Lourdes. She glanced out of the window, into the yard below. The sofa, the old fridge, the empty bottles …

Her eyes drifted back to the fridge.

She retraced her steps down the staircase and clambered through the broken window, out into the yard. The fridge door squealed in protest as she prised it open. There was nothing inside. She turned to leave but something made her take another look.

There was a Tesco bag in the freezer compartment. Inside was another bag. Clear plastic, sealed with a Zip-loc. It contained a mobile phone.

Morgan felt a shiver run through her. She had found Quirke's 'insurance'.

Forty-Seven

1989

After Leo's release from prison, Morgan let a week elapse before plucking up the courage to ask forgiveness.

'I'm sorry I wasn't more understanding,' he told her during a blustery walk along the pier. 'Too wrapped up in my own misery.'

But his voice lacked conviction. Meanwhile, Ursula continued to nurse a grudge, keeping the pilot light burning under a flame of jealousy and resentment. Her stepdaughter's disloyalty had been reprehensible. How could Leo even think of forgiving the girl?

Morgan came to understand that Ursula was determined to stoke the father-daughter rift in order to strengthen her own position. At the same time, she was forced to admit that her stepmother had remained steadfast, never doubting his innocence.

With Leo not even pretending to look for a job – reputation ruined, spirit crushed – Ursula was forced to go out to work. She found a position as a dentist's receptionist and hated every minute. Each evening, she slammed into the house at six twenty-five, brimming with resentment and finding fault with Leo's efforts at making supper.

'If I'd wanted a house-husband, I'd have married a man who could cook.'

Morgan bought her father a book called *DIY Divorce* but he told her not to be impertinent and gave it to the Oxfam shop.

Late one evening Morgan led Danny to the white cliffs. She had chosen an isolated spot, screened from the path by bushes. There was no need for words, he knew why they were there. Lying on the grass, she guided his hand to her breast. Her lips found his. It was time.

Later, they lay side by side, looking out to sea, talking of their future – hers as a reporter, his as a carpenter – and of her father's marriage.

'At least Ursula's loyal,' said Danny. 'Besides, some men will put up with anything not to be lonely.'

'Dad's not lonely,' murmured Morgan, stroking his hair. 'He's got me.'

'For how long?' said Danny. 'You won't be at home forever.'

He kissed her again, teasing her lips with his tongue, and for a while she forgot about her father.

Later, while Danny was pulling on his shirt, she stared at the waves crashing onto the rocks below.

'These are our cliffs now,' she said.

He turned to follow her gaze.

'You could push someone off here and no one could prove you'd done it.'

She didn't know how to respond, settling for a sigh.

'How romantic.'

The following summer, having been temporarily taken in by his grandparents, Stevie Gamble moved to Australia to live with his mother. His father developed an aggressive form of prostate cancer and died in a prison hospice three years after Leo's ordeal.

When word of Bryan Gamble's death reached number fourteen The Grove, Ursula suspended her 'no alcohol during the week' rule and celebrated with a schooner of Harvey's Bristol Cream. Tongue loosened, she told her stepdaughter that Mr Gamble had had his comeuppance, adding, 'And one day, missy, you'll get yours.'

The nature of the threat became clear on Morgan's eighteenth birthday. Leo took his daughter out for dinner, just the two of them, a double celebration to mark her coming of age and A-level results.

'We're moving,' he said over sticky toffee pudding. 'Next month.'

Morgan's eyes widened in surprise.

'Where to?'

He looked away, his voice suddenly hoarse.

'Not you,' he said. 'Just me and your stepmother. I've got a job in Wales, teaching English. It means she won't have to work. I've rented a cottage there so you can stay in Deal until you go to university.'

Morgan couldn't believe her ears.

'So you're letting her win?'

He pretended not to hear.

'I've done my best, Morgan, ever since your mother died, but Ursula thinks it's time for you to live your own life, make your own way in the world.' He signalled for the bill, unable to meet her gaze. 'I've done my imperfect best and I love you very much. But I don't ever want to be a burden. You'll understand when you're older.'

But she didn't understand. Nor did she when her letters to Wales were ignored and answerphone messages went unreturned. It took a note from Ursula to spell things out.

'Your father doesn't want to speak to you ever again.'

When Morgan raced to Danny's house, desperate for comfort, a dreadful day soon got worse. The Vines, it seemed, weren't the only family undergoing upheaval.

'Mum's marrying Reece,' Danny told her while sanding a piece of wood in the shed. 'He's left his wife and got a job selling timeshare apartments. We're going to live in Tenerife.'

He seemed to be in a state of shock. The feeling was mutual.

Reeling, Morgan couldn't bring herself to wave him off at the airport. She spent the week of his departure in bed, convinced she would die at any moment from a broken heart. Eventually, as reality settled in, she wrote twice a day for a month. At first, he replied with stories of homesickness and sleepless nights.

Then he began to mention Valentina. The caretaker's daughter lived in the same Santa Cruz apartment complex as Danny. She was teaching him to speak Spanish and he was returning the favour by giving her English lessons. His letters took on a distant quality and became less frequent. Soon, they stopped altogether.

Morgan knew her life was over. No one had ever known such misery. How the world kept turning, how the sun kept rising, she would never understand.

For weeks, she'd been saving for a ticket to Tenerife. Wandering aimlessly around Deal's rain-lashed shopping precinct, she spent the money on shoes instead, hoping retail therapy would make her feel better. It didn't.

Four weeks later, she started at Sussex University. Towards the end of her first term, a budding screenwriter gave a talk at the Film Society. Cameron was older, wiser, good-looking and funny. Morgan hadn't laughed in months. So when he asked where to get a late-night drink, she suggested they continue the conversation in her room.

Six weeks later, discovering her period was late, her step-mother's words came back to her yet again.

Man plans, God laughs.

Forty-Eight

Morgan slept in the Mini, never once letting go of Quirke's mobile – his 'insurance'. She was tempted to go home and carry on as normal, regardless of any threat from whoever had broken in. At the same time, she was intrigued by the prospect of what might happen if she spent a second night under Donna's roof. She chose neither option, plumping for a safe, uncomplicated night locked in her car, huddled under a coat and an ancient picnic blanket.

As dawn broke over St Margaret's Bay she took a walk on the cliffs, by the Dover Patrol war memorial, easing the stiffness in her limbs while marvelling at the pale pink and orange sunrise. Then she drove to Dover, passing the ferry terminal, and found a phone shop on the high street, arriving an hour before it opened. Sitting in her car, she turned on the news. No mention of Lissa. She'd been missing for seventeen days and nights. The world had moved on.

The shop opened at nine. Morgan crossed her fingers, hoping the assistant would have the right charger. She was in luck.

Back in the Mini, she connected Quirke's phone to the lighter socket. For a heart-stopping second there was no sign of life. Then came a *beep* as the 'charging' icon flashed onscreen.

Morgan pressed the home button. A keypad appeared. Her face fell. She'd never bothered with passcodes. Quirke had been more security-conscious.

Crushed and deflated (four hours' sleep had done nothing to improve her state of mind), she found a café and ordered scrambled eggs and coffee. Gazing out of the window, she tried to recall anything in Quirke's dingy bedsitting room that might give a clue to his passcode but nothing came to mind.

Her breakfast arrived, delivered by a whey-faced man in need of a shower. Morgan pushed the rubbery eggs to one side, sipped her coffee and rolled a cigarette. Her phone rang. The sight of Donna's name boosted her flagging spirits. She decided not to mention Quirke's mobile. In spite of the policewoman's kindness – and flirtatiousness – breaking and entering was not something the ambitious DS was likely to condone.

'What did you make of Rae Slaughter showing up at Quirke's funeral?' said Morgan.

'Very odd,' said Donna. 'She told me she hated the guy. Plus she's the same build as whoever pushed him under the train.'

'You think she did it?'

'I don't know,' said Donna. 'We're checking her out.'

Morgan took a sip of coffee.

'What about the intruder at my place?'

'SOCO drew a blank on prints,' said Donna. 'But there were fresh scratches around one of the window frames.' She paused then added, 'You're sure nothing was stolen?'

'Pretty much,' said Morgan. 'Which makes me think he was looking for something specific.'

'Such as?'

'I've no idea.'

The conversation continued in an amiable but businesslike fashion, interrupted as Donna was summoned by her boss. There was no hint of the sexual frisson Morgan had found so tantalising two nights earlier. She was grateful. Her daughter was missing; she had no interest in anything else, especially the possibility that she might be attracted to other women. She'd had crushes on girls at school – who hadn't? But she'd never given more than a moment's thought to the idea that she might be gay, or even bi-curious.

And yet . . .

I want to lick every inch of you

She could feel the note in her pocket. Maybe when all this was over she and Donna might share a bottle of wine, see how things panned out . . .

The policewoman was back on the line. Her tone was different. Formal. Something had happened.

'I need to tell you something,' she said. 'Before you hear it on the news.'

Morgan stiffened. Her heart was hammering.

'Tell me.'

A pause.

'There's no easy way to say this. We've found a body.'

'Oh, Jesus . . .'

Morgan stood up abruptly, jostling the table, spilling her coffee.

'I need you to listen carefully. I'm telling you this on the phone because it's better you hear it from us. Do you understand?'

'Yes ... I understand.'

'A man has reported a burned out car. In Margate. On a patch of wasteland. The car was stolen. There was a body inside. Incinerated. We think it's a young woman's.'

'You *think?*'

'It's ... hard to tell.'

'Oh, God. When will you know?'

'Could be a while.'

'For God's sake! Days? Weeks?'

'Certainly days, possibly weeks. When a body's in this sort of condition it's a complicated process.'

'Christ, what am I supposed to do?'

Donna's voice was calm.

'I need you to focus. Two things. Number one: there are thousands of missing people out there. *Thousands upon thousands.* Do you understand what I'm saying?'

'Yes.'

'Number two: I need you to give me the name of Lissa's dentist.'

Morgan stared at the coffee pooling on the plastic tablecloth. For a second she thought she'd misheard. *Dentist?*

Then realisation hit.

'For identification?'

'Yes.'

Somehow, despite the surge of panic, the man's name sprang straight to her mind.

'Sandilands,' she said. 'He's in Folkestone. I don't have the number.'

'We'll find him,' said Donna, sounding more businesslike than ever. 'Now, do you need me to call someone?'

'What ...'

'Someone to be with you. I'd come myself but ...'

Morgan took a breath, her eyes filling with tears.

'No. Just do what you need to do.'

'This will take time,' said Donna. 'And I promise we'll let you know the second we have any news. It won't be today, probably not tomorrow, perhaps not even this week. But you *must* remember: *there are thousands of missing people out there.*'

'OK,' said Morgan. 'I need to go.'

She hung up and sat down. She stared at the eggs.

A burned out car. Stolen. A body. Incinerated.

'You OK?'

The café owner was back, staring at her quizzically. Morgan took a breath, steadying herself.

'Sorry about the mess.'

'No problem.'

Her mobile rang again. She snatched it from the table and glanced at the name flashing onscreen.

Nigel Cundy.

She took a moment to compose herself then answered the call, listening as the shrink relayed the information he'd gleaned from his source.

'Jacqui Farmiloe's husband used to be Area Commander. Had his eye on a top job at the Met but retired when he got ill. He has dementia.'

'I know all of this,' said Morgan, forcing herself to focus, trying to banish the image of a charred body in a car.

'My cousin says there were rumours that Colin Farmiloe couldn't keep his pants zipped, whispers of sexual harassment. Nothing went as far as a tribunal so he swanned off into the sunset. Nice fat pension.'

Morgan frowned.

'So he was a sex pest?'

'You've been reading too many tabloids.'

She ignored the jibe.

'What does your cousin say about Jacqui?'

'A copper's copper. Smart. Tough.'

'Anything else?'

'Like?'

'Like one of her rape cases collapsing because DNA evidence was mysteriously contaminated?'

'Got a name?'

'The victim was Suzi Maitliss,' said Morgan. 'The rapist was Caleb Quirke.'

She could hear Nigel scribbling.

'I'll check it out,' he said. Then he cleared his throat. 'My turn to ask a favour?'

'Don't push your luck. I'm still angry you photographed Lissa.'

'Which is why I'd like to buy you a drink. So I can apologise properly.'

Morgan was quiet for a moment.

'Not now, Nigel. Get back to me about Jacqui and the case against Quirke.'

She ended the call then left the café, striding through Dover's dreary streets. With seagulls circling overhead, she forced her thoughts away from the body in the burned out car and turned her mind to Jacqui's 'sex pest' husband. She recalled their first encounter, when he'd stood before her, naked, and burst into song.

'Washing machines live longer with Calgon!'

And their second meeting – more alarming – when he'd masturbated while staring at her and singing another ancient jingle.

'Unzip a banana.'

What had Donna said about her former boss?

'Bad case of wandering hands.'

Morgan could *feel* she was on the right track. Every day, every hour, new connections were being made, new links appearing: between Danny Kilcannon and Jacqui Farmiloe; between Farmiloe and Caleb Quirke. And in the midst of it all, a missing eighteen-year-old girl. If there was a pattern, something that might lead to her daughter, Morgan couldn't see it but she could *feel* things taking shape.

Suddenly, the image of the burned out car was back. The charred body ... Making a supreme effort of will, Morgan refocused on Donna's attempt to sound reassuring.

There are thousands of missing people out there.

Thousands upon thousands ...

In the precinct, she sat on a bench and smoked a roll-up while watching the passers-by: shoppers, office workers, a boy on a bike, a man arguing with his wife. Normal people doing normal things. How she craved an ordinary day.

Keep busy. Stay calm.

Stubbing out her cigarette, her hands shook as she drew Quirke's mobile from her pocket and pressed the home button. The keypad appeared. She stared at the screen, trying to fathom the phone's secrets. She'd seen countless films in which the hero must crack a passcode to retrieve vital information and save the day but this wasn't a movie. The likelihood of chancing upon the right combination was near to zero.

There was, however, one long shot. It was surely possible that Quirke had recorded the passcode in the yellow notebook stolen from his flat.

By a man who wore red socks.

And kept a key to his house in a basket of dead geraniums.

Forty-Nine

Morgan made it to Holloway Road just after midday. Parking at a discreet distance from Rossiter's house, she sat in the Mini, waiting for a bickering couple to pass. Stepping out of the car, she was assailed by the stench of rotting garbage from the recycling centre. Covering her nose, she scanned the down-at-heel terrace. The unhappy couple had rounded the corner. There was no one else in sight, no sign of Rossiter's car.

Morgan rang the doorbell three times, to make sure the house was empty. She reached into the hanging basket, fingers probing the powdery soil until she found the key.

The house was silent. She started on the ground floor. The sitting-room bookshelves were still crammed with paperbacks on anger management and addiction but there was no sign of the yellow notebook. Entering the kitchen, her eyes roved the room: the walk-in pantry, the outsize American fridge. Sliding open a drawer, she froze as her mobile rang.

Donna Goshawk.

Oh, Christ …

'Yes, Donna?'

The DS was quick to put Morgan out of her misery.

'I'm not calling about the body in the car.'

A surge of relief. *Thank God.*

'Where are you?'

Morgan hesitated.

'London. Seeing a friend.'

'Are you near a TV?'

'Why?' Her heart skipped a beat.

'Watch Sky News.'

Morgan hurried back to the sitting room and turned on the TV. A Botox blonde was interviewing Danny Kilcannon. The high-definition TV made the cuts and bruises on his face appear even more severe than in real life.

'So let's cut to the chase, Danny. You were friends with Lissa's mother, am I right?'

'Yes. Morgan and I were at school together.'

'Childhood sweethearts?'

'Something like that.'

'And she supported you while you were in prison? Believed in your innocence, ran your campaign website, helped to prepare your case for the Court of Appeal?'

Danny nodded.

'She was very loyal. I'm incredibly grateful for everything she did.'

The interviewer couldn't prevent a hint of mockery from entering her voice.

'So, have you spoken to "loyal" Morgan since you slept with her daughter? Since the sex tape went viral?'

'Yes,' said Danny calmly. 'She's very angry. I don't blame her. The fact that what happened between me and Lissa was a private matter between two consenting adults is irrelevant. I behaved disgracefully.'

'Do you know who uploaded the sex tape to the internet?'

He shook his head.

'There are only three possibilities. Unless Lissa shared it with someone else, it could only have been leaked by me, Lissa herself, or the police. They took my phone for analysis.'

The interviewer raised an eyebrow.

'You're saying the police leaked the tape?'

'Or possibly Lissa. It certainly wasn't me,' said Danny. 'As for sleeping with her, I should have known better. I've apologised to Morgan and, if she's watching, I apologise again.'

'What about Lissa?' said the interviewer. 'If she's watching, what would you like to say to her?'

Danny turned to face the camera.

'Lissa, please get in touch with someone – preferably your mum – but just contact anyone – the police, your father, me – so we know you're safe and well.'

Morgan studied those familiar grey-green eyes.

Who can we trust?

'Many people saw you make a similar TV appeal four years ago,' said the presenter, 'when your wife went missing. Despite your acquittal for Zoe's murder, a lot of people say you have questions to answer about Rowena – and now about Lissa. What do you say to those people?'

'I totally understand,' said Danny. 'If I were watching this I'd be thinking, *how can I trust this man*?'

The woman leaned forward. Scenting blood.

'And? How can we?'

Danny spread his hands.

'I'm innocent. I don't expect anyone to take my word for it but the sooner Rowena is found – and the sooner Lissa comes home – the sooner we can all get on with our lives.'

'And what will that mean for you?'

'I'm not sure,' said Danny. 'Some kind of normality.'

The interviewer leaned back in her chair.

'May I ask what happened to your face?'

Danny took a breath before answering.

'A lot of people believe I got away with murder. A bunch of them gave me a beating.' He shrugged. 'It's something I have to live with. But what matters is finding Lissa.'

'Danny Kilcannon, thank you for talking to us.'

'Thank you.'

Morgan watched, bracing herself for 'breaking news' about a young woman's body in a burned out car but there was nothing, just a Christmas ad for Asda. She turned off the television and spoke into her mobile.

'Why would he go on TV?'

'He's rebranding himself,' said Donna. 'Trying to make the world think he's Mr Nice Guy, not a sleazebag who gets off on having sex with teenage girls and ...'

Her voice tailed off. Morgan couldn't stop her mind from finishing the sentence.

... and murdering them.

Donna was saying something else.

'We've news on Lissa. The tech guys have been analysing her phone.'

'And?'

'Just one text since she went missing,' said Donna. 'The one she sent to Danny. No calls, no texts, no web activity.'

Morgan was silent for a moment. She'd been hoping for confirmation that Lissa had been using her mobile regularly and was simply in hiding.

'Can you be sure it was Lissa who sent the text?'

'No.'

'So if Danny had her phone, he could have sent it to himself? To make it appear that she's alive and well?'

'Correct.'

Morgan thought for a moment.

'I need to speak to Jacqui.'

'Hold on.'

She waited, listening to muffled voices in the background, then Jacqui Farmiloe came on the line, her voice laced with sympathy.

'I'm sure it wasn't easy for you to watch Danny just now. And I know Donna's told you about the body in the car.'

'Yes.'

'We're moving as fast as possible, doing everything we can. But it's important to remember, Morgan, there are thousands of missing women. It could be anyone. We simply didn't want you to hear about it on the news.'

Morgan was tired of platitudes, of being tormented by anxiety, of not being able to speak her mind.

'Why did Quirke recant his testimony against Danny?'

Jacqui sounded nonplussed.

'Because he lied at the trial.'

'But why?'

A pause.

'All we know is what he told the Court of Appeal. He was menaced by someone threatening to flay him alive with a Stanley knife. So he lied about what he saw the night Zoe died. But conscience got the better of him so he recanted.' She paused before adding, 'Worst day of my life.'

Morgan was trying to keep her voice steady.

'Why did you drop the Suzi Maitliss rape case against Quirke?'

'What does that have to do with anything?'

'That's what I'd like to know.'

A sigh.

'My hands were tied,' said Jacqui. 'The packaging containing Quirke's DNA was damaged. His sample was contaminated. It would never have stood up in court.'

Morgan frowned. Something wasn't right but there was no sense in antagonising the woman leading the hunt for Lissa.

'Get some rest,' said Jacqui. 'We'll let you know the second we have news.'

Pocketing her phone, Morgan looked out of the window, checking for any sign of Rossiter making an unexpected return. Then she resumed her search for the yellow notebook.

She drew a blank in the study, likewise in the spare room. Entering the master bedroom, she paused in the doorway. There was a stack of books by the bed: a history of meditation, a book on cocaine addiction, a memoir chronicling a woman's struggle with depression.

But it was the document case that drew Morgan's eye – slim, leather. She'd seen it before, on the day Rossiter first came to her house trying to persuade her to spy on Danny. True, the reporter had made what seemed to be a routine offer – just a hack buying up a source. But there had been something odd about the proposal, something underhand. Had he been trying to enlist her help? Or buy her silence?

She picked up the leather case, slid her hand inside and pulled out a yellow notebook.

Caleb Quirke's initials were on the cover. The first page contained a handwritten list of numbers.

Bank account.

NHS number.

National Insurance number.

Halfway down the list was the word *phone* next to a number: 7836.

The hairs on the nape of Morgan's neck prickled as she recognised the digits.

Danny's prison number.

FF7836 was on every letter he'd sent from jail. This was no coincidence – it was a numerical hair-shirt for Quirke, a constant reminder of an innocent man behind bars. Quirke's conscience would have been troubled every time he switched on his mobile.

Morgan entered the number, watching the keypad morph into the most unlikely 'wallpaper' image she'd ever seen. Jesus on the Cross.

She wasted no time trying to fathom the workings of the dead man's mind. What mattered were the contents of his phone. She scrolled through the texts. Nothing of note. Then she tapped the *photos* app and opened the *camera roll*. A grid of thumbnail pictures: a church, a field of poppies, a sunset, but no faces, no people.

Scrolling down, she felt a frisson of anticipation as she saw the arrow that denoted a video clip. Heart hammering, she pressed 'play'.

Darkness, pitch black.

A scream.

A girl.

Light streaming from a window.

The footage is jerky. Takes a moment to work out what she's looking at.

A night-time view of Dover Holiday Park.

Light spills from a chalet. The holder of the camera-phone – Quirke, presumably – is thirty yards away, maybe less. Morgan can hear panting, as though he's been running. Then his voice, a breathless commentary.

'It kicked off a few minutes ago ... Someone yelling in the chalet ... Sounded like a girl, maybe two ... I heard laughter so I thought everything was OK – just kids mucking about ... But now ...'

He breaks off as another scream comes from the A-frame chalet then silence falls. The footage grows jerkier as Quirke walks towards the chalet, stopping in his tracks as the door opens.

A figure emerges.

A man, his face in shadow, oblivious to the fact that he's being observed. Suddenly, he's running, pausing by a lamppost, trying to get his bearings, then haring away. But not before Morgan catches a glimpse of his face.

Clive Rossiter.

The footage shows the reporter vanishing into the night. Then the camera-phone jerks back towards the chalet as a second figure emerges.

A young woman? A girl? Her face is lost in shadow. Morgan watches as she follows the direction taken by Rossiter, running past the lamppost.

Chelsea Farmiloe.

She looks young. Fourteen? Maybe fifteen? As she runs, something – a piece of paper – flutters from her pocket. She doesn't notice, disappearing into the shadows.

Morgan can hear Quirke's muttering, the footage becoming jerkier as he approaches the chalet.

'Holy Mary, mother of God ...'

He stoops to pick up the piece of paper. Morgan can make out a single word at the top – 'contract' – then the camera is jerked away, back towards the chalet. Quirke approaches the door, muttering under his breath.

'Oh, sweet Jesus ...'

Something on the floor, a bundle in the hallway.

No, not a bundle.

A girl ...

A pale, thin arm ...

A pool of blood . . .

A freckled face.

Eyes open.

Staring.

Zoe.

Morgan hears Quirke's voice again, babbling to himself.

'Oh, Lord . . . Oh, Lord, oh dear sweet Lord above . . . please, God, have mercy . . .'

And now the camera is jerking crazily as he breaks into a run. Away from the chalet. Away from the blood. Away from the girl with the lifeless eyes.

The footage cuts out.

Morgan stared at the phone. Head swimming, she got to her feet and focused on making a swift exit. Smoothing the bed, she backed out of the room, eyes darting everywhere, anxious to leave no trace. She hurried downstairs, ensuring she'd left the living room as she found it. Then the kitchen. A last look around.

She froze. A sound in the hall. A key in the door.

Fifty

She stole into the pantry.

Closed the door.

Held her breath.

Listening to footsteps entering the kitchen.

A jangle of keys on the table.

The fridge door opening.

The clink of a bottle.

A cough.

Rossiter was home.

Listening as he poured a drink, she prayed he wasn't hungry, heading for the pantry.

She heard his mobile ringing. His voice on the other side of the door as he answered the call.

'Hello?'

She exhaled silently, listening.

'She's on her way,' he said. 'Any idea what she wants?' He fell silent for a moment. 'I'll call when we're done.'

Surely he could hear her heartbeat? Could sense her presence? He would open the door any second and …

Doorbell.

A long, insistent ring. The sound of trouble.

Morgan focused on Rossiter's footsteps as he left the kitchen. Tucking Quirke's notebook into her belt, she reached for her mobile while straining to hear the reporter's voice – distant now, but still audible. She swiped her phone, found the app she needed and took another deep breath.

'Come in.'

Footsteps entering the kitchen: Rossiter's and the visitor's.

'Something to drink?'

'Nope.'

A female voice. Curt, bordering on rude. It took a moment for Morgan to identify the speaker.

'Let's get straight to the fucking point, yeah?'

Chelsea Farmiloe.

'I must get the name of your charm school,' said Rossiter.

'Fuck off.'

Morgan heard the sound of a cigarette being lit.

Rossiter again. 'Feel free to smoke.'

Chelsea ignored his sarcasm.

'I need money. Ten grand.'

A stunned silence. Then Rossiter again – incredulous.

'You're not seriously trying to blackmail me?'

'Don't talk shit. Just sort the money.'

A pause before he spoke again.

'Your mother knows you're here.'

'Like I give a fuck.'

'If it weren't for her you'd be in prison.'

'Makes two of us,' said Chelsea. Morgan could hear steel in the girl's voice. 'Ten grand or I tell everyone you killed Zoe.'

'But I didn't,' said Rossiter.

Clutching her phone, Morgan's knuckles were white, her body rigid with tension as she listened to the stand-off. The journalist was struggling to keep his voice even.

'Your playmates will testify about your "virgins for sale" scam,' he said.

In her mind's eye, Morgan conjured the scene outside the Pleasureland Hotel. The seedy-looking sixty-something man in the blazer and cravat, sitting next to Chelsea in the white Range Rover. The other girl, the one in school uniform. Thirteen? Fourteen at most.

Virgins for sale.

'Will you tell everyone how you were planning to fuck Zoe?' said Chelsea, her voice laced with mockery.

'Not true,' said Rossiter. 'I was following up a story.'

'Off your fucking face,' said Chelsea, temper flaring. 'Half Colombia up your nose and enough alcohol to sink a ship.'

'*You* dragged Zoe into your sleazy little scheme,' said Rossiter. His anger was starting to simmer. '*You* were the one coked out of your skull. *You* hit Zoe with the hammer.'

'Shouldn't have backed out, should she?'

'I would never have gone through with having sex with her.' The reporter was getting agitated. 'I was there for one reason only: to get the story. "Cop's daughter pimps underage virgins".'

'Bollocks,' said Chelsea. 'You were off your face and you'd have fucked her if she'd let you. Why else did you bring all that cash?'

'To look like a punter. To get the story.' The reporter's voice was rising. 'It was you who ran to Mummy. You told her what happened in the chalet, not me.'

'Who else would have dug us *both* out of the shit?' Chelsea was yelling now. 'Who else could make Quirke lie about what he saw? Make his rape charge go away? Who else could frame Kilcannon?'

Morgan's heart was pounding.

Who else could frame Kilcannon?

Five words that vindicated him.

The revelation that Danny had been framed by Detective Inspector Jacqui Farmiloe didn't prove that Lissa was alive but Morgan felt a surge of renewed hope. If he hadn't killed Zoe then surely he was the man Morgan believed him to be – incapable of harming her daughter. She was bursting to storm into the kitchen, to confront the liars who had wreaked such havoc in so many lives, but there was no choice but to stay silent and bide her time. Chelsea was still in full flow.

'I hit Zoe with the hammer but you were there, mate. Which makes you an accomplice. It's joint enterprise. And you're guilty as fuck.'

'Of what?'

'Perverting the course of fucking justice!' Chelsea was shouting again. 'Sell me out and I'll go to prison … *but you'll go with me!*'

There was more but Morgan's head was spinning as she tried to focus on what she was hearing. As the showdown continued, two things became clear: it had been Rossiter who had left the white lilies on Zoe's grave – driven by guilt and remorse; he'd also broken into Morgan's house, looking for anything incriminating that she might have found while investigating Quirke.

'Hashtag moron!' said Chelsea. 'Mum says you left the toilet seat up, which meant that Morgan realised someone was snooping. And it's only Mum putting the kibosh on what the SOCOs found that's keeping you from three hots and a cot!'

Morgan could hear beeping. Someone dialling on a mobile.

'Who are you calling?' said Chelsea.

'Your mother. She needs to know you're trying to blackmail me.'

'What do you think she'll do about it? Same as when I told her what happened to Zoe. *Fuck all!* Know why? Because she does whatever it takes to make sure I'm OK. *Because that's what mums do!*'

Silence fell. Morgan felt sure they must be able to hear her heart hammering. When Rossiter spoke again he was making an effort to control his temper.

'I'm not giving you ten grand. Because you're forgetting something. Your mother. She covered up for you ...'

'For *us*—'

' ... she fixed it so Kilcannon went to prison,' continued Rossiter. 'Which means if you go down, I go down. *But so does she.*' He paused for effect. 'And who'll look after your father then? Who'll pay his carers and wipe his arse?'

Morgan heard a tap running, someone clinking a glass. Then Chelsea's voice again. Less confident now.

'Eight grand and you'll never see me again.'

'Get out of my house.'

The sound of the glass smashing.

'Five. Final offer.'

'Out. Now!'

Silence. Then Chelsea's footsteps as she stormed out of the kitchen, pausing in the doorway.

'You're going to regret this for the rest of your shitty life.'

The sound of the front door opening and closing. Then silence.

Morgan heard Rossiter dialling on his mobile. He waited for the call to connect.

'She's out of control,' he said. 'We need to talk.' A pause. 'I'll meet you there.'

Morgan listened as he snatched up his keys and left the kitchen. The front door opened and closed. Silence descended. Moments later, she heard a car drive away. She counted to twenty before emerging from the pantry.

Stepping around the broken glass, she slipped into the hall and opened the front door, just a crack. The street was deserted. She replaced the key among the dead geraniums then closed the door and strode quickly to her Mini. As she settled behind the wheel, she could feel the tension in her shoulders. She hadn't yet relaxed her grip on her phone but only now did she dare tap 'playback' on the voice memo app. She held her breath.

Two voices, faint but audible.

First Chelsea.

Let's get straight to the fucking point, yeah?

Then Rossiter.

I must get the name of your charm school.

As the rest of the conversation began to play, Morgan felt her face crease into a smile.

Fifty-One

She sat at her kitchen table, lit a roll-up and stared at Quirke's phone.

Vindicated.

Four years of fighting. Defying the sceptics. Keeping the faith. Then Danny's betrayal with Lissa. Her disappearance. The suspicion. Sleepless nights. Fear. But now Morgan knew for sure. He didn't kill Zoe.

OK, so he had slept with Lissa. Things would never be the same, but none of that mattered so long as Lissa was alive. So long as the body in the burned out car wasn't Lissa's.

She dialled Danny's number.

'Hi, this is Danny. You know what to do.'

'It's me,' she said. 'Call as soon as you can.'

She couldn't give details, not in a message: too much to say, too much to explain. She flipped open the yellow notebook. A drawing of Jesus on the Cross. Below, a prayer in Quirke's handwriting.

Almighty God, Maker of heaven and earth, I humbly pray thee to look mercifully upon me, thy wicked servant, and forgive my mortal sins.

Another drawing: a second figure on a crucifix. Quirke himself. And underneath, his confession.

The doctors say I'll die within the year. I swear that I will do everything in my power to ensure that an innocent man is exonerated, a wrong righted. Here is my confession.

Danny Kilcannon was not at the Dover Holiday Park on the night Zoe Munro died. I lied to save my own skin and have paid the highest price: no peace in four years and now terminal cancer. I am a sinner, guilty of perjury and rape. I hang my head in shame.

Morgan turned the page, devouring the dead man's bid for redemption.

I forced myself on Suzi Maitliss. She took her own life. May God forgive me. DI Farmiloe arrested me. DNA proved that I'd had sex with Suzi against her will. But I'd seen the name 'Farmiloe' on the virginity contract dropped by Chelsea. I told DI Farmiloe that I'd witnessed her daughter running from the chalet on the night Zoe was murdered. I showed her a photocopy of the virginity contract, with her daughter's signature on it, and told her that I have the original, along with video footage of Chelsea at the scene.

I vowed to take my secret to the grave if she guaranteed the case against me would never come to court.

Forgive me, Father, for I have sinned.

Morgan re-read the confession then flipped to another page of the notebook. A sheet of A4 was stapled inside – the piece of paper Chelsea had dropped while running from the chalet.

Contract

This is to certify that I, Zoe Munro, swear I have never EVER had sex with anyone and am a total virgin. I promise to have sex with _____ in exchange for £1,000 (one thousand pounds) cash. I promise to give half the money (five hundred pounds) to Chelsea Farmiloe who introduced me to the man whose name is above.

Signed_____ Zoe Munro

Witness_____ Chelsea Farmiloe

Morgan remembered Danny confiding in her about Zoe stealing money in order to leave home. *'I need two grand then you won't see me for dust.'*

She stubbed out her cigarette and tried his number. Still no response.

Who can we trust?

Scrolling through her contacts, she found Nigel Cundy's name. She hesitated. The shrink had tried to atone for photographing Lissa but he wasn't someone Morgan could rely on. She was tempted to call Cameron, but what use was he, six thousand miles away? Come to think of it, when had he ever been any use?

She scrolled to another name. Donna answered after two rings.

'How's it going?'

'Are you with Jacqui?'

Donna sounded confused.

'No, why?'

'We need to talk.'

'Is this about the body in the car? We've contacted Lissa's dentist but these things take time—'

Morgan interrupted.

'It's about your boss.'

A pause.

'What do you mean?'

'Can you come to my place?' said Morgan. She didn't want to elaborate on the phone. 'It's important.'

No hesitation this time.

'I'm on my way.'

Morgan tried to calm herself by taking a long, hot shower. She stood at the kitchen window, sipping wine and marshalling her thoughts. Had Jacqui Farmiloe corrupted the expert witness at Danny's trial? Had the crucial blood-spatter evidence been rigged? If so, the DI's wall of secrets and lies was set to come crashing down.

Two tasks remained. Find Lissa. Get justice for Zoe.

As Morgan lit the roll-up she saw a car crunching over the shingle, Donna at the wheel. Pulling to a halt, the DS gave a wave and a smile. Morgan didn't smile back.

Twenty minutes later, they were side by side on the sofa, staring at Quirke's phone. Morgan had showed Donna the video and played the recording of Rossiter's showdown with Chelsea. Wearing latex gloves, the policewoman was flipping through Quirke's notebook, her eyes wide with disbelief.

'This is so unreal.'

'It's real,' Morgan said. 'Your boss framed Danny to save her daughter's skin.'

Donna was shaking her head slowly.

'Jacqui – *of all people*.'

'What do we do now?'

The DS took a moment to gather herself.

'We go to the Police Commissioner.'

Morgan shook her head.

'I don't trust anyone. Especially at the top.'

Donna nodded.

'Understood.' She thought for a moment. 'I've a contact at the Independent Police Complaints Commission. We'll drive to London, see him tonight.'

Morgan felt a wave of relief.

'OK,' she said. 'Let's go.'

She watched as the DS sealed the phone in an evidence bag, along with the notebook, then got to her feet.

'This is going to be the mother of all shit-storms,' said Donna. 'Are you ready?'

Morgan nodded.

'I've been ready for years.'

Darkness was closing in as they drove away, Donna at the wheel, Morgan cradling the evidence bag on her lap. She tried to imagine how Donna was feeling. Her boss's career would end in disgrace and prison. For Chelsea, too, a lengthy sentence loomed. As for Rossiter, he deserved everything he got.

Donna sighed.

'It's all *so* fucked up.'

Morgan's mobile rang.

Cundy.

'Hello, Nigel.'

'I talked to my cousin. About the Quirke rape case.'

'Too late,' said Morgan. 'I've got all I need.'

'Including the fact that Jacqui Farmiloe is having an affair?'

Morgan stiffened, pressing the phone to her ear.

'I'm listening.'

'Been going on for years.' He paused for effect. 'Here's the kicker: her lover's a woman.'

Morgan felt a rush of blood to the head.

'Do you have a name?'

'No,' said Nigel. 'Just someone she works with.'

Morgan fought to remain calm.

'Thanks for calling.'

She pocketed her phone, feeling Donna's eyes on her.

'Who was that?'

'A friend.'

She fell silent, heart pounding, mind racing.

The single-track road was deserted. No sign of life on the flatlands, just the open spaces Morgan knew so well. She turned to the policewoman.

'Where are we going?'

Donna frowned.

'I told you,' she said. 'My friend at the IPCC.'

Morgan glanced at the locket nestling above the woman's collarbone. She inched her hand down to release the buckle on her seatbelt then reached across and snatched the locket, yanking the chain *hard*.

'What the fuck ...?'

Donna stamped on the brake. Morgan prised open the locket.

A photograph of Jacqui Farmiloe.

The car juddered, skidding across the road.

Grabbing the evidence bag, Morgan pushed open the door and rolled out, hitting the ground then crying out in pain and rolling over on the tarmac. Scrambling to her feet, she raced across the shingle and into the darkness.

Running, running, running.

Fifty-Two

The torch beam was getting closer. Lying flat, shards of flint digging into her ribs, Morgan peered over the shingle ridge. She watched the policewoman combing the beach, the torchlight ranging over an abandoned boat, a cluster of sea kale, a heap of rusting scrap.

Raising her eyes to the skies, Morgan gave silent thanks for the bank of thick cloud. No moon, no stars. The Dungeness road was unlit, the darkness total apart from the power station lights in the distance.

Donna was less than fifty yards away. Morgan could hear pebbles crunching under her feet. The shack behind which she was hiding was padlocked. Breaking a window was not an option: her pursuer was within earshot and getting closer with every passing second.

Morgan could feel her heartbeat. Her hands and face were bleeding, grazed during the fall from the car. She'd lost a shoe, her legs were bruised, her jeans tattered and torn.

The torchbeam cut through the darkness, heading in her direction. Ducking below the ridge, her fingers closed around a piece of flint. She waited until the torch was aiming away from the shack then got to her feet, drew back her arm and hurled the stone as far as she could. The clatter was barely audible above the waves but it did the trick. The beam of light jerked away as Donna scrambled over the shingle, directing her search closer to the shoreline.

Bent low, Morgan searched for her mobile but her pockets were empty. It had fallen from her jacket during her tumble from the car. Her spirits crashed – until she remembered Quirke's phone. She reached into the evidence bag and drew it out. The screen was shattered – another casualty of the fall. She pressed the home button.

Nothing.

She counted to ten, trying to remain calm. The phone itself was irrelevant, so long as there was a way to retrieve the data. She prayed the video had not been damaged. She had no idea how the technology worked. Was the footage stored somewhere? The Cloud? Whatever the Cloud was.

She backed away from the shack and hobbled towards the track that carried the Romney, Hythe & Dymchurch Railway across the shingle. The stones dug into the sole of her bare foot.

Forget the pain. Mind over matter. One step at a time.

The torchlight was still visible, distant now but ranging tirelessly across the shingle ridges. Morgan increased her pace, keeping low as she stumbled through shallow quarries, across dunes and the flotsam and jetsam of the beach.

No lights in the nearby houses, no sign of life. Staying parallel with the road, Morgan hobbled on, towards the one place certain to be inhabited: the twenty-four-hour petrol station. She glanced over her shoulder. The torchlight had gone. Had Donna given up the hunt? Or was she even now calling Jacqui? Maybe Rossiter, too? Morgan scrabbled over a clump of sea kale, eyes piercing the darkness, watching for movement, light, *danger*.

As she rounded the headland, there it was, in the distance: the garish glow of the petrol station. She could make out the pumps on the deserted forecourt. She glanced over her shoulder. No headlights, no sign of her pursuer. But it was getting harder to ignore the pain in her foot. The cuts were red, raw, stinging. Her legs ached. Dare she leave the safety of the beach? Hobble onto the tarmac?

A few hundred yards more ...

Then what?

Call the police ... I'm in danger.

Who from?

A police officer.

Even if the attendant believed her, what if Donna arrived, flashing her smile, *her ID*?

Morgan would take her chances.

A hundred yards from the forecourt, she could see the attendant. Alone at the till. Not a customer in sight.

But now ... the sound of a car. Morgan ducked behind a ridge of shingle, gasping at the searing pain in her legs. The car cruised past the petrol station. At the wheel, Jacqui Farmiloe.

Morgan held her breath and watched the woman drive past, eyes focused on the forecourt, the shop. The car picked up speed. Morgan watched its tail lights recede then walked towards the petrol station. Yards away from the forecourt, she could see the attendant replenishing cigarette packs behind the counter. She saw herself through his eyes: torn clothes, dishevelled, bleeding. She felt a surge of optimism. Surely he would *have* to help. But the flicker of hope was extinguished by the sound of the car returning. Jacqui was back.

Morgan darted to the left, zigzagged across the shingle then flung herself to the ground. She watched Jacqui pull to a halt on the forecourt. The DI walked into the shop and flashed her ID at the man behind the till. Morgan backed away, retreating into the shadows.

A minute later, she watched Jacqui emerge from the shop and cast a final glance around the forecourt before driving away. Asking for help was no longer an option. Farmiloe had made sure of that. Lying on the shingle, Morgan gathered her wits and stared up at the night sky, listening to her own breathing.

And now the sound of another engine, the rumble of a sports car. Morgan propped herself on her elbows and saw a red Porsche pull onto the forecourt. The driver was a petite blonde in her forties. Stepping out of the car, tottering on high heels, she began to fill the tank with petrol while checking her mobile.

Moments later, a white Transit van arrived, pulling up next to the Porsche. A burly man got out and busied himself with the pump, yards from where Morgan lay. She saw him take stock of the high-heeled blonde, following her every movement as she click-clacked into the shop. The van driver watched as the woman paid for her petrol. Finished at the pump, he followed her inside. Morgan saw the woman turn as he spoke to her. The attendant joined in. Laughter all round.

But Morgan's attention was no longer on the shop. In his eagerness to talk to the woman, the van driver had left his door ajar. The keys dangled from the ignition. Morgan got to her feet, tucked the evidence bag into her belt and hobbled towards the forecourt. The man was addressing the blonde woman, his back to the pumps. Morgan climbed into the van and started the engine. The driver turned, eyes wide in alarm, and raced out of the shop as Morgan floored the accelerator, missing him by inches. His face was contorted with rage.

'*Fuck you!*'

She swerved wildly then steered the van onto the road. Tyres squealing. Adrenaline surging. Speeding towards the one person she could trust.

Rain was falling as she drove along the coast, wipers screeching across the glass. She checked her reflection. The cuts to her face were worse than she'd feared.

Driving through coastal towns and villages, she made sure to stay within the speed limit and keep a lookout for police. It wouldn't take long to circulate the van's registration number along with her description. She was trying to fend off a burgeoning sense of paranoia, but there was no way of knowing just how many police officers were party to DI Farmiloe's secrets and lies.

The radio told Morgan what she already knew. Police were still working to identify the remains of the body in the burned out car. No mention of the victim's gender.

Please God, let it not be Lissa.

As Dover Castle came into view, dominating the hill over-looking the port, Morgan felt a wave of relief. Passing another landmark – the Martello tower – she turned onto the lane leading to Danny's cottage. The tree-lined track was deserted. She drove into the layby at the rear of the tower, hiding the van from sight and turning off the engine.

The silence was broken by seagulls in the distance. Morgan locked the van then hobbled along the track, turning her collar against the rain. She caught a glimpse of something stirring in the trees. Owls? Bats? She kept up her pace, walking as fast as her aching limbs would allow.

Rounding the bend, she could see the cottage at the end of the lane. As she drew closer, her spirits sank. No Mercedes, no lights, no sign that Danny was home. She thought back to the last time she'd seen him – on TV appealing for Lissa to get in touch.

Had he listened to Morgan's messages? Was he still refusing to speak to her? Or had he returned her calls, leaving a voicemail on the mobile that lay on a beach miles away?

The cottage was still scarred by graffiti.

Kiddie killer!

Scum!

She rapped on the door. No response. She walked around the side of the cottage. Peering into the sitting room, she pressed her face against the window, then stepped backwards and called out, into the darkness.

'Danny!'

Silence.

'Danny! I know what really happened to Zoe!'

Her eyes searched the windows. No sign of movement. The rain was falling harder now, her bare foot wet, bloody and numb, the chill spreading through her body. She retraced her steps along the track. Time to regroup. Get warm. Plan the next step.

Reaching the van, she fumbled for the key. Then she stood still as she heard a noise.

Rhythmic.

A *clanking* of metal on metal.

Clank. Clank. Clank.

The noise stopped. Morgan held her breath. She was on full alert, senses straining to catch the slightest sound.

Clank.

She stared at the van. Was the noise coming from inside?

Clank. Clank.

No.

It was distant. Faint. Rhythmic.

Clank. Clank. CLANK.

She stepped away from the van. The sound was louder now. It was coming from the Martello tower.

Fifty-Three

Ivy had taken hold of the brickwork, infesting every inch of the circular walls. Morgan walked around the base of the tower – the size of a small house – her ears straining to catch the slightest sound.

Clank. Clank. CLANK.

The noise was distant, rising from underground. As it died away, the only sound was rain falling through the trees. The remnants of an iron ladder clung to the wall of the tower, leading to a boarded-up doorway on which someone had daubed graffiti.

Asylum Seekers Out!

Morgan placed a foot on the bottom rung, applying tentative pressure. The iron was old and had rusted but remained firm. Six steps took her up to a platform that was level with the doorway. The wood was splintered and rotten. Her first kick made no impact. A second made a dent. A third made a hole.

Clank. Clank. Clank.

Morgan kicked again at the weather-beaten wood, widening the hole until it was large enough to stick her head through. She

kneeled on the platform, staring into the musty-smelling blackness. Reaching for her lighter, she held out its flickering flame.

Clank. Clank.

She waited ... but there was no third *clank* – the first variation
in rhythm. This was no mechanical noise, this was sound made
by a person.

'Hello?' Her voice echoed in the darkness.

Clank. Clank. Clank.

The noise was louder now, more insistent.

'Can you hear me?'

Clank. Clank. Clank.

Her mouth was dry.

'Lissa?'

Clank. Clank. Clank. Clank. CLANK ...

'Lissa!'

ClankClankClankClankClankClankClank ...

'If this is Lissa, knock three times.'

Silence.

Then the sweetest sound she had ever heard.

Clank.

Clank.

Clank.

Morgan kicked at the rotten boards. Tore at the hole with her
hands. Wrenching the splintered wood until the cavity was large
enough to climb through, she bent her head and stepped inside
the tower. She could smell the centuries of damp, feel the ancient
bricks and timbers beneath her feet. Stretching out a hand, she
steadied herself against a crossbeam.

'Lissa?'

Clank.

Clank.

CLANK.

Clutching the beam, she took one careful step after another, reaching out to touch a wall. Another step, this time with her bare foot. She gasped as her toe stubbed something solid, a ring of metal the size of a horseshoe.

No, not a horseshoe – a handle. An iron handle protruding from a pile of stones and rocks. She began to move them, one by one, piling them in a heap. They covered what appeared to be a trapdoor.

She tugged. The timbers wouldn't budge. Clamping the lighter between her teeth, she grabbed the ring with both hands and heaved.

It *was* a trapdoor. And it was moving.

One final heave raised the timbers. Morgan dragged the trapdoor aside then lost her balance and fell to the ground. The lighter fell from her mouth.

Clank.

Clank.

CLANK.

The noise was louder now. She groped in the darkness, feeling for the lighter.

'I'm here, Lissa. I'm coming!'

Reaching into the cavity, her fingers closed around an iron bar. She extended her arm further and found a second bar. Then a third.

A ladder.

She paused for breath. Probing the ground by her feet, she retrieved her lighter. Its glow illuminated the dirty-white chalk of the tunnel. Dimly recalling what Nigel Cundy had said about Dover's ancient network of subterranean defences, she began to climb down the ladder, descending into the darkness one step at a time.

Five steps.

Clank.

Fifteen.

Twenty.

Her feet hit the ground.

Clank.

Clank.

Stooping, she groped her way towards the noise. After a hundred yards, the tunnel curved around a corner. Her hands made contact with another piece of wood. She flicked the lighter again. Saw a low doorway, dark against the chalk walls.

Clank.

Clank.

CLANK.

The sound was coming from the other side of the doorway.

'Lissa?'

CLANKclankCLANKclankCLANK.

Stepping back, her leg brushed something solid. She ran her hands along the rusting metal. An iron pole – three feet long, one end wedged into the ground, the other propped at forty-five degrees, preventing anyone on the other side from opening the door. Morgan tugged hard. The pole began to move. A second heave did the trick. Flinging the bar aside, she thumped on the door.

'Push, Lissa! *Push!*' She hammered with her fists. 'Push! Kick! *Hard!*'

The timbers began to budge. She could hear banging on the other side of the door. Suddenly, it collapsed onto her. She hit the ground, winded, but feeling a surge of joy as she heard a whimper.

'*Mum ...*'

A hand reached out of the darkness. She flicked her lighter and gasped.

Her daughter's face was gaunt. Streaked with grime. Hair matted. Clothes torn. Fingernails bleeding. Teeth chattering.

But she was alive.

Wriggling free of the heavy door, Morgan's mind flashed to the first time she'd held her daughter – impossibly tiny. Exhausted but exhilarated, she'd been flooded with relief after seven hours' labour. She'd known then that nothing could ever surpass that feeling. But she'd been wrong. This was the shining moment. But it lasted no more than a second. Lissa was saying something, over and over again.

'He cut her up. He cut her up. *He cut her up ...*'

Morgan pulled Lissa to her, holding her tight, feeling her hard, skinny body.

'It's OK,' she said. 'I've got you. It's OK.'

But Lissa pulled away. Trembling, eyes wide with fear.

'Danny cut her up. *HE CUT HER UP!*'

Morgan gripped Lissa's hand.

'I don't understand what you're saying.'

Lissa took a deep breath. When she spoke, her words came out in short, staccato bursts.

'I woke in the night. Couldn't find him in the house.' She wiped her mouth with the back of her hand. 'I went to his workshop. He had his back to me and he was wearing this weird stuff: shower cap, overalls, mask ...' She broke off, closing her eyes and shaking her head, as though trying to rid herself of a memory too excruciating to bear. 'He had a hacksaw.' Her voice dropped to a whisper. 'And he was *sawing* ...' Her shoulders heaved. 'Bones ... I thought it was some kind of animal ... decomposed.' She gasped for air. 'But it was a body.'

Rowena.

Morgan tightened her grip on her daughter's hand.

'The *smell* ...' Lissa tailed off, still shaking her head from side to side. She stared at her mother, taking stock of her cuts and grazes.

'What happened to your face?'

'I'm fine,' said Morgan. 'Go on.'

Lissa swallowed hard.

'He sensed I was watching. Turned and grabbed me. Then he opened a trapdoor, forced me down here and locked me in.' She wiped her nose on her sleeve. 'At first he kept coming back with food and water. Said he knew I'd have to tell people what I'd seen. He was sorry but he needed time.'

'Needed time for what?'

'To work out what to do. But then he stopped coming. And I've been down here days and *days.*'

'Why didn't you make a noise before?' said Morgan. 'I've been here *so many times.*'

'I didn't dare. In case *he* heard me. But I got so *desperate ...*'

Lissa tailed off again, sobbing. As the tears flowed, Morgan took her hand and led her along the tunnel, towards the ladder. She needed to get her out of here. To hospital. Or home. Anywhere but this dark, dank place.

'Stay close.'

Numb with cold, she kept moving, hand raised, illuminating the way with the lighter. A hundred yards on, peering into the gloom, she came to the low timbered doorway. Something scuttled across her foot. Morgan let out a cry and dropped the lighter.

'Rats,' whispered Lissa. 'They're everywhere.'

Shuddering, Morgan steeled herself then crouched on her haunches, groping for the lighter. As her hand made contact with the bar that had held the door shut, she froze. The darkness was total, the silence absolute.

But someone was there.

On the other side of the door.

Around the curve.

Morgan knew Lissa could sense a presence too. She tightened her grip on her daughter's hand. Lissa crouched down beside her as Morgan's eyes roved the darkness, ears straining to catch the slightest movement, the slightest sound.

And there it was.

Almost inaudible.

Someone breathing.

He was yards away. Motionless. Listening.

Then a sound – *click*.

And the tunnel was flooded with light.

He entered through the doorway. The torch beam was blinding. Morgan raised a hand, shielding her eyes. Her fingers tightened their grip around Lissa's wrist. She heard Danny's voice.

'I wish you hadn't done this.' He took a step forward. 'It makes everything worse.'

Dazzled by the light, she could make out his silhouette, the toolbelt around his waist. He stared at Morgan's face.

'Why are you bleeding?'

Before Morgan could reply, Lissa's anger erupted.

'You sick *bastard*!'

Morgan dug her nails into her daughter's arm, silencing her. She kept her voice steady. She had only one card to play.

'I know you didn't kill Zoe,' she said. 'Get us out of here and I'll tell you how she died.'

He lowered the torch.

'What do you know?'

'Who killed Zoe,' said Morgan.

'Who?'

She studied his eyes. His face was set hard.

'*Who?*'

There was no softness, no sign of the boy she had once known, just a wild-eyed stranger with a hammer dangling from his belt, a desperate man who had been covering his tracks, strewing her path with false clues.

'You left Lissa's phone on the beach, to make me think she'd been nearby?'

A nod. Morgan took a breath, her mind racing.

'Take us somewhere safe,' she said. 'I'll tell you everything.'

He didn't move. Morgan could feel Lissa's anger rising. She tightened her grip on her daughter's arm.

'Let's go, Danny.'

His eyes blazed.

'Tell me what you know. Now!'

She watched his hand inch towards the hammer and made the only decision she could – to tell him everything. How Jacqui Farmiloe had framed him to protect her daughter. How Rossiter had colluded with the cover-up, desperate to save his own skin. How Quirke had lied to avoid being tried for rape. How the video on the dead man's mobile would ensure that Farmiloe and Rossiter got their just deserts – Chelsea too.

'But only if we get out of here.'

She let the silence stretch. Danny lowered the torch and sank down on his haunches, the handle of the hammer grazing the ground. The iron pole was by his feet.

'It's over for me.'

Morgan shook her head.

'You can do the right thing.'

'I'll be done for false imprisonment.' He nodded towards Lissa. 'And for what happened to Rowena. *But it was an accident ...*' His voice was thick with self-pity and despair. 'If she'd trusted me, everything would have been different. But she said I was capable of killing Zoe. My own stepdaughter ...'

'Why would she say that?'

He hung his head.

'I'd been violent.'

'To Rowena?'

A sheepish nod. Morgan thought back to his trial: the allegations of domestic violence, unsubstantiated until now.

'I hit her. But only twice.' He swallowed. 'She was going to tell the jury. My own wife saying I was capable of murder. It would have totally fucked my defence.' He wiped his mouth with the back of his hand. 'That's what the argument was about. But I swear it was an accident. She fell. Hit her head.' He stared at the ground.

'You hid her body?'

His jaw tightened. A nod.

'In the tunnels. Taped up in bin bags so the sniffer dogs wouldn't find her.'

Lissa's eyes widened.

'She's been rotting while you were in prison? For years?'

Another nod, almost imperceptible.

'I had to give her a proper burial when I got out. I even made a coffin. But Farmiloe was going to widen the search. *So I had no choice.*' He swallowed hard. 'I had to make Rowena … disappear.'

Lissa's voice was full of disgust.

'With a hacksaw?'

Danny studied the floor.

'Prison changes you,' he said. 'You … do things. Then you come out and you think you can go back to who you were. But you can't. What would have been unthinkable once becomes the only way to survive.'

'Like leaving me to die?' said Lissa.

He lowered his head further. Morgan kept her voice steady.

'What now, Danny?'

He said nothing for a moment then raised his head to meet her gaze.

'I can't go back to prison.'

Maybe it was the fear in his eyes, or his tone of voice, but Morgan knew she had to act. In a sweeping motion, she lashed out with her foot, kicked the torch from his hand then snatched up the iron bar, raising it with both hands and swinging it against the side of his skull. He staggered back then fell to the ground, motionless.

'Oh my God!'

Lissa's eyes were wide. Morgan grabbed the torch. She aimed the beam at Danny's body.

'Is he dead?' whispered Lissa.

Morgan took her daughter's hand.

'Let's go.'

But Lissa was rooted to the spot. Morgan pulled her away, dragging her through the doorway, along the tunnel, towards the ladder.

'Climb.'

Lissa obeyed, starting to sob as she hauled herself up.

One rung.

Two.

Three.

Morgan followed, dodging Lissa's feet as they flailed above her face.

'Keep going!'

She could smell the change in the air as they neared the surface. Lissa climbed the final rungs then hauled herself from the tunnel. Morgan followed suit, collapsing onto the floor of the tower, panting. The evidence bag was still tucked into her belt; she could feel the contents digging into her hip. Reaching out, she squeezed Lissa's fingers then lay still, gathering her breath.

'Is he dead?' said Lissa.

Morgan didn't reply straightaway.

'I don't know. But I had no choice.'

Lissa fell silent. When she spoke her voice was barely audible.

'I know it doesn't matter in the scheme of things,' she said, 'but I'm *so sorry* – about me and him ...'

Morgan cut her short.

'Not now.' She clambered to her feet. 'We need to call an ambulance for him, then we ...'

She broke off, hearing the sound of a car. Stepping forward, she peered through the hole in the boards.

Two vehicles were pulling to a halt alongside the white van. One was a police car. Its driver – a uniformed officer with a beard – stepped out into the rain and hurried towards the second car. He leaned into the passenger window and addressed the occupants.

Jacqui Farmiloe. Donna Goshawk.

Morgan strained to catch their conversation. It seemed the patrol officer had chanced upon the stolen van and reported his discovery.

'Nicked by a woman, apparently.'

He relayed the description of Morgan. She heard Jacqui's voice.

'OK, we'll take it from here.'

The policeman said something Morgan couldn't make out then got into his car and drove away. She watched as Jacqui made a brief call on her mobile then stepped out of the unmarked car, turning up her collar against the rain.

'*Who is she?*' whispered Lissa.

'*The one who framed Danny.*'

Morgan could see the fear in her daughter's eyes. Peering into the layby, she watched as Donna stepped out of the car. Silhouetted by the headlights, the DS stepped forward and shone a torch into the van's cab. Her boss snapped on a pair of latex gloves and opened the rear doors. She motioned for Donna to shine the torch inside the empty van.

As the policewomen conferred, another car pulled to a halt. The driver stepped out.

Rossiter.

Morgan watched as the reporter had a hurried exchange with Jacqui and Donna. Then her heart began to race as he took hold of the torch, turned towards the tower and shone the beam directly into her eyes.

Fifty-Four

She steered her daughter towards the ladder. Lissa's voice was a fearful hiss.

'I can't go back *down there*!'

Morgan grasped her shoulders.

'We have no choice,' she hissed. 'These are *bad* people.'

Lissa closed her eyes and turned her head away.

Danny's body ...

The darkness ...

The rats ...

Morgan watched her daughter take a deep breath then lower herself into the mouth of the tunnel. She tucked the torch in her belt, alongside the evidence bag. Then she followed Lissa down the ladder, listening to their pursuers entering the tower. As her feet touched the ground, the tunnel was flooded with torchlight from above. She heard Jacqui's voice.

'Morgan! We just need to talk!'

Without hesitating, she pulled Lissa into the tunnel, hobbling one minute, running the next. Switching on the torch, she rounded the curve then stooped through the doorway, steeling herself as she neared the spot where Danny had fallen.

No sign of him. Just a smear of blood on the ground.

'Oh my God …' said Lissa.

Morgan raised the torch, illuminating the chalk-white shadows that stretched into the distance. Behind them, she could hear Jacqui, Clive and Donna descending the ladder. She grabbed Lissa's hand.

'Run!'

They bent low, hurrying through the tunnel. Morgan switched off the torch. The darkness was absolute. She crept on, leading the way, feeling the curve of the walls with her hands. Reaching a fork in the tunnel, she glanced over her shoulder and saw a distant glimmer of light. She heard the faint sound of Donna's voice.

'Morgan!'

She quickened her pace, Lissa following on. Moments later, the glow from the torch had disappeared and the footsteps were no longer audible. Had their pursuers opted for the tunnel's other bore? Or were they creeping closer, taking advantage of the darkness? Morgan gripped Lissa's hand then stumbled onwards, into the blackness, trying to visualise the landscape above their heads: the hills behind Danny's cottage; the woods beyond his garden; the forbidding castle overlooking the Channel.

The air was musty, cold and dank. And now another smell – sweet but acrid. Ammonia? Her hands made out a second fork, another intersection. Following the left-hand curve, she hobbled on – ten yards, twenty – then missed her footing. The ground beneath her disappeared. She fell into a dip. Lissa followed suit, tumbling onto her mother. They lay there, gathering their breath. Listening.

Distant footsteps. Low voices. *Getting closer.*

Reaching out, Morgan's hands found a recess in the wall. The smell of ammonia was stronger now, stinging her eyes.

'Rat piss,' whispered Lissa.

Morgan shuddered, quelling the urge to retch. Should they hide in the recess, hoping their pursuers would pass by? A forlorn hope, but what choice did they have?

The footsteps were louder now, drawing closer with every second.

'Morgan?'

Jacqui's voice echoed along the tunnel. Morgan saw a distant glimmer from the torch. She heard another noise coming from inside the recess: a scratching followed by a frantic scurrying at her feet. Without thinking she snatched blindly into the darkness. Her timing was perfect. She could feel the rat squirming, struggling to escape her grip. Sinewy. Bristly. Then came a sharp, searing pain as the creature bit into her flesh.

Tightening her grip, she sprang to her feet and hurled the rat into the tunnel, towards the torchlight. It skittered away. A second later, she heard cries of revulsion in the distance.

Donna's voice.

'Jesus Christ!'

Rossiter.

'Fuck ... Fuck!'

The torchlight began to fade, along with the sound of receding footsteps. Soon the noise faded altogether and silence descended.

Reaching out, Morgan found Lissa's hand. The diversionary tactic had merely postponed the inevitable. Their pursuers would be back. She switched on the torch and glimpsed three more rats scurrying away into the shadows. This time, her disgust was tinged with a flicker of hope. If the creatures could get in, surely they could get *out*.

They moved on. There seemed no logic to the subterranean maze but as the ground began to slope upwards, they rounded a corner and saw a shaft of light shining from above.

Morgan heard Lissa's whisper.

'I think this is it. His workshop.'

The light illuminated a retracting aluminium ladder extending down into the tunnel. Morgan hesitated, straining to catch the slightest noise.

There it was again. The sound of footsteps.

Trying to ignore the pain in her bare, frozen foot, Morgan clambered up the ladder. At the top, she poked her head into the workshop. Rain hammered on the roof. Her eyes were wide, her pulse racing as she scanned the workbench, the racks of tools. No sign of Danny. Hoisting herself out of the tunnel, she turned and reached out to help Lissa take the final few steps.

Down below, the footsteps were closing in. Morgan raised the trapdoor on its hinge. Looking down, she saw Jacqui Farmiloe's upturned face, twenty feet below. They held each other's gaze.

'What kind of person are you?' said Morgan, her voice echoing down the shaft of the tunnel.

'One like you, Morgan.' The DI was panting, out of breath. 'We're mothers. We protect our own. Whatever it takes.'

Morgan held the woman's gaze.

'I am *nothing* like you.'

She saw Donna and Clive arriving, staring up at her. As the journalist began to climb the ladder, she let the trapdoor slam then rammed the bolt home. Her hands were shaking.

'Stay close,' she told Lissa, heading for the door.

They ran across the garden, buffeted by the wind and rain. The cottage was in darkness, the back door ajar. They crept inside. The kitchen was deserted. Tiptoeing into the hall, they headed for the front door. Morgan froze as she heard Danny's voice.

'This is all *so* fucked up.'

She turned. He was descending the staircase. Blood trickled down one side of his face, seeping from the wound Morgan had inflicted.

He was holding his shotgun.

'Danny ... this is *me*.' She gestured to Lissa. '*Us*.'

No trace of a smile. His voice was flat and lifeless.

'Don't talk.'

He gestured with the shotgun, indicating a small wicker basket on the window ledge.

'Keys.'

She stared at the shotgun then dipped her hand into the basket and grasped a set of keys. As she did so, her fingers closed around something else – something small, smooth and round. Without looking, she knew what it was. She showed him the pebble, holding it in her open palm. He stared at it but if she had been hoping to trigger a flood of rose-tinted nostalgia that would turn back the clock and change everything, she was disappointed.

'It's a pebble,' he said. His voice was expressionless. 'Plenty more on the beach.'

She gazed into his grey-green eyes. A stranger stared back.

And suddenly her fear was engulfed by a wave of exhaustion and crushing disappointment. She'd reached the end of the line, come so far, given so much. All that remained was to see this through to the end.

'What now?'

He opened the door and gestured with the shotgun.

'Car.'

'Mum?'

Lissa was trembling.

'Do as he says.'

She clasped her daughter's hand and hurried out to the Mercedes, through the lashing wind and rain. Raising his voice, Danny turned to Morgan.

'Drive.'

She sat behind the wheel. Lissa clambered into the rear. Danny got into the passenger seat and closed the door.

'We're not the people you need to punish,' said Morgan, trying to sound calmer than she felt. 'They're locked in the tunnel. Rossiter. Farmiloe. They're the enemy, Danny, not us.'

She could see his mind racing.

'You got in through the tower?'

'Yes.'

'OK,' he said. 'Let's go.'

She drove along the unmade road, gathering speed as she splashed through puddles and jolted over muddy ruts. The storm raged harder, rain pounding the car as she pulled to a halt in the layby. Danny got out. Brandishing the shotgun, he motioned for Morgan and Lissa to climb the ladder and enter the tower. He followed suit. Inside, rain dripping from his hair, mingling with streaks of blood on his face, he stared into the mouth of tunnel. He listened but there was no sound, no sign of life.

'Seal it.'

He watched as they dragged the trapdoor into place.

'This is insane,' said Morgan, panting. 'You can't leave them here.'

Danny jerked the shotgun towards the pile of rocks.

'Weigh it down.'

Morgan and Lissa did as instructed, dragging the rocks into a heap. When the trapdoor was covered, he brandished the gun again, forcing them out into the storm, back into the car.

'This needs to end, Danny,' said Morgan. 'Now.'

He ignored her.

'Drive to the cliffs.'

Morgan frowned.

'Which cliffs?'

He met her gaze.

'Our cliffs.'

They drove in silence, following the road that led to the coastal path. There was no traffic. The only sound was Lissa snivelling in the back and the rain hammering on the roof. After a mile, the headlamps picked out a turning.

'Here,' said Danny.

Morgan followed the unmade track. The rain was torrential now, the wind buffeting the car as they neared the expanse of grassland. Out at sea, a flash of sheet lightning illuminated the night sky. They bumped along the pot-holed lane, drawing to a halt yards from the edge of the cliff. He ordered them out of the car.

As the rain whipped her face, Morgan recalled a warm evening long ago. Two fifteen-year-olds locked in each other's arms, trying out the world for size. She remembered the far-away look on his face as he'd stared at the waves crashing onto the rocks below.

You could push someone off here and no one could prove you'd done it.

'I won't let you do this,' she said. 'Not to Lissa.'

He raised the shotgun, pointing it at her waist.

'Turn around.'

She heard her daughter's sob.

'Mum!'

He flicked the safety catch.

As a second flash of lightning lit up the night sky, Morgan sprang forward, launching herself into the air like a cheetah leaping on a gazelle, bringing Lissa crashing to the ground. She shielded her daughter's body with her own, clasping her hands over her head and waiting for the gunshot.

One.

Two.

Three.

But the sound never came.

Instead she heard the roar of the engine. She raised her head. Danny was at the wheel of the Mercedes, reversing at speed, retreating from the cliff edge. He braked, jerking to a halt. Gunning the engine, he held Morgan's gaze. Then he turned to face ahead, towards the sea, and closed his eyes.

The car lurched forward, gathering speed. As it sailed off the cliff it seemed to hang in mid-air, illuminated by a sky-wide flash of lightning, before plummeting down towards the storm-tossed waves and disappearing into the blackness below.

Fifty-Five

Arriving at the gates of the crematorium, Morgan steered the Mini through a crowd of reporters, doing her best to ignore their questions. Only one merited a response, from a chubby man in a parka.

'Are you and Lissa on speaking terms?'

'Absolutely. She's my daughter. I love her to bits.'

Not what he wanted to hear.

'So are you happy about Kristina handling Lissa's media career?'

'If Lissa's happy, I'm happy.'

It was the best she could do.

'Have you forgiven her for having sex with Danny?'

'There's nothing to forgive,' said Morgan as the photographers surged forward. 'But this is a funeral not a press conference so ...'

She drove through the gates, checking the rear-view mirror to see who had captured the interest of the paparazzi. A black limo was pulling up behind her, its tinted windows shielding the occupants – Lissa and Kristina – from view. Apparently, treating Danny's funeral service like a red-carpet event was an integral part of 'creating the character-based glamor, intrigue and drama that mesmerizes billions of fans of reality TV around the world'.

According to the press release, Cameron's twenty-four-year-old girlfriend had 'developed her media manifesto while working in the highly competitive US entertainment industry'. Morgan felt sure she'd scribbled it on a napkin during the flight from LA. Either way, Lissa no longer seemed interested in her mother's advice, preferring a more hard-nosed approach towards building a 'multi-platform, multi-media career'. *'In Ukraine we have a saying: when opportunity knocks, open the door.'*

Together with Lissa, the Louboutin-heeled 'celebrity consultant' was holed up in a suite at the Dorchester Hotel, fielding offers from ratings-hungry TV channels, glossy magazines and celebrity websites. Just this morning Morgan had left three messages on Lissa's voicemail. Her daughter had yet to call back. Meanwhile, Cameron was marooned in LA, wrestling with 'emergency rewrites' on his latest movie. *Puh-lease ...*

As Morgan climbed out of the Mini, her eye was drawn to the passenger seat, strewn with newspapers.

Killer-cannon Death Plunge.

Top Cop Covers Up For Killer Daughter.

The *Post* had capitalised on its own reporter's role in Zoe's murder and the subsequent cover-up.

LIAR ROSSITER! THE POST'S ENEMY WITHIN!

Meanwhile, the red-tops continued to mine the saga's sex angle.

Lissa Exclusive! My Dungeon Ordeal by Killer-cannon Sex-tape Teen.

Two weeks after Danny's death, the fallout from the revelation of the journalist's collusion with Jacqui Farmiloe was starting to fade. But for the key players the consequences were just beginning.

Tipped off by her mother, Chelsea had been arrested while attempting to board a ferry to Bilbao. She'd been remanded in custody, unlike Jacqui, Clive and Donna. (*Twisted Cop's Secret Lesbian Lover!*) All three of them were on bail, awaiting trial for conspiracy to pervert the course of justice. Rossiter was also likely to face prosecution for Zoe's murder, charged alongside Chelsea under the laws relating to joint criminal enterprise. There was a further charge against Jacqui's daughter: inciting a child to engage in sexual activity. The tabloids had binged on the 'virgins for sale' angle.

Top Cop's Girl Masterminds Virginity Scam.

Meanwhile, in a bid to limit the damage to their reputation caused by Farmiloe's abuse of power, the police had launched an investigation by the Independent Police Complaints Commission. They'd also moved swiftly to dredge Danny's body from the sea and recover Rowena's remains from a storm drain near his cottage. The charred remains of the woman in the car were still to be identified.

Leaning against the Mini, Morgan watched the limo pull to a halt outside the chapel. Lissa stepped into the wintry sunshine, followed by Kristina. Both sported designer sunglasses and funereal black. Registering Morgan's presence, the tall, svelte Ukrainian flashed an unconvincing smile and moved in for an air-kiss. Morgan sidestepped the advance, reaching her daughter's side in three quick strides.

'Are you OK?'

Lissa nodded, casting a sulky glare in the direction of the Mini.

'Why didn't you want to come in the limo?'

Morgan ignored the question.

'Didn't you get my messages?'

'We had a meeting.' Lissa's tone was unapologetic. Kristina's smile widened, revealing her dazzlingly white teeth.

'*Playboy*,' she said. 'They want to know if the press are correct about Jacqui leaking the sex tape.'

Morgan frowned.

'Why?'

'Better for Lissa's image if it got into the public domain without her help. Makes her the injured party.'

Morgan's frown deepened. She'd been told, off the record, that Jacqui *had* confessed to leaking the tape. The DI had needed to cast suspicion on Danny during the hunt for Lissa, painting him as a serial seducer of teenage girls. The aim: to make him seem more guilty than ever of Zoe's murder, keeping suspicion away from Chelsea.

'*Playboy*?' said Morgan, fixing Kristina with a stare. 'Tell me you're not serious.'

'I'm exploring all options for my client.'

'Your client,' said Morgan, 'my daughter.'

Before Kristina could reply, her mobile rang.

'Fox TV. I need to take this.'

Answering the call, she tottered away on her high heels. As Morgan watched her go, she raised her face towards the low winter sun.

'Is this what you want? *Playboy*?'

'Don't start,' said Lissa. 'No harm meeting people. Kristina's setting up loads of opportunities to …'

' … launch a career out of being swept up in a sick, horrible …'

Lissa cut her mother short.

'We've *so* had this conversation.'

True, they had. And not just in the days following Danny's death but en route to meet Kristina at Heathrow, a journey made at Lissa's insistence. The argument had been heated.

She's coming to help me!

No, she's coming to exploit you.

'Anyway,' said Lissa, glancing around the crematorium, 'pot, kettle, black.'

'Excuse me?'

'How is *my* cashing in worse than *yours*?'

Morgan blinked.

'I'm not cashing in. I'm writing a book.'

'About the cover-up of Zoe's murder.'

'Among other things.'

'Like how Danny was framed,' said Lissa. 'How Rossiter kept writing articles to make him seem guilty. How Jacqui got the sex tape from my phone and leaked it online.'

Morgan didn't answer immediately.

'It's a book,' she said. 'It's different.'

'If you say so.'

They fell silent. Morgan resisted the urge to roll a cigarette. Lissa scanned the grounds of the crematorium.

'Where is everyone?'

'We are everyone.'

'Not even his mum?'

'She says she's too broke to fly in from Tenerife. And too ashamed of what he did to Rowena.'

Lissa stiffened, glancing towards the crematorium gates.

'Oh my God,' she said quietly. 'He's here.'

Morgan followed her daughter's gaze. The photographers were jostling to capture the arrival of the hearse. It glided slowly through the gates and pulled to a halt outside the chapel. The coffin was covered with white lilies.

'Who ordered the flowers?' said Lissa.

Morgan looked away. Her voice was barely audible.

'Come on,' she said, taking her daughter's arm. 'Time to say goodbye.'

Later that day, she stood in the porch of the Sandwich Bay Care Home and rang the bell. Gazing out to sea, she watched seagulls dive-bombing a fishing boat. Scavengers, like the hacks at the funeral.

Maybe Lissa was right – maybe she was no better. But at least the days of trying to flog articles on celebrities' pets were over. And the literary agent had been persuasive, waving a languid hand around the hardbacks lining his Soho office.

'This is your *carpe diem* moment, Morgan. *"There is a tide in the affairs of men"* and all that.'

True, the deal she was set to sign would make her name, and there was no doubt she was uniquely qualified to tell the inside story of Danny Kilcannon ... of Zoe and Rowena ... of Jacqui and Clive. All the same, her daughter had a point. No matter how tacky Lissa's plans, Morgan had no right to be holier-than-thou.

'May I help you?'

A nurse stood in the doorway. Starched white uniform. Professional smile.

'I'm here to see my father.'

'Of course,' said the nurse. 'What's his name?'

'Leo Vine.'

The smile faltered.

'Morgan, is it?'

'Yes.'

'I'm sorry.' The nurse had the grace to look abashed. 'We have instructions not to allow you on the premises.'

'I just need ten minutes.'

The nurse's smile stiffened.

'Would you like to speak to my supervisor?'

Before Morgan could reply, she detected the smell of vanilla and heard another voice, familiar from long ago.

'It's all right,' said Ursula, appearing in the doorway. 'Let her in.'

The nurse retreated and disappeared down a gloomy corridor.

'This way,' said Ursula.

Her tone was businesslike. She ushered Morgan through the hallway and into the residents' lounge, a gloomy, over-heated room furnished with high-backed chairs.

'We'll talk in here,' said Ursula. 'The residents are having tea.'

The BBC news channel blared from the TV. A reporter was standing outside Dover Priory station, bringing the 'breaking news' that Allan Maitliss had been arrested, charged with pushing Caleb Quirke in front of a train.

'Goodness gracious,' said Ursula, staring at the screen. 'It's all coming out now.'

Like almost everyone Morgan had encountered during the past fortnight, her stepmother was mesmerised by the fallout from the Killer-cannon case.

'The police are conducting a case review alongside the IPCC investigation,' said Ursula, parroting what she'd gleaned from the news. 'They've been re-checking anything connected to Danny – including Maitliss's alibi for when Quirke was murdered. Surprise, surprise, it collapsed.'

But Morgan didn't want to talk about Allan Maitliss or Caleb Quirke. Above all, she didn't want to talk about Danny Kilcannon.

'Where's my father?'

Ursula turned off the TV.

'I'll take you to him in a moment,' she said, lowering herself stiffly into a chair. 'Have a seat.'

Morgan remained standing, taking stock of the grey in her stepmother's hair, the lines on her face.

'I don't want a scene, I just need to see him. And to find out why you've been stalking me.'

The woman nodded.

'I've been expecting you,' she said.

She gestured towards the *Daily Mail*. Morgan glanced at the photo of her own face and the headline above a double-page feature.

Mother's Quest for Daughter and the Truth About Killer-Cannon.

'You've been through quite an ordeal,' said Ursula, her tone as prim as ever. 'It's only natural you'd want to see your father.'

'Hardly the first time I've tried.'

The woman looked away. And suddenly Morgan understood.

'He's dying, isn't he?'

Her stepmother tightened her jaw then met Morgan's gaze.

'There are things you should know,' she said, smoothing a liver-spotted hand over her camel skirt. 'Number one: you won.'

'Won what?'

'What you might call "the battle for his affections".'

Morgan frowned.

'I don't understand.'

Ursula leaned back against the headrest, as though settling in for a fireside chat.

'Your father was diagnosed with early-onset dementia long before he told either of us,' she said. 'Just as you were leaving school, in fact. A big shock but he confided in no one at the time, not even me. Perhaps you can guess why?'

Morgan's jaw tightened.

'Guessing games? Seriously?'

'He was worried you'd insist on looking after him. He feared you might put your life on hold, if only to atone for your behaviour over Stevie Gamble and his disgusting lies.'

Despite the strength of feeling in her voice, Ursula kept her tone even.

'He couldn't let you sacrifice your youth, the way he'd sacrificed his for his mother. So he abandoned you. Or that's how he made it seem. But by spiriting us away to Wales he was being cruel to be kind.' The woman leaned forward and gave a chilly smile. *'By placing the entire burden of caring for him on me.'* Her voice was suddenly a hiss, the smell of vanilla more cloying than ever. 'His way of making up for giving you a wicked stepmother.'

She leaned back, adjusting the pleats of her skirt. When she spoke again, her voice had resumed its steady formality.

'As his illness got worse he made me promise to act *in loco parentis*, to ensure that you came to no harm.' She tucked a wisp of grey hair behind one ear. 'When Zoe was murdered, I was sure Danny was guilty. So when they released him I had to act. Obviously you wouldn't listen to a word *I* said so the messages were all I could do to try and scare you off.'

She plucked a piece of lint from her skirt then looked Morgan in the eye, a note of defiance entering her voice.

'I did it to keep you safe, Morgan. To keep my promise to the man whose bottom I wipe, the man I've visited twice a day for twenty years.' There was a catch in her voice. 'In sickness and in health, till death do us part.'

Morgan closed her eyes for a long moment feeling the crushing weight of the years. When she opened them again, Ursula was staring at her.

'Thank you for looking after my father. Now I'd like to see him.'

Her stepmother nodded then rose from her chair and headed for the door. Morgan followed her along a dingy corridor, wrinkling her nose at the smell of disinfectant.

'Stay here,' said Ursula, pausing at a door. She entered the room without knocking. Morgan waited, straining to make out the murmuring inside. Then the woman was back.

'He's tired,' she said. 'Let's get this over with.'

Following her into the room, Morgan recognised the piano music tinkling gently on the radio. A Schubert sonata.

The room was in darkness, the bed-ridden man thin to the point of emaciation. Rheumy eyes stared from a gaunt, unshaven face. Morgan struggled to compose her features into a smile.

'Hello, Dad.'

He raised his eyes towards Ursula, seeking reassurance.

'It's Morgan,' she said gently. 'Your daughter.'

Leo's eyes flickered in Morgan's direction.

'Daughter …?'

'Yes, Dad. It's me.'

He stared at her, furrowing his brow.

'What's the matter?' he said.

'Nothing.'

'Then why are you crying?'

'I don't know,' said Morgan. 'Maybe I'm happy.'

'Funny way of showing it. Did you bring biscuits? They usually bring biscuits. Or those green things.'

'Grapes,' said Ursula.

'That's it. Grapes.'

'Sorry, Dad. I'll bring some next time.' She glanced at Ursula. 'Maybe tomorrow?'

The woman hesitated then gave a nod. Morgan took her father's hand. His skin was smooth and soft, his thin wrist almost weightless.

'Do I know you?' he said.

Morgan felt a tear trickle down her cheek.

'I love you, Dad.'

He stared at her for a moment then slowly raised his head. The effort seemed to take all his strength. In a surprisingly clear voice, he began to sing "You Are My Sunshine".

After a moment, he tailed off, exhausted by the effort. Morgan felt the feeble squeeze of his fingers as he lay back against the pillows.

'Don't forget the biscuits next time.'

'No, Dad. I won't forget the biscuits.'

As she emerged from the care home, the sun was setting against a cloudless sky. Her mobile rang.

Lissa.

'Kristina's on her way to the airport. Going back to LA.'

'Why?'

'I won't do *Playboy.* She said I needed to get serious about my career strategy and stop wasting her time. *Such* a bitch.'

'So, are you?' said Morgan.

'Am I what?'

'Serious about your career strategy.'

A pause.

'I don't know,' said Lissa. 'Are you serious about yours?'

Morgan stared out to sea. The fishing boat was still on the horizon, surrounded by the shrieking gulls. As the decision settled inside her, it seemed so obvious, as if it had merely been waiting for her conscience to catch up with the rest of the world. She would call the literary agent first thing in the morning, ask him to wriggle out of the contract and resubmit her original proposal. *Trial & Error: a history of miscarriages of justice.* The advance would be a fraction of what she'd been offered for the book on Killer-cannon but it beat writing Me and My Fridge.

'If I have a career strategy,' she said, 'it might need a rethink.'

'Makes two of us,' said Lissa.

Another pause.

'Where are you?' said Morgan.

'The Dorchester. Kristina pre-paid the suite. Fancy a free night? The bar's packed, the men are hot.'

Morgan hesitated.

'I don't think I'm really a Dorchester person.'

'Fine,' said Lissa. 'Whatever.'

'You can come home anytime you like.'

Another pause.

'Are you angry with me?' said Lissa. 'About him?'

'Not even slightly.'

Her daughter's voice brightened.

'OK,' she said. 'I'll think about it.'

Morgan kept her tone light.

'Great. Let me know.'

Hanging up, she walked to the water's edge, slipping the phone into the pocket of her jeans. Her fingers made contact with the pebble. She took it out and stared at it, feeling its weight in the palm of her hand. Then she drew back her arm and skimmed it across the waves, watching it bounce.

Once.

Twice.

Gone.

Acknowledgements

Huge thanks to the brilliant Caroline Michel and the team at Peters Fraser + Dunlop. Thanks to first readers Deborah Moggach and Olivia Lichtenstein for their wise counsel; and to Matilda Forbes Watson for hers.

Joel Richardson, Claire Johnson-Creek, Mark Smith and their colleagues at Twenty7 Books and Bonnier Publishing are as smart a bunch of people as one could hope to work with and astonishingly nice too.

Above all, my thanks to Melanie McGrath. For all kinds of everything.

Morgan Vine returns in 2017

Anjelica Fry is serving a life sentence for the
murder of sociopath Karl Savage, father of her
six-month-old baby. Protesting her innocence,
she begs for Morgan's help.

Morgan isn't convinced. Every prisoner claims
to be innocent.

But then, in the dark of night, she sees
Savage outside her own isolated home.
Very much alive and kicking . . .

@SimonBooker @BonnierZaffre

DISCOVERING DEBUT AUTHORS
PUTTING DIGITAL FIRST

Twenty7 Books is a brand new imprint, publishing exclusively debut novels from the very best new writers. So whether you're a desperate romantic or a crime fiction fiend, discover the bestselling authors of the future by visiting us online.

twenty7